THE SHARING KNIFE

HORIZON

THE
SHARING
KNIFE

Volume Four
HORIZON

Lois McMaster Bujold

An Imprint of HarperCollins*Publishers*

THE SHARING KNIFE, VOLUME FOUR: HORIZON. Copyright © 2009 by Lois McMaster Bujold. All rights reserved. Printed in the United States of America. No part of this book may be used or reproduced in any manner whatsoever without written permission except in the case of brief quotations embodied in critical articles and reviews. For information address HarperCollins Publishers, 10 East 53rd Street, New York, NY 10022.

HarperCollins books may be purchased for educational, business, or sales promotional use. For information please write: Special Markets Department, HarperCollins Publishers, 10 East 53rd Street, New York, NY 10022.

FIRST EDITION

Designed by Joy O'Meara

Eos is a federally registered trademark of HarperCollins Publishers.

Library of Congress Cataloging-in-Publication Data

Bujold, Lois McMaster.
  The sharing knife. Volume four, Horizon / Lois McMaster Bujold. — 1st. ed.
    p.   cm.
  ISBN 978-0-06-137536-1
  I. Title. II. Title: Horizon.
  PS3552.U397S57   2009
  813'.54—dc22   2008049054

09 10 11 12 13   OV/RRD   10 9 8 7 6 5 4 3 2 1

THE SHARING KNIFE

HORIZON

1

The Drowntown day market was in full spate. Fawn's nostrils flared at the strong smells: fish, clams, critters with twitching legs like giant crawdads packed in seaweed; frying funnel cakes, boiling crabs, dried fruit, cheeses; piles of used clothing not well laundered; chickens, goats, sheep, horses. Mixed with it all, the damp tang of the river Gray, stretching so wide its farther shore became a flat blur in the winter morning light.

The lead-colored water shimmered in silence beyond the bright busy blot of folks collected under the bluffs that divided Graymouth's Uptown from its noisier—and, Fawn had to admit, more noisome—riverside. The muddy banks were lined with flatboats at the ends of their journeys, keelboats preparing new starts, and fishing and coastal vessels that came and went more in rhythm with the still-ten-miles-distant sea than with the river's moods. The streets dodged crookedly around goods-sheds, rivermen's taverns, and shacks—all built of dismantled flatboats, or, in some cases, not dismantled but drawn ashore intact on rollers by oxen and allowed to settle into the soil. The owners of the latter claimed to be all ready for the next flood that would try, and fail, to wash the smells and mess of Drowntown out to sea, while Uptown looked down dry-skirted. It seemed a strange way to live. How had she ever thought of the rocky creek at the foot of her family's farm back north as a river?

Fawn shoved her basket up her arm, nudged her companion Remo, and pointed. "Look! There's some new Lakewalkers here this morning!"

At the other end of the square, where all the bigger animals were displayed by their hopeful owners, two women and a man tended a string of half a dozen leggy horses. The three all wore Lakewalker dress: riding trousers, sturdy boots, shirts and leather vests and jackets, not so different in kind from the farmers around them, yet somehow distinctive. More distinctive was their hair, worn long in decorated braids, their height, and their air of discomfort to be surrounded by so many people who weren't Lakewalkers. Upon reflection, Fawn wondered if anyone else here realized the standoffishness *was* discomfort, or if they only thought it high-nosed disdain. She would have seen it that way, once.

"Mm," said Remo unenthusiastically. "I suppose you want to go talk to them?"

"Of course." Fawn dragged him toward the far end of the market.

The man pulled a horse out of the string and held it for a farmer, who bent and ran his hands over its legs. The two young women looked toward Fawn and Remo as they approached; their eyes widened a bit at Remo, whose height, clothes, and long black braid also proclaimed him a Lakewalker patroller. Did their groundsenses reached out to touch the stranger-kinsman, or did they keep them closed against the painful ground noise of the surrounding farmers?

The southern Lakewalkers Fawn had seen so far tended to lighter skin and hair than their northern cousins, and these two were no exception. The taller woman—girl—she seemed not so very much older than Fawn, anyhow—had hair in a single thick plait as tawny as a bobcat pelt. Her silvery-blue eyes were bright in her fine-boned face. The shorter woman had red-brown braids wreathing her head, and coppery eyes in a round face dusted with freckles. Fawn thought they might be patrol partners, like Remo and Barr; they seemed unlikely to be sisters.

"'Morning!" Fawn called cheerfully, looking up at them. The top of her own dark curls came up just past the middle of Remo's chest, and not much farther on these women. At almost-nineteen, Fawn had given up hope of gaining further inches except maybe around, and resigned herself to a permanent crick in her neck.

The reddish-haired woman returned a nod; the bobcat blonde, seeming uncertain how to take the odd pair, addressed herself to a height halfway between them. "'Morning. You all interested in a horse? We've some real fine bloodstock, here. Strong hooves. One of these could carry a man all the way up the Tripoint Trace and never pull up lame." She gestured toward the string, well brushed despite their winter coats, who gazed back and flicked their tufted ears. Beyond, the Lakewalker man trotted the horse toward and away from the farmer, who stood hands on hips, frowning judiciously.

"I thought Lakewalkers only sold off their culls to farmers?" said Fawn innocently. The redhead's slight flinch was more from guilt than insult, Fawn thought. *Some horse traders.* Suppressing a grin, she went on: "Anyhow, no, at least not today. What I was wondering was, what camp you folks hailed from, and if you have any real good medicine makers there."

The blonde replied at once, in a practiced-sounding tone, "Lakewalkers can't treat farmers."

"Oh, I know all about *that*." Fawn tossed her head. "I'm not asking for myself."

Two braided heads turned toward Remo, who blushed. Remo hated to blush, he'd said, because the awkwardness of it always made him blush worse than the original spur. Fawn watched his deepening tinge with fascination. She could not sense the flick of questing groundsenses, but she had no doubt that a couple went by just then. "No, I'm not sick, either," Remo said. "It's not for us."

"Are you two together?" asked the blonde, silver-blue eyes narrowing in a less friendly fashion. *Lovers together,* Fawn guessed she meant to imply, which Lakewalkers were emphatically not supposed to be with farmers.

"Yes. No! Not like that. Fawn's a friend," said Remo. "The *wife* of a friend," he added in hasty emphasis.

"We still can't help you. Medicine makers can't fool with farmers," the redhead seconded her companion.

"Dag's a Lakewalker." Fawn shouldered forward, keeping herself from clutching the Lakewalker wedding braid circling her left wrist under her sleeve. Or brandishing it, leading to the eternal explanation and defense of its validity. "And he's not sick." *Exactly.* "He used to be a patroller, but he thinks he has a calling now for making. He already knows lots, and he can do some, some *amazing* things, which is why he needs a *real good* guide, to help him along his next step." *Whatever it is.* Even Dag did not seem sure, to Fawn's concerned eyes.

The blonde turned her confused face to Remo. "You're not from around these parts, are you? Are you an exchange patroller?"

"Neeta," said the redhead, with a proud gesture at the blonde, "is just back from two years' exchange patrolling in *Luthlia.*"

The blonde shrugged modestly. "You don't have to tell everyone we meet, Tavia."

"No, I'm not exchanging, exactly," said Remo. "We came down from Oleana on a flatboat, got here about a week back. I'm, I've . . ."

Fawn waited with grim interest to see how he would describe himself. Run away from home? Deserted? Joined Captain Dag No-Camp's muleheaded campaign to save the world from itself?

He gulped, and fell back on, "My name's Remo."

A tilt of the braid-wreathed head and a bouncing hand gesture invited him to continue with his tent and camp names, but he merely pressed his lips together in an unfelt smile. Tavia shrugged, and went on, "We came down from New Moon Cutoff Camp yesterday to sell off some cu—horses, and to pick up the week's courier packet." Clearly identifying herself and her partner to this tall, dark, northern stranger as patroller women, carrying mail between camps being a patrol task. Fawn wondered if she'd recognize patroller flirting if she saw it, and if it would be as dire as patroller humor. "The best medicine maker in the district is at New Moon," Tavia continued, "but I don't think he's taking apprentices."

"That would be Arkady Waterbirch?" Fawn hazarded. "The one they say is a *groundsetter*?" That last had been a new term to Fawn, but the local Lakewalkers seemed to set great store by it. At the redhead's raised eyebrows she explained, "I've been asking around for the past few days, whenever I saw a Lakewalker in the market. They always start by telling about the makers in their own camps, but they all end by mentioning this Arkady fellow."

Tavia nodded. "Makes sense."

"Why is he not taking apprentices?" Fawn persisted. All the medicine makers she'd ever met had seemed hungry to find new talent for their craft. Well, unless that talent was trailing a farmer bride. "Is he full up?" She added conscientiously, "Not that Dag's looking to be an apprentice, necessarily. He might just want to, um, talk."

The two women exchanged guarded looks. Neeta said, "You'd think Arkady would be looking for a new apprentice, about now."

"I'm not so sure. He was pretty upset about Sutaw. He took a lot of shafts about it."

"He wasn't even there!"

"That's the complaint that stings the most, I gather."

Uncertain if the girls would explain this camp gossip to a mere farmer, Fawn nudged Remo. He cast her down a pained look, but dutifully asked, "What happened?"

Tavia rubbed her round chin and frowned. "A couple of months back, one of the youngsters at New Moon was badly mauled by a gator. When his friends ran to the medicine tent for help, Arkady was out seeing another patient, so his apprentice Sutaw went to take the boy on. He groundlocked himself, and died of the shock when the boy did."

Remo winced; Fawn quelled a chill in her belly. Remo said, "Wasn't there anyone else there to break the lock?"

"The boy's mother, but she waited too long. Some other youngsters, but of course they couldn't realize. There was a lot of bad feeling, after, between the parents of the mauled boy and Sutaw's tent-kin, but it's pretty much settled down now. Arkady's been keeping to himself."

"Not that you can tell the difference," said Neeta. "He always was as grim as a knife maker. Maybe a new apprentice would be good for him." She smiled at Remo. "Your friend could ask, I suppose. But you'd likely better warn him old Arkady's kind of . . . difficult, sometimes."

"Yeah?" Remo shot an ironic look at Fawn. "That'd be right interesting."

The two girls from New Moon Cutoff were picturing Dag as a young patroller like Remo, Fawn realized. She decided not to try to explain the more . . . difficult aspects of her Lakewalker husband. *He's not banished, not really . . .*

The New Moon man finished counting coins into his wallet from the farmer, slapped the horse on the rump in friendly farewell as it was led away, and turned back toward his companions. Fawn was reminded that her market basket ought to be piled high and handed off to Remo to lug by now.

"Well, thank you." Fawn dipped her knees. "I'll pass the word along."

The two returned nods, the shorter girl's bemused, the taller blonde's a trifle grudging, though both watched after Remo with considering glances as Fawn led him off across the square once more. But their attention was soon diverted as another potential customer strolled up to eye the horses.

Remo looked back over his shoulder and sighed in regret. "Barr would have charmed their socks off."

Fawn dimpled. "Only their socks? I'd think Barr would be more ambitious. Least to hear him tell it."

Remo blushed again, but protested, "They're *patroller* girls. They'd keep him in line." But after a longish glum moment, added, "If they wanted to."

Fawn shook her head, smiling. "Come on, Remo, cheer up. We got us a wedding party to fix." A flash of color caught her eye, and she stepped along to a fruit cart to bargain for blocks of dried persimmon and bright round oranges packed in straw, both astonishing southern fruits she had tasted for the first time only a few days ago. Another Graymouth woman sold Fawn a jar of molasses, sweet as the maple syrup cooked up on the Bluefield farm each spring, if with a much stronger, stranger flavor. It would go well with biscuits, Fawn thought, or maybe with something using up that last barrel of wrinkling apples that had ridden with them all the way from Oleana.

"So," said Remo thoughtfully as they made their way to the next vendor on Fawn's mental list. "If Dag wants to find himself a medicine maker that much, why isn't he doing the asking around?"

Fawn bit her lip. "You've heard him talking about it, haven't you?"

"Oh, sure, couple of times."

"He's said even more to me. But Dag's a doer, not a talker. So if he keeps talking, but doesn't do . . . it seems to me something's wrong somewhere."

"What?"

Her steps slowed. "He's scared, I guess."

"Dag? Are you joking?"

"Not physically scared. Some other kind of scared. I don't have the words for it, but I can feel it. Scared he won't get the answers he wants, maybe." *Scared he'll get the answers he doesn't want.*

"Hm," said Remo doubtfully.

As they wended back to the riverbank and up the row of flatboats to where the *Fetch* was tied, Fawn's thoughts reverted to the horrific tale of the groundlocked apprentice. *That could be Dag, all right.* A youngster in danger, a desperate fight for survival—despite being partnerless, he would dive right in and not come out. With him, it wouldn't even be courage. It'd be a blighted *habit.*

When Dag had first talked about giving up patrolling to become a medicine maker to farmers, it had seemed a wonderful plan to Fawn: it would be a safer line of work, it wouldn't take him away from her, and he could do it all on his own, without needing other Lakewalkers. Without needing other Lakewalkers to accept *her,* to put it bluntly. All of these promised benefits appeared to be untrue, on closer look-see.

My thoughts are all in a tangle, Dag had complained to her. What if it wasn't just his thoughts? What if it was his ground, as well? Which would be no surprise after all the chancy groundwork he'd been doing, lately. *Miracles and horrors.* Maybe he really needed another maker to help straighten it all out.

Groundsetter. Fawn rolled the word over in her mind. It sounded mysterious and promising. Her chin ducked in a firm nod as her feet rapped across the *Fetch*'s gangplank.

∾

The wagon roads from the lower to the upper halves of Graymouth wound around the far ends of the long bluff, but several sets of stairs zigzagged more breathlessly up the steep slope. They were built, inevitably, of old flatboat timbers, generously enough for folks to pass four abreast in places. Dag turned his head for a quick glimpse of the busy riverside laid out below, with the gleaming river receding into level haze in both directions. He breathed in the cool air of this midwinter noon, contemplating the array of people about to officially become part of, well . . . his family, he supposed. Tent Bluefield. The growth of it had happened so gradually over the weeks of their disastrous quest, Dag was almost shocked to look back and realize how far they'd come, and not just in river miles. *Yet here we all are.*

The *Fetch*'s party climbed two by two. In the lead wheezed Berry's uncle Bo, gnarled riverman, the one member of the young flatboat boss's family back in Clearcreek who had volunteered to come help her on this long journey. Beside him thumped Hod, an arm ready to boost Bo along, but Dag judged the wheezing misleading; Bo was as tough as the old boot leather that he resembled, and the knife slash in his belly was almost fully healed. Hod had become far more than a mere boat hand after all their shared adventures, being as near as made-no-never-mind to adopted into the *Fetch*'s family.

Berry's eleven-year-old brother, Hawthorn, came next, his pet raccoon riding on his shoulder, both boy and animal sniffing the air in bright-eyed curiosity. There had been some argumentation over whether a raccoon was a proper ornament to a wedding party, but the creature had ridden with them all the way from Oleana, and had become something of a boat's mascot over the downriver weeks. Dag was just glad no one had extended the argument to Daisy-goat, equally faithful and far more useful. A bit more of Hawthorn's swinging wrist stuck out of his shirtsleeve than when Dag had first met him, and Dag didn't think it was because the cloth had shrunk with its rare washings. When his straw-blond head finally grew to overtop that of his sister Berry, he would be an impressive young man. Three more years, Dag gave it; *forever,* Hawthorn moaned; Dag tried to remember when three years had seemed forever.

Next, the bride herself, supported by Fawn. Fawn had spent a good long time earlier this morning with her clever fingers plaiting Berry's straight hair, usually tied at her nape, up into Lakewalker-style wedding braids. Somewhere in the Drowntown day market Fawn had found fresh winter flowers, either local to these southern climes or grown under glass, Dag was not sure. She'd arranged all the big white blooms she could fit in around Berry's straw-gold topknot, with ivy trailing down in the silky fall of hair behind. Her own hair she'd gathered into a jaunty horsetail at her crown, with sprigs of scarlet flowers seeming to glow against the dark curls. Climbing behind the two women, Dag enjoyed the effect. There had been no time for new bride clothes, in these hasty preparations so far from home, but there had been a lot of laundry done on the *Fetch* yesterday after Fawn had returned from the market with Remo. Shabby and travel-worn the whole party's workaday garments might be, but they were all clean and mended.

As they reached a turn in the stairs and reversed direction, Fawn's little hand gripped Berry's in a gesture of encouragement. Berry's work-hardened fingers looked unusually cold and pale. Dag had seen Berry face down raging shoals, snagging sandbars, rough rivermen, sly goods-dealers, murderous bandits, knife fights, heartbreak, and hangings, *high water and low* as the riverfolk put it, with unflagging courage. Any who would dare chuckle at her pre-wedding nerves . . . had never faced a wedding ceremony themselves, Dag decided.

Fawn's brother Whit, climbing beside Dag, had chuckled merrily at his sister and Dag six months ago when they'd tied their knots in West Blue. He wasn't laughing now, and the corners of Dag's mouth tucked up at the pure justice of the moment. No one, looking at Fawn and Whit together, would take them for anything other than brother and sister even before they opened their mouths. Both had the same dark curls and clear skin, and though Whit topped Fawn by a head, he was still a sawed-off Bluefield. More height he would likely never gain, but his shoulders had broadened this fall, as the strain on his shirt seams testified. And, without losing his still-sometimes-annoying humor, his eyes were graver, more thoughtful; more than once lately Dag had seen him start to let fly with a witty or half-witty barb, then stop and swallow it instead. He, too, had come a long way from West Blue.

Enough to be ready for his wedding day? No, probably not; few folks ever were. Enough to be ready for all the days that followed? That also was a matter of learn-as-you-go, in Dag's experience. *But I think he will not betray her.* He sent an encouraging glint of a smile down at his . . . brother-in-law, in farmer parlance, tent-brother, in Lakewalker terms, and thought that Whit had met the tests of both roles. Whit put his shoulders back and managed a ghastly grin in return.

Behind Dag, Remo's and Barr's long legs took some of the shorter uneven stairs two at a time, in step with each other. Either would likely be shocked to learn Dag now thought of them as part of his peculiar farmer-Lakewalker family tent, but Dag imagined both partners would admit to being his patrollers. As difficult as their present circumstances were, Dag was glad they had become entangled in his little band, whatever one might name it. One Lakewalker among farmers was an oddity. Three were . . . a start, maybe.

They all exited the walkway into Uptown. Dag stared around with interest, this being his first jaunt up the stairs to the bluff. Today was nearly windless in the watery light, but Dag imagined that in high summer Uptown would catch whatever mosquito-removing breezes there were. The streets, better drained than those below, were not as muddy, and were laid out in tidy blocks with boardwalks lining them—more sawed-up former flatboats, no doubt. The houses and buildings looked substantial, less haphazardly cobbled together, free of high-water stains. The people seemed not too different: boat bosses and goods-shed men, drivers and drovers, innkeepers and horseboys; some of the women seemed better dressed, if more soberly than the fancy getups worn by the girls from the bed-boats tied along the Drowntown shore.

The Graymouth town clerk's office was not the front room of some villager's house, as Dag had seen back in tiny West Blue, but a separate building, two stories high, built of sturdy brick probably floated downstream from Glassforge in far-off Oleana. Fawn pointed out the brick to Hod, who grinned in recognition and nodded. The *Fetch*'s party clumped up onto the porch and inside.

Berry and Whit had ventured up here the requisite three days ago to register their intent to wed and to secure an appointment with a recording clerk—the town employed several, Dag understood. The big, busy room to the right of the entry hall had to do with boats and the shipping business; to the left, with land records. Berry and Whit both gulped, grabbed each other's hand, and led the way upstairs to a smaller, quieter chamber.

The rather bare upstairs room held a writing table by a window and half a dozen wooden chairs pushed back to the wall, not quite enough for the crew of the *Fetch*. Hod saw that Bo took a seat with Fawn and Berry. Dag rested his shoulders on the wall and crossed his arms, and Barr and Remo, after a glance at him, did likewise.

The wait was neither long nor uncomfortable, at least not for Dag. He wouldn't vouch for Whit, who kept readjusting his shirt collar. In a few minutes, a man carrying a large record book and a sheet of paper bustled in. Dag judged him maybe a decade older than Whit or Berry; he might have been a cleanly goods-shed clerk working up to owner. He looked up to see Dag, and stepped back with a small *uh*. His eyes flicked down over the hook that served in place of Dag's left hand, to the long knife at his belt, back up to his short-trimmed if still unruly hair, and across again to Barr and Remo with their more obviously Lakewalker-style hair and garb. Both Remo's long, dark braid and Barr's shorter tawny queue were decorated for the occasion with ornaments new-made from shark teeth and pearl shell.

"Ah," the clerk said to Dag, "can I help you fellows find the room you're looking for? There's a marriage registration due next in this one, the Bluefield party."

"Yes, we're part of that patrol," Dag replied amiably. He gave a nod toward Berry and Whit, who popped to their feet, smiling nervously.

The fellow Dag took to be the clerk tore his gaze from the Lakewalkers to glance at his paper and say, "Whitesmith Bluefield and Berry Clearcreek?"

Both ducked their heads; Whit stuck out his hand and said, "They call me Whit."

"I'm Clerk Bakerbun," said the clerk, who shook Whit's hand and, after a brief glance at Fawn, nodded at Berry. "Miss Clearcreek. How de' do." He laid his big book out on the table. "Right, we can begin. Do you each have your principal witnesses?"

"Yes," said Berry. "This here's my uncle Bo, and that's my little brother Hawthorn." Both rose and nodded, Hawthorn tightly clutching his raccoon, which made a noise of indolent protest.

Whit added, "Yeah, and this is my sister Fawn and her husband, Dag Bluefield." His gesture taking in Dag made the clerk blink.

"I'm sorry, I thought you were a Lakewalker," said the clerk to Dag. He looked up into Dag's gold-tinged eyes. "Wait, you are a Lakewalker!"

Whit raised his voice to override the inevitable spate of questions: "And these here are Hod, Remo, and Barr, all friends and boat hands from the *Fetch,* which is Berry's flatboat out of Clearcreek, Oleana, see. They'll sign as witnesses, too. She goes by Boss Berry down on the river, by the way." He smiled proudly at his betrothed. Berry usually had a generous grin beneath wide cheekbones that made her face look like a friendly ferret's; now her smile was stretched thin with nerves.

The clerk looked at Hawthorn, who grinned back more in the usual Clearcreek family style. "Ah, um . . . this youngster looks to be well under twenty years of age. He can't be a legal witness, not in Graymouth."

"But Berry said I could sign. I been practicin'!" protested Hawthorn. He undid one arm from under the fat and sleepy raccoon and held up ink-stained fingers in proof. "And now that Buckthorn and Papa was killed last fall, I'm her only brother!"

"I did promise he could," said Berry. "I didn't know. I'm sorry, Hawthorn."

Bo added gruffly, "Oh, come on, let the little feller sign. It won't do no harm, and it'll mean the world to him. To both of 'em."

"Well . . ." The clerk looked nonplussed. "I don't think I can. It might compromise the validity of the document should it be challenged."

Dag's brows drew down. Farmer customs could be so baffling. All that paper and ink and fuss over property and witnesses. He considered his own wedding cord wound around his upper arm, concealed beneath his jacket sleeve, braided by Fawn's own hands and containing a thread of her live ground, proof of their union to anyone with groundsense. She wore its twin on her left wrist, peeping like a hair bracelet from her shirt cuff, humming with a bit of Dag's ground in turn. Not that any Lakewalker camp wouldn't seize on a wedding as an excuse for a party, and not that the tent-kin on both sides didn't mix in till you were ready to wrap some spare cords around their necks and twist, but in the end, the marriage was solely between two people, tracking its traces in their inward selves. Even if the couple should be cast among strangers, the cords silently spoke their witness for them.

"Never mind, Hawthorn," said Whit to the crestfallen boy. "I bought Berry and me a new family book to start, and you can sign in that. 'Cause it's ours, and doesn't belong to these Graymouth folks." He added to Berry, "It's my first wedding present to you, see." Her pale face lightened in a real grin.

Whit reached into the cloth bag he'd been toting and pulled out a large volume bound in new leather of the sort in which good-sheds kept their records. He laid it on the table, opening it to the first blank white page. Dag was thrown back in memory to the aging family book he'd seen at West Blue, three-quarters full of entries about Bluefield marriages, births, and deaths, and land or animals bought, sold, or swapped, which he and Fawn and for that matter Whit had all put their names in, as principals or witness. That volume had been the latest of a series going back over two hundred years, all carefully kept in a trunk in the parlor. The precious family books would pass in turn, along with the farm itself, to Whit and Fawn's eldest brother and his bride. As the fourth son, Whit was on his own. And, Dag guessed, not sorry for it now.

Fawn measured the book's thickness, a good two fingers, and grinned. "Ambitious, Whit!" Hawthorn looked it over in approval, evidently consoled. Would the old Clearcreek family book pass to Hawthorn, then, not to Berry? It was all so backward to the way a Lakewalker eldest girl inherited the family tent from her mother.

"Hm," said the clerk in a tone of doubt, but did not pursue his quibble. He laid his own big book, its leather cover stamped with Graymouth's town seal, on the table beside Whit's, and opened it to a new page. "If I'm to make two clean copies, best we get started." He sat at the table, drew the ink pot toward him, shot back his cuffs, selected a quill from the jar, and looked up again at Berry and Whit. "State your full names, your parents' names and residences—or, if they are deceased, places of burial—your dates of birth, places of birth, and occupations."

It took a few minutes to get all this down, twice. The fellow did have nice handwriting, Dag decided, leaning over for a peek. Since this caused Bakerbun to stop writing and stare over his shoulder in alarm, Dag returned to his wall space. Berry gave her occupation as *boat boss,* and after a moment, *and fiddler;* Whit, after the briefest hesitation, said not *farmer* but *boat hand.* Dag fancied he could almost hear the twang as Whit's last tie to West Blue parted.

"Next, do you give your sworn words you have no impediments? No other betrothal, marriage, or indenture?"

They both murmured their nays, although Berry winced a little at the *other betrothal* part.

"Good, that's easy," muttered the clerk. "You came up from Drowntown, so I don't guess you have any substantial property to worry about.

I must say, Drowntown folks don't usually bother to come up here to us for this, but that's Drowntown for you."

"I have the *Fetch*," said Berry.

The clerk hesitated. "Flatboat, you say? Not a keel?"

"That's right."

"We don't have to count flats. What about you, Whitesmith Blue-field?"

"I have my earnings for the trip."

The clerk waved this away. "Real property. Land, a house, a building for business? Expectations of inheritance?"

"No. Not yet," Whit amended, with a distant look. "I have a family due-share from the farm in West Blue, but I don't rightly know when I'll get back to collect it. It's not much, anyhow."

The clerk frowned judiciously.

"You should have your papa's house and the hill in Clearcreek, Berry," Bo put in. "You and Hawthorn."

The clerk came suddenly alert. "Do you know how it was left? What terms?"

"I can't rightly say. Don't think no one in Clearcreek even knows Berry's papa is dead, yet. He disappeared on the river last fall, see, along with her older brother, so that's what this trip was for, mainly, to find out what had happened to 'em. Which we did do."

A sudden spate of questions from the clerk drew out the information that the house was substantial, or at least large and rambling, and the hill, too steep for farming but where Berry's family harvested the timber to build their yearly flatboat, was a good square mile in extent. And no one knew for sure if Berry's papa might have left Hawthorn's guardianship to some other relative than Berry in the event of his death, a notion that clearly alarmed Hawthorn very much. Any records were back in Clearcreek, fifteen hundred river miles away.

"This is all very confused," said the clerk at last, rubbing his nose and leaving a faint smear of ink on his upper lip. "I don't think I can register this marriage."

"What?" cried Whit in alarm, in chorus with Berry's dismayed "Why not?"

"It's the rules, miss. To prevent theft by runaway or fraudulent marriages. Which has been tried, which is why the rules."

"I'm not a runaway," said Berry indignantly. "I'm a boat boss! And I got my mother's own brother with me!"

"Yes, but your marriage would give Whitesmith, here, some claims on your property that your other kin might not want to allow. Or if that house and hill is all left to the tad, here, as your papa's only surviving son, he presumably owes you some due-share, but he's too young to administer it. I've seen this sort of tangle lead to all sorts of fights and disputes and even killings, and over a good deal less property than your Oleana hill!"

"In Graymouth, maybe!" cried Berry, but Bo scratched his chin in worry.

"Better you should wait and get married back in Clearcreek, miss," said the clerk.

"But it could be four or six months till we get back there!" said Whit, sounding suddenly bewildered. "We want to get married now!"

"Yeah, Fawn's baked the cake and fixed the food and everything!" put in Hawthorn. "And she made me take a bath!"

"Something like this sort of problem must have come up before." Dag pitched his voice deep to cut across the rising babble of protest. "In a town with as many strangers passing through for trade as Graymouth gets. Couldn't you just leave out all mention of the property, let the Clearcreek clerk write it all in later?"

"I should have kept my fool mouth shut," muttered Bo. "Sorry, Berry."

The distress from the folks assembled in the room was rising like a miasma around Dag, and he closed himself tighter against it.

"That's what the marriage registration is for, to settle all these critical matters!" said the clerk. "Not that I'd expect a Lakewalker to understand," he added in a low mutter. "Don't you fellows trade your women around? Like bed-boat girls, but with big knives, and not near so friendly."

Dag stiffened, but decided to pretend not to hear, although Remo stirred in annoyance and Barr's sandy eyebrows rose.

The clerk straightened up, cleared his throat, and gripped the edges of the table. "There have been variances made, from time to time," he said. Whit made an eager noise. "The fellow puts up a bond with the town clerk in the amount of the disputed property, or a decreed percentage. When he brings back the proper documents or witnesses to prove his claims, he gets it back, less a handling fee. Or, if his claims don't fly, the woman's kin comes to collect it, for damages."

"What damages?" said Hawthorn curiously, but Bo's grip on his shoulder quelled him.

Whit's nose abruptly winkled. "Just how much money are we talking about here?"

"Well, the worth of that hill and house, I suppose."

"I don't have *that* much money!"

The clerk shrugged helplessly.

"We've still to sell off the *Fetch*," said Berry dubiously, "but it won't run to anything near the value of our place in Clearcreek. And besides, we need that money to take home to live on next year."

Remo glanced at Barr and cleared his throat. "Barr and I—anyway, I still have my salvage share from the cave," he offered. "I could, uh, pitch in."

Barr swallowed, and with an effort, got out, "We."

Whit, Bo, and Berry began vigorously explaining to Clerk Bakerbun all the reasons why his legal demand made no sense; the clerk's shoulders stiffened, and his face set.

Fawn slid back under Dag's arm, and whispered up to him, "Dag, this is crazy! These Graymouth folks have got no right to Whit's money, or even some part-fee. They didn't work hard or bleed or risk their lives to earn it. Wedding papers shouldn't cost that much! Do you think it's a cheat? Does that fellow figure us for up-country folks just bleating to be skinned?"

"How would I know?"

She cast him up a significant look. Dag sighed and eased open his groundsense, despite the discomfort pressing on him from all the suddenly unhappy people sharing the room. Less the raccoon, who was now dozing on a chair.

"His ground feels more stressed than sly," he whispered back. "But if he's setting up to angle for a bribe, I'm blighted if I'll let my tent-brother pay it. Not for this."

Fishing for an illicit bribe would be easy enough to handle. Just troop downstairs in a body and loudly demand explanations from as many folks as possible. The truth would out, and then the clerk would be in hot water. Dag didn't take the fellow for that sort of foolish. No . . . Dag guessed this mulishness as overblown conscientiousness, crossed with an underlying contempt for odd shabby people from Drowntown. Arguing with the man might merely make him climb up on his high horse, send Whit and Berry off on their journey unwed, and be happily confirmed in his low opinion of the morals of river folks. Dag's annoyance increased.

Irrelevant as all this paper ceremony seemed to Dag, it meant a lot to Whit and Berry, both so far from home; possibly even more to Whit than Berry, this being his first venture into the wide world, and anxious to do right by his hard-won river maiden. Blight it, the happy day that Fawn and Berry had worked and planned so hard to create should not tumble down into distraught confusion, not if Dag could help it. *And I can.*

Quite quietly, from behind the clerk, he stretched out his left arm, and with his ghost hand—ground projection—shaped a reinforcement for persuasion. Such subtle work was invisible to all eyes here, but not to Barr's or Remo's inner senses; Remo's eyebrows climbed. Barr's jaw dropped, then his lips shaped outraged words, *You dare . . . !*

Dag did not attempt too much detail, just a general trend of feeling. *You like these hardworking young folks. You wish them well. You want to help them out. That far-off Clearcreek woodlot isn't your responsibility. Let that lazy Clearcreek village clerk do some work for a change. These youngsters are going to go away up the river and you'll never see them again. No problem for you. Such a cute couple.* He let the reinforcement spin off his ghost fingers and into the back of the clerk's head. As an added bonus, the clerk wouldn't have a headache for the next several days . . .

Necessarily, Dag accepted the little backwash from Clerk Bakerbun's ground into his own, so as not to leave the man blatantly beguiled.

The clerk rubbed his forehead and frowned. "You say you're heading back upriver right away?"

"Yes, pretty soon," said Berry.

"It's irregular, but I suppose I could leave out mention of the disposition of the property . . ." He paused in an internal struggle. "If I put in a notation for the Clearcreek village clerk to add the information later. It's his task, properly."

"Very sensible," Dag rumbled. He followed up with a wave of approval. With no groundsense, the clerk would not be able to tell whether this happy feeling was coming from outside his head or inside.

Fawn glanced appraisingly at the clerk, at Barr and Remo, at Dag, and pressed her lips together.

The clerk rubbed his forehead again, then turned a brighter look upon Whit and Berry. "You seem like nice young folks. I guess I'm obliged to get you off to a good start . . ."

After that, events followed a course more like what Dag had experienced in West Blue. The clerk had a set of standard promises written out, prepared to lead the couple in their spoken responses. He seemed surprised when both were able to read them off the paper for themselves, each adding a few variations stemming, Dag supposed, from Clearcreek and West Blue local custom. Whit and Berry bent and signed both books, the clerk signed and stamped, and the witnesses lined up to take their turns with the quill.

The clerk seemed equally surprised when he was not called upon to countersign anyone's *X*. Bo's handwriting was labored but legible, as was Hod's, but only because he'd been practicing along with Hawthorn. Fawn caught her tongue between her teeth and wrote her name square and plain. She hesitated over what to put for occupation, glanced up the page at Whit's entry, and settled on *boat cook*.

She then looked up, suddenly awkward. "Dag, what's our place of residence?"

"Uh . . . just put Oleana. For now."

"Really?" She gave him an odd look that even his groundsense could not help him interpret, bent, and scribbled.

Dag's turn came next, and he also found himself unexpectedly flummoxed by the empty, inviting *occupation* space. Patroller? Not anymore. Medicine maker, knife maker? Not for sure. Vagrant? *Mage?* His own unsettled ground gave him no clue. In some desperation, he chose *boat hand,* too. It wasn't a lie, even if it wasn't going to be true for much longer.

Remo, after his name, signed *Pearl Riffle Camp, Oleana,* and *patroller,* adding after a check up the page at the general trend of things, *and boat hand.* Barr copied him. Berry and Whit made sure Hawthorn had his turn in the new Bluefield-Clearcreek family book, Whit hovering with a handkerchief ready to mop any accidental blots. None occurred. And it was done, apparently. Or at least Whit and Berry blew out their breaths, looked at each other a bit wildly, and fell into a heartfelt hug and kiss—part joy, but mainly relief.

The clerk dutifully shook hands all around and offered congratulations. Dag made sure the company did not linger. He didn't know how fast his persuasion would wear off, though he hoped it would last for some days, by which time the events would be well blurred in Clerk Bakerbun's mind by the press of his other work, and he would be in no mood to reexamine the dodgy fix-up.

No more than I.

2

Descending the steps to Drowntown, Berry shot a wide grin over her shoulder at Fawn; Fawn grinned back in equal delight. They'd switched places, Whit and Berry holding hands hard, Fawn clutching Dag's hand scarcely less tightly. Barr and Remo followed. But when they came to a landing where the stairs doubled back, Barr's grip fell on Dag's shoulder.

"Hold up, Dag," he growled. Dag came to a halt, staring blandly out over the riverside.

Fawn turned, surprised by Barr's tone. Remo, after a glance at the two tense faces, waved Whit and the rest of the party on. Whit raised his brows, but thumped on down the boards after the rest of his new Clearcreek in-laws.

Barr's strong teeth set. Through them, he said, "You planted a persuasion on that clerk fellow."

Dag's eyelids fell, rose, in that peculiar Daggish I-am-not-arguing look he got sometimes. It could be very aggravating, Fawn knew, to the person on the wrong side of the non-argument. She touched her lips in dismay. *I thought that might have been what happened back there.* Though she could not perceive groundwork directly, Barr and Remo evidently had. Remo didn't look angry like Barr, but he looked plenty worried in his own way. More so than usual, that is.

"You tore the blighted *hide* off me for trying to plant a persuasion in Boss Berry that time, and I didn't even make it work!" said Barr.

Dag blinked again, and waited patiently and unencouragingly. He didn't deny this, either, Fawn noted.

"So how come you get to persuade farmers, and I don't?"

Remo offered uneasily, "It settled the fellow down. You wouldn't have wanted to let all his nonsense about land and wills and due-shares wreck the wedding, would you?"

"No, but—but that's not the point! Or maybe it is the point. Persuasion's allowed if it's a good deed? *Mine* was a good deed! I was just trying to get Remo to come back to Pearl Riffle with me, which is what I was sent after him to do—that wasn't just a good deed, it was my duty! If you're gonna make up rules for me and then go break them yourself, how can I trust anything you say?"

"Maybe you shouldn't," said Dag dryly.

Before Barr could get out some heated response, Fawn cut in. "Dag, you didn't leave that fellow beguiled, did you?"

"Of course not."

"So you took in a little of his ground."

"I'll just have to add it to the collection, Spark."

Fawn's mind ran down all the bits and pieces of strange grounds that Dag had absorbed into his own during these past weeks, either through the trick of unbeguiling all the folks he'd done his healing work on, or the odd experiments with food and animals, or the darker deed of ground-ripping the renegade Crane. "It's getting to be a pretty queer collection."

"Yeah, well . . . yeah."

Barr started to renew his protest, but was stopped by his partner's grip on his arm. Remo gave him a headshake; Fawn wasn't sure what else passed between the pair, except that something did. Remo said, "We can take this up later. Let's catch up with the others. It's Fawn's birthday, too, remember."

"Yeah, I need to get back to the *Fetch* and finish cooking dinner," Fawn put in anxiously.

Barr let his breath blow out; he shot one last glower at his fellow Lakewalkers, but produced a smile for Fawn's sake. "You're right. It's not the time or the place to settle this." He added in a mutter, "It's going to take more time. And a bigger space."

Remo gave a satisfied nod; Dag said nothing, though his lips twisted. They all started down the stairs once more. Fawn could only think: *I'm in Barr's camp on this one.*

～

The combined wedding-and-birthday-supper chores didn't fall too heavily on Fawn, as everyone pitched in to help, dodging around the little hearth in the kitchen-and-bunk area at the rear of the *Fetch*'s cabin. She served up the inevitable ham, potatoes, and onions, but also fresh fish from the sea, golden yams, the bright oranges and chewy sweet dried persimmon, and molasses to go along with the last of the salt butter for the biscuits. Bo's gift was a new keg of beer, and if it was darker in color and stronger in taste than the paler brews Fawn had encountered up along the Grace Valley, well, maybe it wasn't made that way just to hide the murkiness of Graymouth water, because it did a fine job of washing everything down.

The birthday-wedding cake was mostly apple flavored. There had been a debate over candles, as, properly, a birthday cake should have them but a wedding cake was decorated with flowers. Hawthorn had begged for candles mainly for the fascination of making Dag light them, so Fawn put thin beeswax sticks on top and flowers around the edge. Hawthorn happily had his eyebrows nearly singed off as Dag waved his hook, and, Fawn presumed, ghost hand across the top, and nineteen little flames sprang up behind with a satisfying *foomp*.

Confronted with the bright warmth, reflected in Dag's flickering smile, Fawn realized she'd been too busy fixing up the party to think of a wish. Watching Whit and Berry grin at each other, she considered wishing them well, but really, that's what this whole day was about for everyone. The birthday-wishing-candles part was all Fawn's own.

With a sudden catch of her breath, she thought, *I wish to go home.*

It wasn't homesickness, exactly, because the last thing in the world she wanted was to go back to her parents' farm in West Blue. She'd been fascinated by life on a flatboat, but the *Fetch* had been a very cramped shack floating down a very wide river, and not always bow first, either, and anyhow it had come to the end of its travels. Fawn wanted a real house, planted in solid ground, all her own, hers and Dag's. With an iron cookstove. *I want my future.* She wanted these people in it—she glanced up at them all, Dag, Whit and Berry, Remo and Barr, Hawthorn and Bo and even Hod, waiting to applaud her when she blew out the flames. And, with an ache so abrupt it hurt her heart, she wanted the new ones in it, the shadowy children she and Dag had not yet made together. *I want us all home safe. Wherever our real home turns out to be.* She took a deep, deep breath, shut her eyes, and blew until the lights no longer glowed red against her eyelids. When the clapping started she dared to open them again, and smile.

After cake came the presents, birthday and wedding both. Normally, wedding presents were practical items to outfit the young couple's new house or farm, or tent if they were Lakewalkers—the same aim, Fawn understood, if different in detail. But Whit and Berry still had a long way to travel to get back to the debatable house in Clearcreek. So any presents had to be small, light, and packable. Barr had somehow come up with new shoes made of red-brown alligator hide for both Berry and Fawn, which actually fit, and not by chance; he'd slyly sneaked off old shoes to compare. Hawthorn and Hod proudly presented Fawn with a bound blank book, found at the same place Whit had bought his, but smaller to fit in her saddlebags, and likely in their budget.

Fawn gave two new pairs of cotton drawers each to Whit and Berry, because she'd found good cotton cloth ready-made in the market here cheaper than raw cotton fiber back in Oleana, and it was all too splendid to pass up. The straight seams and simple drawstrings had kept her fingers flying the past few days, but it wasn't as if she hadn't made drawers for Whit before, underclothes being one of the first things her aunt Nattie had ever taught Fawn to sew. For good measure, she'd made up a pair for orphaned Hod, who wiped thrilled tears on his shirtsleeve when she surprised him with them, then disappeared into the dark recesses of the forward cabin to put them on right away. Too shy to parade them for the company, he did make Whit come look before he put his trousers on again, which Whit agreeably did. Whit had a funny look on his face when he came back, and fingered his own pairs thoughtfully before folding them away with rather more care than he'd ever shown to Fawn's taken-for-granted work before.

Whit and Remo then tiptoed out mysteriously, leaving Fawn and Berry smiling at each other while everyone else took care of the cleaning up. Of all the gifts this day had brought, gaining a sister ranked the highest in Fawn's heart. Berry, too, had grown up sisterless—and had become, not long after Hawthorn had been born, motherless—without even the older female company afforded Fawn by her mother and her aunt Nattie. When Berry was smaller the house in Clearcreek had been run, she'd told Fawn, by a succession of older female cousins. But one year no such woman could be found when it was time to launch the flatboat and catch the rise, so Papa Clearcreek had simply packed all three of his children along on his six-months-long round-trip. To the amazement of all their kin, no young Clearcreeks gratified their dire predictions by falling overboard and drowning, so he'd taken them every year thereafter. It seemed a colorful life to Fawn's eyes, but flatboats and keelboats both were thin of female companionship. She suspected Berry thought Fawn was Whit's best present to her, too.

Loud clumping from the front deck brought the whole company out to find Whit holding the reins of a small piebald mare, and Remo muffling the smirk of a successful conspirator. Dag's chestnut gelding Copperhead, sharing the pen with Daisy-goat, pinned his ears back in jealousy, but Dag promptly settled him down. To Fawn's utter shock, Whit handed the reins to her.

"Here you go," he said. "To make up for me making you leave your mare in West Blue. Berry bought you the saddle and bridle, and Remo came up with the saddlebags." The gear was secondhand, but looked to be in good condition; someone had cleaned it up. "Though if I'd known what horses go for in Graymouth, I'd have brought Warp and Weft along to sell here!"

"Whit! Remo! Oh—!"

"It's all right—my window glass went for a jaw-droppin' price, too," Whit allowed, shrugging off her hug in smiling embarrassment. "Berry was right to make me hang on to most of it till we got down here." He tossed a salute at his new wife and old boat boss, who accepted it with a contented nod.

"Wait," said Fawn to Remo, "isn't that one of the horses those

Lakewalkers from New Moon Cutoff were selling in the square yesterday?"

"Yep. I took Whit back, later," Remo said smugly. "Don't worry; this mare's sound. Lively little thing, rising four, I think. They were only culling her because she's too small to be a patrol horse."

Truly, the mare looked as if she'd have to take two steps to leggy Copperhead's one, but she also looked as if she wouldn't mind. Fawn fell to petting her with delight; Berry, less horse-savvy, stroked her mane more cautiously.

"And I found out those girls' tent names, too." By Remo standards, he sounded almost cheerful.

"What girls?" asked Barr.

"Oh . . . just . . . some girls. They're gone now."

"Huh?" Barr regarded him with some suspicion, but then was drawn into the general admiration of the new mare. After Fawn took a first short ride up and down the muddy riverbank, Dag watching closely, she let Hawthorn and Hod try her gift horse's paces, too. They settled the mare back aboard tied to the rail opposite Copperhead, with an armload of hay all around. At length Fawn went back inside, trying to think of a name. The first black-and-white thing that came to her mind was *Skunk,* which seemed both unkind and ungrateful. She would have to think harder.

After testing the level of beer left in the keg, they all settled around the hearth with their tankards. Fawn was just sighing in contentment and considering asking Berry to get out her fiddle and give them all some tunes, as a birthday present Fawn wouldn't have to pack, when Whit said suddenly, "Hey, Dag! What did *you* get Fawn for her birthday?"

"Ah," said Dag. He looked down into his tankard in discomfort. "I was trying to make her a surprise, but it didn't work out." He took a sip, and added, "Yet, anyway."

"Oh, what?" asked Fawn in eager curiosity. Given that he only had the one hand, Dag hardly ever attempted carving or any sort of complicated craft work. It came to her almost at once; he'd meant *making,* Lakewalker groundwork. Magic, to farmer eyes, although Fawn had nearly trained herself out of using that word. But it seemed his attempt had failed, whatever it was, and he was feeling the failure. Especially after Whit's grand present of the mare. She added, "Sometimes you have to give up on the surprise part. Remember your birthday, when I gave you one sweater sleeve?"

Dag smiled a little and touched the finished garment, which he was wearing now against the damp chill seeping back into the boat as the bustle of dinner wore off. "Indeed, Spark. Thing is, you already knew you could finish that promise. You didn't have to stop and invent knitting, first."

"All right, now you have to say," said Whit, leaning back. "You can't trail that sort of bait across the water and then just haul in your line."

"Aye, give us the tale, Dag," said Bo, a bit sleepily. "A tale is as good as a coin, some places."

"Well . . ." Reluctantly, Dag shoved his hand down into his pocket, leaned over, and deposited a black walnut, still in its shell, on the hearthstone. The farmers around the fire all looked blankly at it, and at Dag, but Barr and Remo both sat up, which made Fawn prick her ears, too.

"Dag, what in the world did you do to that poor walnut?" asked Remo. "Its ground is all . . . shiny."

Dag touched the hard ridges with a finger, rolling the green-black sphere around on the stone, then sat back and stared glumly at it. "A shell protects and shields life. It seemed a good natural essence to try to anchor an involution on. The way a knife maker anchors an involution into the bone of a sharing knife, although that cup is made to hold a death, and this . . . was going to hold something else."

Dag had made his first sharing knife bare weeks back, in the aftermath of the horrors of the bandit cave. Barr and Remo had been wildly impressed; having met Dag's knife-maker brother Dar, Fawn had been less surprised.

"I've been trying and trying to think," Dag went on, "what might protect farmers the way ground veiling protects patrollers."

"Absent gods, Dag, how could farmers veil?" said Remo. "It's like turning your whole ground sideways to the world. It gave me conniption fits, when I was first trying to learn. Not even all Lakewakers can catch the trick of it."

Dag nodded, not disagreeing. "But see . . . Fawn can't feel me in her marriage cord the way I can feel her in mine, the way any married Lakewalker does, but last summer I was able to do a shaped reinforcement in her arm that let her feel something like it, leastways for a while until her ground absorbed it again. It wasn't the same thing, but it accomplished the same end."

Fawn nodded vigorously. "It was better, actually. Old Cattagus said you can't tell direction with regular cords, just if your spouse is alive or not. But I could tell which way you were from me. Roughly, anyhow."

Barr's brows rose. "From how far away?"

"Over a hundred miles, part of the time." Fawn added scrupulously, "I don't know if it would have faded at bigger distances."

Remo's brows climbed, too.

"See, the thing is," Dag went on, "nobody's *trying* to do groundwork on farmers. Except to sneak some healing now and then out of pity, which as like as not leaves an accidental beguilement, or the occasional"—he cleared his throat—"illicit persuasion. The strongest makers don't much get outside their camps, and patrollers don't do complex or clever making."

"If you show clear talent for making," said Barr, "they don't send you for patroller. So how did you ever get let out on the trail, Dag?"

"I . . . was a difficult youngster." Dag scratched his head ruefully, but did not expand, although eight people perked up in hope of the story. "I don't know what's not done because it's impossible, or what's not done because it's never been tried. Or tried and kept secret, or discovered and then lost again."

"That still doesn't explain why you wanted to give my sister a walnut for her birthday," said Whit.

"I thought she could put it on a string, wear it like a necklace."

"She probably would. Just like you wore that silly-lookin' straw hat she wove you."

"That hat was very practical," Dag said defensively.

"So what's the use of a walnut, again?"

Dag sighed. "None, apparently. I wanted to make something that would protect her ground."

"What from?" Fawn asked.

Dag took a short breath. "Anything. People like Crane, for one."

Fawn refrained from pointing out that the renegade had actually threatened her with a perfectly ordinary steel knife, not with any magic. *What's going on in that murky head of yours, beloved?*

"Also, maybe some sort of shield could blur or soften farmer grounds so they wouldn't strike on Lakewalker groundsense so hard," Dag went on.

So she wouldn't, Fawn realized he meant, have to walk around ground-naked in front of Lakewalkers. So that her presence in a Lakewalker camp wouldn't disturb the neighbors?

"In other words," said Berry slowly, "you're thinking of something that would work like those wash-pan hats that Barr made up were supposed to, and didn't."

Barr winced. "It was just a stupid *joke,*" he muttered. "I *said* I was sorry."

A few slow smiles around the circle, as the crew of the *Fetch* recalled the uproar back at Pearl Riffle when Barr had hoaxed a gang of flatties into believing they could protect themselves from Lakewalker magic by wearing iron helmets. Iron helmets weren't usual boat gear, but iron cook pots were; the results had been pretty entertaining, for a time. Fawn thought if Barr ever encountered any of those fellows again, he'd better be ready to run really fast.

"Oh my, Dag," said Whit, his eyes suddenly aglow. "If you want something for Lakewalkers to sell to farmers for cash money, you've hit on it. Magic up a bunch of these walnuts, and you could likely peddle them at any price you wanted to name!"

"Yeah," said Bo, "and by the next afternoon at the latest, there'd be folks selling off fake ones, too. It'd be a right craze, it would." He looked suddenly thoughtful. "A feller could make a killing, if he timed it right."

"Absent gods." Dag wiped his left sleeve across his forehead, a look of some horror rising in his eyes. "I never thought of that. You're right. I just wanted to protect Fawn. Makers wouldn't . . . but if . . . never mind, it doesn't matter. I couldn't make it work anyway."

"Dag," said Fawn, "if it involves my ground, wouldn't you have to work *with* my ground? Like you did, um, with that extra reinforcement in my arm?"

"Yes. Well, maybe not just like that. Although that would certainly make selling ground shields to farmers an unusual enterprise . . ." With an effort, he untwisted his reminiscent smile. "It might need to be bonded to its user, yes. Custom-made. The way sharing knives are bonded to the grounds of their pledged donors," he added in explanation all around. And Fawn thought it was a high mark of how far they'd all come that what he got in return were understanding nods.

Dag heaved a despondent sigh. "Except that all I've been able to do so far is make an unbreakable walnut."

"Really?" said Berry, rocking back in doubt.

Hawthorn, entranced by this promise of more Lakewalker magic, scuttled up to go find a Tripoint steel hammer and test the proposition. Many thwacks later, entailing flying chips from the hearthstone and turns taken by Barr and Remo, everyone agreed that it was one blighted unbreakable walnut, all right.

Whit scratched his head and stared at the little dark sphere. "That's pretty useless, I admit. You wouldn't even be able to eat it!"

"Oh, I dunno," drawled Bo. "I 'spect you could win bets with it. Wager some o' those big strong keeler boys they can't crack it, and watch the drinks roll in . . ."

He shared a long, speculative look with Whit, who said, "Say, Dag . . . if you don't want that ol' thing, can I have it?"

"No!" cried Fawn. "Dag made it for me, even if it doesn't do what he wanted. Yet. And anyhow, you aren't planning to go tavern crawling with Bo tonight, are you?"

Berry gave Whit's hair a soft tug, which made him smirk. "No," she said definitely. "He ain't."

Fawn scooped up the walnut and thrust it into her own skirt pocket. It was growing dark outside the cabin windows, she noted with approval. There was one advantage to a midwinter wedding—early nightfall. Bo put another piece of driftwood on the fire, and Berry rose to light an oil lantern. Fawn caught Dag's eye and gave a jerk of her chin.

As planned, Dag levered himself up and invited the crew of the *Fetch* out to a nearby boatmen's tavern for a round of drinks on him. Hawthorn's helpful observation that they hadn't run out of beer yet was ignored, and Hod and Bo shepherded him off. Fawn paused to exchange a quick farewell hug with Berry, who whispered, "Thanks!" in her ear.

"Yep," Fawn murmured back. "I 'spect we'll be out most of the evening, but Hawthorn and Hod'll make sure Bo doesn't stay out all night. Don't you worry about us." She added after a moment, "I'm sure we'll make plenty of noise clomping back in."

She left Berry and Whit holding hands, looking at each other with matching terrified smiles, and sneaking peeks at their new bed nook. Formerly, the boat boss had slept in one of the narrow, three-high bunk racks at the side of the kitchen just like her crew, except that her bunk had been made a tad more private by curtains strung on a wire. Fawn and Berry together had rearranged the bedding last evening, in the space freed up by the sold-off cargo, making two little curtained-off rooms on either side of the aisle. The task had ended with them going up on the roof for a really long, nice private talk. Berry, as she put it, wanted a pilot for the snags and shoals of the marriage bed. Because while Berry was a brave boat boss, and an experienced riverwoman, and a couple of years older than Fawn, Fawn had been married for a whole six months. So Fawn tried her best to explain it all. At least Berry was smiling and relaxed when they came back in.

Whit, in the meanwhile, had taken a long walk with Dag, and returned looking pale and terrified. Fawn took Dag aside, and whispered fiercely, "You know, if it was just Whit, I'd let you exercise your patroller humor to your heart's content, but I won't have any of it fall on Berry, you hear?"

"Don't fret, Spark. I controlled myself," Dag assured her, eyes glinting gold with his amusement. "I admit, it was a bit of a struggle. Two virgins, oh my."

"Really?" said Fawn, with a surprised peek around Dag's side at Whit, hunkering down to warm his hands at the fire. "I would have thought Tansy Mayapple . . . oh, never mind."

"They'll be fine," he'd promised her.

Now, as they strolled away into the darkness after the rest of the crew, and Fawn turned to look over her shoulder at the glow of the lantern hung up on the *Fetch*'s bow, Dag repeated, "They'll do fine, Spark."

"I sure hope so." Fawn reflected that it was likely just as well that everything about this wedding was as different as it could possibly be from the one that Berry had planned back in Clearcreek with her dead betrothed Alder. No reminders. Because while bad memories were plainly bad, it was the good memories, lost in them, that hurt the worst.

The tavern was crowded and noisy tonight, so after Dag had done his duty buying the first round, Fawn bequeathed her barely sipped tankard to the table and drew him back outside for a walk despite the dark. Partway up the steps to Uptown, Fawn found the lookout point that she'd spied earlier that day. She ducked under the rail around the landing and picked her way along the damp path, inadequately lit by the half-moon riding overhead between fitful clouds. At its end, a board propped up between two piles of stones made a smooth, dry seat, with a fine view over the serene river, all hazy silver in the night mist.

In summer, Fawn guessed couples came here to spoon. Even for northerners like themselves, this wasn't quite outdoor spooning weather. She cuddled in gratefully under Dag's right arm. Though the view was romantic, and Dag shared warmth generously, it was plain he was not in a romantic mood. He was in his worrywart mood, and he'd been stuck in it for days, if not weeks. *Plenty long enough, anyhow.*

Fawn fingered the walnut in her pocket, and said quietly, "What's troubling your mind, Dag?"

He shrugged. "Nothing new." After a long hesitation, while Fawn waited in expectant silence, he added, "That's the trouble, I guess. My mind keeps looping and looping over the same problems, and never arrives anywhere different."

"Same paths do tend to go to the same places. Tell me about them, then."

His fingers wound themselves in her curls, as if for consolation or courage, then his arm dropped back around her and snugged her in; maybe she wasn't the only one feeling the chill.

"When we two left Hickory Camp at the end of the summer—when we were thrown out—"

"When we left," Fawn corrected firmly.

A conceding nod. "My notion was that if I walked around the world with my eyes new-open for a time, the way you've made them be, I could maybe see some way for farmers and Lakewalkers to work together against malice outbreaks. Because someday, the patrol won't be perfect, and a malice *will* get away from us again, not in the wilderness or even by a village like Greenspring, but by a big farmer town. And then we'll all be in for it. But if Lakewalkers and farmers were already working together before the inevitable happens . . . maybe we'd have a fighting chance."

"I thought the *Fetch* was a good start," Fawn offered.

"Good, but . . . so small, Spark! Eight people, and that's counting you along-with. For six or so months of trying."

"So, that'd be, um, sixteen folks a year. A hundred and sixty in a decade. In forty years, um . . ." A long hesitation while Fawn secretly tapped her fingers in her skirt. "Six or seven hundred."

"And if the crisis breaks next year, and not forty years from now?"

"Then it won't be any *worse* than if you hadn't tried at all. Anyhow"—*really, you'd think despair was his favorite corn-husk dolly, the way he clutches it*—"I think your count is way off. There was all my kin in West Blue you talked to, and those teamsters from Glassforge, and Cress that you healed in Pearl Riffle and all *her* kin, and boatloads of boatmen along the river. And your show at the bandit cave with Crane; gods, Dag, they'll be talking about that up and down these rivers for at least as many years as folks'll be trying to wear those stupid pots of Barr's. This river, I've figured out, is a village—one street wide and two thousand miles long. It's been a *great* place for you to tell your tale. Because river folks get around to gossip. And swap yarns like they were barter. And sometimes, change each other's minds even when you aren't looking on."

Dag shook his head. "The absent gods may know what kind of path I blazed down the Grace Valley. I sure don't. Did I light a fire, or was it all a damp sputter and right back to the gloom?"

"Why are *all* or *nothing* the only two choices, here?" Fawn asked tartly. "What *I* think is—"

Dag looked down, brows rising at the resolve in her voice.

"What *I* think is, you're trying to carry a lazy man's load. Inside your head, you're trying to lift the whole world all by yourself, in one trip. No wonder you're exhausted. You've got to start smaller."

"Smaller! How much smaller can I get?" Dag motioned down at the riverbank, by which Fawn guessed he meant to indicate their modest flatboat. A rhetorical reply in any case, so she paid no heed to it.

"Your own ground. I know it's true because you told me so yourself, and you never lie to me: the first thing a maker has to make is himself. But nobody ever said he had to do it *by* himself."

"Do you have a point, Spark?"

She ignored his stung tone and answered straight out. "Yes. It's true for cooking or sewing or boatbuilding or harness making or crafting arrows—so I don't guess it's false for groundwork. Before you tackle any new job, first you have to get your own tools in order, clean and sharpened and tidy and laid out ready to hand. The main tool for groundwork is your own ground. And yours, from everything everyone has ever told me about such things, has got to be in the most awful mess right about now.

"What *I* think you need is another maker. Not a farmer girl, much as she loves you, and not just a couple of earnest patroller boys, as much as they want to help, because they don't know beans about that trail, either, but instead someone like Hoharie or Dar." Fawn took a breath, shaken by a moment of panic when she realized that Dag, unlike any member of her family ever, was actually *listening* to her. The notion that a man so strong might actually change or do something differently on the basis of something she'd blathered was alarming. Back when she'd longed in vain for any sign that she was heard, had she ever imagined also accepting responsibility for the results? *Well, they're in my lap now.* She gulped. "So . . . so I've been asking around. Every visiting Lakewalker I could get to talk to me up in the day market, I asked about the best medicine makers in these parts. They told me about a lot of different folks, but the one they all talked up is a fellow named Arkady Waterbirch. Seems he's to be found at a Lakewalker camp called New Moon Cutoff, which is less'n thirty miles northeast of here, right off the Trace. Not much more'n a day's ride away for ol' Copperhead." She added in anxious appeal, "They call him a *groundsetter,* whatever that means."

Dag looked taken aback. "Really? That close? If . . ." But then he rubbed his forehead with his left arm and smiled ruefully. "Oh, gods, Spark. Wouldn't I just . . . but it won't work. It would be Dar and Hoharie all over again, don't you see?" His teeth set in unfond memory. "I've patrolled down this way a time or two. These southern Lakewalkers haven't got any more use for farmers than the ones back in Oleana do—and more land jealousy, what with the camps being squeezed up between farmer areas. And with malices so seldom found in these parts, the farmers don't even give their patrollers that thin gratitude we get in the north. Though when a southern patrol does find a little sessile, 'bout once in a lifetime, you'd think it was the Wolf War breaking out again, the way they carry on . . . anyway. I doubt the pair of us would be any more welcome at New Moon Cutoff than we were at Hickory Lake."

"Maybe, maybe not, if we made it plain we were just visiting. Seems to me it was mainly your tent-kin who thought I was a problem they had to fix."

"Mm," said Dag.

Fawn swallowed. "Or you could go without me. At least to see the man, and ask. I'd be all right staying with Berry and Whit."

"You're the light that I see by, Spark. I'm not letting go of you again." The flash in his eyes reminded her of the lantern reflection off Crane's knife blade, held tight to her throat, that had shimmered across Dag's face just before . . . just before.

"Then we'll both go, and I'll deal with whatever I'm dished out. If it's no better than Hickory Lake, it'll be no worse, either, and I survived that." She pulled the unbreakable walnut from her pocket and rolled it curiously in her hand. "What you're doing now all by yourself isn't working, you say. If any of the rest of us could help you, we would have by now. Time to try something else. Stands to reason Dag! And if this Arkady fellow doesn't work out, either, well, at least you can scratch him off your list, and be that much farther along."

She watched his face scrunch up in doubt so intense it looked like pain, and added, "I can't be happy while you're hurtin'. We have some time to pass anyhow, waiting down here at the edge of the world for the cold to end before we travel. You've kept all your promises to show me the river, and Graymouth, and the sea. Now you can just show me New Moon Cutoff for dessert. And if it's not as fine as the sea, at least it'll be new to me, and that'll be good enough." She gave a determined nod, which made him smile, if a bit bleakly.

"If that's what you really think, Spark," he said, "then I'll give the fellow a try."

3

Two days of cold rain masked Dag's disinclination to travel to New Moon Cutoff, so Fawn did not badger, but she did draw Barr and Remo into the project. When the next day dawned clear, the three of them had Dag on the road north, if not early, at least before noon. Barr and Remo claimed to be interested in buying horses for a better price than found in the Drowntown market, where the flatboat men not wishful to join keeler crews bid for mounts to carry them back home on the Tripoint Trace. Fawn wasn't sure Dag was fooled, because he looked pretty ironic about it all, but he didn't say anything cutting. Fawn rode rather guiltily on her new mare, now named Magpie; three sets of saddlebags were piled onto Copperhead, led by his master; the patroller men strode.

Or tried to. Outside of Graymouth, the road became a quagmire. It was nearly impassable to wagons—they paused several times to offer help to farmers with wheels stuck up to the hubs; and once, the man was so desperate that he even accepted the offer, despite the three tall strangers being Lakewalkers. Though his thanks, afterward, were brief and worried, cast over his shoulder as he urged his team into motion once more. Pack trains of horses or mules made fairly good time on the hoof-pocked verge—a couple of them passed by southbound, bringing in loads of cotton, tea, and other mysterious local goods to the river port. Barr, however, complained bitterly about slogging in his farmer-made boots, new bought in Graymouth.

"Don't they fit right?" Fawn asked. "I thought you said you'd broken them in. Do they leak?"

"No more than you'd expect," said Barr. "But look!" He raised one knee to display a boot.

From her saddle, Fawn looked blankly down at it.

"There must be ten pounds of mud stuck to each foot!" fumed Barr.

Fawn glanced at Remo, standing with his hands on his hips and grinning at his partner, and realized that his boots, though damp and stained, were largely clump-free. "Hey, Remo, how come your boots aren't like that?"

Remo held out a leg and smugly rotated his ankle. "My cousin made these for me. They're groundworked to shed the mud."

"Cheer up, Barr," Dag advised, smiling faintly. "I'll help you fix them when we make camp tonight. Didn't you learn how to renew leather-work when you were on patrol back in Oleana?"

"Well, yes, but—"

"He usually sweet-talked one of the girls into doing it for him," remarked Remo, staring off artlessly over sodden fields.

"I was going to say, *renew,* yes, but these boots have never been worked at all! I thought that needed to happen while they're first made."

"Usually, but I'll see what I can lay in," said Dag. "It's not like I haven't done trail fix-ups on leather gear 'bout ten thousand times."

They trudged onward past a hamlet boasting an inn of sorts, but they still had two hours of daylight left for walking; only Fawn looked back in regret. When dusk descended, they found a high spot off the road to make a camp. Fawn was not impressed with its comforts, although the boys did get a fire going despite the damp. She unpacked their food and shared it around.

Dag and Barr were soon heads down over the offending boots. Dag, quite adeptly it seemed to Fawn, instructed Barr in how to persuade them to be more waterproof. Muddy boots. Soon to be un-muddy boots, but which would not then walk on their own, nor force their owner to dance through the night, nor stride leagues at a step. So much for glamorous Lakewalker magic, wicked necromancy, rumors of cannibalistic rites. *If only other folks could see these fellows as I do . . .*

"Hey, Fawn!" Remo called from beyond the firelight, where he'd been rustling around along a weed-choked drainage ditch. "Want an alligator?"

"No!" she cried back in alarm. "I *don't* want one!" Had he *found* one? How big? Could it smell her new shoes from there? If so, would it be angry? And if Remo caught it, instead of being promptly bitten in trap-like jaws as his carefree enthusiasm deserved, would he make her try to cook it . . . ?

Remo came tromping back out of the darkness with a wriggling form stretched between his two hands. Boot magic was temporarily abandoned as Barr jumped up to look, too. Dag, unhelpfully, sat on his log and grinned at Fawn's expression. Which would have annoyed her more except his grins had grown too rare, lately.

"It's . . . small," said Fawn as the beast was eagerly presented to her gaze. A foot and a half of struggling lizard; Remo had one hand firmly clamped around its long snout and the other stretching its lashing tail. It hissed protest and churned its short legs, trying to claw its captor.

"Just a baby," agreed Remo. "They hatch from eggs, they say. Like chickens."

The bulging yellow eyes, with vertically slit pupils, looked even less friendly than a chicken's. Baby or no, this was not, Fawn sensed, an animal that would welcome cuddling. Bo's tale of the boy, the bear cub, and the thorn would have come out very differently in the end, if the boy had drawn the barb from the paw of a creature like this.

When the Oleana boys had finished exclaiming over the catch, they then squabbled over whether to let it go again. Fawn gave this plan no encouragement. Even barring what horrors a malice might make of such a creature, those things grew, presumably, into what had mauled that boy at the Lakewalker camp. And if she *volunteered* to cook it, it couldn't end up introduced alive into her bedroll later, although she supposed the boys would be more likely to try that game on each other than on Dag. They weren't her *own* brothers. Their ruckus would still disrupt her sleep.

They toasted the meager fragments over the coals. Fawn found that alligator meat tasted like some off cross between pork and the boiled crab claw she had tried in the Drowntown market—and like campfire smoke, of course, but everything tasted of that. It would beat starving, but Fawn did not foresee a future in alligator farming. Treating the skin did keep the patroller boys occupied for the rest of the evening, leaving Fawn to cuddle with Dag in their reptile-free bedroll in a vain attempt to get warm.

When the camp finally settled for the night, she murmured into his collarbone, "Dag . . . ?"

"Mm?"

"I thought what you and Remo discovered about unbeguiling, back up on the Grace, was pretty exciting. I figured you'd be talking about it to every new Lakewalker we met. Instead, I don't recall as you've even *spoken* to any Lakewalker we've passed."

He gave an unrevealing grunt. The verbal equivalent to that thing he did with his eyelids, she decided.

"I been wondering why not," Fawn finished, refusing to be daunted.

He sighed. "It wasn't quite that simple. Yes, my trick works to unbeguile farmers, I'm sure of that part, but I still don't know what the effects are on the Lakewalker, to be taking in all that strange ground. I'm willing to experiment on myself. I'm less willing to put others at risk, till I know——" He broke off.

"What?"

"What I don't know yet."

She wanted to reassure him, to say, *Well, at least we're heading in the right direction to find out,* but for all she knew she'd dragged them out on a fool's errand. Tomorrow would—might—tell. "You will let this Arkady fellow know all about it, though, won't you? Promise?"

"Oh, yes," he breathed, stirring her curls. "Sleep, Spark."

∾

Midday, on a side road striking west from the Tracc, they passed from fallow fields into woods; Dag guessed they were crossing out of farmer-owned land onto that of the Lakewalker camp. The camp itself came up sooner than he'd expected, only a few miles farther on. Magpie, recognizing her former home, tried to pull ahead, and for the first time Fawn had to rein back to her companions' walking pace. The road climbed a low rise that proved to be a former river bluff, and Dag's heart gave an odd lurch when he glimpsed the familiar glint of lake water through the leafless trees. *I've been long away from home, this patrol.* This cutoff was an old watercourse of the Gray River, which had ages ago looped thirty miles west instead, leaving this crescent-shaped lake and the groove of land in which it lay.

A quarter mile along the crest, the road dodged left again, descending to the shallow lake valley. A spur curved back down the slope into the woods. Just past where the tracks met, two flanking tree stumps cradled a peeled pole across the road at knee height; not so much a gate as the idea of a gate. Less cursory were two armed patrollers, taking their turn at this light camp duty between patrols. They watched Dag's little party approach with alert curiosity. Dag presumed their open groundsenses—his was nearly closed just now—assured them that their visitors bore no ill will.

"Oh, hey!" said Remo, his spine straightening. "It's those two girls who were selling horses at the Drowntown market last week!"

"Oh?" Barr followed his gaze, brows climbing. "Aha! So, partner, why didn't you take me along to help buy that birthday horse, huh?"

"Didn't think you were interested in horses," said Remo blandly.

They all paused before the level pole.

"Well, if it isn't the quiet fellow from Oleana!" said one of the patrollers, who had red-brown braids wreathing her head. "How de', Remo. What brings you here?" Her taller blond companion looked approvingly at the boys, curiously at Dag, and doubtfully at Fawn. The redhead added more anxiously, "That piebald mare is working out all right, isn't she?"

Remo ducked his head and smiled. "Hi again! Yes, the mare's fine." Fawn nodded friendly confirmation from atop Magpie, who stretched out her nose and snuffled at her former handlers. "We've just brought our, uh, friend Dag here along to see that Arkady Waterbirch fellow you two told us about."

Remo having apparently become spokesman, Dag was inclined to let him continue; he merely added a nod and touched his forehead in polite greeting. Then he wondered exactly what Fawn and Remo had said about him, because the two women stared at him in some surprise. He rehitched Copperhead's reins around his hook and waited.

Barr chipped in, with a fine white grin, "Hi, my name's Barr. I'd be

Remo's partner who he forgot to mention. I'm from Oleana, too—Pearl Riffle Camp, way on up the Grace. Real malice country up north there, y'know. Seems he also forgot to tell me your names . . ." He trailed off invitingly.

There followed an exchange of pleasantries in which Barr smoothly managed to extract the patroller girls' names, tent-names, projected patrol schedules, family situations, the fact that the tall blonde had just returned from exchange patrol but the shorter redhead had never been beyond the territory of her home camp, and whether either had any pretty sisters—or ugly brothers. Dag would have been tolerably amused, if he hadn't been so tired and strained.

Remo listened with growing impatience. Giving up on waiting for a natural break in the flow, he gripped Barr's arm and overrode him: "And where would we find Maker Waterbirch?"

"Oh," said the redhead, Tavia. She swung around and waved her arm toward the lake. "If you follow this road down and take the right-hand fork along the shoreline, you'll pass the medicine tent about half a mile in. Old Arkady's is the third tent after that, set apart. There's these two big magnolia trees flanking his front path, you can't miss them." She glanced up at the listening Fawn, collected a nudge from her blond partner Neeta, and added, "If you follow this side road off east here, back down the slope, there's a shelter and camp for farmers who come here to trade. Has its own well and all. Your farmer friend can wait there."

"She's with me," said Dag.

Tavia gave him a politely embarrassed smile; her blond partner frowned.

"Farmers aren't allowed in camp," said Neeta. "The shelter's not bad, and there should be a stack of firewood for the hearth. Nobody else is there just now."

Dag's jaw set. "We go in together or not at all."

Remo and Barr exchanged alarmed looks. "Dag," said Remo uneasily, "we just walked two days to get here."

"If Fawn isn't allowed in, neither this place nor its people are any use to me. If we start now, we can be halfway home to the *Fetch* by nightfall."

"Wait, wait!" said Barr as Dag made to turn away. But when Dag paused and raised his eyebrows, he could not immediately come up with a counter.

Fawn, who'd listened to this exchange with her fist stuffed in her mouth, took it away to say placatingly, "It's all right, Dag. Doesn't sound like anybody would bother me at that shelter, and I could build a fire. I could wait out there for a while, anyhow, while you go in and talk to the man. And then we'd see."

"No," said Dag.

"Um . . . who is she, to you?" asked Tavia.

"My wife," said Dag.

The two patroller women looked at each other; the blonde rolled her eyes. The alarm in Barr's eyes was shading over into panic. *Blight it, boy, I don't know what bur is getting under your saddle. I'm closed down as tight as that walnut. I can't possibly be leaking any mood.* Vile as that mood was growing . . .

Tavia glanced at Dag and addressed herself prudently to Remo. "What did he want to see Arkady for, anyway?"

"It's . . . complicated," said Remo helplessly.

"A complicated problem with groundwork," Fawn put in. "And medicine making. Likely not something to discuss in the middle of the road. You two aren't either of you makers, are you?"

The blonde looked offended, but Barr added hastily, "Yes, probably this Arkady fellow should be the one to decide. A couple of patrollers really aren't fit to guess what a maker would want. I know I'm not! That's why we're here!" He blinked and smiled winningly at the women. "*I* thought it was important enough to walk two days for, and in bad boots at that. It seems crazy to stop just half a mile short. If you can't let Fawn in, and believe me I know how stuffy patrol leaders can be about camp rules, couldn't one of you go in and ask him to come out here and talk? And then whatever got decided would be off you and on him, where it belongs." Barr blinked eyes gone liquid as a soulful puppy's; Dag could have sworn his blond queue grew fluffier even as his smile brightened to near blinding. Remo pinched the bridge of his nose and sighed.

Tavia's brow wrinkled, but a crooked smile was drawn unwillingly from her in response. "Well . . ." she said weakly.

"All," growled Dag, "or none."

Barr made pleading hand gestures and kept smiling in a way that reminded Dag of Bo's story about the fellow who grinned a bear out of a tree. Some forms of persuasion, it seemed, had nothing to do with illicit groundwork, because Tavia rubbed her neck and repeated, "Well . . . I suppose I could walk down quick and ask him, sure. Mind, after that it'll be up to him."

"Tavia, you are a jewel among gate guards!" cried Barr.

"Barr, it's just the sensible thing to do," said Remo quellingly. He gave Tavia a respectful salute of thanks. She strode off with a saucy glance over her shoulder that seemed equally divided between the two patroller boys. Neeta shook her head.

Silence fell for a time as Neeta retreated to a more firm-chinned patrol stance, and Remo rubbed his chapped hands and stole glances at her. At length Fawn said, "I suppose we could go water the horses at that well while we wait. Take a look around."

Dag grunted, but didn't balk when she reined her mare around and led off. Barr followed, grabbing Remo and bringing him along. The farmer trade camp proved to be a large clearing, the shelter three log walls with a fieldstone hearth, snugly roofed, all tidy and in reasonable repair. Remo and Barr drew up several buckets of water and emptied them into a trough, where Copperhead and Magpie gulped enough to make it seem worthwhile.

When they returned to the gate, Tavia was just turning onto the bottom of the road, a tall man striding at her shoulder.

"Blight, Barr," muttered Remo. "This is the first time I've seen your talents have a use."

"Yeah?" Barr muttered back. "*I* find them useful. This is just the first time you've ever appreciated them."

As the pair climbed nearer, Dag studied the groundsetter warily. Arkady Waterbirch wore clean trousers, shirt, and an undyed wool coat to the knees, open in this moderate chill. His hair was blond streaked with gray, pulled back in a neat mourning knot at his nape; in the pale light of this winter noon, it shone silver gilt. His hairline was not thinning yet, but seemed to be thinking about it. As he drew nearer still, Dag eyed his tawny skin, with fine lines at the corners of his eyes and around his mouth, and found himself unable to guess the man's age; his silvering hair said older, his unweathered skin suggested younger; in any case, he was likely not far off from Dag's own generation. His hands, too, were smooth, with the cleanest fingernails Dag had ever seen even on a medicine maker. His eyes were bright copper shot with gold. The general effect was a trifle blinding.

What the man's ground was like Dag could not tell until he opened his own, shuttered most of the time since . . . since Crane, really. As the maker's gaze swept him in turn, Dag grew conscious of his own travel-worn appearance. Two days of trudging through the mire and sleeping rough last night had returned him to his patrol look: clothing shabby and sweat-stained—although, thanks to Fawn, neatly mended;

cropped hair uncombed; jaw unshaved, because they'd all been eager to leave last night's damp camp and move along. Most of his old scars were covered by his clothing, but for the first time in a while Dag felt an impulse to hold his maimed left arm behind his back.

The boys were tidy enough, for patrollers; their youth, Dag thought with an inward sigh, could have made rags look good on them, though they did not know it. Fawn, still atop Magpie, was her own fair, small, strong self, brown eyes bright with hope and worry, every scant inch a farmer girl. He was reminded of the day she'd told the formidable Captain Fairbolt Crow to go take a jump in Hickory Lake, during another not-altogether-easy introduction, and almost smiled.

As the maker came to a halt and took in the folks awaiting him, he seemed more and more nonplussed. After a second sweeping look over the party, pausing on Remo, he addressed himself to Dag: "Tavia's tale seems a trifle confused. But if that's your boy, there, I can tell you right now he hasn't the ground to apprentice for a medicine maker. He's a patroller born. If you've come all this way for a different answer than you had at home, I'm sorry for it, because I can't give it to you."

Remo looked taken aback. "No, sir," he said hastily, "that's not what we're here for. And Dag's not my father, he's my . . . um. Captain, I guess."

Captain No-Camp, the ill-fated Crane had dubbed Dag; the name seemed to be sticking, along with a few more unwanted gifts.

The copper-gilt eyes narrowed on Dag's hook. Arkady said more gently, "Ah. You may have been misled by rumor. On a day with the right wind at my back, I can do some useful things, but I don't make miracles. I'm afraid there's not much I can do for your arm. That injury's far too old."

Dag unlocked his voice. "I'm not here about my missing hand, sir." *I'm here about the hand that came back.* So bluntly confronted, Dag found it hard to explain his needs. "It's not Remo who's interested in training for medicine maker. It's me."

Arkady's eyes flew wide. "Surely not. Maker's talents, if you have them, should have shown by age twenty. Even a groundsetter's potential should be starting to show by age forty."

"I was long gone for patroller by then, and no one much could have stopped me. My maker's calling was . . . delayed. But everything changed for me this year, from my name to my ground." Dag swallowed.

"Anyhow," Fawn put in, "Dag doesn't just think he can be a medicine maker, he's *been* healing folks, all down the Grace and Gray valleys. He fixed Hod's busted kneecap where the horse kicked him, and Cress's infected gut, and Chicory's busted skull and that other fellow's cut throat after the fight at the bandit cave, and who knows what all else there, and he healed Bo's stab to his stomach that we all thought sure was going to kill him. *And* he made a sharing knife. Before that, he did patrol healing on the trail I guess, but since last summer all this other has come roaring out. I don't know why now, but talent he has. He *needs* instruction. So as not to make bad mistakes from not knowing things, which is a regret *I* could tell you all about."

Arkady's head rocked back. His eyes narrowed at Dag, then fixed on Remo. "Have you seen this?" he demanded.

"Yes, sir," said Remo. "Well, the kneecap I saw later, after it was part healed, and I wasn't there for the woman at Pearl Riffle, but all the rest, yes."

"And more," said Barr, his lips twisting.

"If so, why wasn't he invited—snatched up!—by the makers at one of those camps along the river?"

"All the folks he healed were farmers," said Fawn.

Arkady recoiled; he wheeled on Dag. In a voice of suppressed fury, he said, "You unspeakable fool! You went and left all those poor people mad with beguilement?"

Dag's lips curled up. "No, sir. Because between Fawn, Remo, Hod, and me, we cracked unbeguilement as well. I could see it was the first thing had to be done, if I meant to be a medicine maker to farmers. Which I did and do."

All three New Moon folks were staring at Dag openmouthed. And seeing . . . not much; he still held his ground veiling tight-furled. None could tell if he was concealing lies or truth, only that he was concealing himself.

"You're raving," said Arkady abruptly. "And I can't be dealing with a renegade."

"I'm no renegade!" said Dag, stung on the raw. *Are you so sure, old patroller?* He was going to have to unveil, open himself to those copper-gold eyes and whatever lay behind them, which he hadn't wanted to do at this gate. *Or at all*, he admitted to himself.

"Deserter?" said Neeta suspiciously. She glanced at Fawn, and her voice grew edged with scorn. "Oh, of course. It's obvious. Banished for farmer loving, back in Oleana."

"No!" Although the latter had come too close to being true. "I resigned from the patrol in good order. My old camp captain knows where I went and why." The problem was huge, complex, with snarled strings running down into the most intimate aspects of his ground and up and out into the whole wide green world. *Blight, it's impossible to speak this tangle plain.* But Fawn's eyes were urgent on him. He must not disappoint her appalling trust.

"Renegade, deserter, banished, or just plain mad, it's clear you're unfit to be a medicine maker," said Arkady coldly. "Off with you. Get out of this camp." He began to veer away. Fawn's hand went out in pleading; he did not glance at her.

We pretend to save farmers, thought Dag, *but in truth we turn our backs . . .*

Opening his ground here, now, felt like tearing off a bandage stuck to a half-healed wound. Dag nearly expected to see blood and pus flying. For the first time in weeks, he extended his ghost hand in its full power.

And ground-ripped a strip from the back of the maker's left hand, right down to the matter. Blood burst from it like a cat scratch. Arkady hissed and wheeled back.

Open at last to the man, Dag bent before the density of his ground, a subdued brilliance like the sun behind a cloud. What Arkady would make of the dark mess that was presently Dag, there was no guessing. The maker's face worked with ripples of emotion: shock, outrage, chilling anger.

Arkady touched the bleeding scratch with the finger of his other hand; the blood stopped flowing. Some floating part of Dag's mind marveled: *Ah! He can do groundwork on himself!*

Dag said, in a dead-level voice, "Open as you were, I could have reached in and done that to the artery from your heart just as easily. At your first heartbeat, it would have burst, and you'd have been dead in the next. And I'm walkin' around loose out here. If I'm not to turn into a real renegade, a man who just needs killin', I need *some* kind of a pathfinder. Because right now I'm almost as lost as I've ever been." Save for after Wolf Ridge, and the death of Kauneo. Nothing would ever be as dark as that again; the realization was oddly consoling.

The two gate guards both had their knives out, tense with alarm, but Arkady waved them back. He was plainly shaken; his lips moved on a—name?—*Sutaw.* He straightened himself, fastidiously flicked the trailing red drops from his fingers, inhaled, and said coldly, "*That* was an inexcusably clumsy piece of groundsetting. If you were an apprentice of mine, I'd have your hide for groundwork that ripped into a patient like that."

All the blood seemed to drain from Dag's head, so deep was his relief. *He's seen this. He knows what it is. It looks normal to him. It's a known groundsetting technique. Not malice magic. I'm not turning into a malice . . .*

Dag only realized he'd fallen to his knees when Fawn appeared at his side, her voice anxious. "Dag? Are you all right? Are you laughing, or crying?" She pulled his hand away from his face. His shoulders shook.

"I'm not sure, Spark," he groaned. "Both, I think." Only now, when it was so abruptly removed, did he realize just how much that secret terror had been riding him, sapping his strength. Had he been a fool? Maybe not.

Arkady rubbed his chiseled chin. And, at length, sighed. "You all had better come down to my place. I don't think I can deal with this in the middle of the road."

"All of them, sir?" said Neeta, with a dubious look at Fawn.

"They seem to come as a set. Yes, all. Tavia, tell the women I'll be having four guests for lunch today." He walked over and extended his right hand to Dag.

Indeed, I need a hand.

Dag took it, hauling himself upright again.

4

A half-mile walk, leading the horses, brought them all to Arkady's place, and Fawn stared in astonishment. After her experience at Hickory Lake Camp she'd thought she knew what Lakewalker tents were like: crude, deliberately temporary log cabins, usually with an open side protected by hide awnings, clustered in kin groups around a dock space or central fire pit. The dwellings she'd glimpsed at Pearl Riffle had been similar. This . . . this was a *house*.

Two huge trees laden with dark green leaves like drooping tongues—but not a blossom in sight at this season—bracketed a stone-paved walk. Atop a foundation cut into the slope and lined with fitted stones, several rooms rambled, built of silvery-gray weathered cedar planks, roofed with split-wood shingles, and connected by a long porch. The windows gleamed with real glass. Barr and Remo, Fawn was consoled to note, also stared openmouthed; by camp standards, it was practically a palace. Dag seemed less surprised, but then, Fawn wasn't exactly sure if he was paying attention. After his brief, scary breakdown at the gate, he'd recovered himself and was looking awfully closed. Again.

They tied the horses to the porch rail and followed Arkady into what appeared to be a main room, pausing to wipe their feet after him twice, once on a mat outside and again on a rag rug just inside the door. The far wall had a whole row of glass windows and a door onto an unroofed porch overlooking the lake. A large hearth to the right was fitted up for cooking, which Fawn suspected might include cooking up medicines. By the hearth stood a sturdy table, waist height for working, but near the windows was a lower, round one that seemed just for eating. It boasted real lathe-made chairs, with stuffed cloth cushions tied on. At Hickory Lake, folks had mostly made do with trestle tables and upended logs.

"You can wash your hands at the sink," Arkady directed, and busied himself with his water kettle and a teapot, of all things. Fawn guessed that he was buying time to think about what to do next; he'd said almost nothing on the walk from the gate, beyond laconically pointing out patrol headquarters and the medicine tent, bracketing the entry road. Those, too, had been plank-built and houselike.

Beneath a lakeside window, the tin-lined sink had a water barrel with a wooden tap to its right, a drain board to the left. Fawn filled the washbasin and took her turn with a cake of fine white soap, watching while Dag did his one-handed trick with the soap and water after her. Arkady, she noticed, paused to covertly watch that, too. The patroller boys followed suit; the very dirty water was dumped down a drain, where it gurgled through a wooden pipe leading outside. It was all as handy as a well-furbished farm kitchen, and as hard to shift. Fawn fancied she could almost hear Dag thinking, *Sessile!* and not in a tone of approval.

They sat five around the table and watched while Arkady poured out tea into fired clay mugs, and offered a pitcher of honey. Fawn sipped the sweet brew gratefully, wondering who was supposed to start, and if it would be up to her. To her relief, Arkady began.

"So—ex-patroller—how have you come to me? New Moon Cutoff seems a long way from Oleana." He took a swallow and settled back, watching Dag narrowly.

It was a—deliberately?—broadly worded question. Dag looked somewhat desperately at Fawn. "Where to begin, Spark?" he asked.

She bit her lip. "The beginning? Which would be Glassforge, I guess."

"That far back? All of it? You sure?"

"If we don't explain how your knife got primed at Glassforge, you won't be able to explain what you did with it at Bonemarsh, and Hoharie herself said she thought that was magery."

Arkady's eyes widened slightly at the word. "Who is Hoharie?"

"Hickory Lake's chief medicine maker," Dag explained.

"Ah." Arkady went still, taking this in. "Do go on."

"How about if I start?" said Fawn. Their tale *had* to convince the groundsetter to take Dag seriously, despite Dag's running off to mix with farmers. Because if they could be let into the camp on this man's bare word, they could surely be thrown out the same way. *Plain and true.* Nothing else would do. Just as well; Fawn didn't think she could tell fancy lies to that penetrating coppery stare.

"It was coming on strawberry season last summer in Oleana, and I was going to Glassforge to look for work on account of—" She took a breath for courage. The intimate parts of this tale would be new to Barr and Remo, too; it was almost harder to speak it in front of them than this shiny stranger. "On account of as I'd got pregnant with a farm boy who didn't care to marry me, and I didn't care to stay around and deal with what my life would be at home once it came out. So, the road. Dag's patrol was called down there to help search for a malice that was running a bandit gang in the hills. A couple of the bandits—a mud-man and a beguiled fellow—snatched me off the road *because* I was pregnant, it seems."

Remo's eyes widened, and Barr blinked, but both kept their mouths shut tight. Arkady's hand touched his lips. "So it's true that malices need pregnant women for their molts?"

"Yes," said Dag. "Though they'll also use pregnant animals if they can't get humans. It's not actually the women they crave, it's the fast-growing ground of the youngsters they bear, and the, the *template* of bearing. To teach them how, see. I arrived . . . almost in time. There was this cave. The malice ripped the ground from Fawn's child about the time I hit its mud-man guards. I was carrying a pouch with two sharing knives in it, one primed and one bonded to me. I tossed the pouch to Fawn, who was closer, and she put both knives in the malice, one after the other."

"Wrong one first," confessed Fawn. "The unprimed one. I didn't know."

"You couldn't have," Dag assured her. He stared rather fiercely at Arkady, who in fact showed no signs of wanting to criticize this.

"It had me by the neck at the time, which is where these came from," Fawn went on, touching the deep red dents marring the sides of her throat, four on one side and one on the other.

"So *that's* what those are!" said Arkady, startled into leaning forward and peering. He drew his hand back before actually touching her. "I didn't think to find blight scars on a farmer. Those are the freshest I've ever seen. That sort of ground injury doesn't often come our way down here."

Barr leaned back, his brow wrinkling; belatedly figuring out just how close to a malice Fawn had come, she thought. *If I have malice fingerprints on me, the malice couldn't have been more than an arm's length off, you know.*

"Count yourselves lucky," said Dag dryly. With this start, he seemed willing to take up the tale. "In any case, my bonded knife ended up primed with the ground of Fawn's child. Hickory Lake's chief knife maker and I each have different ideas as to why, but they don't matter now. Anyway, on the way to take the knife to my camp and see about the puzzle, we stopped at West Blue—Fawn's kinfolk have a farm just up that river valley—I thought they'd want to know she was still alive. We were married there. Twice over, once by farmer customs and once by ours. Here. Roll up your sleeve, Spark."

He shrugged awkwardly out of his jacket and rolled up his own left sleeve, revealing the arm harness that held his wrist cap in place, and above it, his wedding cord that Fawn had braided. He normally kept his sleeve rolled down in front of strangers, but Fawn supposed this maker, like a farmer midwife, had to see what was going on in order to do his work, so you just had to get past the shyness. Almost as reluctantly, Fawn pushed up her left cuff to reveal her cord that Dag had braided.

Dag hitched his shoulder forward. "Does your groundsense say these are valid cords?" he asked. Growled, more like.

"Yes," said Arkady cautiously. Fawn sighed with relief.

"Thank you for your honesty, sir." Dag sat back with a satisfied nod. "We had some blighted stupid argumentation about that at Hickory Lake, later."

Arkady cleared his throat. "Your tent-kin did not welcome your new bride, I take it?" Your very *young* bride, Fawn fancied his glance at her added, but he had the prudence not to say it aloud.

"Your aunt Mari and uncle Cattagus were pretty nice to me, I thought," said Fawn, in what defense she could muster of Dag's home. "Wait, Dag, you left out the glass bowl. That has to be important. It was the first time your ghost hand came out." She turned to Arkady. "That's what Dag called it at first, because it spooked him something awful, but Hoharie said it was a ground projection. You'd better tell that part, Dag, because to me it just looked like magic."

"There was this glass bowl." Dag waved his hand. "Back at West Blue, just before we were wed. It meant a lot to Fawn—she'd brought it back from Glassforge as a gift for her mama. My tent-mother, now. It fell and broke."

"Three big pieces and about a hundred shards," Fawn added in support. "All over the parlor floor." She was grateful that he left out the surrounding family uproar. Angry as she sometimes was with her kin, she would not have wanted to see them held up as fools before this Arkady.

"I . . ." Dag made a gesture with his hook. "*This* came out, and I sort of swirled the glass all back together through its ground. I'd seen bowls like it being made back in Glassforge, you see. Its ground had a hum to it . . ." His lips shaped, but did not blow, a note.

Arkady, Barr, and Remo were all staring at his hook—no, not the hook, Fawn realized. At the invisible, elusive ground projection that took the place of his lost left hand. Which she would never see, but could sometimes—she suppressed a smile—feel. Dag eased back, as did the other three Lakewalkers, and she guessed he'd let the projection go in again.

"First I heard about that bowl," muttered Barr to Remo. "Ye gods. Did you know about it?" Remo shook his head and motioned his partner to shush.

"Before things came to the point at Hickory Lake," Dag went on, "there was that big malice outbreak over in Raintree. Did you hear much about it, way down here?"

"A little," said Arkady. "I confess, the patrollers here follow the news from the north more closely than I do. There always seems to be some excitement going on, up your way."

"Raintree malice was more than that. It promised to be every bit as bad as the Wolf War in Luthlia twenty years back. Worse, because it was fixing to tear across thickly settled farmer country. Malice food on a platter."

Arkady shrugged. "But you were from Oleana—you said?"

Dag's lips thinned. Fawn put in quickly, "Raintree sent out riders for help. Hickory Lake's sort of next door, being in the far northwest of the hinterland. Fairbolt Crow—camp captain at Hickory Lake—chose Dag to be company captain of the force they sent out. Explain about ground-ripping the malice, Dag."

Dag drew breath and twisted his left arm, turning his hook. Ghost hand displayed again, or just referred to? "That thing I did to you at the gate, sir. For which I apologize, but I had to . . . anyway. What did you make it out to be?"

Arkady, reminded, touched the back of his hand, now scabbed, and frowned at Dag. "A projection for groundsetting, applied too power-fully and damaging the overlying tissue. Deliberately, I take it. Although there are occasions when such tearing is a valuable tool—used rather more precisely, I must say."

"Used vastly more powerfully and not at all precisely, it's the same as the ground-ripping a malice does," said Dag.

Arkady's brows flew up. "Surely not." His eyes flicked toward Fawn's throat.

"Surely is," said Dag. "I've seen it coming and going, and there's no mistake—I can show you the old malice scars on my legs, later. Like that glass bowl, the first time I did it I was pretty upset—we had closed on the malice, and it was trying to ground-rip one of my patrollers. I just reached out . . ." Dag drew breath. "Free advice, boys, bought at the usual cost. Don't ever try to ground-rip a malice. Its ground sticks to yours, and is deadly poisonous. That's how I got *these* scars . . ." He gestured to his left side generally. He wasn't pointing to his body, Fawn realized, but to its ground.

"Oh," said Arkady, in an odd voice. "I couldn't imagine what had caused those dark ripples."

Dag hesitated. "You've never seen a malice, have you, sir?"

Arkady shook his head.

"Ever patrolled at all?"

"When I was a boy, they had me out a few times with the others my age. But I showed for a maker very young."

"Ah, the camping trips with the kiddies," muttered Barr. "I hate those." The riveted Remo poked him to silence.

"So you've never seen a live mud-man," sighed Dag.

"Ah . . . no." Arkady added after a moment, "The medicine maker who trained me at Moss River Camp had a dead one that he kept on display. Dried, though, which made it hard to make out any distinguishing details. It fell apart after a short while. Pity, I thought."

"And you've never seen a mud-man nursery, either. That's going to make what came next hard to explain."

Arkady paused for a long moment with a peculiar look on his face, swallowed some first response, and said instead, "Try."

"All right. We found all this out bit by bit, mind. The malice, before we did for it, had taken a place called Bonemarsh Camp. Most of the Lakewalkers got away"—Dag's swift glance around Arkady's house whispered *sessile* again to Fawn—"but it captured half a dozen makers. It ground-locked them together—"

Arkady gave a little flinching hiss.

"Oh, there's worse to come. It anchored this huge, complicated involution in their grounds to slave them to make up a batch of about fifty mud-men, which the malice had growing from local animals. A half-formed mud-man is about the most gut-wrenching thing you've ever seen, by the way. You want to kill it quick just for the pity of it. When my company got back to Bonemarsh, we found the groundlock still holding, the makers seeming unconscious. I'd thought the lock would break when the malice died, y'see, but I was wrong. Worse, when anyone opened their grounds to try to reach in and break the lock, they were sucked into the array as well. Lost three patrollers finding that out."

"That's . . . astonishing," said Arkady. Fawn's first fear, that Arkady would toss them out before they got their tale half told, eased. Beneath his quelling reserve, she thought he was growing quite engrossed. *He likes the parts about groundwork.*

Dag nodded shortly. "This was a very advanced malice, the most fully developed I've ever seen."

"And ah . . . how many have you seen?"

Dag shrugged. "I lost count years back. That I've slain with a knife in my own hand, twenty-six or so. That's counting the sessiles, which I do. Anyway, back at Bonemarsh—I stupidly tried to match grounds to steady the heartbeat of a dying maker in the array. And I got sucked in, too. Which is how I found out about the involution—I saw it from the inside. And after that the story has to go to Fawn, because the next few days were all a gray fog for me."

Fawn decided on a simplified version. "I came to Bonemarsh with Hoharie, because Dag had sent back for her help with this horrible groundlock thing. None of the Lakewalkers seemed to know what to do about it, which made me about half crazy, watching and waiting. Then Hoharie tried some experiment—I never did find out what, though I think she suspected about the involution."

"She did." Dag nodded.

"Anyhow, then *she* was drawn in, and Mari, who was in charge by then, said, *no more experiments.* But that night, I thought of one more. If an involution is a cut-off piece of a maker or a malice, which it seems to be, maybe this leftover piece of malice just needed a separate dose of mortality in order to destroy it. So I took my sharing knife"—she gulped in memory—"and stuck it in Dag's leg. Because when I slew the malice back in Glassforge, he'd said I could stick it in anywhere."

Dag smiled, and murmured, *Sharp end first.* Fawn smiled back.

"I think it worked to give it into Dag's ghost hand, the way his arm jerked up, but he'll have to tell that part," Fawn concluded.

Dag frowned and scratched his head. "Strangest experience I ever did have. We all know what it feels like to have a body and no ground, from being youngsters before our groundsense comes in, or in veiling. While I was slaved in the malice's groundlock, it seemed like I *was* my ground—but not my body. I felt the knife come into me, and I knew it at once—it had been bonded to me, and still had affinity with my blood. But Fawn's child's ground lacked affinity with the malice—very strange and pure, it was—so there was no resonance, no, no . . . *calling,* to break open the knife's involution and release the dying ground. So I broke open the involution myself, and added some affinity from my ghost hand. It was like *unmaking* a knife, all backward. It tore up my ghost hand something fierce, but it destroyed the malice's groundwork, and cleaned out those poison spatters as well. Fawn's sacrifice—well, with that little extra groundwork from me—got all ten of us out of the lock alive." He blinked at Arkady, who was staring with his hand before his parted lips as if to stifle an exclamation, and added apologetically, "It wasn't like I saw it, and figured it out, and did it. It was more like I saw it, and did it, and figured it all out much later."

Remo said, in downright peeved tones, "You never told me about all that, Dag! You only told me about Greenspring!"

"Greenspring was the important part, seemed to me."

Fawn shivered in memory; Dag, grimacing, reached across the table to briefly grip her shoulder as he might console a young patroller.

Arkady took his hand from his mouth and said, "So what was Greenspring?"

Dag sighed. "When I'd recovered enough to ride, we all went home by way of the blighted farmer village that malice had emerged under. When we arrived, we found some folks had come back and were having a mass burial of those who hadn't got out. Which was about half, of a thousand people. That first feast was the secret of how that malice had grown so quick, so strong."

He shared a look of understanding with Fawn, who picked up the thread: "They'd finished planting the grown-ups, mostly women and old folks, and were just starting on the children." She took a breath, measured Arkady, and dared to say, "I'm told New Moon Camp lost a youngster a couple of months back. There were—how many children, in the row in front of that trench, Dag?" Laid out all stiff and wan, there had seemed no end to them.

"One hundred sixty-two," Dag said flatly.

"The ground-ripping had kept them from rotting in the heat," explained Fawn, and swallowed hard. *Pale ice-children.* "It didn't help as much as you'd think."

Arkady shut his ground just then, Fawn thought; he went something more than expressionless, at any rate.

"It took me some thinking, after," said Dag. "How Greenspring was let to happen, and what could keep it from happening again. It's an Oleana problem; in the south there's nearly no malices, and in the far north there's nearly no farmers. Where there's both . . ." He held up hand and hook, but was frustrated in a gesture of interlacing fingers; Fawn thought everyone could imagine it, though. "It was plain something needed done, and it was plainer no one was doing it. And that we were running out of time to wait for someone smarter than me to try to figure out what. That's why I broke with my kin and camp and quit the patrol. They thought it was over Fawn, and it was, but it was Fawn led me to Greenspring. Roundaboutly." Dag gave a sharp nod, and fell silent.

"I . . . see," said Arkady slowly.

He glanced toward his front door; annoyance flashed across his face, but then shifted to a shrewder look. He rose and was halfway to it when a knock sounded. Sticking his head out, Arkady exchanged murmurs with his caller; Fawn caught a glimpse of a middle-aged woman, who craned her neck in turn, but did not enter. Arkady turned back holding a large basket covered with a cloth, which he thumped down upon the table. "Some lunch all around would be as well just now, I think."

Fawn, Remo, and Barr all jumped up to help Arkady set out tools and plates; Dag sat more wearily, and let them. The break from the tension was welcomed by everyone, Fawn suspected, even Arkady. The basket yielded a big lidded clay pot full of a thick stew, two kinds of bread wrapped in cloths, and, almost to Fawn's greater astonishment than this farmer-style fare, what were identifiably a couple of plunkins, spheres half the size of her head with brown husks. Cut open, they revealed a solid fruit both redder in color and sweeter than the plunkin she'd encountered at Hickory Lake.

"Why don't you have this kind up north, Dag?" she asked around a mouthful.

"Longer growing season, I think," he answered, also around a mouthful. Judging from the munching, all the northern Lakewalkers at the table plainly thought it was a treat. Arkady explained that these were grown in the shallow ends of the crescent lake.

Arkady did not pursue his interrogation while they ate—thinking, or did he just have medical notions about guarding digestion? Nor did Dag volunteer anything further. The boys, Fawn thought, wouldn't have dared to say boo. *But Arkady wouldn't be feeding us this good if he wasn't at least thinking of keeping us, would he?* Or maybe he just reckoned wild patrollers, like wild animals, could be tamed with vittles.

Finally growing replete, Fawn thought to ask Arkady, "Where did all this food come from? Who should we thank?"

He looked a trifle surprised at the question. "My neighboring tents take it in turns to send over my lunches and suppers. Breakfasts I do for myself. Tea, usually."

"Are you sick?" she asked diffidently.

His brows went up. "No."

He busied himself making another pot of tea while Fawn and Remo repacked the basket and set it outside the front door at Arkady's direction. He washed his hands again, sat, poured, frowned at Dag. Dag frowned back.

"Your wife," said Arkady delicately, "does not appear to be beguiled."

"She never has been," Dag said.

"Have you not done any groundwork on her?"

"Quite a bit, time to time," said Dag, "but she never grew beguiled with me. That was half the key to unlocking unbeguilement. Hod was the other half."

A sweep of Arkady's clean hand invited Dag to continue. Maybe this subject would be less fraught than Greenspring?

"You know beguilement can be erratic," said Dag.

"Painfully aware." Arkady grimaced. "Like most young and foolish medicine makers, I once tried to heal farmers. The results were disastrous. Lesson learned."

Fawn wanted to hear more of this, but Arkady waved Dag on again.

Dag sighed, as if steeling himself for this next confession. "Hod was a teamster's helper out of Glassforge—we hitched a ride with his wagon down to Pearl Riffle. My horse kicked him in the knee, which made me feel sort of responsible. I remembered what I'd done with that glass bowl, and set myself to try a real healing. Which I did do—pulled his broken kneecap back together good. But it left him beguiled to the eyebrows, which we found out when he made to follow us on our flatboat. And Fawn said, *Take him along and maybe you can figure out why, but if you leave him you never will.* And she was right. Come to it, me, Fawn, Hod, and Remo all sat in a circle and traded around little ground reinforcements till we figured it out. I don't think anyone who didn't have both a beguiled and an unbeguiled farmer to compare at the same time could have seen it."

Remo said, "Even I could see it, once Dag showed me. I can't quite do the unbeguiling trick yet, though."

Arkady's glance went in surprise to Remo. "And what did you see?" he asked.

"Don't tell him, Dag," said Fawn. "Show him." She felt uncomfortable volunteering to be the Demonstration Farmer, but from his expression she suspected Arkady had some pretty stiff-set ideas on the subject that mere assertion would not shift.

"Elbows again?" said Remo.

"That'd do," agreed Dag. "Watch close, Arkady, as the ground transfers."

Remo reached across the table and touched Fawn's left elbow; she felt the spreading warmth of a tiny ground reinforcement. She tried to decide if it also made her feel any friendlier toward the boy, or made him look finer to her eyes; since she already liked him well, it was hard to tell.

Arkady looked across at Dag in some puzzlement. "So?"

"Now watch again. Watch for a little backflow of ground from Fawn to me, almost as it flows from me to her. It's like it flows back *through* the reinforcement."

Dag smiled and reached his left arm toward her right elbow. As before, she saw nothing; but Arkady swore—the first she'd heard him do so, she realized.

"Absent gods. That explains it!"

"Yes. You just saw an unbeguilement. The farmer ground tries to rebalance itself through a ground exchange, the way it happens when two Lakewalkers trade ground, but if the Lakewalker is closed—rejects it—it bounces back and sets up this odd, um . . . imbalance in the farmer ground, which the farmer experiences as longing for another reinforcement. Obsession, if the imbalance is bad enough."

"No, yes . . ." Arkady reached up and almost mussed his carefully tied hair. "Yes, I see, but not that alone. Is *this* why your ground is such a ghastly mess? How many of these have you been *doing*?" His voice wasn't quite a shriek. Fawn stared at him with disappointment. She felt Dag's discovery should be due *much* more applause.

"I unbeguiled every farmer I did healing groundwork on, of course. Once I'd figured it out, that is," Dag added a bit guiltily. Fawn wondered how Cress was getting along.

"And then there were the oats," Fawn put in. "And the pie. And the mosquito, don't forget that, that started it all. Your poor arm swelled up so bad you couldn't get your arm harness on after you ground-ripped that mosquito, remember?"

"You took in ground from *all* those things?" said Arkady in horror. "It's a miracle you're still alive! Absent gods, man, you could have killed yourself!"

"Aha!" said Fawn in triumph. "I told you ripping that thorny tree would be a bad idea, Dag!"

Dag smiled wearily. "I sort of figured that out for myself, sir. Well . . . Fawn and I did. After a bit."

"A properly supervised apprentice," said Arkady, somewhat through his teeth, "would never have been permitted to contaminate himself with such dreadful experiments!"

"Groundsetter's apprentice, you mean?"

"Of course," said Arkady impatiently. "No one else would be capable of the idiocy."

Dag scratched his stubbled chin, and said mildly, "Then he wouldn't ever have been able to discover unbeguilement. Would he. Might be a good thing I started out unsupervised."

"Is it still?" asked Arkady.

Dag lost his glint of humor. "No," he admitted. "Because then came Crane."

Arkady, leaning forward to vent something irate, sat back more slowly. In a suddenly neutral voice, he said, "Tell me about Crane."

"The boys were there for that one," Dag said, with a tired nod at Barr and Remo.

Remo said, "Crane was a real Lakewalker renegade. Nastiest piece of work I ever did see. Which is why, sir, you shouldn't ought to call Dag one." Awed till now by the groundsetter, quiet Remo flashed genuine anger with this; Arkady's head went back a fraction.

Barr put in, "Crane was an Oleana man, banished from a camp up there for theft and, um, keeping a farmer woman. He'd set himself up as leader to this bandit gang on the lower Grace River, taking and burning boats and murdering their crews—horrible stuff. If it wasn't for us Lakewalkers being aboard, our flatboat would have been tricked like the others, I think."

Remo went on, "Dag set us to gathering all the other boats and men that came down the river that day to make an attack on the camp and clean it out. Which we did. Dag, um, captured Crane himself. Barr and I were up the hill dealing with another bandit just then, so I didn't exactly witness . . ." He trailed off with a beseeching look at Dag.

Dag said, in an expressionless voice, "I dropped him by ground-ripping a slice out of his spinal cord, just below the neck. Once saw a man fall from a horse and break his neck about there, so I had a pretty good guess what it would do."

"That . . . seems extreme," said Arkady, in a nearly matching voice. He regarded Dag steadily.

"He was holding a knife to my throat at the time," Fawn put in, nervous lest Arkady go picturing Dag as some cold-blooded killer, "and his men were about to get away with our boat. I don't think Dag had much choice."

"If I had it to do over," said Dag, " . . . well, if I had it *all* to do over, I'd leave more men to guard the boats, regardless of how shorthanded it made us at the cave. But if it were all the same again, I'd do it again. I don't regret it. But it left me stuck with this last mess in my ground . . ." A general gesture at his torso.

Arkady frowned judiciously. "I see."

"Aren't you going to tell about the sharing knife?" said Remo anxiously.

"Oh." Dag shrugged. "We found an unprimed sharing knife in the bandits' spoils, that they'd apparently taken off a murdered Lakewalker woman. Cranc was due to be hanged with the rest, so I gave him the choice of sharing, instead. Which he chose. Surprised me, a little. I boiled the old bonding off the knife and reset the involution, and bonded it to Crane. And used it to execute him, which was dodgy, but everything else about the man was dodgy, so I figured it fit. First knife I ever made. I'd like to have your camp's knife maker look it over for soundness, if I get a chance, though I'm pretty sure there's no such thing as a half-made knife. It either primes or it doesn't."

"And," said Arkady, "you thought you could do this . . . why?"

Dag shrugged once more. "My brother is a knife maker at Hickory Lake, so I've been around the process off and on. But mostly I learned how from taking apart the groundwork of my knife at Bonemarsh."

"And, ah . . ." Arkady said, "the other kind of why?"

What gave Dag the right, does he mean? Fawn wondered.

Dag regarded him steadily back. "I needed a knife. I hate walking bare."

A little silence fell, all around the table.

"You know, Dag," said Fawn slowly, "we've spent since last spring being knocked from pillar to post so bad it's a wonder we've had time to breathe. But when you lay it all out in a row like this . . . don't you see a kind of pattern to things?"

"No," said Dag.

She looked up at Arkady. "Do you, sir?"

She thought his face said *yes,* but he pushed back his chair instead of answering. He said, "You folks look as though you all slept in a ditch last night."

"Pretty near," Fawn admitted. Infested with scary swamp lizards, at that.

"I'd think you'd all enjoy a hot bath, then," said Arkady.

This won blank looks from all three patrollers. Fawn, appalled by a vision of heating pots and pots of water on the hearth, said hastily, "Oh, we couldn't put you to so much trouble, sir!"

"It's no trouble. I'll show you."

A little . . . smugly? Arkady led them outside and down some stairs from the lakeside porch to an area of flagged pavement. At the far side was a remarkable setup: a shower bucket with a pull rope on a post, made private by a cloth-hung screen, and a big barrel, its bottom lined with copper, over a fire pit. Coals still glowed underneath.

"You can take the path down to the lake to get more water, all you want"—Arkady pointed to a pair of buckets on a yoke—"and heat it in the barrel. More wood's in the stack behind those forsythia bushes. Put the hot water in the shower bucket, soap up and rinse down, soak in the barrel after. Take your time. I need to go talk with some folks, but I'll be back in a while." He paused and studied Dag. "Er . . . do you shave?"

"Now and then," said Dag dryly.

"Now, then."

Arkady went back in, popped out a few moments later with a stack of towels and a new cake of soap, and disappeared again, this time for good. Fawn stared after him, bewildered by this turn, though not ungrateful.

"Do we stink that bad?" asked Remo, sniffing his shirt. Barr was too busy delightedly examining the mechanism of the shower to answer.

"We aren't too pretty, compared to Arkady," Fawn allowed.

"And this keeps us occupied here for as long as he wants to talk to . . . folks. How many folks, I wonder?" said Dag, sounding less impressed.

Oh. Of course. Fawn's gratitude faded in new worry. How many people in the camp had more authority than this groundsetter, that he needed to consult them? It answered Dag's question, if in an unsettling fashion: *not many.*

But Dag assisted Fawn to take the first turn, and then took one himself with apparent enjoyment. She thought Barr very gallant to volunteer for the last turn, till he refused to come out again. Granted, soaking in the barrel, which steamed in the chill air, was blissful. He was still pickling in there when Arkady returned, to find the rest of them dressed and clustered around the hearth drying their hair. Dag's system was to run a towel over his head once, but Remo fussed more over his than Fawn did over hers.

Arkady put his hands on his hips and looked Dag over. "Better," he allowed. "I can't have you following me around the camp looking like some starveling vagabond, after all."

"Am I to do so?" asked Dag warily. "Why?"

"It's how apprenticing is done, normally."

Fawn almost whooped with joy, but Dag merely rubbed his new-shaved chin. "I take your offer kindly, sir, but I'm not sure how long we can stay. My work is up north, not down here." He glanced at Fawn.

Arkady answered the question beneath the question. "You can all stay here at my place for the moment. Including your farmer bride, though it's asked that she not wander around the camp unescorted."

Fawn nodded glad acceptance of the rule, though Dag frowned a trifle, which made Fawn wonder belatedly, *Asked by who?*

"You'll just be watching and listening at first, you understand," said Arkady, "at least till I can figure out some way to cleanse your dirty ground. If I can."

Dag flicked an eyebrow upward. "I'm good at listenin'. So am I to be your apprentice—or your patient?"

"A bit of both," Arkady admitted. "You asked—no, *she* asked," he corrected under his breath, "if I saw a pattern in your tale. I did. I saw a man coming late and abruptly into groundsetter powers, totally unsupervised, making the wildest mess of himself."

"You know, sir, you don't sound too approving, but my two top notions were that I was going mad, or that I was turning into a malice. I like your version better."

Arkady snorted. "Normally, the development you've experienced would have unfolded over five or six years, not five or six months. Naturally you found it confusing. And—how old are you? Mid-fifties?"

Dag nodded.

"Well, your talent's around fifteen years late showing, to boot. I don't know what you were doing all that time—"

"Patrolling," said Dag briefly.

"Or why it's all released now," Arkady continued.

Dag smiled across at Fawn.

"*Do* you think your farmer girl has something to do with it?" demanded Arkady. "I admit, I don't see how."

Dag's smile deepened. "My tent-brother Whit, who I grant has a mouth on him that's going to get his teeth busted one of these days, once said he didn't know if I was robbin' cradles or if Fawn was robbin' graves. I think it was the second. I'd pretty much lain down in mine just waiting for someone to come along and throw the dirt in on top. Instead, she came along and yanked me out of it. I will say, sir, it was a lot more restful than what I've been doing since, but it was pinching narrow. I don't hanker to go back in."

Fawn's heart lifted.

Arkady just shook his head. He turned toward the door, took two steps, then turned back. "Oh, Dag?" He held up both his hands.

Fawn saw it only by reflection, but well enough at that; Barr and Remo looked startled and impressed and Dag—Dag's face lit right up. *Arkady has ghost hands, too!*

"We'll have to see what we can do about your little asymmetry problem, later," said Arkady. "Among other things." He jerked his chin at Remo. "Come along, patroller boy. I'll show you where to take your horses."

5

Dag's apprenticeship began sooner than he or, he guessed, even Arkady expected. They were all at the table finishing breakfast from a basket sent to sustain the enlarged household—bread, plunkin, and hard-boiled eggs, with more tea—when after the briefest knock at the door, a breathless boy burst in and blurted, "Maker Arkady, sir! Maker Challa says to tell you they're bringing in a hurt patroller, an' if you would be pleased to step 'round."

"Very well," said Arkady calmly. "Tell her I'll be right along."

The boy nodded and departed as abruptly as he'd arrived.

Arkady swallowed his tea. Dag said uneasily, "Shouldn't we go at once?"

"If the patroller's condition were that dire, I doubt he'd have lived to arrive," said Arkady. "You have time to finish your drink." He set down his mug, rose without haste, and added, "For the real emergencies, Challa rings a big bell she has up on a post in front of the medicine tent. Two rings and three. All the makers' tents are within earshot, one direction or another. Then, we run."

Now, evidently, they strolled. Dag gave Fawn a hug good-bye, nodded thanks at her whisper of "Good luck!," shrugged on his jacket, and
followed Arkady out. The morning was not young; weary from their
thirty-mile trudge, Barr, Remo, and Fawn had all slept in, although
even so they were up before their host. Dag had wakened at first light,
with all of the uncertainties that had chased one another around in his
head last night ready for more laps.

After taking Remo to settle the horses yesterday afternoon, Arkady,
evidently deciding that Dag cleaned up well enough to be displayed, had
escorted him to the medicine tent for introductions. To his surprise,
Dag had learned that Arkady was not New Moon Cutoff's chief medicine maker; that post was held by a much older woman, saggy, baggy,
and cheerful. Maker Challa had eyed Dag shrewdly and shown him
around her domain, introducing him in turn to the herb-lore master
and his two apprentices, and to her own partner, a woman more nearly
Dag's age. They didn't ask Dag as many questions as he'd feared; it was
plain that Arkady had discussed his odd stray with them already. *Provi-
sionally accepted.* But just what were the provisions?

A five-minute walk along the shore road brought the medicine tent
within sight. It was a rambling gray structure like Arkady's house, and
not much larger. At the railing out front was a rig Dag recognized from
patrol procedure, two saddled horses fore and aft of a makeshift litter
of cut sapling poles. Challa and a lean, brown-haired patroller were just
lifting a more heavily built, gray-haired patroller to his feet, drawing
his arms over their shoulders and aiming him inside. At every step, the
older patroller mumbled, "Ow. Ow. Ow . . ."

"Well, Tapp," said Arkady with callous cheerfulness as they came up
even with the group. "And what have you done to yourself?"

"Nothing, blight it!" snapped the gray-haired man, whose plait was coming undone. "*All I did* was fling my saddlebags up on my horse, just like I've done ten thousand times before. I swear! A fellow's insides shouldn't come popping out just from saddling his blighted horse. Ow. Ow!"

Arkady opened the door for them. The lean patroller bent to undo his partner's boots, then maneuvered him through the first room, crammed with shelves devoted to records, into a bright chamber with glass windows overlooking the lake. All four of them helped lift the hurting man onto the narrow bed at table height that stood out in the center of the room. Tapp was clammy and gasping with pain, but he still eyed Dag, and his left arm, curiously.

Arkady and Tapp's partner between them shucked him out of his trousers, and Challa briskly rolled down his drawers to groin level, raised her white eyebrows, and pointed at a reddened bulge at the side of his abdomen.

"Yep," said Arkady. "Come over here, Dag, and tell me what you sense."

Tapp watched Dag uneasily. "Who the blight is he?"

"Clean up your mouth, Tapp," chided Challa.

"If a fellow can't swear at a time like this, when can he?" Tapp complained.

"Not in my tent," said Challa firmly.

Tapp snorted, then winced. "Yes, ma'am, Maker-ma'am." His wandering gaze returned to Dag. "Aren't you a patroller?" he asked querulously. "Not one of ours. Courier?"

"I was, once," said Dag. "Now, um . . ."

Arkady waited with cool interest to see how Dag would explain himself.

"You know how we exchange young patrollers to other camps in the hope that someone else will have better luck knocking sense into them?" said Dag.

"Yes?" said Tapp.

"You can think of me as an exchange maker. On trial." Dag cleared his throat and added, "It's only my first day, see."

"Arkady, Challa, no!" cried Tapp. "You always turn your ham-handed novices loose on me . . . !"

Arkady grinned. "Calm yourself, Tapp. Dag here's just observing." He lifted a suddenly sharp coppery gaze to Dag. "And what do you observe?"

Dag cupped his right hand above the bulge and, reluctantly, opened himself. "His sudden move lifting his bags likely split open a weak place in his belly muscles, and a piece of his gut has worked through, and has got itself twisted around pretty bad. It's all hot and swollen, which doesn't help a thing. I'd guess he tried to tough it out too bli—"—Dag glanced at Challa, watching him as closely as Arkady—"too long—*I don't need a litter, I can ride*—"

The partner barked a laugh. "The very words!" Tapp glared at him.

"And made it worse getting here," Dag went on. "How far out was your patrol?"

"A two-day ride," the partner said. "We were up northwest almost to the banks of the Gray."

"Sometime on the ride his gut got knotted back on itself like this, and the hole swelled tight, and now he's in a bad way and no mistake. I'm thinking he's lucky it wasn't a three-day ride."

Arkady tilted his head in reluctant respect. "Very good. And what would you do about it?"

Dag said cautiously, "I knew a fellow up in . . . a place I once patrolled, had something like this. The makers stuffed his gut back inside somehow, persuaded the hole shut, and put him on camp rest till it finished healing. I don't rightly know how the gut-stuffing part was done."

"If there's no torsion, and the rip in the muscle sheet is large enough, you can actually do it pressing with your fingers," said Arkady.

"I did it that way five times on the way here," Tapp complained, "but my gut kept falling out again, till it all swelled shut."

Challa winced.

Arkady sighed. "And I suppose you insisted you could eat, too?"

"Not after the first day," Tapp said in a smaller voice.

Arkady rolled his eyes, and muttered, "Patrollers!" He drew breath and turned again to Dag. "Twisted and tight as this is now, it's going to take some careful groundsetting to restore the gut without rupturing it and spilling blood and rotting food into the abdominal cavity, which is a recipe for infection."

Dag nodded understanding. "Like a knife wound to the belly."

"Correct. Challa, if I may trouble you to dump a dense ground reinforcement into the inflamed area, we'll see if we can relieve the tightness a bit before attempting to manipulate anything."

Challa nodded, laid her hands on the lump, and closed her eyes. Dag sensed the flow of her unshaped ground-gifting into Tapp's unhappy flesh. The extra ground would support and speed the body's own attempts to heal, and so ease the swelling and pain. The simplest of procedures; any number of patrollers learned at least that much groundwork, even the younger Dag. The focus of Challa's groundwork was much finer, however, and its density impressive.

"While we're waiting for that to take effect," Arkady went on, "let me tell you more . . ."

Dag, willingly, and Tapp, much less willingly, were then treated to a detailed description of half a dozen other ways Dag would never have imagined that folks' insides could end up in places where they did not belong, and what to do about it. Dag was especially impressed, or appalled, by the version that had the stomach squeezing through the little hole in the diaphragm where the gullet connected, and ending up half on one side and half on the other. About the time Tapp must have been wishing he'd never been born, Arkady wrapped up his talk and cupped his hands gently around the bulge. Dag extended his sensitivity to his utmost. *Down and in.* Arkady glanced up keenly at him, then returned his attention to his task, closing his eyes in concentration.

Arkady's ground-fingers shaped themselves in unfingerlike ways to gently widen the hole, tease the gut knot apart, and slide the strained tissue back inside. In a sallow sweat, Tapp whimpered; his partner gripped his hand hard and watched him in concern, all patroller-humor extinguished.

The power, thought Dag. The power to so readily move matter through its ground was immense, yet Arkady's ground projection danced as delicately as if he were laying out flower petals that he was trying not to crush. He persuaded the two sides of the ripped hole back together, then set a neatly shaped ground reinforcement to hold them that way. Tapp's strained face and grip eased, and he lay back bonelessly on the table. It had all been done in less than ten minutes, without ever breaking the skin.

"I'll send one of the ham-handed novices down to your tent tonight to give you another reinforcement," Arkady told Tapp, and glanced up. "Has anyone told his wife yet that he's home early?"

"I sent the boy," said Challa.

Indeed, Tapp's wife arrived in a few minutes more, irate with worry, and the *Tapp, what did you do to yourself?* and *It wasn't my fault!* conversation was repeated, with variations. Arkady prudently gave most of his instructions to her—bed rest and no food till tomorrow, camp rest till Challa decreed otherwise. Dag helped carry Tapp back out to the horse litter and saw him trundled off, escorted by his partner and his wife. Staring after them, Dag turned his hook this way and that, trying to imagine the groundwork that would persuade half of someone's stomach back to its proper position through such a little hole without bursting it under the heart.

Arkady, stretching his back beside Dag, said, "He'll recover well if he doesn't overdo. It didn't help that he was two days fooling around with the rupture and telling his patrol leader he'd be fine before he even started home, his partner says. Patrollers have no sense, sometimes."

"Goes with the territory," Dag said. "Sensible people don't go looking for malices."

"I suppose you would know."

"Forty years at it, sir."

"Huh. I guess it would be about that." He frowned at Dag's hook. "Before and after the hand, then? Because it looks like that's been off for about twenty years, there."

"Aye," said Dag. "Just about that." But if Arkady was angling for an old patroller story, he was doomed to disappointment. A more important question occurred to Dag then. "Sir—why didn't you get cold and shaky after doing that groundwork?"

Arkady's head turned. "What, do you?"

"After all my healings, pretty much, and that glass-bowl episode knocked me on my tail. My flesh felt like clay, and my stomach heaved."

"Well, then, you were doing something wrong."

"What?"

"We'll have to figure that out." Arkady rubbed his mouth with the back of his hand and stared curiously at Dag, but did not pursue the matter at once. Instead, he turned Dag over to Challa while he went off to, he said, check on a few folks.

Challa showed Dag her tent's record-keeping methods, more pleased than was quite flattering to learn that the shabby northerner could read and write. They were interrupted once by a woman whose toddler's oozing sore throat had not responded to home ground reinforcements, and a second time by a boy, frog-marched in by his father, in need of having his bloodied head stitched after a fight with his brother. A rock seemed to have been involved, presented as evidence, or possibly a souvenir, by the irate and dizzy loser.

As she worked, Challa kept up a gentle and seemingly habitual flow of instruction and commentary that Dag drank in—with the growing sense that he was just the latest in a long line of apprentices to pass through her tent. Dag was painfully aware that he was of no help in stitching up the flap of scalp, but at least his hook provided a useful diversion while the sewing was going on. The boy ingenuously demanded the tale—severely abridged by Dag—of how the missing hand had been bitten off by a mud-wolf, then set his quaking lip and endured his own little ordeal under Challa's curved needle with fresh determination. Challa suppressed a smile and complimented his courage.

Barr popped in then with the news that the lunch basket and Arkady had both arrived back at the house. Dag paced silently beside him up the road, his head awhirl with his morning's tutorials. The range of things he didn't know seemed to be expanding at an alarming rate.

ᕰ

This lunch basket yielded ham sandwiches and plunkin, swiftly consumed. While Fawn, Remo, and Barr cleared away the plates and crumbs from the round table, Arkady arose and went to one of his shelves. He returned with a piece of paper and sat again across from Dag. Instead of presenting it to read, he turned it over and tore it in half.

"Now," he said, "let's just see what it is you're doing that's giving you trouble. Watch. Ah—with your groundsense, please."

What is he about? Dag opened himself and attended, summoning the concentration of the morning against a drift toward a postlunch nap.

Arkady eased the two pieces back in line, held them down on the table, and ran his thumb down the tear. Behind the barely perceptible ground projection, the paper hissed back together. He held it up and snapped it, then turned it and tore it in half again. Fawn and the boys abandoned the sink and slid hastily back into their chairs to watch.

It had been so swift, Dag was barely certain what he'd sensed, but he dutifully positioned the halves on the table in front of him, edged them together as best he could, extended his ghost hand, closed his eyes, and found that strange level of perception, *down and in,* that he had first discovered while healing Hod. Paper, it seemed, was much like felted cloth, a mass of tiny threads all matted together—torn away from one another, now. He was put in mind of how Fawn had spun the threads for their wedding cords, making the fibers twirl around and catch hold. So freshly separated, these fibers' grounds still held the echo of their former friction. *This will be easy.* He smiled and drew his hook down the edges, his ghost thumb persuading them back together.

And opened his eyes in consternation as the paper burst into flame along the line of his repair. He beat it out in hasty embarrassment.

Barr ducked the flying char and said, "It's not anybody's birthday, Dag! Take it easy!"

Dag brushed futilely at the scorch marks on Arkady's table. "Sorry. Sorry! I'm not sure what happened just there."

"Mm-huh," said Arkady, leaning back with narrowed eyes and not sounding the least surprised. "As I thought. You're expending far more strength than the task warrants, and exhausting yourself prematurely. The waste you shed becomes, in this case, heat."

"But Hod's knee didn't burst into flames!" Fawn objected. Adding after a reflective moment, "Luckily."

"That was a much greater task, and living beings absorb ground on levels mere objects don't possess. The cure for the unpleasant aftereffects you experienced, the chill and the nausea, isn't some special trick. It's the result of a general habit of efficiency in one's work. Don't do with groundsetting anything that can be done physically, or even by another medicine maker; pace yourself, because you never know how soon another patient will turn up; and never use more strength than is truly needed. It's not merely less wasteful; it's more *elegant*." Arkady rolled the last word off his tongue quite lovingly.

Dag scratched his head in doubt.

Barr sniggered. "I don't know as Dag does elegant."

Fawn bristled, opening her mouth to begin some hot defense. Dag interrupted smoothly, "Ground-veiling drills. When was the last time you and Barr did your ground-veiling drills, Remo? Back before Whit and Berry's wedding, wasn't it?"

Remo shot an acid look at his partner. "Yes, sir." He did not add, *You were there, Dag!;* some former patrol leader had evidently cured him of any leaning to risky backtalk.

"Now, half an hour. Down on the lakeshore will be a good place. No one will interrupt your concentration there."

Remo loyally arose, glowered at Barr, and jerked his chin. Barr grumbled up and followed him out, casting a last look of frustrated curiosity over his shoulder. Peace of a sort descended.

Beyond an upward twitch of his silvery brows, Arkady made no comment. Instead, he drained his mug of tea, set it sideways to the table, and with a sharp crack broke off its handle.

"Oh!" said Fawn, startled, then closed her lips tight. She glanced at the door through which the boys had left and folded her hands primly in her lap in a superfluous effort to appear small.

Arkady pushed the two pieces across to Dag. "Try again. Don't try to contain the whole cup, or even the whole handle, although hold awareness of their essential ground in mind. Think surfaces. Again, let your muscles do as much as possible. Hold the parts together tightly—" He broke off; a tinge of color heated his cheeks. "Er . . ."

"Fawn, lend me your hands over here," said Dag.

She nodded understanding, rose, licked her finger to pick up a couple of tiny fragments still left across the table, deposited them again in front of Dag, and gripped the cup and handle, fitting them back together. "Just like the bowl, huh?" Her dimple flashed at him, as if to say, *You can do it.*

"Uh-huh." Dag shot Arkady a challenging glance, but the maker made no comment. *Surfaces, eh?* Dag closed his eyes, reached out till his hook clinked, and dropped down and in, finding the ground of the bowl, of the handle. Of the two interfaces. This fired clay had a rougher voice than the high chime of the glass bowl, a mumbling little growl. The recent break still vibrated with the rupture, though the clay was far more inert than the ends of broken blood vessels that Dag had several times worked back together. But they still had a good catch. The two flakes rose through the air, seeking their slots. Catch. Catch. Finer and finer, catchcatchcatchcatch . . . And finer still . . .

"Good," said Arkady. "Stop."

Dag gulped and opened his eyes.

Gingerly, Fawn released the handle, which remained in place. Even more gingerly, she grasped the handle and released the cup. The mending held. "It's warm," she reported, "but not near so hot as that bowl was, Dag. You could barely touch that bowl, even after it stopped glowing." She peered more closely. "I can just see a line in the glaze."

The two crumbs of stray clay were also back in place, faintly outlined.

"How do you feel?" Arkady asked Dag. His voice and gaze were both level.

"Not . . . bad," said Dag, a little surprised. "Something's taken out of me, sure, but I don't feel dizzy or cold. And my lunch is staying put." This mending lacked the soaring exaltation and violent collapse of his prior ones, of the glass bowl or Hod's knee or Chicory's head; it was more like . . . interest and ease. Less exciting, to be sure. *But less wearing, I do admit.*

Arkady rose and returned with another wrinkled note. He sat, tore it in half, and shoved the pieces across to Dag once more. "Try again. *Less* hard."

Dag nodded understanding and aligned the scraps. Fawn slipped back into her chair, still clutching the cup, and watched wide-eyed. In anticipation of another conflagration her hand crept toward the damp dishcloth she'd been using to wipe the table, but then returned bravely to her lap.

This time, Dag deliberately slowed himself down, drawing his ghost hand back until it was barely projecting. He took his time, easing along the rip, peering warily through his lashes for any untoward flash of flame. Finishing, he opened his eyes, staring down at the repaired paper. Good as . . . old.

"Strange . . ." he said. "In a way, this is harder than Hod's knee. The body seems to cooperate with its own healing in ways that dead objects don't."

"Huh," said Arkady. "You already know *that,* do you . . . ?" Dag glanced up to catch an unblinking frown. Arkady went on, "Do that one more time. More gently still, if you can."

Dag ripped the page in half himself this round, smoothed it, pulled it back together once more. Handed it to Arkady.

"Good," said the maker simply. "Something of the same technique works to hold together skin, as well. Best to save it for tissues you can't reach with a needle, however."

"That . . . would be all of them, in my case," Dag noted gently.

"Ah." Caught out for the second time, the maker grimaced. "My apologies. Habit, I'm afraid. I'll try to be more heedful."

"I'm used to it," said Dag.

Did Arkady wince? Hard to tell. But he only said, "That does bring up . . . Have you ever attempted a ground projection from your right hand?"

Dag shook his head. "It came out from the left side all on its own, seemed like. I thought it was . . . well, I'm not just sure what I thought it was."

Fawn said loyally, "To me, it didn't seem any stranger than the rest of what you did."

"Yes . . . it *was* you first guessed it was something I should have, that got delayed." He smiled to remember just when she'd said it, too. "Seems you were square on."

She shrugged. "Stood to reason, I thought."

"Try now," said Arkady. "Right hand."

Dag did; nothing happened. His ground on the right side remained firmly intertwined with the flesh that generated it, just as always.

"Did Dag mention," said Fawn, "that at the time his ghost hand first came out, his right arm was busted? All tied up with splints in a sling. Though I had to keep making him put it back in the sling."

Arkady sat back. "Really?" It was more a noise of surprise than disbelief. "That's . . . interesting." After a moment, and another glance at the hook, his brows drew down in puzzlement. "My word. How in the world did you manage everything?"

"I had a little help," said Dag.

"Who you callin' little?" Fawn breathed at him, dimpling deeply. He couldn't help smiling back.

Arkady rubbed his brow and sighed.

Dag straightened self-consciously, clearing his throat. "Besides me bein' so lopsided," he said, "you talked about doing something to, ah, cleanse my dirty ground. What did you have in mind?" Or was the cure for contamination, like that for the aftereffects of groundsetting, to be simple, tedious self-regulation? *Pace yourself* could be pretty useless advice, in the midst of some pressing emergency.

"Well . . . I admit, I don't know yet. You're an odd collection of puzzles to turn up at my gate."

"At first it seemed to me that my ground cleansed, or healed, or remade itself all by itself, over time. The way anyone absorbs a ground reinforcement—or the ground of their food, for that matter. Figured the problem was that I'd just taken in too much, too fast."

"Both of those, certainly. Though one might argue that any farmer ground is too much."

Anyone, or *Arkady*? Dag frowned at the evasive wording. "Except the ground I most choked on was pure Lakewalker." Or, considering Crane, impure Lakewalker. "I actually found the ground of food strengthening. At least after I learned to limit myself to the life-ground of things like seed grains, instead of ripping right down to the matter."

Fawn said, "Yeah, that mess you made of my pie didn't sit too well, did it? Because it was cooked and dead, do you reckon?"

"Maybe," said Dag. "Which reminds me, I meant to try a live fish— minnow!" he corrected hastily at her dismayed look.

Arkady swallowed a noise of horror. "No! No! For the next several days—in fact, till I give you permission—don't ground-rip anything! At least until I can get some sense of whether your disruptions are clearing on their own. Which reminds me . . ."

He rose and went to his shelves, returning with a quill, a bottle of ink, and what Dag now recognized as a medicine maker's casebook.

He laid them all out, opened the book to a fresh page, dipped his quill, and scribbled. He glanced up and added in an abstracted tone, "Open yourself, please." A couple more minutes passed while he jotted what Dag, squinting sideways, read as notes upon the present condition of his ground, although between the handwriting and the abbreviations he could hardly guess what Arkady thought it was. Arkady's own strange bright-shadowed ground was equally unrevealing.

"There," said Arkady, finishing. "I should have done this yesterday. It goes without saying that—no, I suppose it doesn't. You are to do no ground-gifting till I tell you, either, understood?"

"Sir?" said Dag uncertainly. No medicine making at all? Observation could only go so far as a teaching method . . . *It's only the beginning,* Dag chided himself. *You'd think you were a sixteen-year-old on your first patrol again, stupid with daydreams of instant achievement.* He couldn't even argue, *But now there's the problem of Greenspring!* since the problem of Greenspring had been sitting out there all his life, unnoticed. Yet all this attention to the particulars of his own ground, here in this quiet southern camp, seemed a long way from becoming help for the beleaguered north.

"We don't want that ground contamination of yours spread all around the camp. At least till we know how much of your present problems stem from it."

Dag nodded reluctant acknowledgment. About to ask, *But could I heal farmers? They won't care how dirty with farmer ground I am,* he realized that the necessary unbeguilement would violate Arkady's ban against taking in strange ground, too. He sighed, resigning himself to his— temporary, he trusted—quarantine.

6

Dag mulishly chose to share Fawn's ostracism, keeping to Arkady's house when he wasn't on duty, but the medicine tent brought the camp to him. He divided his time between what traditional apprentice dog chores Maker Challa could think of that a one-handed man might do, and close observing. Perforce, he learned names, tent-names, personalities, and, more intimately, grounds of a growing string of New Moon folks; what they made of him he was less sure. But it was plain that a camp medicine maker must come to know his people over time the way a patroller memorized the trails of his territory.

Barr and Remo, meanwhile, wasted no time in going off to explore the camp at large, with the result that they'd shortly cooked up a scheme to go out on patrol as exchange volunteers. Dag approved; it would make good use of their time, take the burden of feeding them off Arkady's neighbors for a couple of weeks, and pay the camp back something for their welcome here. It soon came out that their gingerliness in presenting the plan was not because they needed Dag's permission, but because they wanted to borrow Dag's sharing knife.

Carrying a primed knife marked a patroller as tried and trusted, and they'd both earned that from him. In this camp's patrol territory, where not even a sessile had been found for over three generations, Dag was nearly certain to get his knife back intact. It was his own workmanship, not Barr and Remo's dependability, that Dag doubted. So the next afternoon, he gathered up his knife and his nerve and sought out New Moon's senior knife maker.

Her name, he'd been told, was Vayve Blackturtle. Her work shack, a neat cypress-wood cabin overlooking the lake near its south end, was instantly recognizable by the small collection of human thighbones hung to cure along its eaves. As he climbed nearer Dag found, more unexpectedly, signs of a garden surrounding it—not of practical food, but of flowers. Even in this drab dawning of the year, a spatter of bright purple and yellow crocuses poked up from tidy mulch beds, and the unopened buds on the flowering shrubs were fat and red.

As he wasn't sneaking up on a malice's lair, here, Dag forced himself to leave his ground partly open. So he hadn't yet mounted the porch steps when a woman emerged to stare down at him. She looked alarmingly like a younger version of Dag's aunt Mari, lean and shrewd of eye. Her brown hair was drawn back in the usual mourning knot that makers wore while working, but her soberly cut skirt and jacket were embroidered with recognizable dogwood flowers. The stern air common to knife makers hung about her, yet her look was not that of an offended recluse—Dag thought of Dar—but of open curiosity.

"Maker Vayve? M' name's Dag Bluefield." He left off the *No-Camp* part. "May I trouble you with a question about a knife?"

"Oh, would you be Arkady Waterbirch's prodigy? I've heard of you. Step on up." Her roofed porch had hospitable seats, with stuffed cushions; the woven wicker creaked as Dag lowered himself. She took the next seat, half around a low plank table.

Dag wondered at her description of him. He'd certainly done nothing prodigious here. He dragged the cord Fawn had fashioned over his head, held the leather sheath to the table with his hook, and drew out the plain bone blade. "Some weeks back, up on the Grace River, I was called upon to rededicate and bond—and prime—a sharing knife. Under emergency conditions, more or less."

"You were traveling with those two young patrollers who smoked out a nest of river bandits, I heard. All Oleana men, aren't you? You're a fair way from home."

Dag decided not to pursue just what Barr and Remo had been saying about themselves, and him. *We drifted downriver till we ran into bandits* could easily be misconstrued as *We were sent downriver to destroy bandits*, dodging awkward questions about how the partners had come to be trailing Dag.

Leaving out the preamble of Raintree, Dag gave much the same truncated account of Crane and his death to Maker Vayve as he had to Arkady. As he spoke, her grim frown deepened.

"A sharing knife," she said, "is made as an instrument of sacrifice and redemption—not of criminal execution."

"This one was all three, in its way. Crane paid far less than he owed, but all that he had. I'm not asking you to judge the morality of its making, ma'am. Just its workmanship. First knife I ever made, see. Will it kill a malice?"

"The gossip I heard wasn't clear if you were a patroller or a medicine maker." Politely, she left out the renegade/deserter/banished/or-just-plain-mad part. "How did you know how to make any knife at all?"

"My older brother is senior knife maker back at Hickory Lake Camp in Oleana. I've been around the craft quite a bit, time to time."

Her brows twitched up in some doubt. "If lurking underfoot was all it took to create talent, I'd have better luck with my apprentices." But she picked up the knife and opened her ground to examine it, holding it to her lips and forehead in turn, eyes closed and open. Dag watched anxiously.

She laid it gently back on the table. "Your involution is about four times stronger than it needs to be, but it's sound and shows no sign of leakage. I see no reason it wouldn't break open properly when exposed to the disruption of a malice. I grant it seems an unusually dark, unhappy knife, but primed knives are seldom chirping merry."

"Crane was as close to a mad dog in human form as makes no nevermind, but he wasn't stupid. I think he liked the irony of tying this around my neck," Dag admitted. But it seemed this knife was safe to lend; he would do so.

A damp breeze, almost warm, set the bones to faintly clinking along the eaves. Reminded of another concern, he asked, "Do you chance to have any spare blanks? My brother usually did. There were always more bones than hearts."

"Why do you ask?" she returned.

"I'm without a bonded knife myself just now. My old one was . . . lost. Been meaning to replace it when I found the chance. I should like to make it for myself, under better supervision—if you'd be willing, ma'am."

"It seems you're a trifle past an apprentice's test piece." She nodded at the knife on the table. "Do you mean to take up the craft? I don't know that I'd dare steal you from Arkady."

"No, ma'am. I just want more confidence, if I ever have to face such an emergency again."

"Confidence? Nerve, I'd call it." She regarded him with a warring mixture of curiosity and disapproval. "That murdered woman's bonded knife *belonged* to someone, and it wasn't you. And you took it without a second thought, as nearly as I can tell."

"I had thoughts in plenty, ma'am. It was time I lacked."

She shrugged. "This not being an emergency, you would have to ask for the donation from the tent-kin."

"No bones were left in your care for the general need? Or by the kinless?"

Her expression and her ground both went a little opaque. "Not at present."

In other words, this dodgy Oleana fellow was going to have to do his own begging. Perhaps he could, later, if he made more of a place for himself here.

Vayve glanced up. Climbing the path to her shack were the two patroller girls Dag had met that first day at the gate. The leggy blonde was half veiled and not happy about something. They looked up in surprise to see Dag, and he furled himself a little more, slipping Crane's knife back into its sheath, and into his shirt. Both partners' eyes followed it.

"Hello, Tavia, Neeta," said the maker cordially. "What brings you up here?"

"Oh, Vayve!" said Neeta, her voice distressed. "Something terrible's happened to my primed knife—well, it was going to be my primed knife. My father had promised it to me when I came back from Luthlia, but this morning when we went to take it from the chest—well, look!"

She mounted the steps, slid the knife she was clutching from its sheath, and laid it on the table in front of the maker. The dry bone blade was cracked, split up half its length. Traces of tattered groundwork still clung to it, but its involution and the death it had contained were gone.

"He swears it was fine when he last put it away, and nobody dropped it—what happened to it? Vayve, can you fix it?"

"Oh, dear," said Vayve, picking up the knife. "Just how old was this, Neeta? It's not of my making."

"I'm not exactly sure. My father carried it when he was younger, and his uncle before him. Did we do something wrong—should we have oiled it, or, or . . . ?"

The maker turned the blade, studying the split. "No, that wouldn't have made any difference. It was simply too old, Neeta. The groundwork on knives doesn't last forever, you know."

"I was going to take it on patrol tomorrow!"

The patrol Barr and Remo were joining—so, the reasons for their urgency to volunteer were revealed, one blond, one red-haired. Dag didn't think he allowed his amusement to show in his face, but Tavia, watching him inquisitively, returned an uncertain half smile.

"Isn't there anything you can do?" Neeta went on. "Was my tentkin's sacrifice just *wasted,* then? Thrown into the air?"

Dag had been through this scene before, with distraught younger patrollers. He said gently, "If that knife was carried on patrol for many years, it wasn't wasted, even if it was never used on a malice. It upheld us all the same."

Neeta shot him a *Who the blight are you to say?* look. "But I might have taken this one to Luthlia instead of the one grandmother gave me, and used it last year on that sessile my patrol found. And then we'd still have had the other."

Most young patrollers who exchanged north of the Dead Lake took primed knives from home along; it was something of a customary fee for their training. Dag himself had carried primed knives to Luthlia that way twice, early in his long tally. About half the patrollers returned, ready to take up expanded duties. None of the knives did. A steady stream of sacrifice, flowing northward.

"You can't know that," soothed Vayve. "I believe that knife you took with you was quite old as well, wasn't it? Their fates might simply have been reversed."

"Then maybe I should have taken both." But Neeta's hands unclenched, and she sighed. She added wryly, "I just don't know when I'll have a chance at another, is all. All of my tent-kin are disgustingly healthy."

Patroller humor, but Tavia put in more seriously, "No one ever wants to share around here. Nobody in my tent will give me a primed knife because nobody even *has* one. Mama won't even give me permission to bond to a blank! She says I'm much too young. Neeta claims that in Luthlia, they say if you're old enough to patrol, you're old enough to pledge!"

In Oleana, too. Dag thought of his patroller cousin who'd shared at age nineteen. *Much too young.* Both sides in this argument seemed right to Dag, which wrung his brain a bit. Or maybe it was his heart.

Bestirring himself to give the young patroller's mind a more hopeful turn, Dag inquired, "So, will you be patrol leader tomorrow?"

"Not yet," Neeta said glumly, then added, "But our camp captain promised me the next place to open up."

"How many patrols does New Moon Cutoff field?"

"Eight, when we're at full strength." She frowned at him. "You're a funny fellow. Those Oleana boys say you're obsessed with farmers."

"You should stop by Arkady's place and talk with my wife Fawn," said Dag, driven to dryness by her tone. "You could compare malice kills. She slew one, too, did Barr or Remo tell you that? Up near Glass-forge." *And it wasn't a mere sessile.*

Her nose wrinkled. "It sounded pretty garbled. You had to lend her your knife, didn't you?"

Dag tilted his head. "We're all lent our knives, in the end."

"But she can never share in return."

And glad I am of it. But even that was only half true. The strange tale of Fawn's lost babe was nothing he wanted to repeat here, if the boys had actually had the wit to keep it close. "Many Lakewalkers never share, either—weren't you just now complaining of that?"

Dag had, he realized, an audience of three, far from warm, but bemused enough by this upcountry stranger to not bolt. Neeta had taken the last seat, Tavia leaned comfortably against one of the porch posts, and Vayve seemed in no hurry to return to whatever task he'd interrupted. He swallowed, and swung abruptly into what he'd come to think of as the ballad of Greenspring, much as he'd explained it to Arkady, and to dozens before him. Dag's words were growing all too smooth-polished with use, but, he hoped, not so glib as to fail to carry the weight of his horror. By the time he came to his description of the children's burial trench, his listeners' eyes were dark with pity, though their mouths stayed tight.

"Your answer's simple enough, it seems to me," said Neeta, when he at last ran down. "Chase all your farmers back south of the Grace. Not that we want them."

"You ever try to run a farmer off his land? There's nothing simple about it," said Dag.

"That part's too true," said Vayve. "A hundred years back, New Moon folks still used to change camps, winter and summer. Then it got so that if you left your land for a season, you'd come back to find it cleared, plowed, and planted. We finally had to hold our territory by sitting on it, dividing tents between here and Moss River. And send folks from the camp council down to Graymouth and get lines drawn on pieces of farmer paper to say we owned it! Absurd!"

"The cost to us of teaching farmers is nothing to the cost everyone will pay if we don't," said Dag stubbornly.

"In your north country, maybe," said Tavia.

"Everywhere. We have to begin where we are, with whatever piece we have in front of us. Never miss a chance to befriend and teach—there's a task anyone can start."

Vayve made a little gesture at Dag's upper arm, the wedding cord beneath his jacket sleeve unconcealed from her groundsense. She said dryly, "I'd say you took *befriending* a bit far, Oleana man."

Not nearly far enough, yet. Dag sighed, rose, touched his brow politely. "I'll check back about those bone blanks. Good day, ma'am. Patrollers."

∾

Over the next week Dag grew increasingly absorbed by the work in the medicine tent. Not that he hadn't been in and out of the hands of the makers plenty before, but this shift in his angle of view, looking down the throats of such varied problems, made a bigger difference than he'd have guessed. As a patroller, he'd never visited the medicine tent except as a last resort; now, as part of that last resort, he found himself not only understanding, but actually reciting, that annoying maker chant of *Why didn't you come in sooner?*

A half-dozen folks a day turned up with minor ailments or injuries, although once a man was carried in with a broken leg, and a day later, more interesting and much more difficult, an aged woman with a broken hip. Still more delicate was a woman with an ugly tumor in her breast, which Arkady was treating daily by pinching off its blood supply, tiny vessel by tiny vessel. His explanation of why he didn't try to destroy it by ground-ripping gave Dag chills—tumor ground could be nearly as toxic as malice spatter, it appeared. Arkady began taking Dag with him on his daily round of tent visits, too, although Dag was uncertain how he'd earned this advancement, since though he might fetch, carry, or hold, he was still not allowed to do even the simplest groundwork.

The old casebooks packed on the shelves, once Challa taught him how to interpret them, proved unexpectedly gripping. They reminded Dag of patrol logs: stained, tattered, with terrible handwriting and baffling abbreviations. But also like patrol logs, the more he read the more he began to see what was between the lines as well as what was on them. The folks trickling into the tent showed Dag how the makers treated some complaints; the books taught him about things he hadn't yet seen, and so he squinted at their pages daily till the light failed. With his late start as a maker's apprentice, he felt urgent to catch up any way he could, and he overcame his halting north-country tongue to ask Challa and Arkady as many questions as Fawn might.

His head was bursting with it all when he came back to Arkady's place one midafternoon for a forgotten bundle of tooth-extraction tools, to find Fawn curled weeping in their bedroll. He lowered himself beside her as she sat up, hastily drying her eyes and pretending to yawn. "Oh, you're back! I was just having a nap. It always makes me all rumpled and funny-looking, sleeping in the daytime." But her smile lacked its dimple, and her big brown eyes were bleak.

"Spark, what's wrong?" He ran his thumb gently down the moist tracks from her eyes.

"Nothing." She shook her dark curls, abandoning, to his relief, her shaky subterfuge. "I'm just . . . being stupid, I guess."

"It's not nothing. Because you're not stupid. Tell me. You can tell me anything, can't you?" He hoped so. Because here, so far from home and kin, he was all she had.

She sniffed dolefully, considered this, nodded. "I'm just . . . it's just . . . it's all right at night, when you come back and talk to me, but it's been so quiet all day since Barr and Remo left. And I ran out of things to *do*." She waved her empty hands. "I finished sewing the last of the drawers, and I ran out of yarn for socks, and there's not even any cooking or cleaning, because Arkady's neighbor women do all that. It's too gray and cold to sit outside, so I just sit in here, and, and do nothing. Which isn't as much fun as I'd 'a thought." She rubbed her face, then said in a lower voice, "I can't possibly be homesick for

West Blue, because I don't *want* to go back there. Maybe it's just my monthly coming on. You know how that makes me cranky."

He bent and kissed her damp temple, contemplating both her notions. It was perfectly possible, as he well knew, to be homesick for a place one didn't want to go back to. And her monthly was indeed coming on. *All true,* he thought, *but incomplete.* "Poor Spark!" He lifted her hands one by one and kissed them, which made her gulp and sniff again. "*Nothing* is just what the problem is. Your hands have got all lonely, that's what. They're not used to resting folded up."

"Can you get me—does this camp have Stores, like Hickory Lake? Can you get me some more wool or cotton or something?" She frowned. "Oh. But I guess we don't have any camp credit here."

"No, we don't." He stared down at her. Had his head truly been stuffed so full as to drive all care for her out of it? Each night her eyes had sparkled, her lips parted, as she listened eagerly to his tales of his day, and so he'd thought her content. He should have noticed how she'd had less and less to offer in return. Her days should be laden with new things right along with his; absent gods knew her head was better built for learning than his had ever felt.

She sat up more sternly. "Never mind me. I promised I'd take whatever this camp dished out till you got what you needed, and I don't mean to go back on my word. I'll be fine."

"Shh, Spark. Surely we can do better than that." He hugged and comforted her as best he could, till her faked cheer grew less wobbly, then went to find Arkady.

∾

"Out of the question," Arkady said, when Dag finished explaining his request. "A farmer can't learn our techniques."

Dag was unsurprised. He forged on nonetheless. "I always figured to train her myself, later, but having her just settin' around like this is a huge waste of her time. *And* of a camp resource. Fawn can learn anything you can teach—except groundwork—we always meant her to be my spare hands, if ever I got out among farmers as a real medicine maker. You haven't seen it, but I have. When she's by my side, farmers calm right down and stop being afraid of me, despite what a starveling vagabond I generally look. The women because they can see she's not scared, and the men because she's so blighted cute they forget to worry about Lakewalker death magic. And if I'm ever to treat farmer women and girls, which I guess'd be about half my customers, I'd need her with me before I'd dare touch them." He thought of Arkady's breast-tumor treatment, and other even more intimate women's ailments, and shivered. "Absent gods, yes!"

Arkady finished the brief note he'd been jotting about the tooth extraction, set down his quill, and frowned across at Dag. "It's not by any means concluded that you'll be turned loose to treat farmers. As for placing Fawn here in the medicine tent—I grant you she has clever hands, but that bright ground of hers, always open, would be a distraction to patients and makers alike."

"It's not a distraction to me," said Dag. "These are the same fool arguments Hoharie made back at Hickory Lake. One little farmer girl's open ground is only as much of a botheration as folks choose it to be. Lakewalkers can deal fine with Fawn around when they want to."

"Yes, but why should they want to?"

Dag bit his lip. "I'm a stranger here. I've earned no trust from this camp. I know I can't ask this of folks." His eyes caught and held Arkady's, and he dropped his voice to his company captain's growl—not a gift of Dag's that Arkady had guessed at, judging from his faint recoil. "But you can. I've seen how this camp respects you, and I've more than a notion by now of why. You can make this happen if you choose, and we both know it." Dag let his voice and his look lighten. "Besides, what's to lose? Try her for a couple of weeks. If Fawn doesn't work out here, we can think of something else. It's not like me and my farmer bride are asking to join your camp permanent."

"Hm," said Arkady, lowering his eyes and closing his casebook. "Is that what you think? Well. Perhaps I could talk to Challa and Levan."

∾

Fawn was ecstatic when Dag told her the news, which made him right proud of his husbandly insight. The next morning as he took her along to introduce to her new task makers at the medicine tent, she skipped down the road, caught his amused eye upon her, stopped, tossed her head, then skipped again. But she was walking sedately by the time they arrived.

Dag watched her welcome carefully, not above letting it be seen that he was watching. Challa was politely resigned. Levan, the aging herb master, had the air of a man with a long view enduring a temporary burden. His two female apprentices and Challa's boy, at first stiff and cold, grew more pliant as they realized that Fawn would be taking over many of their most tedious chores, from washing pots and bedding to peeling stems and sweeping the floor. As the first days passed, her uncomplaining cheer and enthusiasm softened the older makers, too. Within half a week more, even camp residents stopping in for treatment or to pick up medicines ceased being surprised to find her about the place.

Dag's own heart was comforted and mind eased by having her so often within his sight and hearing, and by her obvious happiness at being so. Gradually, Dag began calling her over to give him a hand, as opportunities presented, and gradually, the other members of the tent became used to the picture. The first time Challa absentmindedly assigned a two-handed chore to the *pair* of them, Dag smiled in secret victory.

❧

One morning, as Dag made to rise from the breakfast table, Arkady said, "Wait."

Dutifully, Dag sat back down.

"Have you made any further progress overcoming your asymmetry?"

Dag shrugged. "Can't say as I have." Which seemed better than *I've hardly given it a thought.*

"Try now."

Dag laid his right arm out on the table and attempted a ground projection, with the same lack of results as before.

"Uh-huh," said Arkady, and walked over to rummage on his shelves. He came back carrying a couple of lengths of rope and a penknife. After tying one rope around Dag's hook, he bent Dag's left arm behind him, and wove the end through the chair back and around to secure firmly in front. Dag cooperated uneasily.

"There. Will that hold?"

Dag tugged. "I expect so."

"Right arm feel free?"

Dag wriggled his fingers. "Aye." Fawn finished packing up the breakfast basket and slid back into her chair to watch. She met Dag's look and grinned. Arkady had evidently paid better attention than Dag had thought to Fawn's words about how his ghost hand had first emerged.

Arkady lit a candle by waving his hand over it, sat on Dag's right, and picked up the sharp little knife. "You claim you've reattached blood vessels before, in your farmer healing?"

"Aye," said Dag, watching in worry as Arkady began passing the knife blade through the candle flame. "In Hod's knee, and Chickory's busted skull. They're stretchy, and coil up when they're busted, but the ends seem to want to find each other again after. Just the bigger ones. They got littler and littler till I couldn't follow them down and in without risking groundlock."

"Mm, yes. I've always wondered if the little arteries empty into a pool in the tissues, and then the veins suck up the blood again, or if they're connected all the way through, unimaginably tiny. If only Sutaw had advanced enough to pull me out of the deep groundlock, I thought I might try . . . well. Never mind. That doesn't concern us today." He held the knife in the air to cool. "Let's give you something more interesting than a piece of paper to work on, shall we?"

He drew the tiny blade across the back of his own left hand, slicing through a plump vein. Fawn squeaked as blood began to well. Arkady laid his oozing hand down in front of Dag.

Dag, eyeing the red trickle with a mixture of alarm and annoyance, attempted once more to coax a ground projection from his right hand. His left arm jerked at its bindings behind him, but from the right . . . nothing.

"What," said Arkady, "you're just going to sit there and watch while your teacher bleeds? For shame, Dag."

Dag flushed, grimaced, clenched and stretched his fingers. Shook his head. "Sorry. I'm sorry."

Arkady waited, then shrugged, passed his right hand over his left—the flash of ground projection went by almost too fast for Dag to perceive—and mopped at the drips with a napkin. The bleeding stopped. He tilted his head for a long moment, eyeing Dag in a shrewd way that made him feel even more of a fool.

"Ye-es," Arkady drawled. "Perhaps . . ." Taking the second length of rope, he knelt by Dag's chair. "Fawn, give me a hand, here. I want to tie his feet firmly to the chair legs."

"Why?" asked Dag. "No one does ground projections from their feet."

"Safety precaution."

Fawn touched Dag's shoulder in encouragement and knelt on his other side; she and Arkady passed the rope back and forth and consulted on the knots. Fawn was inclined to be thorough. Dag craned his neck and tried to see what they'd done, but couldn't quite. He flexed his ankles against their restraints, which held tight, and waited while the pair seated themselves, flanking him once more. Arkady cooked his knife blade in the candle flame again, looking bland.

Then, abruptly, he pounced across the table, yanked Fawn's hand down in front of Dag, and sliced across its back. "Ow!" she cried.

Dag nearly fell over, trying to lunge out of his chair. *Safety for who, you blighter?* He strained at his bindings, clawed at the knot in front, thought wildly of ground-ripping the rope apart, then barely controlled his rocking as Arkady continued to press Fawn's hand down, squeezing to make it drip. Her eyes were wide, and she gasped a little, but she did not struggle to withdraw. Instead, she looked hopefully at Dag.

"You can fix this. Can't you?" Arkady purred in Dag's right ear.

"Blight your eyes . . ." Dag growled. Arkady hadn't plotted this with Fawn in advance, hadn't asked her permission; her surprise and distress had been spontaneous and loud in Dag's groundsense, for all that she'd quickly overcome both. Her pain lingered, shivery sharp like shards of glass.

Arkady let Fawn's hand go and leaned back as Dag extended his right hand above it, fingers not quite touching her pale skin. The slice was barely half an inch long, precisely placed across the blue vein. Dag forced himself to breathe, to open his ground, to concentrate. *Down and in*. The back of Fawn's hand expanded in his perceptions, the wider world tilted away. He felt for the shuddering vein ends. The ground of his right hand seemed to spurt and sputter. *Blight you, Arkady, I've no skill on this side . . . !*

Skill or no, Dag managed to push his ground beyond the confines of his skin. Clumsily, he caught up the two cut ends of the biggest vessel, guided them back together—they seemed to seek each other, which helped—and shaped a strong—no, not quite that strong, right—ground reinforcement to hold them there. *There*. He forced himself to calm, lest he set Fawn's hand afire and do more damage than Arkady had. Down and in . . . he found the living fibers of skin, and began weaving them back together. Farther down, farther in . . .

He was broken from his beginning trance not by a ground-touch, but by Arkady simply slapping him on the side of his head. Dag came back blinking and shaken to the morning light of the room. He inhaled, looked down. Fawn was wiping the blood from her hand with Arkady's napkin. Nothing showed of the attack but a faint pink line.

Dag drew a deep breath. "You like living dangerously, do you, Arkady?"

Arkady's shrug was devoid of apology. "It was time to move you along. It worked, didn't it? Now, let's see that projection again."

His right-side projection felt weak and clumsy, but it was there. And again. And again. Dag was light-headed and nauseated when Arkady at last ceased his badgering and allowed Fawn to untie him.

Dag shook out both his arms, stretching his aching back. The only reason he didn't then stand up and slug the maker across his close-shaved jaw was the sudden thought—*Does this mean I'm almost over my quarantine?*

7

On a bright day that breathed promise of an early southern spring, Fawn helped Nola and Cerie, the herb master's apprentices, pack up a handcart to take to the New Moon Camp farmer's market. The three young women dragged their load around through the sapling gate and down over the hill to the clearing where the horses had been watered that first day. The tree branches were still bare against the cool blue sky, but the buds swelled red, and a few low weeds winked green in the flattened and brownish grass.

It was at last made plain to Fawn why the medicine tent's kitchen was always so busy. After concocting enough remedies for the needs of the camp, the herb master and his helpers produced yet more for the local trade. Some medicines were not so different from what Fawn's mama and aunt Nattie compounded, but Maker Levan himself did groundwork on others that made them much more effective and—he seemed to think this an important point—uniform. Unlike the cure-all nostrums Fawn had seen hawked in the Drowntown market, which Dag claimed were mostly spirits—you might still be sick, but you'd be too drunk to care, Barr had quipped—the Lakewalkers made limited claims for their medicines. Dewormers for people, horses, cattle, and sheep; effective remedies for bog ague and hookworm, neither plague to be found in West Blue but common here, especially in the long, hot summers; a bitter pain powder from willow bark and poppy just like the northern one Fawn had seen Dag use when his arm had been broken; a tincture of foxglove for bad hearts; a gray powder much trusted by the locals to sprinkle on wounds to fight infection.

In the clearing, a number of Lakewalkers unrolled awnings from under the eaves of the shelter and set up trestle tables beneath them. Today they offered mostly handwork of a sort Fawn had seen before: fine leathers that would not rot, nearly unbreakable rope and cord, a small but choice selection from the camp blacksmith—tools that would not rust, blades that would hold their edge. Fawn helped the two apprentices lay out the medicine tent's offerings fetchingly on their table, then they all settled down on upended logs to await their customers.

It wasn't long. As the sun marked noon, a few farmers began to trickle in to the clearing, some driving rumbling carts or wagons, some with packhorses or mules. It would be a slow day, Nola informed Fawn; the market was busier in the summer, when the roads were better. Most people here on both sides seemed to already know their business, as well as one another's names, and deals were struck quickly and efficiently, as when two cartloads of fat grain sacks were traded for several kegs of animal dewormer and some sets of unbreakable traces.

A well-sprung wagon drawn by a pretty team of four matched palomino horses swung into the clearing, and five people climbed down: a very well-dressed farmer with streaks of gray in his hair, a maidservant shepherding a small boy, a horseboy, who went immediately to unhitch and rub down the animals, and what had to be the graying man's wife. She was half a head taller than he, but equally well dressed, in a traveling skirt, close-fitting jacket, and fine boots, with her sandy hair coiled up in tidy braids. She strode without hesitation to one of the armed patrollers lurking around the edge of the clearing, and spoke to him. After a moment he nodded, if a trifle reluctantly, and trotted away up the road.

"Look! *She's* back," muttered Nola.

"I see," murmured Cerie.

The little boy grabbed his father's hand and towed him around the shelter to see the fascinating contents of all the tables. The tall woman glanced over the array and walked straight to the medicine table. Fawn sat up and blinked as she drew closer. Despite her farmer dress, the woman had the fine-boned features and bright silvery-blue eyes of a full-blooded Lakewalker.

She looked down at Fawn, on the other side of the table, with quite as much surprise as Fawn looked up at her.

"Absent gods," she said, in an amused alto voice. "Is New Moon taking in farmers now? Wonders and marvels!"

"No, ma'am," said Fawn, raising her chin. She almost touched her temple the way Dag did; then, afraid it might be mistaken for some sort of mockery, gripped her hands in her lap. "I'm just visiting. My husband's a Lakewalker from Oleana, though, studying groundsetting with Maker Arkady for a stretch."

"Really!"

Uncertain what the woman's exclamation meant, Fawn just smiled in what she hoped seemed a friendly way. Then the woman's eye fell on the cord peeking from Fawn's left jacket cuff, and her breath drew in. She leaned forward abruptly, reaching out, then caught herself, straightened, and motioned more politely. "May I see that? That's a real wedding braid, isn't it?"

Fawn pushed back her cuff and laid her arm out on the table. "Yes, ma'am. Dag and I made them for each other back in Oleana."

The little boy came galloping around the side of the shelter and, suddenly shy, clutched his mother's skirts and stared at Fawn. The man strolled after, putting his arm possessively around the woman's waist.

A brief stillness flashed in the woman's face that hinted at ground-sense extended. "How?" she asked, sounding amazed.

"Dag wove his ground into his in the usual way for Lakewalkers. When we came to mine, we found that my ground would follow my live blood into my braid as I plaited it, and Dag could make it stick."

"Blood! I never thought of that . . ."

The man was watching his wife's profile warily. She glanced side-ways at him, raised her chin, and said distinctly, "It doesn't matter. I don't need it." Fawn wasn't sure what emotion warmed his eyes—pride? relief? In any case, the woman selected some pain powder, some ague remedy, and half their stock of the anti-nausea syrup highly rec-ommended, Fawn had learned, for morning sickness. She paid for it all with good Graymouth coin from a heavy purse, and she and her husband and son returned to the wagon, where the maidservant was setting out a picnic lunch.

"Who was that woman?" Fawn asked her companions. "She looked like a Lakewalker—is she from here?"

"She was," said Nola in a disapproving tone. "She was a patroller, but about ten years back she ran off to marry—if you can call it that—that farmer following her."

"They say he owns several mills in Moss River City," Cerie added, nodding toward the wagon, "and built her a house overlooking the river three floors high, with flower gardens that go all the way down to the water."

"Was she banished?"

"She should have been," said Nola. "But her tent didn't ask it of the camp council."

"Banishing deserters is a joke," sighed Cerie. "Hardly any of them come back, so all it means is that their tent-kin can't speak to them or visit them out there in farmer country. If their kin chase after them and drag them back here, they mostly just leave again at the first chance. And hardly anybody wants to hunt them down and hang them. Some claim if anyone's that disaffected, it's better to let them go, before they spread their mood around the camp."

"Are there very many who leave?"

Cerie shrugged. "Not really. Maybe a dozen a year?"

Compared to the *Unheard of!* at Hickory Lake, that seemed like a lot to Fawn. And if the outward leak was like that at every camp in the south, it would add up. That peeled pole barrier at the camp gate only worked in one direction, it seemed.

In a while, three Lakewalkers appeared from the rutted road, an older woman and two sandy-haired adults. They sat down to the picnic with the Moss River family, speaking quietly. Once, the older woman stood up on her knees and measured the little boy against her shoulder, and said something that made him laugh, and once, the Lakewalker woman in farmer dress put her hand to her belly and gestured, which won strained smiles from the others. At length, the family packed up, made sober farewells, and drove off. The older woman turned her head to watch them out of sight, then the three vanished up the road again.

Fawn's companions were looking impatiently at the shifting sun and their dwindling stocks of medicines and customers when a light cart drove up to the shelter, drawn by a rather winded mare. As she dropped her head to crop the scant grass, a young man jumped down and fetched out some slat crates. He glanced around, then carried them up to the medicine table and went back for two more. Fawn peeked over to see they were jammed with a jumble of glass jars and bottles packed in clean straw.

Almost as winded as his horse, the fellow set down the last boxes and said, "I'm not too late? Good! I don't have much coin, but figure what these are worth to you."

Cerie and Nola actually looked pleased by the offered barter—good glass containers were always in demand in the medicine tent—and circled the table to kneel down and inventory the boxes. The young man's stare lit on Fawn, and he looked taken aback. "Well, hello there! You're no Lakewalker!"

"No, sir." The *sir* was a trifle flattering, but there was no harm in it. She recited her well-worn speech, repeated to nearly every buyer they'd had today: "But I'm married to one. My husband is a Lakewalker from Oleana learning medicine making here."

"Go on! You don't look old enough to be married to anyone!"

Fawn tried not to glower at a paying customer. She supposed she'd know herself a woman grown when that remark began to be gratifying and not just annoying. "I'm nineteen. People just think I'm younger on account as I'm so short." She sat up straight, so he could see she was much too curvy to be a child.

"Nineteen!" he repeated. "Oh." He looked about nineteen himself, fresh-faced, with brown hair and bright blue eyes. He had a wiry build like Whit, but was, of course, taller. "I guess your, um . . . husband must be pretty important, to get you into the camp. They don't usually let farmers past their gates here, you know."

Fawn shrugged. "New Moon hasn't taken us on as members or anything. We're just visiting. Dag found me a job here when I ran out of stuff to spin and got to pining for home. He used to be a patroller up Oleana way, but now he feels a calling to be a medicine maker. To farmers," she added proudly. "No one's done that before."

His mouth opened in surprise. "But that's not possible! Farmers are supposed to go crazy if Lakewalkers use their sorcery on 'em."

A surprisingly accurate comment, but maybe he was a near neighbor and so less ill-informed than most.

"Dag thinks he's cracked beguilement, figured out how to make that not happen." She added honestly, "He's still working out whether or not it'll do something bad to the Lakewalker. He's just a beginner as far as medicine making goes. But he figures, if he can make it work . . . His notion is that Oleana farmers need to learn a lot more about Lakewalkers, on account as we have so many more malice—blight bogle—outbreaks up our way, and it's dangerous for folks to remain so ignorant. He figures healing would give him a straight road to teaching people."

"Are there really—are the bogles really bad, up that way?"

"No, because the Oleana patrol keeps 'em down, but their job could stand to be made easier."

The young man rubbed his mouth. "A couple of my friends keep talking about walking the Trace, maybe moving up to Oleana. Is it true there's free land there, just for the taking?"

"Well, you got to register your claim with whatever village clerk is closest, and then clear the trees and rocks and pull the stumps. There's land for the back-busting *working* of it, yes. Two of my brothers are homesteading that way, right up on the edge of the great woods the Lakewalkers still hold. My oldest brother'll get our papa's farm, of course."

"Yeah, mine, too," sighed the young man. He added after a moment, "My name's Finch Bridger, by the way. My parents' place is about ten miles that way." He pointed roughly southeast.

"I'm Fawn Bluefield," returned Fawn.

"How de'!" He stuck out a friendly, work-hardened hand; Fawn shook it and smiled back. He added after a moment, "Aren't the winters tough in Oleana?"

"Nothing like so bad as north of the Dead Lake, Dag says. You prepare for it. Lay in your food and fodder and firewood, make warm clothes."

"Is there snow?"

"Of course."

"I've never seen snow here but once, and it was gone by noon. In these parts, we mostly just have cold rain, instead."

"We have some nice quiet times in winter. And it's fun to have the sleigh out. Papa puts bells on the harnesses." An unexpected spasm of homesickness shot through Fawn at the recollection.

"Huh," Finch said, evidently trying to picture this. "That sounds nice."

Nola and Cerie finished their count and came back around the table, and Finch dug in his pockets to lay out a few supplemental coins. "Let me know how far this goes . . . I need this, and this . . . and I can't leave without this, or I'll be skinned."

He took up all their remaining stock of anti-nausea medicine. Fawn raised her eyebrows. "You don't look old enough to be married, either."

"Huh? Oh." He blushed. "That's for my sister-in-law. She's increasing, again, and she's so sick she can barely hold her head up. That's why I was let off chores to drive over here today."

"Well, that nice syrup's bound to help her keep her food down and get her strength back. It doesn't even taste bad, for medicine." Fawn sure wished she'd had some, back when. She banished the bleak memory. Her own child had been lost to her before becoming much more than a sick stomach and a social disaster; she had no call to picture her as a bright-eyed little girl the size of that Lakewalker woman's half-blood child.

The Bridger boy packed his medicines carefully on his cart, then made two trips to a table on the other side of the shelter, lugging half a dozen bulging sacks like overstuffed pillowcases. Fawn didn't see what he'd acquired in return, but he circled back to her table with a similar sack, scantly filled. He thrust it at her. "Here. You can have this."

Fawn peeked in to find several pounds of washed cotton. "What else do you need? I don't know how to value this." She glanced to Nola for help.

"Nothing. It's a present."

"For me?" said Fawn, surprised.

He nodded jerkily.

"I can't take this off you!"

"It was leftover. No point in hauling it back home again."

"Well . . . thanks!"

He nodded again. "Well. Um. It was nice talking to you, Fawn Bluefield. I sure hope everything works out for you. When are you starting back north?"

"I don't hardly know, yet. It all depends on Dag."

"Um. Oh. Sure." He hovered uncertainly, as if wanting to say more, but then glanced at the sun, smiled at her again, and tore himself away.

At the end of another half hour, the last farmer bought the last item left on their table, a jar of purple ointment meant for cuts on horses' knees, and rode off. All three girls helped the remaining Lakewalkers take down the trestles and roll up the awnings. Cerie and Nola were cheerful at having a good haul of coin to show for the day, as well as the valued glass. They trundled the handcart, reloaded with all their barter, back up the rutted road. Fawn glanced back over her shoulder at the tidied clearing, thinking, *This place isn't quite what it looked at first glance.*

Was anywhere? She remembered the little river below the West Blue farm in winter. All hard, rigid ice, seeming utterly still—but with water running underneath secretly eroding its strength until, one day, it all cracked and washed away in ragged lumps. How close were these southern Lakewalker camps to cracking apart like that? It was an unsettling notion.

∾

Dag was watching Fawn unpack the day's lunch basket on the round table when the distant clanging of a bell echoed through the quiet noon. Arkady shot to his feet, dropping his bread and cheese, though he managed one gulp of hot tea before saying to Dag, "Come on." And, after a fractional hesitation, "You, too, Fawn."

They sprinted up the road to the medicine tent. Arkady fell to a rapid gasping walk as they found themselves crowding up behind a makeshift litter being maneuvered through the door. He grabbed Dag's arm.

"I thought I'd have at least another week to drill you," he muttered. "Never mind, you'll do. Come along, do exactly what I tell you, and don't hesitate. Drop that hook, it'll just get in the way."

"What about my contaminated ground?"

"For the next half hour, we have more urgent worries."

Dag rolled up his sleeve and worked on his buckles, following after. He'd recognized the pregnant woman on the litter and her tent-kin carrying it almost as fast as Arkady had, because he'd visited her daily in Arkady's wake.

Somewhat to Dag's discomfiture, Arkady had dragged him along to every childbirth in New Moon Cutoff Camp since his arrival. As a terrified young patroller, Dag had once delivered a child on the Great North Road under the direction of its irate but fortunately experienced mother, so he was long past mere embarrassment, but he still felt an intruder in these women's tents. Two births had progressed quite normally, and Dag had been given no tasks but to sit quietly, listen to

Arkady instruct him, and try not to loom. In the third, the child had to be shifted into better position inside its mother's body, which Arkady accomplished with a combination of handwork, groundwork, and, Dag was almost certain, lecturing it.

It was all a much more complicated process than Dag had imagined. *What, did you think women were stuffed with straw in there?* Arkady had inquired tartly. And gone on to explain that about once a year, all the medicine makers' apprentices in the area were assembled to witness a human dissection, when someone gifted their body to the purpose, at which all the shifting, sparkling ground the young makers directly perceived was mapped to the secret physical structures that generated it. Arkady promised, or threatened, to make sure Dag observed the next such demonstration. But today Dag would glimpse inside a body still alive. *Maybe.*

Tawa Killdeer's complication horrified Dag. The mysterious, nourishing placenta had grown across the mouth of her womb, instead of up a side as it was supposed to. Her labor must rip apart the supporting organ long before the child could emerge to breathe; without aid, the result would be a dead blue infant and a mother swiftly bleeding to death. The proposed treatment was drastic: to cut the child directly from its mother's belly. The chance of saving the child this way was good; the mother, poor; without groundwork, impossible. But Dag now realized why Arkady had pushed him so hard learning to control blood flow in their practice sessions.

Tawa's kin, Challa, and Arkady all helped shift the pregnant woman up onto the waist-high bed in the bright far room. Challa was already washing her straining belly with grain spirits as her sister pulled off her clothing. A wad of cloth between her legs was bright with blood.

She didn't have a bonded sharing knife with her, nor did any of her kin carry one. A northern woman would have . . .

"Here, Dag," snapped Arkady. "Open yourself. Down and in." He grabbed Dag's left arm and positioned it over Tawa's lower belly. The room tilted away; before Dag shut his eyes to concentrate on Tawa's ground, he had one glimpse of her pale face, her set jaw stifling outcry. Her sister held one white-knuckled hand, her frightened husband the other, and Challa's boy coaxed her clenching teeth apart to insert a leather strap for her to bite. The last time Dag had seen a look like that was on the face of a fellow patroller closing on a malice. Staring down death, eyes defiantly wide open.

Arkady's voice in his ear: "Placenta's parting too soon and bleeding underneath. Let your left-side ground projection sink down and in. Spread it as far as you can. Hold pressure just like stopping any other bleeding wound, but you're working from the inside out. Good . . ."

Dag shaped his ghost hand like a broad lily pad, pressing against the inside of Tawa's womb. His right-side projection as well, from the opposite direction, providing counterpressure. The flow of blood between her legs slowed to a trickle. From the corner of one eye, barely open, he saw Challa lean in, the flash of a sharp knife, felt as well as saw flesh part. Two cuts, one of the abdominal wall, a second of the womb itself. Arkady worked across from her, following the blade with his ground-hands, stemming bleeding. Dag caught a glimpse of a tiny, slick purple body sliding out from the cut feetfirst, the flash of the infant's distressed but *alive* ground. Other hands took it from Challa. Choking noises, a thin wail.

"One down, one to go," Arkady muttered.

Tawa's pain and fear flooded Dag's ground, which he had matched to hers as closely as a man's could match a woman's. He thought of the look on her face and endured. He'd soaked up the like before, in rough-and-ready treatment of patroller injuries on the trail. The sister and husband also partitioned the load of pain and stress, the sharing rendering it more bearable to Tawa; the senior makers had mastered the trick of closing grounds to pain but not to the person, and worked on steadily. Dag hoped the pair was watching out for potential group groundlock.

The sharing wasn't bearable to everyone. The two herb master's apprentices had been holding down Tawa's ankles. One was now head-down in the corner, sobbing, fighting black faintness, her ground snapped shut; her place had been taken over by a dogged-looking Fawn. She grinned back at the glint of his eye, scared, determined—confident in him. Dag remembered to breathe.

"Now," Arkady murmured in Dag's ear, "you have to let go the placenta without letting go the pressure, so we can get it out of there and close up. Let your projection slip down *through* the tissues . . . a little tug on the cord, oh good, we have it all . . . that's right . . . hold . . ."

Arkady and Challa together closed the inner cut, he weaving tissues back together in a fragile splice, she setting strong reinforcements. Then the abdominal wall, the support here applied physically, with curved needle and stitches. More washing of the wrinkled, flaccid belly with grain spirits, then dry cloths and dressings. Tawa's chest heaved, tears of pain dripped down her temples, but her eyes flashed and she nodded weakly as her sister displayed a blanket-wrapped and red-faced little girl to her. Her husband was weeping unashamed, overwhelmed. *You blighted should be,* Dag thought, not disapprovingly.

A small eternity passed before Arkady murmured in Dag's ear again: "Ease up gradually, let's see where we are. The vessels in the womb wall should close on their own at this stage   it's their good trick. Ah. Yes. It looks like they're behaving . . ."

Slowly, Dag withdrew his ghost hands. The broad, natural wound left by the placenta within Tawa was raw but only oozing slightly. She stifled a cry as his breaking ground-match returned her pain to her. He backed away, and the kinswomen closed in to take care of the rest of the cleanup.

Dag blinked, aware again of his shivering body, cold as clay. Fawn appeared under his shoulder. They made it through the room's other door and out onto the bright porch before he bent over the rail and heaved. The sun, strangely, still seemed to be at noon. Dag felt as though it ought to be sunset.

Arkady came out and handed him a cup of hot tea with a hand that shook slightly. "Here."

Dag clutched it and sipped gratefully. Arkady lowered himself to a seat against the wall, warmed by the nearly springlike sun, and Dag sat beside him, with Fawn on folded knees at Dag's other side.

"It was throwing you off the deep end of the dock, but I'm glad you were here today. We don't often beat those odds," said Arkady.

He didn't, Dag noticed, accuse him of inelegant inefficiency this round. "Will Tawa live?"

"If infection doesn't set in. I'll send everyone who can give ground reinforcements down to her tent in turns over the next couple of days." He added after a moment, "You kept your head well, patroller. Usually my apprentices get wobbly, first time we have to open up someone with knives."

"I expect I'm older than your usual apprentice." Dag hesitated. "And I've opened up folks with knives before, but never to *save* their lives."

"Ah." Arkady sipped.

Dag shared a swallow from his cup with Fawn, and thought about the other complications of childbearing Arkady had described to him. The placenta tearing away from the womb wall prematurely, hiding lethal bleeding till too late; babies turned the wrong way 'round pinching off their own cords; a child too large to pass its mother's pelvis. Without groundwork, farmer midwives sometimes had to break such a child inside its mother and draw it out dead. Even with groundwork that was sometimes the only way. "How do you make such choices? When it's one life or the other?" Dag wondered if Arkady understood his question was practical, not despairing.

Arkady shook his head. "Best chance, usually. It varies, and often you can't know till it's right up on you." He hesitated. "There is one other you should know about. And it's not a choice.

"Sometimes—very rarely, fortunately—the placenta doesn't implant in the womb at all, but roots in that little tube that runs from the sparkling organ down to it. A child can't live or be born from there. Instead it grows till it rips the mother apart from the inside, and she dies of the bleeding and rotting. The pain is dreadful, and the fear. It's not a quick death, nor a merciful one. What you must do if confronted with one of these is to *immediately* strip the life-ground from the conception. You don't let the mother or kin argue with you. You may be able to coax the material fragments down into the womb to be flushed out in her next monthly, though often by the time you see it, the tube is ruptured already, and all you can do is lay in ground reinforcements and hope the body will clean up the mess itself."

"Ground-rip," said Dag through dry lips. "Like a malice." Like what the Glassforge malice had done to Fawn's child; by her set face, he saw she realized this too.

"Ground-strip," said Arkady, "like a groundsetter. In forty years I've only seen this three times, and thank the absent gods that the first time I was with my own mentor, who talked me through it. I could not have done it else."

"So that ground . . . would end up in me."

"Just like your experiments with food, I'm afraid, yes. It's quickly absorbed." But not, it seemed, quickly forgotten, judging by the bleak shadows rippling through Arkady's bright ground.

Dag took a swallow of tea against his rising gorge. Fawn pried the cup from his fingers and took one herself, possibly for the same reason.

"I've never been sure," said Arkady, "if I wanted to pray I'd never encounter one of those again, or pray that the next woman would at least encounter me. In time."

Dag had always known that senior medicine makers kept secrets of their craft not discussed with outsiders. He was beginning to see why. "I always thought medicine making would be less harrowing than patrolling."

"Today was happy." Arkady finished his tea and grunted to his feet. "Hold on to that."

Dag followed suit. For the first time, he wondered why the brilliant Arkady was wifeless. Since he'd arrived at New Moon, he'd been too blighted busy to notice that inexplicable absence. He would ask Challa, he decided. Some other time. Because there were certain possible answers he wasn't up to hearing, just now.

∽

Two nights later Dag sat with Arkady at the round table and armwrestled himself. Or at least, tested his right-side ground projection against his left. The left side always won, which was a bit boring. He glanced at Fawn, sitting by the fire and spinning up a bag of cotton she'd acquired at the farmer's market, and thought he could devise a better practice drill and go to bed early with her at the same time, very efficient. Arkady cleared his throat as the projections failed under Dag's inattention. But before Dag could recover himself, a knock sounded at the door. Arkady nodded, and Dag rose to answer it.

Two people, his half-furled groundsense told him. But without urgency, unlike most night knocks for Arkady. He opened the door to find, to his surprise, Tawa Killdeer's husband and sister.

"How de', folks! Come on in."

The sister shook her head. "We can't stay. But the Killdeer tent wanted you to have this, Dag." She thrust a long narrow bundle wrapped in hemmed cloth into his hand. "We heard you were in want of one."

Heard from who? Dag felt through the wrapping and knew the contents at once.

"Tawa's great-uncle left it to the tent a year or so back," explained the husband. "He was an exchange patroller to the north, back in his youth."

"Well—thank you!" It was hardly a gift he could refuse, even if he'd wanted to. Which he did not. A diffident smile turned his lips. "Thank your tent, and Tawa."

"We will." New father and new aunt walked away into the chilly night, happy, unbereaved.

Yes, thought Dag, his hand closing on the gift.

He brought the bundle to the table and unwrapped it in the lantern light. Fawn came to his shoulder, smiling at his smile. As the human thighbone was revealed, her smile faded. Dag ran his hand along the smooth length: clean, dried, cured, and ready to carve into a knife blank. Strong, too; bones donated by the very old were often too fragile to carve. Someone had scratched the donor's name and tent name into the far end with a pin. That part of the bone would be cut away when the tip was shaped to a malice-killing point. Dag would burn the name on the finished blade's side, he decided, so that it would not be lost to memory.

In a distant and somewhat strained voice, Fawn said, "You going to make that up into a knife?"

"Yes. Maker Vayve as much as said if I could get a bone she'd help me." Which was not a lesson to be scorned—in either direction.

"And bond to it?"

"Yes." He stroked the smooth surface. "It's an honorable gifting. It feels right, see. For something that intimate, you want it to feel right." Crane's bones, for example, buried with him on the banks of the Grace, would have felt . . . well, Dag wasn't just sure what they'd have felt like to a stranger, but they would have given *him* the horrors.

Fawn bit her lip, drew breath. "I know that's a thing you wanted, and I can't say nay to it. But . . . promise me you'll not prime that thing while I'm still aboveground and breathing!"

"I'm not likely to, Spark." But after she . . . *That doesn't bear thinking about*. In the natural course of events, it was likely they'd both grow old together.

"I was just remembering that horrid ballad."

"Which horrid ballad?"

"The one about the two patrollers."

That still didn't narrow the choices much, but he realized which one she meant—a dramatic tale in which two partners, separated from their patrol, found a dangerous malice. Neither carried a primed knife, but both bore bonded ones. The argument over which self-sacrificing loon was to share on the spot and which was to carry the news back to the grieving widow or betrothed, depending, had taken three heart-wrenching stanzas. It was a popular song in the north; people danced to it. Not that similar events had never happened in real life, but Dag suspected the circumstances were not so tidy.

"It was just a song," he protested.

Her mouth set mulishly. "Promise me anyway."

"I promise, Spark." He kissed those lips to soften them.

After, she drew back to search his eyes, then nodded. "You'd best believe it."

8

Fawn returned late one evening from the medicine tent along with
Dag and Arkady—there had been another child with an intractable
fever—to find the dinner basket left by their door with a letter propped
up on it.

Arkady read the inscription and raised his brows. "For you," he said,
handing it to Fawn. "Courier must have brought it by."

Surprised, she made out her name and Dag's, and *Arkady's Place, New
Moon Cutoff Camp*, in Whit's crabbed handwriting. Whit was a reluctant
correspondent; any letter from him had to be important. She took it to
the round table while Arkady stoked the fire for his endless tea. Dag set
down the basket, lit the brace of table candles, then came to her shoulder, looking concerned. "Anything wrong?"

"No, not really," she reported, tilting the paper to catch the flickering light. Whit's scrawl was actually legible, in a painful sort of way.
"Whit says Berry found a buyer for the *Fetch* who wants it for a house-
boat." The *Fetch* had been much better built than most makeshift crafts
launched from the upper Grace feeder creeks by venturesome Oleana

hill boys. Berry would be happy that her papa's last boat wouldn't be broken up for timber, or worse, firewood. Daisy-goat was slated to be sold with her floating home, alas. "He also says Berry's found them all work with a keeler boss she trusts, heading upriver soon to catch the last of the winter fall. All on the same boat—Whit and Bo and Hod for hands, Hawthorn for boat boy, and her for the fiddler." Berry had been holding out for just such a collection of berths, though exactly when she would find it had still been up in the air when Dag and Fawn had left Graymouth. Whit had talked idly about the whole crew joining the long-planned overland ride up the Trace, but the money would be much better this way. "Whit says if we want to change our minds, we should meet them in Graymouth before the end of the week, and if not, to write and let him know when to look for us back at Clearcreek."

"Ah," said Dag.

She glanced up at him. "I better write back soon, or the letter might not reach him before they shove off. So . . . what are we doing, Dag? When we started out for New Moon, I thought we might be here a few days, but it's already been more 'n a month."

Dag delayed answer by going to the sink to wash his hand before dinner, a ritual Arkady insisted upon with more than maternal firmness. Fawn followed suit. They laid out the contents of the basket, and Arkady brought over the tea, before Dag spoke. "I've hardly finished training up for medicine maker."

Arkady, pouring, snorted. "You've hardly started. I'd give you two years. Most apprentices take three or four."

"Two years!" said Fawn.

Dag merely nodded. "I begin to see why."

"Really," said Arkady, "medicine makers don't ever stop learning from each other, and from their patients. The common ailments become routine very quickly—and I will say, you're the most relentless student

I've ever had—but some experiences can't be sped up. You just have to wait for them to occur."

Dag bit into his bread and butter, chewed, swallowed. "When would you guess I'd be fit to start actual groundwork?"

Arkady didn't answer right off. Instead he went to his shelf, took down a familiar little book, and paged through it. He eyed Dag steadily for an unnerving minute, then, with some danger of mixing ink and crumbs, jotted a few notes and blew on the page to dry them. "Tomorrow," he said.

Dag looked startled but pleased. "What about all my so-called dirty ground you were so worried about?"

"As I hoped, the best remedy was time. Your ground is cleaning itself out quite nicely, and will continue to do so as long as you don't contaminate yourself again. The permanent cure, of course, is to *stop doing that*."

Dag took a slow sip of tea. "That's . . . not enough, Arkady. If I'm ever to treat farmers and not leave them crazy with beguilement, I'm going to have to go on absorbing all sorts of strange ground."

Arkady glowered at him.

"It was all mixed together in my head for a while," Dag went on, "but looking back, I'm less and less sure how much of my upset was from taking in strange ground, and how much was just from dealing with Crane and his bandits, which was plenty to give any thinking man nightmares."

"Mind and ground—and emotion—do intersect on the deepest levels," Arkady conceded. He glanced, oddly, at Fawn.

Dag nodded. "Because for all the things I took in—barring Crane—it seems to me I just kept getting stronger and better at groundwork all the way downriver. 'Cept for the part about being *untidy*, just what about having dirty ground unfits me for medicine making?"

"Every bit of strange ground you take in changes your own ground, and so how it works. The results risk being uncontrolled."

Dag frowned. "Everything I do and learn—blight, every breath I take—changes my ground. My ground can't *not* change, not while I'm alive. Could be dirty ground is just something to live with, like the bugs and blisters and weather and weariness on patrol."

"Rough-and-ready may do for patrolling. Not for the delicate control needed for groundsetting."

"Groundsetting isn't so sweet and delicate as all that, that I've seen."

"Your projection changes everything you touch with it."

"My hand changes everything I touch with it. Always has. Anyway, I *want* to change folks."

"Dag, you can't treat farmers. Not at New Moon Cutoff."

"What if Fawn falls ill? I will sure enough treat her!"

Arkady waved this away. "That's different."

"Oh? How? Groundwise."

Arkady sighed and rubbed his brow. "I can see I'm going to have to give you the set speech. For my usual apprentices it starts out, *When I was your age* . . . but I suppose that won't do for you."

"When you were my age?" Fawn suggested helpfully.

Arkady eyed her. "A little older than that. Not much, I grant."

Dag eased back and occupied his protesting mouth with another bite of bread. He nodded to signal that Arkady had his full attention.

Arkady drew a long breath. "When I was much younger, and stupider, and vastly more energetic, my wife and I were training up together as medicine makers at a camp called Hatchet Slough, which is about a hundred and fifty miles northeast of here."

What wife? Fawn hadn't seen hide nor hair of a Missus Arkady since she'd arrived, nor, more tellingly, heard any word. Dag nodded understanding—of the geography? Or of something else? She wasn't sure if

Arkady saw the little flinch that went-with. Tales of the ill fates of first wives would likely do that to Dag. Fawn gulped and shut up hard.

"We were both newly come into our full maker's powers. Bryna had a special talent for women's ailments. There were already hints that I'd be a groundsetter when I grew into myself. It seemed we had more enthusiasm than sick or injured to treat at Hatchet Slough. An excess of energy that's hard to imagine, now . . .

"Being young, we talked about the problems of our neighboring farmers. She thought it a grand idea to offer treatments to them—perhaps set up a little medicine tent at the camp farmer's market, next to the table for herbs and preparations. Our mentors put their feet down hard on that before it became more than talk, of course, but you can see how far our thinking had gone. Your notions aren't new, Dag."

Dag's eyes lit. "But with unbeguilement, you could really do that!"

Arkady made a little wait-for-the-rest gesture. "A desperate farmer woman with a dying husband who'd heard our loose talk came to Bryna for help. She went."

"Is this one of those failed-and-blamed tales?" Dag said uneasily. Fawn shivered. Accusations of black sorcery could get a lone Lakewalker beaten up—or burned alive, if the mob was vicious enough. Lakewalkers in pairs or groups were much harder to tackle.

"No. She succeeded. The man wasn't even beguiled." Arkady drew another fortifying breath. "Word got out. Another frantic farmer came, and another. I started going out with her. One sick woman became deeply beguiled, and began haunting the camp. Her husband decided she'd been seduced, and tried to waylay and kill me. Fortunately, there were some patrollers nearby who rescued me and drove him off.

"It all came to a head when there was a riot at the camp gates by the kin of some desperately ill folks, trying to break in and carry us away by force. It was repulsed with a lot of bloodied heads on both sides—one patroller was killed, and two farmers. The camp council decided to break the impasse by smuggling us out in the night. We were taken in secret to Moss River Camp to continue our training. The Hatchet Slough Lakewalkers misdirected anyone inclined to search for us. And that was the end of our experiments with farmers." Arkady sat up straight and fixed Dag with a glare. "As I don't care to relive that nightmare, you will stay away from farmers as long as you reside at New Moon Cutoff. Is that very clear?"

Dag returned a short nod like some unhappily disciplined patroller. "Yes, sir."

Arkady said in a more conciliating tone, "Of course that does not apply to Fawn. She doesn't trail a jealous farmer spouse, nor does she have kin here to foment a riot. She's not likely to create a *camp* problem." He added after a moment, "At least, not in that sense."

Fawn's brows drew down in puzzlement. "But what happened to your wife, sir?"

Dag gave her an urgent head shake, but whether it meant *No, don't ask!* or *I'll explain later*, she wasn't sure.

But Arkady replied merely, "She works at Moss River Camp these days." Voice and expression both flat and uninviting, so Fawn swallowed the dozen questions *that* begged.

"As guests here," Dag said, "Fawn and I are of course obliged to abide by your camp rules. I won't give you trouble, sir."

Fawn wasn't at all sure how to take the skeptical lift of Arkady's brows, but his tension eased; he accepted Dag's assurance with a nod. The maker opened his mouth as if to add something, but then apparently thought better of it, taking a belated bite of his dinner instead.

∾

It wasn't till they were settling down in their bedroll, laid out in the spare room at the house's farthest end, that Fawn found the chance to ask more.

"So what was all that about Missus Arkady? Missus Maker Arkady, I guess. For a horrible minute I thought Arkady was going to tell us she'd been murdered by farmers, but seemingly not."

Dag sighed and folded her in close to him. "I had the tale from Challa a few days back. Seems Arkady and his wife worked together happily in the medicine tent here for years and years. They were partners, as well as spouses, close as close. But they had some of the same problems that Utau and Sarri had."

"No children?" A sorrow that the Hickory Lake couple had solved radically by taking another member into their marriage, Utau's cousin Razi; not the usual course, Fawn had gathered. But their toddlers were darling, however many parents they possessed.

Dag nodded. "Not just no conceptions. Miscarriage after miscarriage, getting worse as she grew older. Arkady was especially frustrated, Challa says, because as a senior medicine maker he thought he ought to be able to fix it somehow. Seems that's why the miscarriages got more dangerous, actually. When the troubles weren't let go early, they were worse when they did break. It's not an uncommon problem—I've seen it in camps all over the north. Two exceptional people get string-bound, and their tent-kin settle back happily to wait for the exceptional children to start popping out, and nothing happens. Kauneo and I . . ." He bit his lip.

She stroked his brow. "You don't have to say."

He nodded gratefully, but went on anyhow. "We didn't have long enough together to find out if we'd be more of that. There was one month we had hopes . . . anyway, Arkady's wife Bryna. She was getting older, time was running out, then suddenly she asked him to cut strings with her."

Lakewalker divorce. Fawn nodded.

"Arkady wasn't too happy, I reckon, but he didn't fight it. They divided up New Moon and Moss River medicine tents between them, more or less, and very soon after, she got string-bound with a widowed patroller from over there. They had two children before she had her change of life. I guess they're nearly grown by now."

Fawn tried to decide if this was a happy ending or not. Half a one, maybe. "You wonder why Arkady didn't remarry."

"Even my groundsense doesn't help me figure what goes on in his head. I do see he's a right sensitive man, and maybe only partly from training his groundsense to a pitch like I've never seen."

"Do you think that's why he's so . . . I don't know how to say it—*tidy*? Maybe turmoil hurts him in his ground."

He raised his brows at her. "Could be, Spark."

She cuddled in closer, planting a kiss on his collarbone. His hand tightened on her hip. Before they gave over talking in favor of other sorts of exchange, she said, "So, what should I write to Whit and Berry?"

He sighed uncertainly. "What do you want to do, Spark?"

She went still beneath his warm grip, stemming her first thought before it could leap off her tongue. *I want to go home* made no sense. The West Blue farmhouse would belong to her eldest brother's wife, in due course. Dag had been all but banished from Hickory Lake. All the home she had was right here beneath her, a square of blanket on somebody else's floor. And Dag. It was enough for two.

But not for three.

Or maybe even more; twins ran in Fawn's family. Two *years* in this place? It seemed a huge stretch of time to her, though Dag no doubt saw it as a hiccup in his much longer existence. A lot could happen in two years. Births. Deaths. Both.

Her thoughts were spinning too wide and loose to snag sense. She coiled them in. A day, a week, a month, that was all she could plan right now. "I've seen the rivers, and it was all good except for that one mile. And I've seen the sea. I'd still like to see the Trace in that lingerin' spring you . . ."—she caught the word *promised* before it could escape to wound him—"told me about. Whichever spring that turns out to be."

He ducked his head, but didn't speak.

Arkady had said how much time it would take to turn Dag into a real medicine maker. He hadn't exactly said outright that Dag and his farmer bride were invited to stay here that long. Was that *I'd give you two years* an observation or an offer?

She drew breath. "I'll write Whit and Berry that we're not coming back to the *Fetch,* anyhow." That floating home might already be passed to its new owner, their things transferred to the keelboat. "Is it possible to send a letter from here all the way up to Clearcreek?"

Dag pursed his lips, seeming to check his mental map—courier routes and camp locations, likely. "Yes. No guarantee of how quick it'd get there, though."

Fawn nodded understanding. It was a slow, hard slog to wrestle a keelboat upriver: four months or more from Graymouth to Tripoint, compared to the six or so weeks it took to float down. The overland route on the Tripoint Trace cut off the corner of the river route, many miles shorter, quicker for the horsed or the lightly burdened, but un- friendly to heavy cargo. They could leave New Moon weeks or even months from now and still beat Whit and Berry . . . *home,* her thought faltered. Or to Clearcreek, anyhow. Where Whit at least had achieved a real home now, with Berry and Hawthorn. She and Dag would be welcome *guests* there, Fawn had no doubt. She swallowed. "I'll tell him if we don't all meet up back at Clearcreek by strawberry season, to look for another letter."

Dag nodded again.

It was plain that tonight even he couldn't answer the question *Dag, what will happen to us?* She didn't ask it. She tilted back her head instead, finding his lips for a wordless kiss.

∽

Dag took Fawn along with him to Vayve's place to work on his new sharing knife, feigning to need her clever fingers even more than he actually did. By the time Vayve had watched Fawn help carve and polish the cured femur, wait in apprehensive but attentive silence while Dag anchored the involution into the bone, and slice his skin with a hot knife to let his blood trickle onto the blade for bonding, the maker had lost her rigidity at having a farmer in her work shack. Another little victory for Fawn's good nature and bright ground; or, considering how far into the core of Lakewalker secrets this making was, maybe not so little.

It didn't take Dag as long to recover from the shuddering pain of setting this involution as it had when he'd done Crane's knife—if not elegant, at least this one was not so anxiously overbuilt. He set Fawn to burning his name and the donor's into the sides of the bone with an awl heated in a candle flame, then borrowed her birthday walnut back from her skirt pocket to place before Vayve.

Vayve's lips pursed as she took it up and examined it. "What was this? Practice in setting involutions? It's far too dense, if so."

Dag shook his head. "I'd another notion altogether. Hoped you might have some ideas. It's been in my mind for a while that I'd like to make something for Faw—farmers that would work to protect them from malices like ground veiling does a patroller. Not the same way, mind; I don't see how farmers could twist their grounds sideways to the world the way we do. It would have to be something else. Something any good maker could produce."

Vayve looked startled. "You would have Lakewalker makers expend themselves creating these shields for farmers? How could we afford the time?"

"Make and sell them, like other groundworked objects."

"You know we only sell trivial things. These shields of yours—if they could be made at all—would not be trivial work."

"So, don't sell them for a trivial price." Dag glanced at his knife on the workbench, its plain lines echoing the bone from which it had just emerged, then over at another blank Vayve had in progress, hung on the wall. The carving on that blade was elaborate. Later, it might be decorated with shell inlay or colored stones, the hilt wrapped with patterned leather. Some designs were exclusive to certain tents or camps, proclaiming the knife's origin to the educated eye; you could always tell southern work at a glance, that way. Great pains and pride went into the makings. In the north, Dag thought, it was mostly just pain. *There's your spare time, Vayve. Don't you see it?*

Fawn put in, "Dag started off with the notion of shielding just me, and only then thought of farmers generally. But I reckon such shields might work to protect Lakewalker youngsters, too. Like the nineteen lost at Bonemarsh. Because it wasn't only Greenspring hit with that sorrow. Stands to reason."

Vayve fell suddenly silent.

So did Dag, blinking. *Of course. Of course . . . !* The intractable problem of how to persuade Lakewalker makers to be interested in this wild notion of his evaporated with startling suddenness, right before Dag's eyes. Vayve's ground roiled with new thought.

Why hadn't *he* taken his idea that one step further? Aside from the fact that his head had been stuffed so full of new things these past months it felt like bursting, and he was so dizzy with it all he didn't know if he was coming or going. Maybe it was for the same reason no Lakewalkers had taken any step—they already had a solution to the problem, or thought they did. A young Lakewalker's tent-kin or patrol mentors were all intent on teaching ground veiling. Why tackle a problem sideways in chancy experiments that could cost lives when you already had a time-proven system?

Dag took an unsteady breath and went on: "I was thinking that an involution might either be expanded into, or anchor, some sort of slippery shield that a malice couldn't get a grip on. At least for long enough for the farmer—or youngster—to run away. If an involution can hold a dying ground, why not a living one?"

Vayve's brows climbed. "But a knife's involution breaks when it's brought in contact with a malice."

Dag ducked his head. "But it doesn't break from the outside. It breaks from the inside, from the affinity of the dying ground with the malice nearby. It's a sort of a vibration. I didn't realize that, for all the twenty-six knives that had passed through my hand to their ends, till I held one that had *no* affinity with a malice."

Dag took a long breath, and began the explanation, again, of how his former bonded knife had become charged with the death of Fawn's unborn child at Glassforge, and the tale of its final fate in Raintree. Vayve asked far more, and more detailed, questions about the events than Arkady had. She proved especially fascinated with his account of the malice's mud-man magery as seen from the inside.

Dag explained, "I recognized it as an involution of a sort, too, but huge, and so complex—anchored in the array of groundlocked makers the malice had slaved together. It didn't just sit there passive like a knife's involution. It was living off the makers, in a sense. It was the first I realized that magery is an *alive* thing.

"I'm not sure just where a ground shield would get such aliveness, though. And it couldn't be working all the time, or it would wear out too quick. I'm thinking it would need to come awake only when challenged, the way a knife only breaks when it actually enters a malice."

"Well," said Vayve slowly, "there would be four possible sources of ground in that moment. The involution itself, the person being shielded, the immediate surroundings, or the malice itself."

Dag frowned. "I don't see how you could put enough strength into an involution to last more 'n a moment, if it came alive like the magery I saw in Raintree."

"It would be clever if you could pull it from the malice itself," mused Vayve. "Like grabbing an attacker's arm and pulling him off balance."

"More like grabbing an attacker's arm and pulling it off," said Dag, "but no. You don't want malice ground getting in you or on you. It's a deadly poison. Blight itself."

"The surroundings could be anything. No way to anticipate them," said Vayve. "That leaves the person being shielded."

"That seems . . . circular," said Dag, trying to picture this.

"If the malice's touch spurred your shield to going," said Fawn, "how would you rein it in?"

Dag frowned. "I expect it would run down on its own pretty quick."

"If it was using up a person's ground to live, wouldn't that be sort of fatal?"

"Um . . ." said Dag, scratching the back of his head.

They debated involutions and groundwork for upwards of an hour, till the light falling through the open door of the work shack and Dag's grumbling stomach reminded him that their dinner basket had likely arrived at Arkady's place. They had not solved any of the problems, but Dag's unsettlement felt curiously heartening. Maybe he'd only stepped back or sideways, and not ahead, but at least he hadn't been dancing alone. *Fawn was right. Makers need other makers.* Like Dag's knife-maker brother Dar, Vayve had plainly been doing the same task over and over in the same way for a long time; unlike Dar, her mind hadn't set solid.

"Come around again if you think of anything else," she told Dag with a friendly smile as he and Fawn made their way down her porch steps.

He smiled back. "You too."

∽

The breeze whispered from the south. The slanting sun burned through the damp air with surprising strength. Fawn could just picture the full spring that would come on in not many weeks more, when the fat buds and shy shoots all unfurled. In any case, it was warm enough this afternoon to sit outside on Arkady's roofless porch overlooking the lake. Seated on the bench pushed up to the plank table, she crouched over her task, her tongue caught between her teeth, tracing with her curved steel cutter around Dag's new bonded knife laid upon a leather scrap. The southern Lakewalkers made their knife sheaths of elaborate tooled leather, inlaid sometimes with silver or even gold, but this one would be plain, in the northern style. Simple and fierce, like her thoughts. She tried to make it her best work, like holding yourself up stiff and straight in pride before the eyes of an enemy.

Arkady wandered out of the house with a mug of tea in his hand, peered for a moment over her shoulder, then drifted to the porch rail, leaning on it to gaze down over the slope. Thirty paces below, Dag sat cross-legged on the stubby dock, his back to the house, bent over his own task.

"*What* is he doing down there?" Arkady muttered querulously. "What does he have in those sacks?"

"A bag of nuts," replied Fawn, not looking up from the cut she was finishing, "and a box of mice. And a glass jar."

"Mice!"

"He's not ground-ripping them!" she added hastily as Arkady straightened up. "He promised me he'd be careful about that." She'd walked down to observe Dag's progress a short while ago. She'd brought him the nuts and the jar, but made him catch his own mice. There were limits to wifely support. Although the sight of several mice marching out of the nearby woods in a ragged line and jumping into the box under Dag's direction had been a memory to treasure. "He says he's about to give up trying to make a shield for the whole body, like that ground-worked leather coat he once had that he claimed would turn arrows. The idea sort of worked, but then the mice couldn't run or breathe." Forcing a second trip to the woods for more mice, earlier, and silencing Fawn's doubts about the enterprise. Dag could make lots of little trials quickly this way, work through the mistakes and dead ends. And scale up to, say, *her* later on. Much later on. "He's gone back to just trying for ground shielding."

"Madness," Arkady muttered.

"If he can make it work," Fawn pointed out loyally, "it could save thousands of lives."

"Thousands," Arkady breathed. "Gods." He leaned and sipped his tea again, staring down the slope with an unreadable expression.

"When your husband first turned up at my gates," Arkady continued after a long pause, "I took him for a simple man, if not a simpleton outright. Shabby, grubby, with that northern mumble that sounds like he has a mouth full of pebbles . . ."

"He's only so word-stiff when he's feeling shy and uncertain," Fawn defended. "He can talk like a stump speaker when the mood gets on him. And he likes being clean as much as the next man"—well, unless the next man was Arkady—"he just doesn't waste time pining for things he can't get right then. He's good at enduring."

"Indeed," murmured Arkady. He swallowed more tea. "I've spent my whole life in three camps, you know. I've traveled between them, but never beyond them."

Fawn's brows flew up in surprise. "What, you never rode down to look at the sea? Or Graymouth? And them so close!"

Arkady tilted his free hand back and forth. "My chosen realm runs beneath the skin. It seemed a vast enough hinterland for me." He stared again down the slope. "Dag, though . . . walks with a foot in each world. He straddles things. Outside and inside. Patroller and maker. North and south." He glanced at her. "Lakewalker and farmer. Knife maker and medicine maker, gods. He may be the least simple man I've ever met."

Fawn had no argument with that. She bent her head for another cut, finished it, and said, "It goes with his knack for mending things that are broken, I guess. Bowls. Bones. Hearts. Worlds, maybe. To fix things you first have to walk all around them, see them whole."

"And this all somehow comes down to sitting on my dock torment-ing mice?" Arkady almost ran his hand through his hair. He did clench his nape knot. "*What* is he doing?" he repeated. Abandoning his mug on the railing, he thumped down the porch steps and strode down the slope. Fawn watched him stand by Dag, speak, wave his arms. Dag's hand returned a level gesture. When she looked up from her next cut, Arkady was sitting cross-legged too, glowering at the jar into which Dag was lowering a wriggling mouse by its tail. They seemed to be still talking. Debating. But when Dag bent over again in concentration, Arkady did too.

Fawn lined up her pieces and picked up her square-nosed awl to make holes for the stitching to come. She would stain the leather black with walnut juice, she decided, and bleach the binding threads pale in contrast. She glanced at the bone knife she'd helped fashion with her own hands, gods spare her heart. Her mortal foe would go most elegantly garbed in mourning colors, soft as whispers against Dag's breastbone when he suspended the sheath from the cord around his neck. Her rival's dark dress would be sewn well, to last for years. Decades. Longer, if Fawn had her wish.

If wishes were horses, we all would ride.

She leaned forward and pressed the first pair of holes through the leather.

9

The Oleana boys returned from patrol in a cold afternoon rain, last gasp of the southern winter. Dag had just put another piece of split wood on the fire that warmed Arkady's main room where they'd all clustered, Dag reading old casebooks, Arkady writing in a new one, Fawn knitting. The partners were heralded by the thump and shuffle of steps on the porch, and Remo's voice: "Better leave our boots out here, and everything else till it dries. You know how Arkady is about his floors." A grunt of agreement. A female voice said, "I'll just stand in the doorway, then." Fawn set aside her handwork and looked up in happy welcome. Dag straightened and turned his head curiously.

The door swung open and the patrollers entered, stomping and blowing. Remo wore wet socks, toes and heels peeking through the holes, and Barr wore none, his feet pale and cold, joints red where they'd rubbed in his boots. Both had hair plastered to their heads by the rain. Their wet jackets had apparently been hung on the row of pegs outside the door, so shirts and vests were not overly sodden except around their necks, but their trousers were flecked with mire in the pattern made by splashing hooves. Neeta, her boots muddy, stopped on the threshold. She wore a sensible hat with a brim that shed the rain beyond her jacket neck, and bore a laden withy basket.

"Welcome back," said Dag, puzzled by the dark mood that hung about the partners. Neeta, though equally damp, smiled across at him as cheerfully as a spring flower.

"I won't come in," she called from the doorway. "My tent will be expecting me. But the patrol wanted you to have this, Dag." She hefted the basket.

He raised his brows, going over to take it from her. It seemed to contain a large smoked ham and some glass jars of what might be fruit preserves, wrapped in cloth. "Well . . . thank the patrol for me," he said, a little nonplussed.

She grinned back at him, her cheeks flushing pink with the cold. Her silver-blue eyes sparkled like stars in a sunset sky. "It's the least we can do, sir. There's this farmer's market we always stop in at on the last day of patrol, you see, when we're homeward bound. It's a bit of a tradition. Well. I'm letting in the cold air, aren't I." What from any other girl might have been an embarrassed giggle came out more of a silvery trill. "Enjoy, sir!" She remained staring him keenly up and down for another moment before she withdrew and let the door snick closed behind her.

Remo, glowering after her, heaved a sigh. Barr snorted.

Fawn relieved Dag of the basket and lugged it to the round table. "Nice ham," she commented. Her own brows rose when she unwrapped the jewel-colored jars to discover the cloth was a made-up cotton shirt, very neatly sewn, in Dag's size. Dag tried to think what he might have done for Neeta's patrol to earn this tribute, and came up blank. He'd only been doing groundwork in the medicine tent for two weeks, they'd treated no extraordinary emergencies lately, and besides, the patrol hadn't even been here.

In any case, neither returnee bore the air of a young man who had wooed and won. Dag was surprised. Generally, exchange patrollers, with the glamour of the exotic about them, found it fairly easy to worm their way into the bedrolls of willing young patrol women—easier, anyway, than it was for the local fellows the girls had been seeing all their lives. The advantage was considered one of the many enticements to go on exchange. All four youngsters in question were healthy and, as far as Dag knew, unattached. The interest had certainly been there. The numbers came out even. But Barr and Remo were plainly not relaxed, or sated, or goofy with delight, or enjoying any other of the happy emotions a woman could induce in a man—Dag smiled across at Fawn. Quite the reverse. If grounds could be made visible, theirs would be knotted into personal thunderclouds hovering over their heads.

Dag said neutrally, "So, how was your first southern patrol?" They could not have found a malice, sessile or otherwise, or the general mood would have been something quite different.

"I don't want to talk about it," Remo said. "Is Arkady's bath barrel out there hot?"

"It was this morning," said Fawn. "The coals are still banked. You could likely put some more kindling on and get it to catch."

"Good," growled Remo. "Been thinking about that for hours." He trudged out the back way.

"Why, yes, Remo, of course you can go first," Barr remarked airily to the closing door. Dag heard Remo's steps thump down the outside stairs. Barr flopped down on the braided rug in front of the hearth and stared bitterly up at the ceiling.

"What's bit him?" Fawn asked in wonder. Her gaze strayed to Barr. "And you?"

Barr made an unconversational noise in the back of his throat, not quite a death rattle.

"Did your, ah, courtships not prosper?" Dag inquired genially, taking his seat again. He really didn't see how they could have failed. "Which one were you sweet on, again? I couldn't hardly tell."

Fawn picked up her needles and plunked down in the padded chair opposite, but didn't start knitting again. Arkady had set down his quill and rested his chin in his hand, spread fingers hiding his smirk, listening shamelessly.

"Tavia," sighed Barr. He waved his arms in the air. "Tavia, Tavia, Tavia. Hair so soft. The rest of her"—optimistically large hand motions above his chest—"so soft, too. A man wouldn't get sliced up by her hip bones like that blond icicle Remo's drooling after, not that it does him any good, either." The arms fell listlessly to the rug.

"And the trouble with all this is . . . ?" prodded Fawn.

"Tavia's gone sweet on Remo. Why? Why? I like her way better than he ever would. I bet I could make her happier, too. I'm an ever-so-much-cheerier fellow. Irony, ah, irony."

"I gather from this that Remo is, er, sweet on Neeta?" Dag inquired. "I shouldn't think she would find him repulsive." He wasn't sure whether to hope to learn Neeta was sweet on Barr, or not. A truly creative patroller with a big enough blanket might do something with that array. He elected not to mention the thought. One mustn't shock the youngsters.

"Oh, he was doing pretty good with her, at first, and I was getting all ready to catch Tavia on the first bounce with his goodwill, till he made the big mistake of telling Neeta who *you* really were."

"Dag Bluefield No-Camp? It's no secret."

"No, who you were up in Luthlia. Dag Wolverine of Leech Lake Camp."

Dag's stomach clenched. "Oh. But that's near a generation ago."

"Neeta's just back from two years' exchange to Luthlia, and full of it.

Did you know they still sing *ballads* up there about Captain Dag Wolverine of the Wolf War?"

"One ballad," growled Dag. And he didn't much care for it. His wife Kauneo had been a heroine of Wolf Ridge, and her brothers, and forty-odd others. Dag had merely been a survivor.

Fawn, eyeing him uneasily, offered, "You can't blame folks for wanting a song to help them remember their war."

"Yeah, well, I don't want to remember it." Although the old memories no longer seared, merely twinged; he had time and Fawn to thank for that. "Besides, that ballad got it wrong. It carved up the truth to fit in its stanzas. Taught the wrong lessons."

Barr groaned from the floor, "One ballad? There's a couple dozen! A whole cycle about the Wolf War. And Neeta learned every blighted one of them while she was up there. She can sing them all. She did. And as soon as Remo let your old name drop, she didn't want to hear anything from either of us except Dag stories."

Dag had endured infatuated youngsters, and some not so young, a time or two before; at Hickory Camp word had eventually got 'round not to bother him, or perhaps he'd simply grown too old and dull. It was always embarrassing, but everyone always lived. He sighed grimly, trying to recall his methods of dealing with it. It had usually involved having Fairbolt send him out with a different patrol till things blew over. Not a method he could apply here, alas.

"Lovely Tavia," Barr went on—bemoaned, actually—"lovely soft Tavia. Tavia, the fool girl, has sheep's eyes only for Remo. Remo lusts after Neeta. Neeta's besotted with Captain Dag Wolverine, who I'm not sure even still exists. Now, if only Fawn would yearn after me, the circle would be complete, but that's not going to happen, we established that." He vented a huge sigh. "So here I ride all alone at the tail of the pack train of love, eating dust."

Dag, about to say something else, paused in stiff suspicion. "Just when and where did this establishin' take place?"

"Back on the *Fetch*," mumbled Barr. "Very early on. Very."

Dag glowered down at the supine figure on the rug, but his prey was too limp even for sport. Besides, if Fawn had suffered serious insult, the corner of her mouth wouldn't dimple at the reminder.

"Remo's taking forever," said Barr at last. "I think I'll go wash up in the lake."

"But the water'll be cold!" said Fawn.

"Good," said Barr savagely, convulsed to his feet, and lurched out.

Arkady muffled a snicker, then let his hand fall to the table. "I suppose if we're going to laugh at them we should do it now, and not in their faces."

Dag cast him a glance of apology. "Sorry, Arkady. I reckoned those two would have had their love lives all arranged by now." The only thing more dismal than one lovesick young patroller underfoot in his host's tent was surely *two* lovesick young patrollers. Dag wondered how soon the pair might be sent back out on patrol.

Fawn said, in a constricted tone, "Is Neeta going to be a problem, Dag?"

"No. I'll just avoid her. It shouldn't be hard; she'll be patrolling, I'll be in the medicine tent."

Fawn raised her brows, but did not voice her opinion of his plan.

Arkady's gaze sobered as he regarded Dag. "What Wolf War?" he inquired.

"You've not heard of it? There's a relief," said Dag. "It was just one of our many northern malice scuffles, 'bout twenty years back. That's where this went, among other things." He gave a vague wave of his hook. The fading Wolf War wasn't relevant to his current ambitions; he didn't need to discuss it here. He tried not to think *Hooray.*

"Excuse me, but——*company captain*? In *Luthlia*?" Arkady persisted.

"It was a short career."

"I thought you were a plain patroller from Oleana."

"I am. I was. It suited me better, after . . ." He waved his left arm again. "Luthlia is a hard hinterland, a young man's country. When I wasn't young anymore, I went home."

"How long were you actually up there?"

" 'Bout ten years." He grew uncomfortable under Arkady's continuing stare. "What about it?"

Arkady was silent a moment, then shrugged. "You keep surprising me, is all. I usually fancy myself more shrewd."

Dag couldn't think of anything to say to that, so he picked up the old casebook and tried to read again. After a moment Fawn returned to her knitting, and Arkady to his writing. All more slowly, with frequent glances to the lakeside windows.

∿

By the time the partners had washed, donned dry clothes, warmed up, returned Dag's knife, and fallen upon the dinner basket like starving dogs, their moods had improved. Fortunately, in Dag's view.

Fawn dared to ask, "Was this southern patrol very different from your Oleana ones?"

Barr and Remo exchanged a hard-to-read glance. Arkady, chewing, watched with interest.

"No . . ." said Remo slowly. "And yes."

"Yes." Barr nodded. "It's funny . . ."

"What is?" asked Dag.

"I always thought I'd like it if things were looser out on patrol." He jiggled his shoulders to indicate a desirable slackness, then added,

"Though the alligator hunt was fun. The farmers whose lands we crossed didn't want us to hunt their bears, they're too rare and valuable here—they want the bear grease and pelts and meat for themselves. But they were happy to grant us all the alligators we could find, the bigger the better. Wild pigs were free game, too. We came back with a stack of raw hides that we unloaded in that farmers market." He took another bite of bread piled high with bright apricot jam from one of Dag's gift jars, and chewed blissfully.

Fawn made a face. "Wasn't it scary? Did you hunt them at night?" She turned to Arkady and explained, "Up in Oleana the Lakewalker patrols cross farms at night, to avoid disturbing folks. You hardly know they're out there."

"No," said Remo, "you couldn't, not around here. There's way too much settled land. You'd run out of night. We just rode across in broad daylight. We didn't bother the farmers, and they didn't bother us."

Barr put in, "Some sort of pretended not to notice us, which felt odd. Some would nod greeting. This patrol had a regular string of farmers' barns we put up at, or campsites in their woodlots. The farmers expected a few coins for the use of them, which the patrol leader doled out."

"So—the farmers around here aren't so ignorant of patrollers as I was back in West Blue?" said Fawn.

Remo scratched his head. "I guess not."

"That's good."

"I'm not so sure." Encouraged by Dag's opened hand, Remo went on, "It seemed like there was nothing much for them to be ignorant *of*. We were no more than a hunting party."

"More party than hunting," said Barr, his brow furrowing. "It wasn't how the New Moon patrollers all slipped in and out of camp at night. I didn't mind that. It was how they were walking their patterns. They were noisy. They broke formation all the time to talk to each other. They sang. *While walking.* Blight, you'd never flush a mud-man that way. Our patrol captain back at Pearl Riffle always said that could be your first sign there was a malice nearby, even without the blight. She'd have had our tongues on a toasting fork for *coughing* during a pattern, but here they just let the ruckus roll on." He looked up at Dag. "Are all southern patrols like that, or was it just this one?"

Dag swallowed his bite, and chased it with tea. "I've only patrolled down here one season, 'bout four years back. I gather that the areas where they've found a sessile within living memory aren't quite so, ah, loose, but there's no question that the more pressing likelihood of malices shapes us in the north."

"Shapeless . . ." said Remo. "Yes, that's what this patrol felt like."

"That's why it's so important that southern patrollers exchange north," said Dag, with a glance at the now-frowning Arkady. "Not just for the extra hands they lend us, but for the training they bring back home. Without them, the southern patrol would be falling apart." *Faster.* "Neeta's more valuable for coming home than any two volunteers who stay on in Luthlia."

"I'm not sure she knows that," said Remo slowly. "This was her first patrol after coming back here with new eyes. She was . . . it's like . . . she was the only one there who realized what we saw. And she was ashamed for her patrol mates. And she hadn't expected to be."

"Wouldn't your patrol leader have trained in the north?" asked Fawn. "I thought they had to."

"He's been back a long time," said Remo. "Decades. I got the impression he'd sort of given up." He glanced up at Dag. "Was the patrol you walked with here like that?"

"Not after a season with me along."

Barr snorted tea through his nose.

Remo ignored him to say, "But you weren't the patrol leader."

"You don't have to be."

Remo chewed a bite of stew, swallowed. "Huh."

∾

It seemed to Fawn that word of Dag's new, or old, fame spread around New Moon Cutoff Camp at an unsettlingly fast clip. She supposed twenty-five gossiping patrollers dispersed to twenty-five tents added up, atop all the folks who'd met them both in the medicine tent by now. Dag wasn't just Arkady's peculiar project anymore, but a man of, apparently, more than local fame. It made her wonder just what all else was in those ballads Neeta had been passing along—Fawn had only ever heard the one, back in Oleana, and it had named no names.

Dag hated it, she could tell. But as the longest-tempered man Fawn had ever met, he endured politely, mostly. Well, he did give pretty daunting shrift to the merely curious, unless it was a patient he was doing groundwork on, when he turned the questions more gently. Children got straight, if brief, answers out of him, but no one else could.

For the first time since they'd arrived, Dag began to get invitations to visit tents around the camp for something other than Arkady's medicine walks. Any that didn't include Fawn he refused bluntly. Any that did, he took pains to point out to the issuer that Fawn was confined to Arkady's place and the medicine tent by camp council order.

Then came an invitation that could not be refused.

"Dinner at the camp captain's tent?" Dag said in confusion that Fawn shared: New Moon patrol's captain was a *member* of the council. "Both of us?"

"All of us. Your patroller boys and me, as well," Arkady told him. "I expect most of the camp council will be there."

Dag blinked. "You think we should go?"

"Of course you should go. This could be your chance."

"Chance to do what?"

Arkady paused. "Fit in better," he said at last.

"I thought we were fittin' in fairly good. For practical purposes."

"Yes, well," said Arkady vaguely.

They went.

It was a pig roast, all outside at the tent—house, really—of the camp captain, making it seem to Fawn quite like Hickory Lake for a change. Captain Antan Bullrush and his maker wife were older folks, their children grown, but there was still a crowd for dinner: three tent-heads, all mature women who were council members this season; spouses and families and grandchildren; and, since one of the council women was aunt to Tavia, both partners. Neeta looked especially pleased. The cookout could almost have been a farmer clan picnic, with different women bringing their dishes to share. But when everyone was stuffed, and the children gone off to play along the lakeside, and lanterns hung in the trees, a more select group gathered on a circle of upturned stumps. And began to interrogate Dag.

They asked about Captain Dag Wolverine of the Wolf War. What they got *told* about was Captain Dag Bluefield of the Raintree malice outbreak, with a side order of Greenspring. The Wolf War was ruthlessly relegated to background, though it had to come in a little to help explain how Dag's company had been able to go through the Raintree malice like, in Fawn's informed view, a hot knife through butter. But if the alternate tale was meant to turn aside interest in Dag's patrol-captaining career, Fawn didn't think it was working all that well.

Arkady chewed his thumb and said little, watching his protégé getting turned on this spit, and sometimes spitting back. He studied the faces of the council quorum, and only winced now and then. It was plain that he wished Dag would take a more compromising tone. It was plain to Fawn that Dag wasn't going to waste such a captive audience. He sure didn't sound like he had a mouth full of pebbles tonight.

At length, the circle broke up to seek desserts. And, judging from the bent heads, to exchange franker opinions privately.

Dag murmured to Arkady, "Any objection if Fawn and I slip away early?"

Arkady pursed his lips. "No, in fact. That would be fine. I need to stay awhile and talk to some folks."

Dag nodded. Fawn refused to go without thanking Missus Bullrush properly, but once that duty was done, she allowed him to lead her off. They stopped by patrol headquarters to check on their horses, idling in the paddock there eating New Moon's fodder since their arrival, then continued down the shore road in the darkening chill.

"So," Fawn said hesitantly. "What was that all about?"

Dag scratched his head gently with his hook. "I'm not just sure. We were being inspected, right enough. You'd think they could come to the medicine tent for that."

"Do you think they're deciding whether to let us stay for your two years?"

"Maybe." He chewed his lip. "Maybe more."

"Dag Bluefield New Moon Cutoff?" She shaped the name in her mouth. Camp names didn't just tell your place of residence. If you bore one, it marked you a member of some greater whole, and even after the better part of a year trailing after Dag, Fawn didn't know all the subtleties that implied. "Is that . . . something you would like?"

"Strange," he sighed. "At the end of last summer, that could have been the sum of my ambitions. It was exactly what I wanted from Hoharie. Train up as a medicine maker together with you, serve in camp. Let my tired feet rest from patrolling. But Hoharie choked on you, and that was the end of it. I think I've made it clear enough to these New Moon folks that we come as partners or not at all—they won't make her mistake."

"I wonder what mistake they will make?"

He snorted. "Hard to say, Spark." His strong, dry hand found hers, and her cold little fingers stole warmth from it gratefully. "I do know Arkady's not keen on spending two years of his time training me up as a groundsetter just to have me go off north and treat farmers. If I—we—became members of this camp, we'd have to abide by camp rules and discipline."

"We?"

He sucked a fortifying breath through his nose. "Wouldn't that be something to have done, though? For the first time ever, get a farmer girl accepted as a full-fledged member of a Lakewalker camp?"

"Would they?"

"I wouldn't stay for less. I hope I made that plain."

Fawn rather thought he had. Her brows scrunched. She felt rattled, and she suspected he did, too. This offer—if it got made—wasn't anything she'd ever expected or planned on, but then, nothing about her life since she'd met Dag had been anything that she could have imagined back when she'd first fled West Blue. *My whole life is an accident.* But some of her accidents had been happy far beyond her dreams, and she had surely chosen to put herself in the way of both good and bad, when she'd first set foot to the road. *Am I Dag's greatest accident, too?*

At Arkady's place Dag lit a lantern against the cool gloom, smiled slowly, and observed, "Seems we have the house to ourselves."

The gold glint in his eye wasn't only from the lantern light. Fawn dimpled back. "That's a nice change," she said agreeably.

Dag had been reticent about offering lovemaking since the patroller boys had returned, only partly due to fatigue from his long training days and, now, occasional draining groundwork under Arkady's supervision. The partners laid their bedrolls in the main room, and there was a door to close between, but wooden walls did not much block groundsense. Tonight Dag and Fawn had a brief gift of privacy, if they could seize it before the beer ran out at the pig roast. They took turns washing up quickly in the sink, then Dag carried the lantern to their end room.

Fawn unrolled their bedding, and helped Dag off with his shirt and arm harness. He returned the favor, folding down her blouse as though it were a flower's petals; they stood facing on their knees, skin to skin, each leaning into the other for support and heat. They'd made love in many different moods, from merry to mournful; tonight, it seemed to Fawn, there was something almost desperate in Dag's grip.

"Gods, Spark," he muttered. "Help me remember who I am."

She hugged him tight. He released his clutch in favor of a caress, long fingers gliding over her bare back, winding in her hair, and she thought, not for the first time, that with all his touch being channeled through his single hand, he paid it a more reverent attention. And so, as a consequence, did she.

She whispered into his shoulder, "Wherever we are, you can always come home to me."

He bent his face to her curls, handless arm tightening around her, and breathed her in. It was gently done; she had no call to think of a drowning man drawing air. "Always," he promised. They sank to their bedroll of residence.

∾

Dag woke slowly in a gray morning light feeling vastly better, and he smiled to remember why. Fawn still slept. He lifted his arm from around her coiled warmth, then rolled over and opened his second eye.

At his face level, half a dozen pairs of beady little eyes stared back at him in unblinking fascination.

"You again!" he groaned at the field mice. "Go on! Shoo!"

Fawn came awake at his voice, sat up on her elbow, and took in their visitors. "Oh, my word. They're back."

"I thought you said you'd got rid of them yesterday. Again."

"I did. Well, I thought I did. I took the box halfway around the lake and dumped them in the woods."

Dag contemplated these leftovers from his frustrating shielding experiments. Survivors all; had they been especially determined? They'd have to be, to trek back across half of New Moon Camp. "I'd think a farmer girl like you would have more ruthless ways of getting rid of mice."

"Well, if they were piddling up my pantry, sure. But the only crime this bunch committed was to fall in love with you. Death seemed too cruel a penalty for that." Her big brown eyes blinked at him in consideration.

"Beguiled," he corrected austerely. "I don't think mice have brains enough to fall in love."

She dimpled. "I never noticed as it took brains."

"There is that, Spark." He creaked to his feet, peered a bit blearily around the room, found his slat box, tipped it on its side in front of the staring mice—whose heads turned in unison to track him—and chivvied them into it. Carrying them out the door onto Arkady's roofless porch, he poured them over the rail. They fell with only a few faint squeaks, bouncing unharmed in the grass below, and, shocked out of their trance, scampered away. For now. Dag shook his head and trod back inside, where Fawn was sitting up lovely-naked and laughing behind her hand.

"The poor things!"

He grinned and opened himself to her bright ground as if basking in sunlight. Then went still, blinking.

Within her vivid swirl spun a brighter spark yet. He knew it at once, from that heartbreaking almost-month that he and Kauneo . . .

Fawn had no groundsense. It was *his* task to track when the brilliant changes in her ground signaled her time of fertility, and switch to alternate forms of pleasuring each other. For all the eight months of their marriage and before, she had trusted him to do so. How had he missed the signals last night? Blight it, he'd known it was almost time . . . !

No, not *blight it,* never in the same breath with this. That breath tangled in his throat in a ball of guilt, terror, and joy. If he'd taken one of Challa's surgical knives and laid open his own chest wall, his heart could not be more exposed in this moment.

It might not catch. More than half of all such conceptions never did; many of the remainder failed in the first few weeks, barely delaying the woman's monthly. It was one of the strongest, if least discussed, Lakewalker social rules to make no comment upon those blazing signs in a woman's ground unless she brought them up herself. Should he say anything until he was more sure? When would that be? Fawn had been pregnant once before; how soon would she recognize her own symptoms? Would they be the same, for this half-blood child? If that spark survived to become a child . . . ?

"Dag?" said Fawn doubtfully. "You feeling all right? Why're you lookin' at me like that?"

He fell to his knees beside her, crouched, gathered her up in his arms, hugged her fiercely and protectively. Feeling as helpless as he'd ever been. "Because I love you," he told her.

"Well, sure," she said, a bit shaken by his fervor. "I knew that." She hugged him back, bemused.

Absent gods. What do we do now?

10

So, when are you going to tell her, Dag?" Arkady asked curiously.

Dag re-furled his reaching groundsense, anxiously following Fawn down the road toward the medicine tent. She was off early to help the herb girls prepare the morning's load for the farmer's market. Five dizzy days it had been since that careless hour in their bedroll . . .

He glanced up to find the Oleana boys grinning at him over their tea and plunkin, and clenched his teeth. He could endure, he supposed, their smirking at him; never at her. For that alone, he ought to tell her soon. Or pound them, whichever came first.

"It's not going to be—we're past that—gods. That horror you told me about. When it plants in the wrong place. And I'd have to—my own first—"

Barr and Remo looked blank.

"Safely past," Arkady soothed him.

Dag let out a pent breath. "That other thing—like Tawa Kill-deer—"

"Not that, either," said Arkady. "It looked this morning like a very nice implantation up in the right rear wall of the womb, just where it should be."

And not twins, as far as Dag could tell. Lakewalker women almost never bore twins, but when they did, Arkady had said, there could be more problems, the added stress on the mother cascading to other troubles, or an even more bizarre tangling together of the children's bodies. And Fawn was so little . . . *Not that, either*, Dag reminded himself. None of that. A whole category of complications he could cross right off.

"You know," said Arkady, "almost all apprentices go through a phase where they're convinced they're coming down with every new disease they've just learned about. I thought you were going to be the notable exception. I suppose I didn't think it through quite far enough."

Barr snickered. Dag didn't lunge across the table at him, and took a moment to feel proud of his self-control. He needed some positive thoughts, just now.

"It's the women's game," Remo assured him, with all the certainty of his vast inexperience. "They look after all that stuff, Dag. Relax."

"It's not a game," growled Dag. "Absent gods. Was I that stupid when I was your age? I suppose I was." And Remo's careless remark reminded him once more that Fawn had no kinswomen here to wrap their care around her like an heirloom quilt.

Barr shook his head. "I've never seen you dither like this, Dag."

I've never been faced with this before, you young dolt . . . ! It's all new! New to him, at least. Old as the world. "Entertainin', am I?" Dag snapped. He rose abruptly. "Come on, Arkady. Let's go talk out on the porch. Leave these two to their swill."

"It's breakfast!" Barr protested in mock outrage. "We don't swill breakfast!"

"Well, maybe the tea," allowed Remo, tipping back his mug.

Arkady followed him out without protest. Dag slammed the porch door on their laughter.

It was better, leaning on the railing in the mild air. The sun was not high enough yet to warm Dag's back, but it lit the golden haze across the surface of the lake and along the farther shore. The first faint green breathed in the trees, with a pink splash of redbud bright against stark gray branches. And, when Arkady leaned alongside him, Dag didn't have to look him in the eye.

"I don't know how it happened," Dag said.

Arkady chuckled. "You can't expect me to believe that."

Dag's hand clenched the rail; he bit back swearwords. "You know that's not what I meant! I thought . . . not till we were more settled. Till we knew what we were doing. With this wedding trip behind us, which has gone on so long now I suppose I better start calling it a marriage trip. I even reckoned it—a child—was something I'd let Fawn choose, where and when. When—where—she'd be safe." His grip tightened. "I don't know enough!"

"You are aware," said Arkady carefully, "nine out of ten women sail through this without special problems. Lakewalker, farmer, or half blood."

Dag brooded. "Those used to sound like *good* odds."

Arkady gazed out over the lake. "New Moon Cutoff would be about the safest place you could find for this, you do realize."

"That thought had crossed my mind," Dag admitted. "Maybe even safer than with her own kin. Certainly safer than somewhere in the north with just me, trying to figure out how to go on."

"Then it might be time for a slightly more, ah, conciliating approach to people around here, do you suppose?" Arkady suggested mildly. "More adaptive?"

"What a delicate tongue you have, Arkady." Dag sighed and turned to lean sideways, watching his profile. "Reckon you could near make lace with it."

"I'd be satisfied if I could make a good groundsetter." Arkady tilted his tea mug in toast to Dag, and drank. "But I think you know that by now."

Dag stood silent for a while, letting the balmy air caress his winter skin. "You could find another apprentice. You always have. Where is the north going to find another Dag 'n Fawn?"

"Service is service. One man can only do his day's work no matter where he is."

"True enough." So much rode on this pivot point of their lives, so unexpectedly aimed at Dag's heart. Strange for such a tiny spark to weigh so heavily; it might move worlds.

Yet it all could still prove in vain. Dag reconsidered Arkady with new respect. How many times had he gone through these same gyrations, only to have his hopes wash away in sorrow? Dag felt abruptly ashamed. "Sorry to be dithering like this. It's my first time, see." It was surely as profound a ground transformation as any he'd experienced this punch-drunk year, when he'd become first Fawn's patroller, then Fawn's husband, then captain, makeshift mage, then not a patroller at all. An uprooted seeker . . . a new maker. And now, once again, Fawn remade him. *Fawn's child's father. When this is over, I will be a different man.* How agonizing was it, to begin such a transformation and then have it break off, incomplete? *Fawn would know,* he realized. He added, "Challa told me about you and Bryna."

"Ah," said Arkady. "Good." And after a moment, "Then you'll understand."

Dag nodded. "Well . . . some." Better than those two giggling louts indoors.

Arkady rubbed his chin and stared out at the morning light, eyes like two new copper coins. And then he said a strange thing: "Don't let fear swallow all your happiness. Don't forget to take joy."

Dag gulped. Both of their grounds were nearly closed; it was Arkady's voice alone that hinted how hard-bought this bit of wisdom might have been, yet the words had been nearly toneless.

Dag considered his most secret fear. *If Fawn dies of this, I will have killed her, sure as if I'd led her out to battle on a ridge against impossible foes.* So was that fear for her, or for himself? He'd known a couple of men whose wives had died in childbed; it wasn't something a man got over, despite how time wore away all things. His remorse would be no novelty. *But I have a new bonded knife, now. I wouldn't have to get over this one.* Not for long. It was a peculiar enticement to courage.

Gods, he was getting morbid. He'd better tell Fawn soon just so she could give him a dose of her calm good sense and cheerful optimism. He could almost hear her voice: *Stands to reason, Dag!*

Well, once she got over being mad at him. With justice. If she threw things, he wouldn't duck, he decided gallantly.

"I'll tell her tonight," he said. "We have a lot to talk about, I reckon."

"Good," said Arkady.

ᴠ

An hour into the farmers market, the medicine table had already enjoyed a fair sprinkling of trade. With the bright weather, and several days for the roads to dry since the last rain, Nola and Cerie thought it might be busy enough for them to sell out early and take a few hours off in the sunshine. Fawn made cordial hellos to their regular customers, smiling at faces starting to be familiar. She'd even begun to recognize folks' rigs, spotting Finch what's-his-name in his open cart as he drove in. His mare was dark with sweat, and stood quietly when he dropped his reins and vaulted down.

He strode quickly to the medicine table, eyes seeking, to her surprise, Fawn. "You're here, you're here, oh thanks be! Can I talk to you privately, Missus Bluefield?"

"Well, sure, I suppose so." Fawn looked around. "Would over by the trees be private enough?"

"Yes, anything." His hand stretched and clenched, as if he wanted to grab her arm and hurry her along, but didn't quite dare. They came to a halt at the fringe of the woods, in sight of the market but out of earshot. Not out of groundsense range, naturally, but she doubted groundsense could make anything more of the agitated farm youth than she did. Finch's tense face was damp with perspiration and flushed with exertion, making his blue eyes look incongruously bright.

"Is your husband still of a mind to treat farmers?" he asked abruptly. He watched her mouth with painful intensity, as if expecting his heart's salvation to issue from her lips.

"Well . . . in the north, in due course, sure. But he's just an apprentice here. He's not allowed."

His hand swept this aside as if he barely heard her. His words fell out in a breathless tumble. "It's my nephew Sparrow. My brother's little boy. He's barely five. He's got the lockjaw. And it's all my fault! I let him run barefoot in the barn. There was this nail, went halfway though his poor little foot. I was supposed to be watching him! He cries and cries, when he can. The fever came on first. The straining started last night. The screams are bad, but the silences are worse, oh gods."

"Yeah, I know lockjaw," said Fawn slowly. "Violet Stonecrop's little brother died of it, oh, years back. They were neighbors of ours, when I was growing up in West Blue. I didn't see, but Violet told me all about it, later." Horrifying descriptions.

"Can he come? Can your Lakewalker husband help?" Finch clutched her sleeve. "Can you ask—him, whatever his name is? Please? My sister-in-law cries, and Mama's so mad she won't even look at me. Please, can you ask him?" The clutch became a shaking grip, painful. "It's all so awful!"

"Dag," said Fawn, answering his least question while trying desperately to think. "Dag Bluefield. He insisted on taking my name when we were wed, the way Lakewalkers do. Took a farmer name to be more Lakewalker. 'S funny." She would have to catch Dag alone, not in front of everyone in the medicine tent. She glanced at the sun. Near noon— he might be back to the house for lunch.

Or she could spare Dag the decision. Because this one was going to be hard no matter what way it played out, though with a youngster involved, she didn't have a lot of doubt which way Dag would jump. She knew the camp rules as well as he did. She could send Finch packing, back to his daylight nightmare, and never share the dilemma. It wasn't a good time for Dag. He'd seemed so strained since the pig roast. Constantly looking at her, as if wondering—what? As if regretting how his farmer bride divided him from his people?

Out in the wide world, there were any number of folks sick or dying right this minute, and what was one more? Arkady would surely forbid it, if he caught even a whiff of the plan. Fawn wasn't even sure Lakewalkers could do anything for lockjaw; she hadn't seen a case since she'd started work in the medicine tent. *This could cost Dag his training.* And how much would that cost others, down the line?

She let out her breath in a slow trickle, knowing her choice was no choice at all. "I can't promise he'll come. But I can ask him. Come along."

Finch exhaled in a long huff, nodded, seemed to realize at last that his grip was hurting her, and let her go. She looked up and gave a wave to

Cerie and Nola, watching her dubiously across the grass, which didn't explain a thing but at least made it look like she wasn't sneaking. There was a path over the wooded ridge that went nearly straight to Arkady's place, much quicker than going around by the gate. The camp's perimeter, she had learned, wasn't as tightly guarded as that gate made it appear.

Nevertheless, she'd better not push their luck. When they were almost in sight of the water, she told Finch, "Stay here, down in this little hollow. Arkady's place is just a couple hundred paces farther on. I'll bring back Dag, or . . . or his word. I might be a little while."

He nodded silently and hunkered down on a fallen log below the earthen banks, turning his face up to a dapple of sunlight, eyes squeezing shut. Fawn hurried down the path.

She found Dag and Arkady just finishing lunch, packing up the basket. The Oleana boys had gone off somewhere, good.

"Fawn!" said Dag, rising from the table in surprise. "I thought you'd be at the market. Are you hungry?"

She gave her head a quick shake.

He hesitated, giving her that uncomfortable penetrating Daggish look. Groundsense, gods, her skin might as well be glass. "Are you all right?"

"Something's come up," she told him, not glancing at Arkady. "Can I talk to you private?"

"Ah, hm," said Arkady, his brows lifting inexplicably. "Perhaps it's as well. I'll walk on back to the medicine tent, Dag. You take all the time you need." With a benign wave, he took the basket with him, setting it outside the front door. Well, this was easier than she'd expected. So far. She wasn't sure that was a good thing. Fawn waited till she could no longer hear his footsteps going up the path.

"Fawn," Dag began slowly, "there's something—" but she overrode him, saying, "Oh, Dag, it's so horrible!"

"Huh?" he said warily. "No, Spark, it won't be that bad, I'll be with you every—"

"It's Finch Bridger's nephew, poor tyke. He stepped on a nail and got the lockjaw. Oh, Dag, I know Arkady won't like it, but can we go to him? He's only five years old!"

Dag blinked. Paused. Blinked again. "Who?"

Rapidly, Fawn related what Finch had told her. "Can we go to him? Do we dare? Can Lakewalker medicine makers even *treat* lockjaw?"

Dag replied, with agonizing slowness, "I've read up on it in Arkady's casebooks. They do groundwork on the nerves, and try to get enough water and food down between the spasms to keep the patient alive till the worst passes. I've only run across two cases. One was a woman at Hickory Lake came down with it—after childbirth, gods, there's another!—Hoharie brought her through somehow. Didn't see that one, only heard about it—tent gossip. Another was a patroller caught way out on the big summer wilderness sweep up in Luthlia. The treatment failed. He shared. Not right away—when he and his patrol couldn't bear it anymore."

"Do you think you could do that nerve work? Despite not having seen it?"

Dag vented a long sigh, scratched his head. "How old did you say this youngster was, again?"

"Rising five, Finch says."

"Absent gods," Dag muttered.

"The Bridger farm is about ten miles off. Finch has a cart. Do you think we could get there and back before Arkady . . . um, no, likely not."

Dag shook his head. "It can take days to pull someone through lockjaw. Or . . . not."

"I can pack up what we need for some overnights in two shakes of a lamb's tail."

"I'd really rather you stayed here."

"And face Arkady alone?" She shook her head vigorously. "Don't you dare leave me to him! He'd make mincemeat of me. It's going to be bad enough when we get back. Anyhow, it would be madness to send you into an upset farmer household without me to ease them along. To know what Lakewalkerish things need explaining to them, and how."

"That is unquestionably true." He stared at her unnervingly. "Well . . . it's not a very contagious sort of disease, in the usual course of things. You might be safe around it."

"Well, of course!"

"If you didn't get too close."

She stared back at him, perplexed. What was he going on about, here? *Never mind.* Once they got to the Bridgers', she would deal with things as they needed to be dealt with, same as always. She wet her lips. Marshaled what had to be said. "Now—you sure, Dag? Because if you're not, I can go tell Finch no myself." That much, at least, she could spare him. "This could cost you Arkady."

He smiled wryly down at her, traced his thumb across her warm cheek. "If it does . . . then his price is too high, and I'm too poor an old patroller to afford him."

She gave a short nod, swallowing the lump in her throat. "We'd best bustle about, then."

She went to their room to pack a sack, and he went to Arkady's work chamber to borrow a few items of equipment he thought he might need. Quite without permission, and Fawn suspected that wasn't going to go down too well with Arkady either. She returned to the main room to find him writing Arkady a brief, truthful note. Well . . . it said he'd been asked away to treat a sick youngster, and not to expect them back at any particular time. If he left out the word *farmer* in front of youngster, it wasn't a lie. Nor even, in all probability, a concealment.

She led Dag back to the sun-speckled hollow to find Finch sitting on the ground with his arms wrapped around his knees, his head bent. When he heard them approaching he scrambled to his feet, wiping his sleeve across his wet face.

He stared in shock at Dag, looking back and forth—or up and down—between them. "Uh . . ."

"This is Dag," said Fawn, grabbing his left arm in a possessive hug. Snapping eyes daring Finch to say boo, defying him to stare at the hook, and if he blurted one word about how short and young she was, or how old Dag was . . .

Dag nodded politely. "Finch."

"Sir!" Finch gulped. "You're, um . . ." He peered sideways. And up. And back to Fawn's tense face. " . . . not what I expected."

"Generally not, but folks get over it," said Fawn rather tartly, then controlled her prickliness. Finch had enough troubles; he didn't need to know what they might be sacrificing in his cause. "I've been thinking. It might be more discreet if we were to circle around and meet your cart at the end of the road, out of sight of the market."

"I don't think it'll make much difference in the end, Spark," said Dag.

"Still, there's no point in going fishing for questions and arguments and delay."

Since Finch nodded vigorously, this plan was adopted. A quick walk through the open woods brought them to the head of the road not long after the cart arrived, and Dag helped her swing their sacks up into the back. She sat next to Finch, and Dag took the rear-facing seat behind them, folding in his long legs with a sigh. Finch slapped the reins across his mare's back, urging her into as fast a trot as the roads would allow.

∾

To Dag's eye, the Bridger farm looked not so snug and rich as Fawn's family place in West Blue, being more crowded and cluttered, its flat yard still full of churned mud from the winter rains. But it seemed to have all the essentials: a big barn, a large woodlot, outbuildings in varied states of repair, fences penning cows, pigs, and chickens, if not their smell. The unpainted wooden farmhouse was two stories high and foursquare. Dag followed Finch into the dim center hall feeling they were a noisy invasion; for a moment, the hush seemed deathly, and he thought, *Too late!*, not knowing whether to be grieved or relieved. But a moan from above-stairs, and a woman's sob, cured that impression as fast as did his reaching groundsense.

They clumped up the stairs into a crowded corner room. On a bed that seemed far too big for him, a small boy writhed in pain. His lips were drawn back in the distinctive near-grin of his disease, his neck rigid, his breath whistling through his tight little teeth. A young woman, clearly his frantic mother, was patting and stroking him as if she could coax his straining muscles to relax. His grim grandmother sat on the bed's other side, holding his clutching hand and looking exhausted.

Both stood and stared at the apparition of Dag, eyes filling with fear and desperate hope. A few days earlier, Dag thought, it would likely have just been fear. Dag swallowed and drew Fawn in front of him like a human shield. His own ground seemed to center itself, drawn like a lodestone to the agony in the bed. "Fawn," he muttered, "deal with them. I need to see to this."

He released his grip on her right shoulder, and she stepped forward, her motion catching the women's eyes. Smiling, Fawn gave her little knee dip, and said brightly, "How de'! I'm Fawn Bluefield and this is my husband, Dag Bluefield. I guess Finch has told you how he met me in the

New Moon farmer's market. Dag here's training up to be a Lakewalker medicine maker."

Good of her to get that *training up* in right away, to stop them from expecting such miracles as Arkady could no doubt produce. Names were offered in return in thin voices: Cherry Bridger, the mama, Missus Bridger, the grandmama. Finch's mother stared at her careless son who had produced this Lakewalker prodigy, new doubt sapping old anger.

"Now," Fawn went on briskly, "the first thing Dag needs to do with little Sparrow here is take a look at him in his ground, and then we can see how to go on from there. So if you could just let him by, ma'am . . ." She pursed her lips and picked the grandmother to draw out of Dag's way.

"Take off my arm harness first, Spark. I doubt I'll need it for anything here." Fawn nodded, folded up his left sleeve, and went to work on his buckles. He bent his head toward her, but watched the others out of the corner of his eye. This ritual, with sweet-faced Fawn making short work of the ugly, threatening hook, always seemed to have a soothing effect on farmer patients. Dag wasn't sure if it was pure distraction, or his display of vulnerability, or a signal, or just a show: *You've all seen a man rolling up his sleeves to get down to work? Well, watch this!*

Dag rubbed the red marks left by the leather straps on his arm, and slipped past the wide-eyed women. He abandoned his attempt to marshal a greeting for a frightened five-year-old when it became obvious the boy was too gripped by his spasms to hear or understand. He muttered in Fawn's ear, "Now, if it looks like I've gone in too deep or am staying too long, slap me on the side of the head the way you saw Arkady do. Hard as you have to. Can you do that?"

She nodded firmly. Dag sank to his knees at the bedside, the visible world already fading from his senses, the swirl of its true substance rising to the fore. Behind him, he could hear Fawn's cheerful voice raised in the beginner lecture: *Now, let me tell you all something about Lakewalker groundsense . . .*

The child's ground was roiling. *Down and in.* The flare of fever was familiar by now, not good but not the main problem. The deep puncture in the foot hadn't been cleaned out properly, and was hot and dirty and poisonous inside despite its deceptively healed surface skin. But it was indeed the frenzied noise along the nerves that drove the relentless muscle spasms. Dag sent soothing groundwork twisting down their branches like releasing dye into a stream, and felt the frenzy slacken.

He fought his way up and out before groundlock set in, and came back blinking to a room that seemed awfully quiet. He sat back on his heels. Looked around vaguely, found Fawn. "How long was I in?"

" 'Bout ten minutes. Dag, it was amazing! You could just see his poor little muscles give way, one by one!"

A new figure had arrived, clearly Finch's older brother, staring hard at the scene. He held Sparrow's mother tightly around the shoulders.

"Is he better? Is he well?" she choked.

"Not yet, ma'am," Dag told her regretfully. "Just a temporary respite. I'm going to have to go back in again when this wears off. But each treatment buys some time. First, we have to get as much drink and food into him as the little fellow can hold, to keep the disease from killing him of starvation. And we need to go in and do a better job cleaning out that puncture. We'll need boiled water—Fawn, can you see to it? And some sort of soft, rich food, but easy to keep down—I don't know—"

Fawn nodded. "I expect oatmeal boiled up with cream and honey would do for a start."

"Perfect."

The women, anxious for something effective to do at last, clattered out in a body. The boy's father—what had they said his name was?—Lark Bridger, that was it—took the chair formerly held by the grandmother. Finch leaned his forehead against the tall bedpost and closed his eyes.

"Papa? Uncle Finch?" A weak little voice.

Lark took up the boy's hand. "Hey, chirping Sparrow!" His voice was hoarse, seeming unaccustomed to such softness. "Good to hear from you at last! Your uncle Finch has brought this Lakewalker fellow here to help you out."

"He's funny-looking," said Finch, "but he's all right."

The boy's head turned. Grave young eyes found Dag, squinted. Sparrow must have agreed with his uncle's assessment, because he didn't recoil, but said the first thing a child, whether Lakewalker or farmer, inevitably asked: "What happened to your hand?"

Dag ignored the embarrassed rustle from the grown-ups, and gave the child a straight answer: "Wolf bit it off."

"Oh!" said Sparrow, sounding impressed as only a five-year-old could; but then, more unusually, blinked sympathetic tears. "Did it hurt?"

"Yes, but it was a long time ago. It's fine now. Hey, now, it's all right, don't cry for me. We still have some work to do healing you, do you know?"

Blinks. Suspicion. "What kind o' work?"

"I know you won't feel like it, but you have to drink and eat as much as you can—all your mama and Fawn bring you. Your muscles are working harder than plowing a forty-acre field, see, and you need your food. Then Fawn and I—she's my wife, that real pretty girl you just saw—are going to clean out your foot a bit more."

In a way, Dag was grateful for this task; it would be visible to farmer eyes, comprehensible, reassuring. Though on second thought, he wasn't sure he wanted Fawn so closely involved with the wound. He made Finch wash his hands in preparation to help, instead.

"I hurt all over . . ." Sparrow moaned to his papa.

I'll bet.

Dag's initial groundwork was already wearing off by the time Fawn came back with the boiled water, the boy beginning to twitch and spasm. As she set up their supplies, Dag went in again. It was easier this time in that he had some idea what he was doing, but he could feel the drain on his ground, and he began to dread the long night to come. When he came back up, Dag set the mother to coaxing a dose of the bitter-tasting pain powder down the boy; Fawn gave him a nod for the wisdom of that. But Fawn clearly didn't understand why he drew Finch into the clean-out work in her place.

"No!" Sparrow whimpered as they turned him over and placed his foot across the towels on his uncle's lap. "It'll hurt! Papa, don't let them!"

"I promise you it'll hurt less 'n a wolf bite, and that's the absolute truth," Dag intoned.

The resistant wriggling paused, and Dag marveled how well that specious argument worked on youngsters. Every time. Fawn, familiar with the ploy, grinned sideways at him.

Dag threw a ground reinforcement into the little foot, did his best to numb the nerves, and bent to the nasty task. One-handed, he reopened the cut with one of Arkady's sharp scalpels, and with a syringe Fawn filled with boiled water, plus groundwork, thoroughly flushed out the poisoned flesh. Working with Finch to rewrap the foot in a bandage was much more awkward than working with Fawn, but the results were adequate. After, Dag handed everything off to the grandmother to be boiled or burned. More hand washing, thinking uneasily of Arkady. And then it was time to go in after the child's sizzling nerves, again.

They fell into a cycle as the day wore on into dusk. Ten minutes of groundwork gave twenty minutes of relief from the spasms, during which Sparrow either was coaxed to eat by one of the women, or rested limply. Then the wrenching twitches and painful weeping would begin again, and Dag would kneel, bow his head, and slip back into his trance. The fever remained high, but they were giving the boy's own body the means to fight back. Another brief respite. And again.

As the task became familiar, Dag found space within it to think and wonder. Could a maker set up some sort of involution containing ground-work to soothe the frantic nerves, something that would last better than half an hour at a time? And why did this disruption remind Dag weirdly of the ground of some snakebite victims? Meditating on that peculiar question, he was only brought out of his trance by a sharp slap to his skull.

He blinked up in the lamplight to find Fawn scowling at him in worry.

"Did I interrupt anything?" she asked.

"No. Thank you. That was right."

"Good."

Blight. He'd thought he could send her off to another room to rest, but it looked as though she'd have to keep this night vigil right alongside him. No one else here could even guess when his trance began to slip dangerously into groundlock. They laid their bedroll on the floor, and slept in snatches.

By morning, they were both growing frayed. When Fawn next slapped him out of his trance, he just grunted at her, horribly irritated. Bending his aching forehead to the cotton-stuffed mattress, he closed his eyes.

"Why do you keep making him stop?" Cherry Bridger demanded nervously. "If he kept on, couldn't he fix it for good and all?"

"*Because,*" Fawn rather snarled, "if Dag gets groundlocked to Spa—to a patient, and the patient dies, Dag could die with him. That's what happened to Arkady's apprentice just before Dag."

"Oh," said Cherry in a smaller voice. "I didn't know that."

"Time you learned. Farmers need to learn more about Lakewalkers so they won't misunderstand how to handle them. They're a dreadfully nervy bunch, you know. High-strung."

Delicately conveying that Dag should be treated carefully; Dag was not ungrateful.

The afternoon was bad. The evening, worse, and Dag began to wonder if coming out with Finch would turn into one of the worst mistakes of his life. But sometime during the night his ten minutes of snatched sleep became twenty, then forty. When Fawn woke him, blinking, after two hours solid, he realized they'd turned some corner. That, and a good farm breakfast, revived him enough to go on.

The lull between bouts lengthening, Sparrow had time, in his restless misery, to grow bored. Dag diverted him with what children's stories he could remember from his distant youth, or Lakewalker ballads recast into tall tale. He wished Bo were here. The other members of the boy's family, as they drifted in and out to help, listened along wordlessly. As the next dawn edged toward noon, then night, Dag felt as though he'd been stuck in this room for about a thousand years.

It was somehow decided, not by him, that he needn't stay by the bedside anymore, but that someone would come get him when more groundwork was wanted, which was now up to three and four hours apart. He was led off to a real bed in another room. With a washstand. And Fawn. It was his first chance to speak with her alone in days—he'd lost track of how many. But shouldn't he have his wits about him for a talk so important? He was fairly sure that he should. And that he didn't.

So he let her pull the brightly colored quilt up over them both, hugged her in hard, and slept like a dead man.

11

Fawn awoke tucked up under Dag's left arm, so early in a misty dawn that the farmhouse was still silent. She was wearing one of his shirts for a nightdress; he was stripped for sleep as usual. She stretched her neck to put her ear to his heartbeat, then glanced up. He was awake, looking down at her.

"Slept out, finally?" she asked.

"Yes, I feel much better now." His hand traced over her neck, breast, belly, and rested there, spread-fingered. His expression grew curiously tender.

She gave him a sleepy smile. "What?"

"You amaze me," he whispered. "Every day, you amaze me."

She cuddled in more firmly. *I think I have the better part of that trade.* She wondered just how refreshed he found himself this morning, and considered lifting the quilt to check. They'd made do with much less privacy than this back on the *Fetch,* time to time, muffling early morning giggles in each other's quick kisses.

But Dag's face grew serious, and he sighed. Yet he made no move to rise. Talk, then? Or maybe talk first, then . . .

"Remember the night of the pig roast?"

She kissed his collarbone. "Yes?" she said encouragingly. She stifled worry. Was he finally going to cough up whatever had been putting him off his stride since then? About time.

"I was a little distracted. I was . . . gods, Dag, stop making excuses for yourself . . ." His mutter trailed off. He drew breath and began again. "Your fertile time was starting up, and I didn't catch it. I . . . we . . . I made you . . . you're pregnant."

She froze in astonishment. His chest had stilled, not breathing. A wave of shock seemed to rise from her feet through her lungs to the top of her head, and for a moment she wasn't sure if it was good or bad or just *immense,* because her whole world was turning inside out. With a squeal of wild joy, she lurched up and kissed him smack on the mouth. "Oh! Oh!"

His squeezed eyes flew wide; he kissed her back, hugged her hard, released her; only then did his chest collapse in a woosh of breath. "Well! That's a relief. Thought you'd be mad at me, Spark."

"Is that why you blurted it out so blunt?" She stared, confused and a trifle alarmed. "I admit, this might not've been my first pick of time 'n place, but you don't expect babies to be convenient. Not if you have a lick of sense. Aren't you happy?"

His arms tightened around her. "Ecstatic. Confounded." He hesitated. "Taken by surprise."

"But we're married. We knew this was bound to happen sometime, that's what marriage is *for.* Surprised today, sure, but not . . . not in *general.*" Her nose wrinkled. "I suppose it could be like patrolling for malices. They're what you went out looking for, but it's still a surprise to find one *that* day."

His deep laugh rumbled in his chest, and she was reassured. "Not my first pick of comparisons, Spark!" The laugh faded. "Except for the part about being scared."

"Scared? When you went out after them again and again? Brave, I'd say!"

He shook his head, his expression growing inward, as if looking into long memory. "No. That wasn't courage, just a kind of numbness. It was like I'd lost all affinity with the world. Now, though . . . oh gods, I care so much I can't hardly breathe." He dotted kisses all across her face, quick, almost frantic pecks. "And I'm scared spitless."

About to say, *It'll be fine, Dag!,* she paused as the complexities of their present situation began to creep back to her mind. Instead she said, "Babies, once they're started, come on in their time, not yours. You just have to scramble around as best you can."

She reached up and set her finger to his lips, stopping whatever he'd been about to say, as her own memory gripped her. The boy who'd fathered her first lost child had feared only for his own threatened comfort. He'd greeted the news of its bare existence with anger, rejection, threats of unforgivable slander.

This astonishing man in bed with her wanted to remake the whole world into a safe cradle for her second. Or *leastways* turn his heart inside out trying.

She'd a sneaking suspicion wisdom was to be found in some happy medium, but on the whole she preferred Dag's approach. "You amaze me, too, Dag," she whispered.

He rolled toward her, folded her in.

She nuzzled his chest hair, then thought of yet another advantage to possessing a Lakewalker spouse. "Hey! Is it a boy or a girl?"

"Too early to tell even for groundsense. It'll be another few weeks till anyone can be sure." He drew her upward to kiss her again, then added, "A girl could carry on our tent name." His attempt at a neutral tone failed to conceal his hopeful interest.

"But if she married a farmer, she'd take her husband's name," Fawn felt constrained to point out.

"Any boy who marries *our* girl will take her name and like it!"

She giggled madly. "You sound so fierce!"

He blushed. "I 'spose I am getting a bit ahead of myself, Spark."

Truly.

Uncertainty began to nibble away at her first joyful surprise. Because her attempt to picture the birth of this child foundered on the first question, *Where?* Somewhere between the surety of this morning's breakfast and the air dream of the child's future wedding lay a whole lot of today's-work. And a need, burning as inexorably as an hour-marked candle, to get things *settled*. Laying in winter supplies on the farm every fall had taught her how to plan ahead, how to make the future happen as it was supposed to. Well . . . it had shown her one way, she reckoned. It hadn't taught her how to follow a long-legged Lakewalker husband over half a continent; that, she'd had to learn as she trotted along. And she was still learning. *How do we do this?* wasn't to be simply answered, *Just like Mama and Papa.*

Dag's hand left off caressing her belly and found a lower spot to admire. She eased her thighs apart to give him room, then hesitated. "I suppose it's safe to . . . ? Must be, stands to reason. Most folks wouldn't even know at this point."

"Yes," he said firmly. "I asked."

"Who?"

"Arkady."

"Oh." She digested this, as well as she could through the distraction of his sweet tickling. "Does he know that I'm . . . ? Oh. Yeah. *'Course* he could tell, if you could." She blinked. "Wait a minute. Did everyone know but me? Barr and Remo, too? And . . ." *Now* she hit him, but it was too late to be convincing.

"Groundsense," he sighed. "You just deal with it." He licked down her neck. "You're smiling."

She suspected she was grinning like a chipmunk with its cheeks full, actually. "So much for my dignity."

"Remember," he breathed, "to take joy."

She was put in mind of what he'd said when planning their wedding night; that it would stand out sharp and clear when a thousand other nights blurred. So far, he'd been proved right, though they weren't even up to a thousand days, yet. She opened mind, heart, and body to him as he set about making sure that, along with all her other recollections of this remarkable morning, she would remember that she was beloved.

After they washed up and dressed, Dag went in to give Sparrow another treatment. The boy seemed so much eased that Finch's unmarried sister, a girl of fifteen, was left to sit with him. Midmorning found Fawn and Dag on their own in the farmhouse kitchen, the rest of the Bridger family having scattered to their relentless farm chores. Fawn rewarmed the pot of grits left out for them, not too stiffly congealed, and fried up ham and eggs to go-with. They were half done with this meal when Dag lifted and turned his head at nothing. It reminded Fawn of the way a cat stared at things no one else could see. *Lakewalkers.* No wonder they made regular folks uneasy.

"What?" said Fawn.

"Just bumped grounds with Neeta, of all people. What's she doing here?"

"Looking for us?" Fawn made to scramble up.

"Seemingly. Sit, Spark, she's still riding in. Finish your breakfast. You need your food." He gave her a fond smile.

She smiled back. Deep inside her head an excited voice was still crying *Babybabybaby, yesnoyes eep!* She wanted to jump up and run around madly preparing *something,* but truly, there was nothing much to do yet, especially here. Except to eat her breakfast. She swallowed the last bite of buttery grits, then followed Dag to the front porch.

Neeta was just cantering into the farmyard, mud splashing from the hooves of her sweating horse, which shook its head as she pulled up, and stood blowing through round, red nostrils. "Dag!" she cried. "Sir! You're alive!"

Had there been doubt? Dag's left arm tightened around Fawn's waist, whether possessively or in warning she wasn't sure.

"Am I in time?" Neeta added breathlessly. She cast an odd look at Fawn, her blond brows tightening as if in confusion or dismay or . . . disappointment?

In a rather deliberate drawl, Dag said, "In time for what, Neeta? I expect we could still rustle you up some breakfast."

She made an impatient swipe of her hand at the levity. "Captain Bullrush can't be more than an hour behind me, and he's hopping mad. You have time to get away if you hurry."

"Away where, and why? I can't believe Antan Bullrush has mayhem on his mind, on such a fine spring morning."

"No, no, of course not, but you can still get back to camp. Slip past him. No one need ever know you were here. Oh gods, I should have brought another horse. I can lend you mine if you like, and I can walk home." She dismounted and climbed the wooden steps as if to present her reins to Dag at once.

Dag stuffed his hand into his pocket. "I should've thought folks knew we were out. Didn't Arkady get my note?"

"Yes, Barr and Remo said. Except they didn't tell us till the *next* night, when the rumors were already all over the place."

An uneasy sigh trickled through Dag's lips. "So, ah . . . you want to begin at the beginning, Neeta?" He let a tinge of patrol-captain sternness seep into his tone—deliberately?

Perhaps, for Neeta straightened her shoulders. "Yes, sir. Well. I guess old Arkady wasn't best pleased when he found you'd gone off— *was* there a sick farmer?"

"Lockjaw," said Dag shortly.

Neeta's mouth made an *Oh;* she looked briefly daunted, but forged on. "I don't know what was going through Arkady's mind, but the next morning when you two didn't come to the medicine tent, he told Challa he'd given you a day of rest. Except that Nola and Cerie piped up that they'd seen Fawn go off into the woods the day before with some cute farmer boy, and she never came back. Well, *Cerie* said she wasn't sure it was like that, but *Nola* thought it was. And Arkady just snorted."

"Wasn't like what?" said Fawn, taken aback.

"That you had eloped with that farmer boy, and Dag had gone chasing after you both." Neeta's lips thinned with as much disapproval as if she had discovered it to be true.

Fawn gasped in outrage at the slander. "I never—!"

Dag squeezed her to silence and removed his hand from his pocket, but only to rub it over his face. "Go on."

"Any gossip that's all over the medicine tent spreads all over the camp pretty shortly. That night Barr and Remo told me and Tavia about your note, but they made us swear to keep our mouths shut, which I for one was just as happy to do. I still thought it could have been a false trail, if you'd gone off with blood in your eye. I don't know how the whole garbled mess came to Captain Bullrush's ear, but next morning he stormed down to the medicine tent to find out what was really going on. He said he wasn't going to be having some blighted murder ballad play out in *his* patrol district.

"He was even more livid when he found out the truth, and that Arkady hadn't warned him. I heard they had the most ferocious argument. They agreed to give you till last night to show up and explain yourself, and then the captain was going to go looking for the answers. Which he is doing this morning. Oh, sir!" Neeta raised a distressed hand toward Dag. "Arkady and I had almost talked the camp into offering you tent rights! I thought you fought so hard for your training—don't you care about it anymore?"

"More than I can rightly say."

"Then there has to be some way to salvage this. Can't you have these farmers swear you were never here?"

Dag wanted, Fawn could see, to slap Neeta with a flat *No,* and leave it at that. But the habits of too many years spent shaping young patrollers cut in before he could gratify himself. "Useless, Neeta. Antan would have the truth out in no time. I won't lie. But I'd be glad to grovel, if you think it would help."

"Oh!" Neeta nearly stamped her foot, Fawn thought; she did clench her fists. "Can't you *please* come away?"

"Not yet. One more day of nerve treatments will slice better 'n a week off Sparrow's recovery, I figure. Have you ever seen lockjaw, Neeta?"

She shook her head, lips tight. "No. But I hear it's gruesome."

"You heard right." Dag straightened and stretched, as if girding himself. "Leave your captain to me, Neeta. It's come on sooner than I would have liked, but these questions were bound to get laid on the table sometime. Best to have it out and done."

"Sir, you . . . you blighted fool, sir!"

"The Bridgers will let you use their barn. Go take care of your horse, patroller." Dag sighed. "You've used him hard this morning."

"To no good purpose, it looks like," muttered Neeta savagely. She stalked off the porch and led her blown mount away around the house.

"I could wish Arkady hadn't taken it into his head to cover for me," murmured Dag. "I wasn't expecting that. Did he lie outright? Ah, gods. This is going to be Hickory Lake all over again. I'm so sorry, Spark."

"I don't think it's the same," said Fawn sturdily.

"Sure puts me in mind. Blight. If only I'd had more time to earn my place, time to persuade. I thought the scheme of a medicine tent in the farmer's market was first-rate, or could be made to be, with unbeguilement. Get it set up and running in two years or three, leave it behind as a seed when we did go north again."

"Planting ideas?" Fawn tested the notion in her mind. "Only works if you're going to stay and water and weed them. And pick off the caterpillars."

"Huh." He dropped a kiss on the top of her head. "It's never simple, is it, Spark?"

∽

Captain Bullrush bumped Dag's groundsense within the hour. Dag went out to wait on the top porch step, leaning against the post. Fawn sat at his feet, her face propped in her little fists. Neeta lounged on the steps opposite Fawn, one booted leg outstretched, scowling. The adult Bridgers filtered out onto the porch, too, Papa Bridger and Lark flanking the front door with their arms crossed, Mama Bridger in her rocker failing to knit, Cherry and Finch anxious on the bench beside her.

"I expect Captain Bullrush will be wanting a word or two with me. I'd take it kindly if you folks won't interrupt his say," Dag cautioned the Bridgers. "Fawn's and my place back at New Moon Camp is at stake, here."

Finch ducked his head at Fawn, his source of many lessons on Lakewalkers over the past four days—though not that one—and said, "I'm so sorry. I didn't know!"

Dag gave him a dry smile over his shoulder. "If you had, would you have done any different?"

Finch glanced up toward the corner bedroom, where his nephew lay peacefully sleeping. "I guess not. Not really."

"Me neither."

The little Lakewalker patrol trotted slowly up the lane. The camp captain naturally didn't ride alone; he'd chosen his age mate Tapp to be his partner for this inquiry. Witness, too, probably. Not surprisingly, Barr and Remo trailed after. They looked relieved to see Dag and Fawn, more confused to see Neeta. The four drew up their mounts in the muddy yard in front of the porch.

From his place in his saddle, Antan Bullrush was almost eye to eye with Dag. He did not dismount, but did ease his reins and lean on his saddlebow. His bent back revealed as much of his state of mind as his mostly closed ground: weary exasperation tempered by confusion and caution. If he'd been younger and less tired, he'd likely have been more angry. Dag understood that one, bone-deep.

His eye fell on Neeta in a way that made the girl flinch. "And what are you doing here, patroller?" he growled.

She raised her chin. "I'm off duty, sir. I'm free to go where I like."

"Is that so?"

She had the prudence to make no reply. Thankfully. Antan turned his gaze to Dag, and went on, "I see your intelligencer has run ahead of us. So which of the tales was true, northerner? Was this an elopement, or an errand of mercy?"

"It was a five-year-old boy with lockjaw. Sir." Dag touched his fingers to his temple in a habitual salute that had very little actual salute in it.

To his credit, the captain's face set in what might have been a sympathetic wince. A flicker of his groundsense extended; he glanced after it toward that corner room, then nodded. "I see. It's as well to have the facts straight, I suppose." Even if they weren't the facts he might have preferred?

"Told him it couldn't be an elopement," Remo muttered.

"Might have been an abduction, though," Barr said judiciously, or mock judiciously—with Barr, it was hard to tell. "I might have believed that."

A sharp downward jerk of Antan's fist demanded silence from the pair.

Papa Bridger stepped sternly forward. "Without this lanky fellow and his little wife, I believe we'd be burying my grandson today."

Dag turned his left arm in what would be a palm-down calming gesture, if he'd had a palm on that side. The faint threat from his hook and reminder of his sacrifice were just a bonus for Antan, he figured.

Antan took in the array of Bridger eyes upon him and said to Dag, a trifle through his teeth, "We would do better without the audience, here."

"They're on their own porch," observed Dag. "You're in their yard." Antan looked sulky, but couldn't very well deny this.

"What *I* think," said Fawn abruptly, standing up, "is that it's time to get everyone here introduced to each other, so's they'll have no excuse for talking over each other's heads." And she proceeded to spend the next several minutes doing so. Antan's attempt to glower continuously at Dag kept getting interrupted by having to acknowledge names and little life stories. By the time Fawn had worked through everything including Tapp's recent gut problems, it was plain that Antan's plan to keep this on his own familiar terms—a stern patrol dressing-down—was slipping through his fingers.

Antan stared at the farmers, rubbed his face, grasped at straws. "How many folks know about this excursion of yours by now, Dag? Just the ones here, or more—neighbors, kinfolk?"

Fawn answered. "Neighbors, married sisters, in-laws—all sorts of folks have stopped by to help in the past few days. It's how farmers do things, you know, sir."

"Uh huh. So any notion that this could be kept a secret is hash?"

"Afraid so, sir," said Dag, understanding his drift, and its hopelessness. "As I tried to explain to Neeta. But I believe she was only thinking about half of the picture."

Neeta glanced over her shoulder at all the Bridgers and blinked uneasily.

Antan gave Neeta an *I'll-deal-with-you-later* look. He said to Dag, "Did Arkady make it clear to you that this sort of thing was forbidden?"

"He made it clear he thought it inadvisable, and explained why." Dag hesitated. "It was clearer to me that I couldn't turn away from a youngster dying in that much agony and still be a fellow I wanted to shave every morning."

Antan was plainly moved by this last—but not far enough. "If we have a repeat of what happened over at Hatchet Slough, *my* patrollers will bear the brunt of it." He glanced at Tapp, at Neeta. Seeing broken heads? Or worse?

Dag was moved, too—but not far enough. "A good idea badly carried out is not the same as a bad idea. With unbeguilement, I believe Arkady's old notion of setting up a medicine tent in the farmers market would be an orderly way to try a new thing, without riots at your gates. It wouldn't have to be Hatchet Slough again."

Antan rocked back in his saddle. "Is that the bee you have in your brain?"

Dag nodded. Oh gods, was this the time, place, and man for this argument? *Never mind, keep going.* "Because someday, when all the malices are gone—when that long evil doesn't mold us anymore—who will we Lakewalkers be? I've seen a boatload of possibilities, this patrol. It's not too soon to start trying new things, especially here. In a lot of ways, the south is a vision of the future of the north."

Antan had gone rigid, like a man fighting inside his own mind as well as outside. "Listen to me, northerner—it's my calling to hold New Moon Cutoff. To defend it, lest our traditions and our blood be destroyed by inches."

Dag snorted. "Our traditions? Really? Where did you exchange when you were a young patroller, Antan?

"South Seagate," the camp captain replied uneasily.

"Pretty far south for north, that is. So when did New Moon hold its last ten-year rededication? I know what a traditional camp looks like, and it's nothing like New Moon. If you were *traditional,* you'd put a torch to every house in it. Because traditional Lakewalkers don't *defend.* We *run.* New Moon has gone as sessile as its farmer neighbors. And you're only clenching your hands so tight because you have *so little left in them.*"

Antan looked down at his reins, and, with an effort, undid his white-knuckled fingers from around them. He frowned across at Fawn. "I'd think you'd be newly interested in defending what's in front of you, Dag."

Dag shrugged. "I'd be very happy to return to New Moon and continue my training." He spared a glance at glowing Fawn, regarding him in unshaken trust. *Absent gods, would I be happy for that.*

"And would you swear not to do anything in secret like this"—a wave around at the Bridger farm—"again?"

Silence. Then, "Can I have a medicine booth, so I wouldn't have to be secret?"

Longer silence.

"That's groveling?" Neeta muttered through her teeth.

Fawn had hunkered next to her on the step; Dag heard her whisper in return, "Dag-style, yep. Watch 'n listen."

Dag went on more urgently, "The future is happening right here, every day. You can swim or you can drown, but you can't choose not to be in the flood. I suppose the real insight is that it's always been that way." He took a breath. "I think we should start learning to swim."

Antan snapped, "Men like Tapp and me have youngsters to defend, too. Everyone's youngsters, not just our own."

Dag gave a conceding nod, but swept his hand around in a loop that took in not only Fawn, but Neeta and the Oleana boys, Finch, and Sparrow and his sister upstairs. "If you really mean *everyone's* youngsters, Lakewalker and farmer alike, then I'm with you. Because they may be our charges now, but they will be our judges when the waters fall."

"Blight," said Antan slowly. "And here I thought you were just dangerous because you were a softhearted fool. You're a real renegade, aren't you? Ten times more than that poor bandit fellow you knifed up on the Grace."

"Well, sir." And what kind of an answer was that? Not a denial.

"Gods, you make me dizzy. I sit here listening to you any longer, I'm like to fall off my blighted horse. Listen, northerner. We didn't have a problem till you walked in. No question that the fastest way to rid ourselves of it is for you to walk out again. I don't have time for this."

Fawn looked off into the air, but her voice grew distinctly edged. "My mama used to say to me, *What, you don't have time to do it right, but you do have time to do it over?*"

Antan broke from her cool stare and returned to scowling at Dag.

"You're not my patroller, Dag Bluefield. Absent gods, you're not even anyone's tent-kin here. If you're so set on dealing with farmers, you can take it up anywhere you like—except within the bounds of *my* camp. And whatever mess you've started here can chase after you, and not end up at our gates."

"My training—" Dag began.

"You should have thought of that earlier."

"I did."

"Then you made your choice. So there's no blighted point in me sitting here arguing with you, is there? Just don't come back to New Moon. We won't let you in again."

He wheeled his horse away. Then his eye fell on Barr and Remo, sitting stricken on their mounts. "Ah." He reined in. "You two. Are you coming with me, or staying with him?"

Remo's lips parted in surprise; he looked at Neeta and back to Antan. "*Could* we stay at New Moon, sir?"

"You can apply. Your patrol leader told me that you were exceptionally disciplined patrollers."

"Oh, not me, sir!" Barr said, in a sweetly cheery tone. "I've been hanging around with renegades way too long. My ground is totally corrupted, y'see. You wouldn't want me in your patrols. Something untidy might rub off on them. Wits, maybe."

Antan's teeth clenched in something not much like a smile. "Right. Then you can bring Dag back his horses and gear." His gaze swung to Remo, scythe-like. "And you?"

Remo looked in anguish at Barr, Neeta, Dag. "I—can I have a little time to think about it, sir?"

"You can have till your partner leaves." Antan's arm veered to Neeta. "*You*, go get your horse and catch up." He jerked his chin at Tapp. "Enough of this fool's errand. Back to camp."

As the patrollers turned away, Barr edged his horse up to the porch. "I guess I'll be back tomorrow with Copperhead and all. Any messages?"

"Tell Arkady . . ." No. Dag could hardly tell Arkady he was sorry for going out, because he still wasn't. Only for not coming back. "Tell Arkady I'm sorry for how things worked out. But will you keep arguing for me back there as long as you can? Because Antan Bullrush isn't the only authority at New Moon. And your mouth has nothing more to lose you at this point."

Barr grinned like a possum and reined after the others.

12

After following Dag upstairs to watch him treat Sparrow, Fawn returned with him to the Bridger kitchen to find a family conference in progress that reminded her of table talk at home in West Blue. They all had plenty of rude things to say about Captain Bullrush, anyhow.

"Well, yes, but I have a deal of sympathy for Antan," said Dag, as Cherry Bridger pushed tea mugs in front of them both.

"But he as much as tossed you out on your ear!" said Cherry. Finch hunched his shoulders and looked guilty.

"The man was trying to protect his camp." Dag repeated Arkady's story of the tragedy at Hatchet Slough, not quite in Arkady's words.

"But that was a long time ago," said Finch. "Before I was born!"

"It's present memory to folks like Captain Bullrush and Arkady, though." Dag swallowed tea, shook his head. "I think Antan senses his ways are starting to be outworn, but he's got nothing to put in their place, so his only answer is to hold harder. There's a lot of folks like him."

"But Dag's trying to change all that," Fawn put in proudly.

"Don't load my boat too heavy, Spark. One man can't change all the world any more than he can change which way the wind blows. The most he can do is learn to read that wind and sail it. I figure a fellow can get quite a cargo safe from shore to shore, if he can do that."

He scrubbed his face. "Gods, listen to me. All wind and water and nonsense. No wonder it all slips through my hand. I need some good farmer dirt to ground me, Spark. It's all about time, see. I deeply do not understand time, and groundsense is no help; it's stuck in time like everything else." He glanced up at a ring of blank faces, and ducked his head. "Sorry. Too many winter nights out on patrol with nothing to look at but stars. It's like to make a man strange."

Fawn thought she could nearly hear the Bridgers thinking, *stranger,* but no one said it aloud. "So, what do we do now, Dag?"

Papa Bridger put in, with heavy emphasis, "You two would be welcome to stay here. For as long as you've a mind." Lark nodded shortly, and Cherry and Mama Bridger murmured something bolstering.

Fawn tried to picture it. Could they make a life as permanent guests in that upstairs room? Doing what? Well, she knew farm chores; she could pull her weight. But she suspected there might be objections to Dag taking up medicine making for farmers this close to New Moon. And . . . with a baby? In some other woman's house? Though Cherry Bridger made a tempting substitute kinswoman. They'd be safe for a time, at least . . .

Finch leaned forward, elbows on the table, face serious. "Fawn, do you remember those friends I told you about, who were talking about moving north?"

"Yes?"

"I passed on what you told me about your country, and it tipped the balance. We decided *someday* should be this spring. We thought we'd all go together, because the Trace is no place for loners. We've been getting our supplies in order—Sage asked his sweetheart to marry him and come along—we were all to start this past week, but then Sparrow got sick, and I was all distracted. I was to take the brown mare and two pack mules for my due-share, and my supplies and tools."

Papa Bridger and Lark nodded.

"Sage has a wagon, so they'll be going slower than a pack train. I figured to catch up when . . . well, I figured to leave one way or another."

If Sparrow had died, Finch had meant to flee the farm in shame, he meant. Fawn nodded understanding. Mama Bridger sighed.

"I'm glad"—Finch glanced at Dag, took a deep breath—"that it's not going to be like that. But I still want to catch up with Sage and the boys. What I wondered was—have you ever been on the Trace, sir?"

Dag's brows flicked up. "I've never walked it end to end all at one time. I've ridden or walked most sections."

"I've never been north of Alligator Hat," Finch said.

The nearest village—some fifteen miles up the Trace, Fawn had learned, charmed by the name. She'd wondered if they in fact sold alligator hats there.

"But you, sir," Finch went on, "if you were meaning to go home after all—if you threw in with us now—you might be a sort of guide. Mightn't you?" He looked anxiously at Fawn.

"Of a sort," said Dag. He, too, looked at Fawn, question in his eyes. "I'm not the medicine maker I meant to be, yet."

She nibbled on her bottom lip. "Before, you'd half a mind to jump into this with no training but patrol medicine."

"Before, I was a blighted fool. A menace."

"A mighty lucky menace, if so. And it's not like you grew *more* ignorant, for our two months with Arkady."

"It sure feels like it. Arkady opened my eyes to a whole new realm.

It's been right humbling. Maker Vayve, too—I thought I knew all about knife making from watching Dar, but Vayve's style was quite a bit different. Between 'em, I feel like someone took my skull and shook it like a bottle of cider, and the cork's about to pop out."

"You don't have to be the best medicine maker in seven hinterlands." Although she suspected Arkady might be. "Yeah, Arkady sets a high bar, though I wonder if some of that isn't your mama's voice in the back of your head. She does make you crazy, you know that, Dag. But all you really have to do is be better than what folks have now. And be *there*."

Dag shook his head gloomily.

"Maybe you can find another medicine maker up in Oleana who'll take you up on your terms. Arkady can't be the only good teacher."

The gloom lightened slightly. "Point, Spark." He scrubbed his hair, studied her. "You want to go home."

Truly, if they were going north this year, it needed to be soon. Early pregnancy was no picnic—she remembered the sickness and mind-draining fatigue—but late pregnancy would be even worse for travel. Hers, anyhow. *Yeah, we need to go before I get too round to move.* Dag was endearingly nervous for her health *during,* a concern she treasured after the frightening isolation of her first experience, but she was more nervous for what would come *after.* She had never been much for other people's babies, though she'd always expected to quite like her own. Still . . . just how scary was it to be handed a baby you couldn't hand back?

She didn't need a substitute kinswoman; she had a real one now in Berry Bluefield. *Best thing Whit ever did for me.* If Fawn was going to end up having a baby in someone else's house, she wanted it to be Berry's place in Clearcreek.

Useless to try to lie to a man with groundsense, but she at least managed, "I want what you need."

A crooked smile. "I think I need to go home, too. *We* need." *We-three,* not *we-two;* she heard that, and had to smile back. Dag straightened. "Go home and get started. Arkady's wrong about one thing; it does make a difference where you put your hand on the lever. But we're not going anywhere without our horses. We'll have to see what Barr and Remo— or Barr, leastways—brings us."

∾

Barr brought Arkady.

Also Copperhead, Magpie, and two heavily loaded packhorses. Dag, strolling out onto the porch when he sensed them, stared openmouthed at the train. Barr was riding Copperhead himself, but trailed a strange horse bearing an empty saddle and his bags. Dag looked in vain for Remo, and his heart sank at that absence.

It had been two days since Captain Bullrush's decree of expulsion. Dag hadn't expected Barr back before yesterday noon at the earliest. A hundred things might have delayed him, most hopefully some Barrish persuasion to reverse Antan's ruling. The longer Dag had waited, the more his hopes had risen. But Barr surely wouldn't have packed all that gear just for a quick return to New Moon, and for pity's sake how had he obtained all those horses?

"What's all this?" Dag asked, bemusedly returning Barr's wave of greeting.

Arkady overrode the answer. "What does it look like, you unutter- able fool? I told you how it would be, did I not? Did I not?"

Arkady's outward appearance was typically fastidious, barring ride- rumpled clothing and a few wisps of hair escaping its knot. But the roil in his usually serene ground and look of wild exasperation in his eyes put Dag forcibly in mind of a cat that had been stuck in a barrel and rolled downhill.

"You broke your word to me!" Arkady went on.

"I didn't seek to, sir. The problem came to me, and I couldn't turn aside."

"Did you have the first notion what was being thrown away? No, of course you didn't. Patrollers! Antan's a bull and you're a mule. The only one who really understands is Challa, and even she didn't come in on my side!"

"Side?" said Dag. His glance at Barr was not enlightening. Barr wasn't actually staring up at the sky and innocently whistling, but he might as well have been.

"It's unconscionable—unconscionable!"

Dag admired Arkady's ability to even *pronounce* such a jaw-breaking word while sputtering with rage, but he was still adrift, here. If Arkady hadn't been sent out to offer Dag a pardon, why was he here? Just to vent his feelings?

"—to waste a talent like yours. Still worse to turn you loose on the world one-tenth trained and wholly unsupervised. So since that pack of fools won't let you come back to New Moon"—Arkady's voice dwindled—"I'm coming with you."

Dag's jaw dropped. "What?"

"You heard me." Arkady's eyes sought the dirt. "I'm coming along with you. To continue your training till it's complete to my satisfaction."

"Where?"

"North, I suppose. That's where you're going, isn't it? Your wife will be homing like a pigeon—women in her condition generally do, you know. That much was obvious."

Dag wanted to say *Not to me,* but came up instead with, "Arkady, you mean to ride the Trace with us?"

Arkady nodded.

"It's eight hundred miles and more, you do know that?"

He nodded again, more shortly.

"What's the longest you've ever ridden at a stretch?"

Arkady raised his chin. "Twenty miles."

"For how many days?"

Arkady cleared his throat. "One."

"And how long have you ever gone without a bath?"

Arkady glared, but didn't deign to answer that one. He straightened his shoulders and dismounted; Barr followed suit. The maker rather absently handed the young patroller his reins, then stepped up to the porch.

"Is New Moon going to allow this?" Dag's staggered wits were finally beginning to work again. If this offer was real, he should fall on his knees and thank the absent gods. Was it? "Do they even know you're out here?"

"They'll figure it out," snapped Arkady. "I warned Antan, *and* the rest of those ditherers on the camp council. If they imagined I was bluffing, well, they'll know better next time."

"You can't live on the road the way you do in camp." Dag looked away at the tree line along the road, hazy in the damp warmth of the late afternoon, looked back, caught Arkady's evasive eyes square. "It looks like I'm going to have a lot more people on my hands this trip than I expected. I can't be your nursemaid, and Barr can't be your servant."

"I will not crumple into a heap from a horseback ride, thank you," said Arkady through his teeth. "Not even one eight hundred miles long."

"The world under the skin is your home hinterland, but the world outside it is mine. My road, my rules. Can you accept that?"

"About as well as you ever did, I expect," Arkady returned. Their stares held each other for an uncomfortable stretch.

"Then you can begin by taking care of your own horse," Dag said at last. "The barn's around back."

Arkady's glare turned scorching. Barr looked very alarmed. But after a long hesitation, Arkady merely said, "All right," and took back his reins. As he started around the house, he added over his shoulder, "When I return I want to inspect what you did to that boy with the lockjaw."

Lines drawn clearly enough; Dag nodded acceptance.

This still left Barr holding the leads of five horses, although Copperhead's ground showed signs of recent heavy persuasion; that and the gelding's ten-mile jaunt this morning doubtless explained why he wasn't trying to tear strips out of his trail mates just now. Dag took him and Magpie off Barr's hands. Barr yielded gratefully.

"Where's Remo?" Dag asked.

Barr's face went bleak. "He stayed."

"Ah." An unexpected exchange. Dag frowned after Arkady. "Barr— is Arkady bluffing, with this crazy gambit? Holding himself hostage, to force the camp council to knuckle under and take me back?"

The corner of Barr's mouth tucked up. "I think he thinks he is. I'm sure they think he is."

Dag nodded somewhat relieved understanding, then shot him a sharper look. "Then what's the use?"

"Well, I got him this far. I figured the rest would be up to you."

"Yeah . . . ?"

Challa made medicine; Arkady made medicine makers. Fawn might dub it the difference between corn and seed corn. When going off to break new land, the latter was clearly the more valuable. So would it be better to call Arkady's bluff, or the camp council's? With a slow smile, Dag thought, *Neither.* Best of all would be to grab your gift of seed corn and run before the original owners could demand it back.

"I'll tell Finch we can all be ready to start north tomorrow," said Dag, and led the horses off toward the barn.

∾

Their departure in the morning was much delayed, but with only fifteen miles to cover till their first planned stop, they hadn't really needed to be off at dawn. Dag and Barr readied their horses with patrollers' efficiency, but either Finch or his mama kept thinking of last-minute items to add to his packs. In a strange way, it reminded Fawn of her leave-taking at West Blue after her wedding, minus the wedding. Finch, too, was a younger child with no land and a meager due-share, and his space was needed for the next generation even more than his hands were wanted for labor.

His family wasn't glad to see him go, but they weren't arguing very hard against it, either. His mama's feelings were likely the most mixed. His papa seemed pleased he'd found a grown-up guide, even if he still found Dag unsettling. Arkady and Barr just baffled the Bridgers, despite Barr's entertaining the family at dinner with an account of their journey on the *Fetch*—although he'd glanced at Mama Bridger and left out the river bandits, to Fawn's relief. Bo's tallest tales could scarcely have won wider eyes; the great river, barely thirty miles west of here, plainly seemed an exotic world to them.

I was more ignorant than that, once. Time seemed tilted, as if ten years of change had been packed into her last ten months. Fawn shook her head in wonder and kicked Magpie after long-legged Copperhead. Finch kept twisting in his saddle and waving, though once they turned onto the road and the budding trees hid the house, he set his face forward eagerly enough.

It was Barr and Arkady who kept glancing back. Fawn suspected Barr was still wishing Remo might change his mind and chase after them, and Arkady had similar hopes about his camp council. Arkady wasn't used to losing arguments, Fawn reckoned. She dropped back next to Barr as they rode along in the soft spring air. He was encumbered with the two packhorses, but they seemed to follow without protest.

"Where did you get the horses and gear?" she asked.

"It's all Arkady's. I gather he barely tapped into his camp credit even after mounting me. Though one whole packsaddle is crammed with nothing but his medicine stuff he didn't want to leave behind. I had to remind him to pack clothes." Barr grimaced. "He said if he didn't take the portable medicine tent, the council wouldn't believe he was serious."

"Is he serious?"

Barr smirked. "Dag is."

"Huh."

It was a promising day for their start, pale blue overhead, pale green alongside, and as the warming afternoon wore on, Fawn found herself nodding. Then yawning and slumping, fighting heavy eyelids and seductive visions of laying a bedroll beneath the bushes and taking a long nap. She blinked awake briefly at the shock of realization. *I really am pregnant.* Her fatigue the past few days at the farmhouse had enough other excuses that she'd not noticed it creeping up on her. If not for Dag's groundsense, this would be her first suspicion. She stared down at her stomach, neatly clad in her riding trousers, in a mixture of awe and alarm. *This time, can I get it right?*

"Sleepy, Spark?" Dag's voice jolted her awake.

"'Fraid so," she mumbled. "Maybe I could tie myself to my saddle, the way you say couriers sometimes do."

"I have a better idea. Why don't you come over here"—he indicated his lap—"and we can double up the way we rode into Glassforge."

She smiled at the memory. "What about Magpie?"

"She's Lakewalker trained. She'll follow."

"Well, if you think it'll work . . ."

Copperhead stepped alongside, and Fawn knotted her reins on her mare's neck and let Dag help her slide across. She tucked up reasonably neatly, arm around his back, her cheek to his heart, and sniffed clean cotton and warm Dag. Happy nose.

"This is so nice," she murmured, cuddling in tight. "But I won't close my eyes. I don't want to miss a mile of the Tripoint Trace." Although so far, all the miles had looked rather alike, flat farm country broken up by shaded brown watercourses. At least all the looming trees, bearded by swags of that gray hanging moss, were different from Oleana. Bald cypress and magnolia and live oak . . . what a dozy afternoon . . .

∾

"Spark?"

At Dag's murmur, she unglued her eyelids. "What? What did I miss?"

"About four miles of nothing. Swamp, mostly."

"I slept for an hour?" She squinted, hoping she hadn't drooled on his shirt. "Your arm must be ready to fall off!"

"It'll stick. But we're coming up on Alligator Hat."

"Oh!"

Dag stopped to let her down, and she seized an invigorating stretch before remounting Magpie. They trotted after the others, which also helped bounce her awake.

Alligator Hat seemed typical of the small villages straggling up the Trace. A few dozen wooden houses were set back from the road, with gardens of varying neatness. Some front gates bore painted signs advertising rooms and stall space for rent for weary travelers. A sturdy bridge led over a weir for a mill. The road widened into a square around which clustered businesses that served both the local farmers and the Trace: a couple of alehouses, a neat two-story inn with its own large stable out back, the village clerk's office, another livery, signs for harness and repair, a wagon wright's, and a big smithy. Finch waved his arm and led their caravan around back into the smithy's yard.

A large wagon was set to one side, tongue to the ground. It was new-painted green with fine, curling yellow stripes, the wheels picked out in scarlet. Under its arching canvas roof, Fawn glimpsed a female shape fussing with some baskets. The double back door to the smithy was flung wide, a red glow winking from the forge inside where a bulky young man waited with his hand on the bellows. Near the door in the better light, a tall, lanky young man held the head of a big brown mule, scratching its poll and making soothing murmurs in its long ears. No twitch looped its cream-colored lip, even though it rolled its eye in worry. A wiry young man held its back hoof trapped between his knees on his leather apron, a nail in his mouth, a hammer in his hand.

He glanced up briefly at Finch and waved the hammer, calling around the nail, "Be righ' wi' you!," then returned to shoeing the mule. The *clack clack* of hammer on hoof echoed around the yard, the nail went in neatly, and he wrenched off the protruding point, clinched it, and filed it down. He sprang back as he released the hoof, but the mule merely sighed and leaned into its ear scratching. The two young men grinned at each other, then the lanky one tied the mule's rope to a ring on a post.

Bulky, lanky, and wiry all came out to the yard. Despite his friend's broader shoulders, it seemed the wiry one was the smith, because he greeted their party with the air of a host. "Finch! You made it!" He came up as Finch and the rest dismounted, and asked more quietly and anxiously, "How's Sparrow?," then blew out his breath with relief when Finch replied that his nephew was going to be all right.

Wiry glanced in some confusion at the rest of the party, clearly wondering if they were customers off the Trace. "What can I do for you folks? Shoeing, repairs?"

It seemed to occur to Finch for the first time that four strangers and six beasts were rather a lot to spring onto his friends' travel party unannounced. He hastened to make introductions. "This is Dag Bluefield, who's the fellow we owe Sparrow's life to. He's a Lakewalker medicine maker who wants to go north to Oleana and treat farmers, and this is his wife, Fawn Bluefield, which is why, I guess." He glanced at Fawn and evidently decided it wasn't necessary to add, *She's a farmer.* Fawn made her little knee dip; the three boys gaped at her in wonder and, after a second look at Dag, the usual surprise. "And this is Dag's, um, friend Arkady Waterbirch, who's going along with him, and Barr, um—did you ever say your last name?"

"Barr will do," the patroller said, staring with interest at these farmer near-age-mates. Barr, who had always looked like a puppy next to Dag, seemed suddenly an older dog.

"And these are my friends, Sage Smith"—wiry—"Ash Tanner"— that was bulky—"and Indigo Axe." Lanky, with deeply tanned skin despite the recent winter, a long face, and an impressively beaky nose.

The woman, meanwhile, had hopped down from the wagon and strolled over to the group. Sage reached out and grasped her hand.

"And this is my wife, Calla," he announced with shy pride. "Indigo's her little brother."

The latter hardly needed stating. Calla Axe Smith was half a head taller than her new husband, as tall and lanky as Indigo, with the same warm skin, long face, and beaky nose. Black hair, scarcely longer than her brother's, was cropped in fine wisps around her head. She wasn't beautiful, but Fawn imagined that once she outgrew her youthful awkwardness she might be striking. Fawn had trouble guessing her age, but thought Calla might be even younger than herself, which would be a nice change. Except that Indigo looked to be in his late teens like the other boys, so Calla had to be older than that.

"How de'!" said Fawn, with another eager knee dip. "I'm right glad to hear there's to be another married woman in the party."

"Are all those folks going with us?" Calla said, not sounding at all delighted. She frowned coolly up and down at the mismatched couple of Dag and Fawn. Indigo regarded them downright warily.

"Dag knows the Trace," Finch put in. "He's been all along it."

"This is our rig." Sage pointed proudly at the wagon, seeming oblivious to his wife's standoffishness, although Dag glanced at her sharply. "What do you think of the new paint, Finch? Calla did the stripes."

"Yeah!" said Finch in admiration.

"It's beautiful, but it's big for the Trace. What do you have to pull it?" asked Dag, in a tone of friendly interest.

"Six fine mules." Sage jerked his thumb over his shoulder at the sturdy beast he'd just finished shoeing. "The team and their tack were Calla's due-share. Calla's family used to make harness."

Calla gave a little grimace, but Sage went on with undaunted enthusiasm. "I have all my tools aboard, and my new anvil Papa gave me. As long as a smith has his anvil, he can make every other tool he needs to make every other tool you need."

"Six mules will likely do till after the Hardboil River, unless you need to pull out of a mud hole," Dag said. "But there's at least three long hills—mountain passes, really—north of the ferry that will need more to get this weight up them. Most folks who take wagons on the Trace do it in groups, and double or triple the teams on those slopes, hauling the wagons up in turns." Dag surveyed the animals standing in the yard. "If you hitch on Finch's two mules and our two packhorses, and maybe take part of your load up separate, it'll likely do. You want to be sure you pack harness for the extra pairs, though."

Sage took in this new information with vast interest. "That's good to know! We only had the one spare set. I'll beg an extra set from Papa before we go."

"Are you going to break land?" Fawn stood on tiptoe to look over the tailboard at the array of tools and supplies neatly arranged inside. Sage pointed out yet more features of his rig, including a folded feather bed; Calla frowned in faint embarrassment, but didn't blush. "Do you know which part of Oleana you're going to try, yet?"

"No plowing for me! That would be Finch and Ash. I'm heading to Tripoint!" Sage took a deep, exultant breath. "Where Tripoint steel comes from! I have to see that."

"Really? You might do well there." Dag extended his left arm and turned his hook, which he'd been holding nearly behind his back till now. "It was a couple of Tripoint artificers made this for me."

"Oh, yeah? When? What kind of steel did they use for that little spring-tongue back of the curve, there? That's clever—gives you a pinch grip, doesn't it? Light but strong—"

Sage was the first person Fawn had yet met who, if not tongue-tied altogether by Dag's maiming, asked about the arm harness and not the hand. Dag, she could see, was rather cheered by this, and the two fell into a discussion about the merits of Tripoint artificers that threatened to run on till everyone else fell over.

Fortunately, an older woman came out from the frame house bordering the yard, and called, "Is that you, Finch? Will you be wanting dinner?"

She proved to be Sage's mama, Missus Smith, leading to a repeat of the introductions all around. She looked taken aback to be presented with five extra mouths to feed within an hour of the meal, and Dag instantly volunteered to take his share of the party down the street to the inn. This, however, she rejected indignantly, especially after learning about Sparrow.

Necessarily the next move in the dance, although Dag didn't seem to realize it, was for Fawn to dip her knees again and say cheerily, "How de', ma'am! What can I do to help out?" Which won a slightly more approving eye, and an invitation into the kitchen in Calla's wake.

Dag grabbed her in passing to whisper, "You don't have to do this, Spark. The inn will feed us, and you can have a rest."

She whispered back, "No, this is better. We're going to be traveling with these folks for the next six weeks. Best chance I'll get to see where they come from."

He hesitated, then nodded understanding.

Fawn glanced up at the rambling but not large house. "We might like a room at the inn later, though. Because I've a suspicion all the boys are going to end up in bedrolls in the smithy loft. Which will be dry and free but not as private."

His lips twitched. "Point, Spark." He let her go, turning back to the men to help deal with fodder and beds for the four-footed guests.

The kitchen featured an iron cookstove of the sort Fawn had coveted up on the Grace River—not a northern import, but a homebuilt imitation that had been presented by Papa Smith to his wife after seeing a real one at Graymouth. By the time Fawn had exclaimed over it, been shown its features, and assured Mama Smith that it was as fine as any Tripoint work, the ice was in a fair way to being broken, at least enough for going on with.

But the kitchen also harbored an unmarried daughter and two unexpected daughters-in-law, wives to Sage's older brothers, the boys who were slated to be the next generation of Alligator Hat smiths. Six women in one kitchen was a crowd indeed. As the guest, Fawn seized bottom place in the pecking order of work flow, dislodging Calla, who'd only been there three weeks, unexpectedly upward. Tall, gawky Calla seemed more tense than grateful.

Mama Smith, her daughter, and both sisters-in-law displayed a decided coolness toward Calla, too, which puzzled Fawn. Truly, there were way too many women in this house already, not to mention Smiths in the smithy, but Calla seemed very much in support of her young husband and his northward trek. Fawn would have thought Calla's mama-in-law would be softened by that, as she was plainly fond of her youngest son. But Fawn's musing had to wait while they put out food for, finally, fifteen adults and two toddlers in the kitchen and dining room and spilling over into the parlor. And then there was the washing up.

Dag had slipped away before dinner to secure their inn room, so was able to free Mama Smith from her dilemma of which family members to dislodge in her packed house to gain a decent bed for unforeseen married guests. As Fawn had guessed, Finch, Barr, and Arkady were offered bachelor space next to Ash and Indigo in the smithy loft, though Fawn could see Mama Smith was a bit doubtful about Arkady.

Barr had done well through dinner, repeating some of his milder river anecdotes in the few edgewise spaces given him. Fawn had said heartening things about Oleana. Dag had let Finch describe his adventures with Sparrow, making his shyness look wise and mysterious. Arkady had said nothing at all. Fawn didn't think any of the household took his well-disguised terror for anything but standoffish Lakewalker pride, which was likely just as well. She wondered if he'd ever been inside a farmer house before last night. Barr did help him get his bedroll up to the loft.

Fawn waved good-bye in the gathering darkness and let Dag escort her across the square.

The inn room proved small, but pretty and clean, and wonderfully quiet. Dag guaranteed it free of crawly pests. Fawn gave her husband a hug for finding it, then rested her head on his chest with a tired sigh.

"Are you all right?" he asked, stroking her hair. "It was a long day for you."

"Plenty more of those to come. No, I'm fine. I do wonder what's going on with Sage and Calla, though. I liked him pretty well, but she's cold as a fish. And his family doesn't like her one bit. But nobody vented to me. Usually, in a family that big, there's at least someone who'll tell their complaints to anyone listening. You can't shut them up."

Dag hesitated. "Didn't you realize?"

"Realize what?"

"Calla and her brother are both half bloods."

Fawn's hand stole unwilled to her belly, spreading protective fingers. "No," she said slowly. "I hadn't realized that."

13

The departure in the morning from the smithy yard was even more of an uproar than the one from the Bridger farm. As he tightened his girths for the second—no, *third* time and swung up on Copperhead, neatly avoiding a welcoming cow-kick, Dag found himself falling into his old patrol leader habit of doing ground checks on every person, animal, and piece of equipment in range. The result was actually heartening: *young, healthy, and in repair* pretty much summed it up. Well, with a couple of exceptions on the *young* part, including Copperhead. But with a portable smithy and a portable medicine tent, together with folks who knew how to work them, Dag's party was vastly better prepared for the Trace than most travelers.

My party? Really? Speaking of habits. Because he was fairly sure Sage thought of it as his party, and Finch as his, and for all Dag knew, Ash felt the same. Arkady was the one certain exception. Despite Dag's stern remarks on self-reliance, Barr as silent conspirator had made sure Arkady and all his gear were loaded in good time, giving him no excuse to either break back to New Moon in a panic, or drag his feet hoping for an envoy of peace to pelt up.

The entire Smith family turned out to send their son off to his new life in the scary north, with lots of little presents popped into the back of the wagon at the last moment. A couple of folks from Ash's family turned up, too. In the mob, it took a while for Dag to notice that there seemed to be no one at all for Calla and Indigo. There might be half a dozen sound reasons for this, starting with prior good-byes like Finch's. But Dag's mind picked at it anyway, as a six-mule wagon, seven riders, and four pack animals turned onto the Trace and struck north.

It was another dry day, thankfully. The Trace along here was well maintained by the villages that lived on its bounty, with deep creeks sturdily bridged, shallow ones with fords that nearly qualified as paved. Even the mud puddles today were minor, to be splashed through cheerfully, and not yard-deep traps for wagon wheels. After a good night's sleep, Fawn rode along on Magpie with her head up, taking in everything. Unaware of how busily that bright ground in her belly swirled, self-making of the highest order. Now, there was true magic, world magic.

After an hour, the caravan sorted itself out and settled into the rhythm of the road. The way here was wide and straight. Dag took the chance to ride up alongside Finch, trailed by his pair of plodding pack mules. Fawn cast Dag a curious glance and kicked Magpie up on Finch's other side. Finch gave them both friendly smiles, making it easy for Dag to start.

"Known Sage long?"

"Oh, years. His papa's was the closest big smithy to us, so we'd go every couple of months for repairs and special shoeing and whatnot. Stayed the night in Alligator Hat, usually. We two tads used to play together while the work got done. As we got bigger, his papa and big brothers let us work together alongside them. They taught me a lot." Finch vented a nostalgic sigh.

"And Ash?"

"He's more a friend of Sage's than mine. Lives near the Hat. His family has a poor strip of a farm, so he always knew he'd have to find another way. He's been talking about the north for years."

"And, ah, Calla and Indigo?"

Fawn shot him a look across Finch's saddlebow, aware, as the boy was not, of the reason for Dag's newly acute interest in half bloods. And hers. Dag could just about see her ears prick up.

"They used to be Sage's neighbors when they were younger. Their folks had a harness shop on the square."

Dag considered his next question carefully. Were Calla and Indigo's bloodlines known to their village? Bastardy was not a Lakewalker concept. Any child born to a Lakewalker woman was a full member of her tent, whether the parents were string-bound or not. *As long as the father is a Lakewalker, too,* Dag reminded himself. Farmers held a stricter view of paternity, tied as it was to their inheritances. If these siblings were the secret gifts of some passing patroller, Dag didn't want to be the first to explode their lives with the news. He finally settled on, "Tell me about their parents."

Fawn's brows twitched; she gave him an approving nod. He'd evidently got that one right, good.

"Oh, yeah, you would be interested in that, wouldn't you?" Finch said blithely. "Their papa was a Lakewalker maker from Moss River. He left his camp to marry their mama, but he took her farmer name just like you did Fawn's. Funny. I'm not sure how they first met; something to do with their trade, I think."

Dag relaxed a little.

Fawn asked, "What happened to them? They weren't out for the send-off this morning, were they?"

"Oh, no. Eight, ten years ago, Alligator Hat had the worst outbreak of yellow fever—they still call it the Fever Summer. Indigo's whole family came down with it. His mama and little sister died, but Indigo and his papa and Calla got better."

Fawn's eyes widened. "Oh my."

Fawn had only seen the south in its more idyllic seasons. Dag was just as glad she'd be spared the full summer, when the heat came down like a hammer and you near choked on the water in the air, and mosquitoes patrolled in clouds almost as bad as northern Luthlian bogs, and for more months running. And lethal fevers of half a dozen sorts raged unchecked till the laggard frosts. "Then what?"

"Well, their papa took a long time recovering, and was pretty unhappy at that. The harness shop failed."

From the loss of the work of his wife's hands? Or from having the heart torn out of the household? And of him, maybe. It was Dag's turn to grow uneasy. While his groundwork might aid Fawn in some dire illness, he'd never pictured being deathly ill himself at the same time.

"He finally set Indigo and Calla with his wife's sister, and went back to his people at Moss River Camp."

"He abandoned his children?" said Fawn indignantly.

"No, not really. He visited and brought their aunt and uncle horses and hides a couple of times a year, and other presents for them—cash money when he had it. Indigo and Calla were happy enough on her farm when they were younger, I guess."

Dag was uncomfortably reminded of the renegade Crane's tale. If Crane had had a more cooperative sister-in-law—or a more cooperative camp—might he have worked out some less disastrous fate? So was it the rigidity of the north, or was it Crane's own chaos that had been the problem? Or both?

Fawn peeked over her shoulder at the wagon rumbling maybe twenty paces back, Sage and Calla on the box, Indigo riding alongside. Out of earshot, for now. "And when they got older?" she asked.

"It was all right till lately." Finch's lips thinned. "Just the last year or so. There were these accusations. I didn't think much of them. I mean, sure, Indigo's good with animals, but a lot of folks are. Calla took it to heart, though, Indigo says."

"Accusations of what?" asked Fawn.

"Er . . ." Finch cast a sidewise look at Dag. "Lakewalker sorcery. Or powers, anyway. Indigo got in a lot of fights about it. And then, of course, if anything bad happened, just bad luck, to folks he was mad at or who were mad at him, there were suspicions it wasn't luck, but some doing on Calla's part, and Indigo got into even more fights over those. Defending his sister."

"Oh, dear," said Fawn.

"Anyway, it got so bad their aunt made their papa take them to Moss River for some sort of testing. I guess they might have been allowed to be Lakewalkers if they'd passed whatever it was, but they didn't, and the camp sent them back. Which you would think would have stopped the rumors, but it didn't."

"Some people," Fawn sighed.

"Testing?" said Dag.

"A kind of Lakewalker magic, I guess. Weaving or something, which doesn't sound too sorcerous to me. I didn't understand it when Indigo tried to explain. I'm not sure he did, either."

"Practice marriage cords, do you think?" said Fawn across to Dag, touching her own.

"Might have been."

"Too bad they didn't know about—never mind. And then what?"

"Well, luckily this spring Sage went sweet on Calla, and things started working out. I was a little surprised she took to him—she's four, five years older. Mostly, older girls look at you like you're a flour beetle in their bread dough." A distinct sigh. "Anyway, Indigo's notion is that up north, they don't need to tell anyone about their Lakewalker papa, so no one will have reason to give them trouble anymore."

Dag considered this plan. It struck him as overly optimistic. True, fellow farmers wouldn't be able to tell the pair were half bloods, but most Lakewalkers would know with one glance at their grounds. And they'd certainly run into Lakewalkers sometime. But for the moment, he just said, "Mm."

Fawn said rather carefully, "I got the idea Sage's family had taken against Calla, some. Is it her age?"

"She's not *that* much older. And there are plenty of other girls around Alligator Hat just as poor. One of Sage's sisters-in-law had no due-share at all. I guess some of his family believed those stupid rumors, though really, if Calla did have powers, I'd think you'd want them on your side."

He did not deny the familial coolness, Dag noted. The bones of the tale all lined up true. With one joint possibly missing, although it would be easy enough to check now that Dag knew where to look.

"Well," said Fawn, "I hope things work out for them all."

Sincerely.

Waving Fawn to continue her amiable chatting with Finch, Dag held Copperhead back till the mule wagon came alongside. He eased closer to Sage, driving, and touched his temple to Calla, and to Indigo riding beyond. "Fine mornin' for your start."

Sage nodded, and came back friendly-like with, "I take it for a good sign."

Calla sat up and turned her head stiffly Dag's way, watching him as if she feared he might leap from Copperhead and attack her. Dag was reminded of his height, his hook, and his general—what was that phrase Arkady had used?—starveling vagabond air. He really did need Fawn by him, to make him look tame. Yet Calla should be far more used to Lakewalkers than the typical farmer girl. Her alarm was something more particular.

Dag smiled vaguely at them all and opened his ground. *Indeed.* Sage's ground was planted with an ill-formed persuasion, fading as it was absorbed over time. He showed not a trace of beguilement, however. Interesting.

Calla's attention sharpened, as did Indigo's. Both plainly possessed a residual groundsense, Calla's much the stronger. Likely not the doubled vision of the world full-blooded Lakewalkers could call up, of light-shot shadows more weighty and true than the forms that cast them. But Dag would certainly seem suddenly more *there* to them, when he opened like this. Did they understand why? Surely this couldn't be new to them.

"What?" said Calla curtly, eyes narrowing. Tension quivered off her tight ground like noise from a badly tuned fiddle. Indigo was less strained, but alert.

Maybe Fawn could help Dag puzzle out the half-blood girl? They were both young women. Dag scraped for inspiration, and came up with, "I was wonderin', Sage. Happens that my wife Fawn is lately with child, which is partly why we're heading home just now. She's holding up right well so far, but she does get weary in the afternoons. I'm thinking it would ease her to have a lie-down in your wagon, later, when the riding starts to exhaust her."

Calla's face fairly cried *No!*, but before she could speak, Sage said cheerfully, "Why, sure! We'd be happy to help her out. She's such a little bit of a thing, she wouldn't add more to my load than a sack of feathers."

"Thank you kindly! I'll let her know." Dag switched his reins from his hook to his hand and raised his left arm as if in acknowledgment. He let his ghost hand trail out and spread like a net, passing through the back of Sage's head, defusing the tattered persuasion into nothingness, accepting the faint ground backsplash. Sage just smiled at him, blinking. Calla looked worried but deeply uncertain.

As I thought. Good. Dag went on, "If there's anything I can do for you folks—*anything at all*"—his eyes bored into Calla's—"don't wait to ask. I've helped train a world of young patrollers about your ages. There's not too much I haven't seen before."

If Calla was struggling to manage rudimentary ground powers, and it certainly appeared that she was, she needed all the help she could get. But she should have had help before now, blight it. What had her maker father been thinking? Or was she a late bloomer—like Dag—dismissed because someone mistook *not yet* for *not*?

She has to trust me, first. Which wasn't going to happen in their first hour of acquaintance. *Patience, Dag.* They had weeks before them, just like a new patrol. He nodded and reined Copperhead away.

Arkady and Barr were trailing their pack string out of range of the kick-up of dirt from the wagon. At Barr's wave, Dag joined them.

Arkady frowned at him. "What did you just do to your ground?"

"Just a little cleanup. I flushed some old groundwork out of Sage. It would have been absorbed in a few more weeks, but I wanted to see exactly what it was."

"That boy with the lockjaw—now this—your ground is going to be back in the same mess in no time if you keep this up."

Dag shrugged. "Afraid so. *Don't do that* isn't going to be a good enough plan, out here. We need to come up with something else."

"What?"

"I was hoping you might get some new notions, once you had more cud to chew on. You're the brilliant groundsetter. Aren't you?"

Arkady gave him a look between annoyance and amusement. "Don't try those trainer tricks on me. I invented them."

"Well, then." Dag's lips curled up in hope. Two days without a new problem to bite on, and already Arkady was getting restive. Dag just had to keep him moving north, and wait.

Barr, apparently wrenching his mind away from a disturbing vision of Arkady as a cow, said to Dag, "So what was the groundwork?"

"Ah," said Dag. "This may prove to come under what Arkady calls medicine tent work. Which means if I explain it to you, it's in aid of someone, and not for tale-telling."

Barr took this in. "This means if I gossip about it, you pound me?"

"This means you don't gossip about it. Period."

Barr opened his free hand in cautious agreement, and set it again to his thigh.

"I believe Calla tried to persuade or beguile her sweetheart Sage," said Dag. "And failed, near as I can tell."

"Persuade him to do what?" asked Barr.

"It seemed to be what a farmer might call a love spell."

Arkady snorted. "Pointless. The boy's besotted with her."

"I wonder if she realizes that?" Dag was put in mind of Fawn when he'd first met her, lumbered with desperate self-doubts. How could all these young women not *know* how lovely they were? "I don't see my way clear yet, but I figure if I wait and watch, it will all lay itself open to me. Meanwhile, we have these two youngsters here with more than a touch of groundsense, and no one at all to instruct them how to go on with it. They seem to be"—he glanced at Arkady and picked his word—"damaged."

"Oh?" said Arkady, straightening in his saddle.

Hooked you. Dag repeated Finch's tale, more or less, of the two young half bloods blundering between worlds, finding no clear path. Or paths deliberately blocked? Dag's curiosity grew.

In a baffled voice, Barr said, "But you just met them yesterday, Dag. They don't even like us. Why are you taking them up?" Dag's and Arkady's matching looks had barely intersected on his skull when he continued, "Oh. Fawn's pregnancy. Of *course* you want to study half bloods now."

Dag drew breath. "That, too. But do you also remember when I met you and Remo? Why did I take you two up?"

"I don't know," said Barr. Reminded, he glanced back over his shoulder at the empty road where, to his obvious discouragement, no wayward partner galloped to catch up. "I . . . don't know."

He looked for aid to Arkady, who merely shrugged. "I don't know that I can put a name to it, either. But it touches the heart of what marks a true maker. I promise that you didn't get me out on this mad road just because Dag can do some tricks."

Dag exchanged a salute even-all for Arkady's considering nod, then turned Copperhead to catch up with Fawn.

❧

Fawn was glad for the invitation to nap in the wagon, and hardly needed Dag's hint to want to make friends with Calla. But the Trace so fascinated her, she stayed upright on Magpie for the whole of that afternoon. The landscape was much the same as it had been since Graymouth—now fifty-odd miles behind them—a succession of swamps, woods, woods in swamps, cleared fields on the higher ground, and little villages. The good weather brought out not only local traffic—farm wagons and riders and pack mules—but road crews. They passed gangs of men and boys shoveling up barrows of dirt from the verges to raise the crown above the wet, or filling in low spots with wagonloads of gravel. It seemed to be a point of pride for each village to maintain the famous road in its vicinity; Fawn learned to spot the debatable boundaries between townships by the ruts.

During a midafternoon break, they were passed by what Fawn thought of as real Trace traffic, a caravan of some forty northbound mules loaded high with crates of valuable black tea. A muleteer strode along for every three beasts, fellows whose rough looks would have alarmed her before her time on the river, though now she could see they were merely ex–flatboat crews working their way home. They stared back at the bright wagon, and at her and Calla, but didn't make rude hoots or anything. Indigo complained that the caravan would grab off the best campsites and their beasts eat all the new spring grass, and leave a lot of alarming-sounding mule diseases in their trampled wake, but Sage allowed amiably that their party could likely find other sites.

Some farms bordering the road made a bit of coin renting fenced pastures by the night for just this purpose. With seventeen animals to feed, this was tempting despite everyone's youthfully slim purses, although the Smith women had loaded on enough gift grub for people that no one was going to have to cook for the first three days. But just before sunset they came upon an open meadow along a watercourse that no one seemed to be demanding payment for, not too eaten down by prior visitors, so they pulled off.

The still, brown channel was overhung with creeper-laced cypresses and thick with mysterious shadows and birdcalls, and Fawn was grateful for the Lakewalkers making an alligator patrol before bed. All they stirred up was a family of scurrying animals that looked to be the unlikely offspring of a possum mating with a turtle. Dag, accused, denied that ancient or recent Lakewalker magery had anything to do with the armor-plated possums. When the boys poked them with sticks they rolled up like pill bugs, inspiring a brief round of creature-ball till they unrolled and scampered indignantly away.

Sodden with fatigue, Fawn fell into their bedroll, pleased to learn the night song of a mockingbird from the circle of Dag's arms; the next thing she knew, morning light tickled her eyes.

This day's start was quicker but not so lively. She wasn't the stiffest, climbing up onto her horse again; Arkady seemed creakier, but his chill squint defied anyone to comment. Dag and Barr mirrored each other in a series of patroller stretches accompanied by a rude, rhyming challenge chant that set them both laughing, but allowed them to lunge up onto their mounts without groans. Indigo was fun to watch, helping Sage hitch up their mules. When he talked to the beasts, coaxing and cajoling and praising, Fawn could almost imagine them talking back, or at least signaling with their big floppy ears. It wasn't near the overwhelming effect Dag had on mice—fortunately, as being followed about by half a dozen entranced mules might get awkward—but put her in mind of it.

But by that afternoon, not all the charms of the Trace could keep her upright in her saddle. She crawled into the warm and creaking shadow of the wagon's canvas roof with a thankful moan, and didn't wake till the light was growing golden. Her mouth felt as if she'd been chewing on cotton, but at least her limbs didn't seem to be dripping off. Recalling her mandate to make friends, she went forward to the box. Calla stiffened at her greetings, but Sage obligingly scooted over so she might sit up on his other side.

"Long way to Tripoint," Fawn observed invitingly, gazing down over the harnessed backs of the mules. She liked the way their ears bobbed like swaying branches as they walked briskly along.

"Yep," agreed Sage. "Though we have a good pace going, so far. If we can keep it up, it might take us a week to hit the Barrens, and maybe two after that to make the Hardboil River ferry. Which will be about the halfway mark, folks say."

The Barrens, Dag had explained to Fawn, were a two-hundred-mile-wide tongue of ancient blight extending due east from the Western Levels that had for long divided north from south. For most of a millennium, the only way across had been around, either down the Gray River or up the eastern seaboard. It had only become safely passable again a few hundred years ago. Because malices did not come up on old blight, no Lakewalkers patrolled that waste, and no farmers attempted to wrest a living from its still-bitter soils. Without camp or village markets, folks crossing it had to pack all their own supplies. Rumor made it bandit country, which went with the lack of patrols, Fawn supposed.

"I saw a bit of the Barrens when we were passing down the Gray on the *Fetch*," Fawn offered. "Scrubby country, all sandy and flat, and no river towns at all. Quiet stretch, but it was still a relief when we got past it and saw green again."

This triggered a string of interested questions from Sage about their river journey. Inevitably, their encounter with the awful river bandits infesting Crooked Elbow came out, but Fawn downplayed it in favor of explaining as much as she could about Dag's dreams for healing the divisions between her people and his. She'd thought his notion of a Lakewalker medicine maker treating farmers might draw Calla out, but the young woman kept stubbornly silent.

Fawn tried a more direct lure, explaining how Dag, she, Hod, and Remo had among them cracked unbeguilement, that memorable day back up on the Grace. "It wasn't something either a Lakewalker or a farmer alone could have figured out. It took all of us, working together."

This finally startled a question from Calla: "Your husband can unbeguile folks?"

"He can do no end of groundwork, these days. Arkady's even better."

This news failed to cheer up Calla; if anything, she looked . . . fearful? Yet Fawn couldn't see how a girl with a Lakewalker maker for a father could be afraid of groundwork. "Didn't you ever watch your papa making?"

Calla shrugged. "I was a child. I couldn't tell that he was doing anything more than sewing leather."

Oh. Right. Groundsense didn't come in till a person was more than half grown, and Calla had been barely that when her mama had died and her papa had left her with her farmer kin.

Calla added after a moment, in an oddly wistful tone, "Folks always wanted to buy his work, though. Harness and bridles and saddles. It was plain, but it was extra pretty, somehow. And it never broke." She straightened, jaw clamping as though she regretted letting even this mild memory escape.

"I remember that," said Sage.

For a little while Fawn was able to get Sage—but not Calla—to reminisce about growing up in Alligator Hat, and she offered tales of West Blue in trade. Then Indigo cantered back from scouting ahead, claiming to have spotted one of those rentable pastures too fine and cheap to pass up. Arriving at the site, everyone agreed he was right, and they turned off for the night.

Sage drew the wagon to a halt in a stand of pecan trees just coming into leaf, overlooking a sparkling creek much too shallow to conceal alligators. Fawn approved. He went off to find the farmhouse and offer his coins, and Fawn followed Calla down from the box, glad to have unmoving ground under her feet. The two came briefly face-to-face, and Fawn smiled brightly.

"*Why* do you keep bothering me?" said Calla through her teeth.

"I'd like to be friends. We've a long road ahead." Why Fawn should feel a *maternal* regard for a girl five or six years older than herself was hard to explain, but she did. Or maybe not so hard. "Seems I'm newly interested in happiness for half bloods."

"If you really wanted to increase happiness, you wouldn't be making *more* half bloods," snapped Calla, and strode away.

Fawn blinked, a bit discouraged. *That did not go well. Yet. Keep trying.* She made her way over to the less-prickly Indigo, who was starting to unharness the mules, thinking up some unexceptionable praise for his animal handling.

ᴠ

As darkness fell, Dag walked the perimeter of the pasture in pure patroller habit, but sensed no danger for a mile in any direction. He wandered back to the creek and eased himself down on a rock, listening to the gurgle of the water and the munching of the mules. Copperhead came over and lipped his hair, and Dag took a moment to impress upon the gelding, again, that there were to be no random attacks upon his pasture mates tonight. Magpie, being more ladylike, needed no such persuasion. The two horses wandered away downstream in search of sweeter grass.

Dag became aware that he was being stalked, more or less. A thin figure approached from the shadows as cautiously as a hunter sneaking up on a bear or a catamount, or some other dangerous beast that might turn and rend. He sat still and waited.

Before long, Calla's hoarse voice demanded, "What do you want?"

"Beg pardon?" said Dag.

"What is it that you'll take, to leave me and mine alone?"

Dag's brows drew down. "Missus Smith, I truly do not understand that question."

"Don't make mock of me!" Her voice was sharp, but with a quaver at the end.

He reckoned a year of living with Fawn must have made him more fluent in female. He could already tell it was going to be one of *those* conversations. "Ma'am, I'm not. I'd take it as a privilege to help you out. And your brother, though it's plain you're the more gifted in groundsense. Someone should have taken you both in hand before this."

"We don't need help. We don't need Lakewalkers." Her voice went lower and, if possible, more bitter. "Lakewalkers don't need us."

"Maybe not at Moss River, but not all Lakewalkers think like that. What was that test Finch was talking about—weaving your ground into a cord?"

"What about it?"

"You should have passed."

Her voice went lower still. "Indigo didn't. So I didn't."

Dag's brows rose. "You deliberately failed?"

"They would have separated us. Kept me, thrown Indigo away. Everyone else had left us, one way or another. I wasn't going to do that to him, not again."

"Whose idea was it to go north? Yours, or his, or . . . ?"

"The boys always talked about it. But it was just talk. After Moss River, I wanted to get away from everything so bad, but it was too dangerous to go by ourselves. I had enough magic to make us targets, but not enough to protect us. We had to have the others, we *had* to."

"Seems sensible thinking to me," Dag said cautiously.

"Please"—her voice broke—"don't take that away from us."

Dag held his ground open wide, in the hopes she might sense he told no lies. "You talking about that attempt of yours to persuade Sage?"

"You sensed it?" A sharp-drawn breath. "Don't touch it, you—! I'll give you—I don't know what. I don't have much money, but I can give you some."

"Absent gods, I don't want your money!"

A long pause. "I've only got one other thing." And from the scrunch in her shoulders, not something she'd be pleased to part with, not to him.

Dag was startled, bemused, and more than a little offended. "Absent gods! No. You're young enough to be my daughter, you know."

"So's your wife." A brittle pause. "Oh, full blood, you have to be older than you look. Granddaughter."

"Now, that's going a mite too far!" He didn't know whether to laugh or be horrified.

Calla stood rigid. "It seemed it might be a fixation of yours. Younger women."

Dag said sternly, "Fawn and I are a long story that you might learn more of if you listen, but in the meanwhile, don't talk ignorant rubbish. Fawn's earned every bit of loyalty I can give her." His voice slowed. "We have a fair trade going on, that way."

Calla flinched.

It finally clicked in. *Oh gods, I'm slow.* "I take it you believe you magicked young Sage into marrying you and taking you and your brother north?"

"You know I did, Lakewalker. His family suspected. His sister told me to my face Sage wouldn't have looked twice at such a horse-faced rack of bones without it."

Dag began to speak, hesitated, and reversed the order. "You figure your spell is still holding? He hasn't treated you any different, the past couple of days?" It was a safe question; there had been a couple of happy grounds in that feather bed just last night, together with some faint, distinctive creaking from the wagon that sheltered it.

"Of course it's holding. Or he'd have cast me off by now."

"Well, no. If you'd had the training you should have, you'd know those sorts of persuasions are absorbed over time, and have to be renewed to keep working. That groundwork of yours faded weeks ago. In any case, I cleared the last of it out of Sage early yesterday."

A faint cry, choked off. She quivered like a filly about to bolt.

"Stand still!" Dag used his old patrol captain's voice; she froze rigid. "Straighten up, girl, and gather the wits you were born with. I'm not saying your initial persuasion didn't cause Sage to take a second look at you, because I think it likely did. But it was what he saw that made him stay. He doesn't love you because you magicked him." Dag's voice softened. "He loves you because you're lovable."

The kindness nearly broke her as the sternness never would; once again, Dag was reminded of Fawn. Tears laced her gasp, but she steadied her breathing. And listened; oh my, she was listening with all her heart now. *Here's your chance, old patroller; go carefully.*

"More to the point," he went on, "Sage was never a bit beguiled by you. And for the same reason that my groundwork on Fawn doesn't beguile her. Your heart was entirely open to him, so your grounds flowed both ways, and he never choked on the imbalance.

"So as he loves you, and as you like him right well, too—and both your grounds prove it—there's not a reason in the wide green world you can't rub along as well or better than any other married couple. You could have set your persuasion into any other youth in Alligator Hat. You picked well when you picked Sage. I think you know that."

"Oh . . . !"

"Though you might care to clear the air with a confession. It's bound to make it easier between you not to be hiding that useless secret. And it will straighten out your ground for your next lessons in groundwork."

"He'll hate me!"

"Well"—Dag scratched his head for show—"I'm not saying he won't be a touch unsettled, but he knew about your powers before, and they didn't scare him off none. He might be flattered. A tall, handsome"— *alarming*—"older girl plucks him out from all the other fellows . . . he might even be proud."

He could tell by her stillness that this was a completely new thought to her.

"And if he has any questions, he can bring them to me or Arkady. I meant it when I said I've helped a passel of youngsters learn to manage their groundsense. And trust me, some of them were even more thorny than you. You may not need Moss River—in fact, it seems Moss River was exactly what you didn't need—but you need *someone* to show you how to go on."

She'd moved close enough for him to see her; her hands clutched her hair. "But I don't *want* this. These powers."

"Then you can choose not to use them. But that's not a choice you *can* make before you've learned to command them. Until then, you'll just be blundering around in the dark bumping into things and hurting yourself—and maybe others—through ignorance."

For the first time, her silence grew considering, and not just frightened. "I can . . . choose not to be . . . ?"

"If you learn enough. And what I can't teach, Arkady surely can. Chance has given you a prize, this journey. Absent gods, girl, seize it. I mean to."

Calla made a faint, confused noise, and Dag explained, "Arkady's my teacher."

"You have a teacher? At your age?"

Dag chose to ignore the second part of that. "Yes. And Fawn teaches me, too. She's taught me more this past year than I imagined possible. The whole world teaches me new things every day, now that she's made me alive to it again. You teach me."

"What do *I* teach you?" Calla stared in bewilderment.

"What half bloods need, to start with. I expect there will be more surprises, as we go along." He rose from his rock, gave her his softest salute. "I can hardly wait. Good night, Missus Smith."

"Uh . . . good night, Mister Bluefield . . ."

He tracked her trudge back toward her wagon and her waiting husband. He was reminded that he had a bedroll warmed by a waiting wife, but detoured through the nearby trees. A long, pale shadow detached itself from a pecan bole as he neared.

"Do you think she has the makings of a maker?" said Dag to Arkady.

"In some small, useful ways, undoubtedly."

"I hope you don't mind me volunteering you, sir."

"No . . ." A shrewd pause. "All in all, that was well done."

From Arkady, who was quite capable of prefacing his milder critiques with *You gormless, ham-handed half-wit!* this was true praise.

"I hope so, sir," said Dag. "I surely do."

14

Over the next few days Fawn was heartened to see Arkady chatting often with Calla, riding beside the wagon or even sitting on the box. Barr helped Indigo with the animals. With each of the half bloods tucked under a suitable Lakewalker wing, Dag rode alone during Fawn's fatigue naps. She watched him curiously over the tailboard, turning that walnut in his hand and brooding over it. *He's working up to something.*

Swampy Alligator Hat lay over a hundred miles behind them when they first hit rain, and even then they only had to pull the wagon out of mire once and warp it across swollen fords with ropes twice. Coming into the last stretch of farmland south of the Barrens, Ash Tanner led them aside some miles for a planned rest at his uncle's farm, where they were made welcome despite the surprise additions to the party. The animals were set to graze for a day, and the people turned to topping up their supplies for the pull ahead.

That afternoon, Dag and Fawn retreated to their bedroll, which they'd laid in the most private corner of the Tanner barn loft—although, Fawn suspected, not for the reason their comrades thought.

They were left strictly alone anyway, which likely suited Dag's purposes just as well.

Climbing down afterward, Dag led her off to seek out Barr and Arkady. A roof on posts along one side of the barn sheltered a work area free of the misting rain. Barr had their saddles and bridles up on sawhorses, giving them a cleaning. If Arkady was doing anything besides keeping him company, it wasn't apparent to Fawn, but they did break off some chat as she and Dag came around the corner.

Dag set her in front of him, hand on her right shoulder, wooden wrist cuff resting on her left. "I need you two a moment," he said to the Lakewalkers.

Barr set down his brush and rag; Arkady, leaning against a post with his arms crossed, lifted his eyebrows.

"What in the world did you do to Fawn's ground?" asked Barr. "It's all . . . shiny." He closed his eyes to—Fawn supposed *see better* didn't quite make sense, and she surely couldn't feel it, but a vague discomfort filled her to be the focus of his uncanny attention. As for Arkady, she didn't even attempt to read the intent stillness of his face.

"Well," said Dag, "that's what I need you to help me test. Barr, try to plant a persuasion in Fawn's ground."

"Er . . . what kind?"

"Whatever you're best at. It doesn't have to be well shaped."

"That's fortunate," murmured Arkady.

Dag shot him a quelling look. "I'll lift it right out again if you succeed. Just anything."

Hesitantly, Barr approached and started to lay his hand on her breast, glanced at Dag, and prudently moved it up to her collarbone. He frowned at the walnut that lay there, held by a cord plaited of her hair. The walnut was not pierced, but trapped in a woven net that continued unbroken into the braid circling her neck. "Huh!" he said after a moment. "I can sense her ground—she's not really veiled—but the work slides off. Like rain on a window."

"Good." Dag turned her; obediently, she shuffled around. He dropped his hand away and said, "Now, Arkady. Try to ground-rip her. The way I did you at the camp gate my first day."

Arkady cocked his head and made a short gesture. Nothing happened. He blinked, came closer, and lifted her hand in his. His other finger traced a line across the back. Fawn felt a twinge like winter sparks in a wool blanket. "Interesting," he said, in a neutral tone. "Her ground seems to dimple away as I try to grip it."

"Dag, have we really done it?" Fawn said breathlessly. "Made a ground shield for farmers?"

He sighed uncertainly. "Maybe. Enough to protect you from ordinary persuasion or beguilement, and the sort of ground-ripping I—a person can do. But a malice is much more powerful, and I don't know how to test for that. It's not like I'm going to set you out as bait."

"Maybe someone"—she glanced at Barr—"could get a patrol to take a volunteer farmer out somewhere to try it. Up north, maybe, where the malices are thicker. Or at least, try it on their youngsters."

Dag shook his head. "I'm still not sure this shield would work on Lakewalker grounds. They're too active."

"So, try one on Barr and find out."

Barr gulped. "Er . . . all right. Makes sense."

Fawn said, "It's too bad we don't have a Lakewalker child to try it on. Maybe later."

Brightening, Dag told Arkady, "At least I've half solved the problem of how to turn it off. All Fawn has to do is remove the necklace, and the link to her ground will break. Thing is, she'd need me to do all that groundwork over again to link it back to her. In the ideal design, the farmer would be able to take it on and off at will. Leastways I've proved the principle of the thing."

Arkady gave him a thoughtful nod. "I didn't think you'd get this far." Brows tightening, he took up Fawn's hand and stroked it with his finger again; she shivered at the prickle. "Now I hesitate to guess how far you can take this."

Dag watched her hand intently. "That contraction seems to be a natural response, of a sort. After I was near ground-ripped by the Raintree malice, Mari said my ground was so tight nobody could get in to help me. Had to take her word for it—I was out cold. She said she'd never seen anyone look more like a corpse and still breathe."

"Even if it doesn't protect farmers from malices, it seems it protects them from Lakewalkers," Fawn said. "Like Barr's cook-pot helmets for real. It *changes* things. Um . . ." She glanced up at Barr and Arkady. "What about—Dag's—someone at Hickory Lake once told me that because farmers couldn't veil their grounds, it was like they were walking around naked, to Lakewalker eyes. What is this doing for that? And don't be polite," she added sharply. "Tell me the truth."

"In ground veiling"—Barr held up his hand and turned it edge on—"it's like the Lakewalker's ground slowly gets thinner and thinner till it vanishes. From the inside, it looks like the world's ground does the same, like going back to being a child when you couldn't sense at all. With this, your ground's density is all still there, but it's like I'm seeing it under moving water. I can't make out the details. If you see?"

Well, being dressed in thin cloth was better than parading around stark. Fawn nodded satisfaction. She wrapped her hand around the walnut. *What an extraordinary birthday present this is turning out to be.* "Should I keep it on?" she asked Dag.

"Yes, I want to see how long that involution will hold up. Sharing knives may last a lifetime, but lesser work fades sooner."

"That's going to hold awhile, I wager," said Arkady.

Fawn slipped the walnut pendant inside her blouse. "I wonder how one would work on Calla or Indigo? Like on a farmer, or like on a Lake-walker?"

Dag's eyes narrowed. "Huh. Good question, Spark." His gaze strayed to her middle. "If they're starting to trust me enough . . . I'll ask them to let me try. Later. Not now. It's going to take me some days to recover from this."

"Talk to Calla before you offer such a shield to Sage," advised Arkady. "I wouldn't want her to take it amiss. I've just about got her taking food from my hand, so to speak, but she's still nervy." He paused. "It's been quite a while since I've instructed a beginner. I'll give her this—at least she doesn't have any bad training for me to undo."

Dag nodded understanding. A sly smile slipped over his mouth and vanished, by which Fawn guessed he was pleased that Arkady was taking his new student seriously.

⟶

Over the next days, the swampy alligator country fell behind. Villages grew poorer and farther apart and the road surface deteriorated, with fewer bridges and worse fords. In places with softer soil, the way was beaten down into a broad track between earthen walls that rose higher than their heads. Farms were replaced by piney woods. In the growing heat, the trees breathed a delicious and oddly northern smell that made Dag smile for no reason Fawn could see, but she was glad of it nonethe-less.

Local traffic thinned out. Their only company on the road became others sharing the long haul. More folks were headed north than south, what with the rivers disgorging their travelers onto the Trace at Graymouth. They passed gangs of flatboat men walking home, and were passed by speedier horse pack trains, including some Lakewalker kin carrying trade between camps. They played leapfrog with that tea caravan for days, and, when Fawn, Dag, and Barr proved conversant in river talk, ended up getting to know some of the muleteers by name.

The last village before the Barrens going north, or the first after coming south, guarded a rope-cranked ferry, a smaller version of those Fawn had seen up on the Grace. The crowd trying to cross at the river-bank held them up for half a day. On the other side, the road climbed again. The piney woods grew more ragged and sad, then thinned out into scrubland inhabited only by mice, hawks, rabbits, and wild pigs. The shadeless stretches turned headache-hot. Roadside camping spots with both water and grazing became harder to find, as prior travelers' beasts of burden had eaten the scanty fodder far back from the road.

Two days into the Barrens and their novelty had worn off for Fawn, to be replaced by her nausea of pregnancy. This lasted till she fled from the campfire one morning to retch in the bushes, and Arkady, with an incredibly smug smirk, produced a bottle of that Lakewalker stomach medicine from his pack. He only made Dag grovel a little for it. In the evenings Arkady took Dag aside for maker ground-projection and sensitivity drills, and Dag retaliated by making Barr and Arkady do patroller ground-veiling drills. The results of the latter left Dag frowning.

One evening, they camped with some friendly flatboat boys who knew the Clearcreeks, and exchanged much river gossip including garbled accounts of the gruesome events at Crooked Elbow, which Dag, Fawn, and Barr tried to amend. Dag treated a flatboat boy's sore foot and seized the chance for his beginner lecture on Lakewalkers; Fawn wasn't sure which of these left Arkady rubbing his forehead. But at least it was a thoughtful rub.

The lack of grazing proved worse than the company had anticipated, and the feed grain they'd so prudently packed along from the Tanner farm ran low, then out. But late one afternoon Ash, whose turn it was to scout ahead, came cantering back all excited. The fertile valley he described seemed too good to be true, but a few miles farther on, at a dip where a river ran between high rocky walls and around a bend, they found a broad sweep of meadow, flecked by wildflowers, that glowed like green glass in the leveling light. Dozens of dogwoods lit up the woods like white flower fountains. New leaves, Fawn realized, weren't just pale green, but shades of bronze and copper red. Both people and animals greeted the sight with the same joyful sigh.

This bliss lasted till Sage, who had gone into the woods bordering the bluffs to gather firewood, came bolting back out waving his bloodied ax in the air and screaming, "Snakes! Hundreds of 'em! And they're all rattlers!"

Fawn, about to unsaddle Magpie, scrambled back aboard and pulled up her toes. "What?"

"There can't be hundreds," objected Finch. "Snakes don't travel in *herds*, Sage. You just panicked."

"Yeah, how many did you really see?" said Ash. "Two? Three?" Although he prudently unshipped another long-handled ax from his pack.

"Actually . . ." said Dag, slowly wheeling about and scanning the rocky slopes.

Disturbed and attentive silence fell, broken only by Sage's panting. Everyone's faces turned to follow Dag, like beguiled mice.

" . . . there *are* hundreds," Dag continued. "Those ledges up there are full of snake dens. They coil up in snake balls to get through the cold times, see. They're all just coming out of their winter sleep."

Finch swung abruptly up onto the driver's box next to Calla.

"You can get up to a couple of hundred rattlesnakes at a time in the bigger dens," Dag went on blithely.

Indigo looked in longing at the rich grass. All the tired, hungry animals had their heads down tearing at it. "We could all hole up in the wagon, I guess, but—would they bite the mules and horses?"

"They might," Dag said. "More usually they'd just slither off. But with so many so thick around here, an accident becomes more likely."

"Can't you Lakewalkers, like, persuade them to stay away?" asked Fawn nervously. "If you can summon your horses, can't you, um, un-summon snakes?"

Ash raised his ax. "If we all worked together, I bet we could clear them out of here permanent."

Arkady remarked, as if to the air, "The most common snakebite victims I've treated are young men. Beer is frequently involved. Mostly, the bites are on the arms, but one fellow managed to get bitten on his ear and one . . . well, I trust it happened in his bedroll. Because it would have taken a great deal of beer to account for it, otherwise."

"Bedroll?" said Fawn.

"Snakes are attracted to body heat," Dag explained. "They like to cuddle up with you under your blankets. In snake country, patrollers learn to wake up very carefully."

"Yeah," muttered Barr. "Especially if there are other patrollers around."

A white grin flickered over Dag's mouth that didn't reassure Fawn one bit. Their bedroll would be laid out on the grass tonight . . . "Dag . . . ?" It wasn't loud enough to be a wail, exactly, but it was quite pitiable nonetheless.

He gave up some inner vision, which she resolved not to ask about till they were miles from here, and motioned to Barr and Arkady.

"Come on. Let's show these farmer boys and girls a patroller snake drive."

Arkady sighed in a *Must I?* sort of way, but didn't argue when Dag assigned him to the other side of the little river. He picked and waded his way across, and trudged up the opposite slope.

"Calla, Indigo—you want to learn how to do this?"

"No!" said Calla, and "Um . . ." said her brother.

"It might be a good trick to know if you ever get snakes on your porch or under your house. Before your children find 'em," Dag remarked.

An arrested look came over Calla's long face. After a brief silence, she nodded and joined Dag. After another moment, Indigo trod reluctantly after Barr. Sage gulped, gripped his ax, and followed Calla. Dag's voice faded in the distance, rising and falling in his patrol-leader lecture cadence, as he led them upstream and angled into the woods.

Fawn stayed atop Magpie. *If I ever find snakes on my porch, I'll yell for Dag,* she decided firmly.

She couldn't spot them at first, but she could see the grass quiver: here, then there, then over there, then seemingly everywhere. And she could hear the rustling, growing louder. Then, at the water's edge, sinuous diamond-patterned forms in brown and dirty white appeared, thick, spade-shaped heads questing. First in ones and twos, and then in tangled dozens, the rattlesnakes slid into the churning water and were swept downstream, swirling in clotted mats like tangled branches.

On the opposite bank, Arkady's snakes approached in neat ranks of ten across, and entered the water in a synchrony that unfortunately broke up as soon as they encountered the rocks and Dag's snakes. Dag and Arkady called rather rude critiques upon each other's snake-herding styles across the water. The *important* part, Fawn decided, was that they were all going *away*.

Dag, Barr, and Arkady and their reluctant apprentices moved down the valley in a wide ragged line, passing out of sight around the river's curve. In about an hour, they all came trudging back. The rest of the company had finally unsaddled the horses and unharnessed the mules, a task somewhat impeded by the big sticks everyone was carrying.

"Mules may safely graze," Dag announced cheerfully. "By the time those poor snakes get out of the water, they'll be chilled through, and then nightfall will keep 'em sluggish. It should take them a few days to find their way home again."

Barr put his hands on his hips, stared down the valley into the setting sun, and shook his head. "You know, if anyone's camping downstream of us, they're going to be in for quite a surprise."

∾

To give the animals time to graze their fill, they made a late start from what Fawn now thought of as Rattlesnake Vale. She was grateful to be on the road before any of the wet and surly inhabitants returned.

As the day wore on, she could see that they were finally passing out of the Barrens. Streams grew more common, and trees taller and more abundant, climbing out of the watercourses to crown the heights once more. There were no farms as yet, though Dag said roving herders brought their flocks up for spring grazing. A debatable country; the southerners called it northern, and the northerners called it southern. Another day, Dag assured her, and the Trace would begin its long descent toward the valley of the Hardboil River, the largest eastern tributary of the great Gray south of the Grace. After that, they'd soon reach the ferry—and beyond, Dag promised her green mountains like vast rolling waves. Fawn stayed awake on Magpie all that afternoon just for the excitement of the thought.

They passed their first crossroad for a hundred miles, and soon after that, another, plainly rutted with wagon-wheel tracks. Riding ahead between Arkady and Dag so as to eat the least road dust, Fawn spotted the return of local traffic: a few riders and walkers not burdened with camping gear, a farm wagon or two, a man, a boy, and dogs with some sheep. The passersby stared and a few times glared back, and Fawn was reminded that not everyone might be as friendly toward a mixed party of farmers and Lakewalkers as the rivermen had proved. Like the rivers, the road passed through places yet was apart from them, no one's native country and everyone's, a space where strangers had to get along with one another will or nil.

Fawn was suggesting they ought to send Barr ahead with Finch tonight to scout for their campsite, just in case, when Arkady turned in his saddle. Coming up around the wagon at an easy lope was a pair of rangy Lakewalker mounts. Their riders were probably partners, Fawn thought; couriers, perhaps. You couldn't tell a patroller man from a patroller woman at a distance by their clothes, but as they neared Fawn saw they were one each, both fit and tall with hair in single braids. The woman wore a long, dark leather coat, loosely open in the warmth, split up the back for riding. Her black braid swung behind her, still as thick as Fawn's arm where it was cut off bluntly to clear her cantle. Her partner's braid only made it past his shoulders, thinning to a sad tail at the end. The woman's face turned curiously toward them as their horses blew past; she had the coppery skin of a true northerner, and her eyes flashed gold.

"Great hair," murmured Arkady. Dag stared, too; Fawn wondered if either man had even noticed the fellow.

"I know that coat!" Dag stood in his stirrups, staring harder. "Could it be—?" He raised his hand to his mouth, and bellowed, "Sumac!"

The woman reined in her mount so hard it nearly squatted on its haunches, wheeling around in almost the same stride. She, too, stood up in her stirrups. Dag switched his reins over and waved his hook.

The woman's gold eyes widened. In an equally startled voice, she yelled back, "Uncle Dag!"

༄

Dag grinned as his niece trotted back to him and pulled up her mount. He gave Copperhead's rein a sharp yank as the gelding attempted to snap. "Now, be nice to the family, old fellow. Redwings are too rare to waste."

Sumac's eyes gleamed with laughter. "I see you still have that awful horse!"

"I see you still have my awful coat." It actually fit her less loosely than it had her older brother, years back, but then Dar's eldest had been a skinny pup during his youthful stint in the patrol. It had then descended through Sumac to her younger brother; Dag had thought it lost.

"You bet I do. I made Wyn give it back soon as he got home from his final exchange. You'll like this—look." She twisted around in her saddle and lifted her thick braid. "See that scratch across the back?"

"Is that new?" It was dyed red, barely visible against the black leather.

"'Bout a year old. My patrol ambushed a malice just going off sessile above Eagle Falls. One of its mud-men yanked a boar spear away from one of my patrollers. Which I made him eat much dirt about later—you'd have been proud. The spear point would have gone straight in and out my chest wall, and just *ruined* my new shirt, but instead it skittered across my back. I let it knock me the rest of the way down and came up rolling, then got inside the swing with my knife and did for the mud-man, very tidy."

Dag concealed the skip in his heartbeat and gave this tale a proper death's-head patroller grin. She had *not* told this story at home, or he would have heard about it before this. With reproaches. "First time that ratty old garment paid for itself, I do believe, after all those years of carting it around."

They were interrupted as the wagon rolled past. Dag waved on a concerned-looking Sage and Calla, and the boys with the pack animals as well. Barr stared over his shoulder, handed his pack string off to Ash, and came trotting back to them.

Fawn's eyes were wide, looking across Dag's saddlebow at tall Sumac. "Is that your old magic coat that was supposed to turn arrows, Dag?"

Sumac's gaze flicked with equal curiosity toward little Fawn. "I've not tried arrows. Rain and spears, definitely. I've become very attached to it, tatters and all. I paid Torri Beaver a pot of coin to renew the groundwork when last I was home, though she offered to make me a new one for not much more. I had her leave the scratch in, for bragging rights. Er . . . you don't want it back, do you, Uncle Dag?"

"Not me. You keep it. My patrolling days are done."

Sumac rolled back in her saddle, fine lips pursing, doubt replacing the merriment in her slitted eyes. "In truth, I hardly recognized your ground. I hardly *do* recognize it."

"Well, it's been what, over a year since we crossed paths? When were you home last?"

"This fall. Just about a month after you left, I was told."

"So you've heard about, um . . . everything."

"And in so many different versions." Her voice slowed. "So . . . is this your infamous farmer bride, Uncle Dag?"

Dag lowered his eyelids, let them rise. "Sumac Redwing Hickory, meet Fawn Bluefield. My wife. You may observe our marriage cords, if you please."

Sumac turned her head, blinked twice. "It seems Dirla and Fairbolt were right about those."

She could have said, *It seems Papa and Grandmama were right about those*; Dag breathed relief. Or maybe Sumac was just being polite. He trusted that her past few years as a patrol leader under Fairbolt Crow had taught her a little more leaderly tact, however much she scorned the mealy-mouthed. "Making me Dag Bluefield, ah . . . No-Camp, at present," he went on.

Her black brows quirked, but she let that pass. "So—Missus Bluefield—I guess that makes you my aunt Fawn, eh?" The two young women regarded each other in mutual contemplation of this absurdity. Sumac shook her head. "Uncle Dag. Who would have guessed?" And after another moment, "What in the world is wrong with her ground?"

"Nothing. It's a little experiment of mine. A ground shield for farmers."

"Groundwork? *You?*"

"It's a long tale."

Fawn put in, "Dag's studying to be a medicine maker. Arkady here is teaching him. He's a real respected groundsetter from the south."

Sumac's astonished lips shaped the word, *Medicine . . . !*

Arkady touched his temple in an almost Dag-like salute. "Arkady Waterbirch New Moon Cutoff, at your service." He'd been almost expressionless, listening to all this family gossip, but now his lips lifted a trifle.

"Maker Waterbirch." Sumac returned a courteous nod, looking deeply bemused.

Barr cleared his throat.

"And Barr from Pearl Riffle Camp, up on the Grace," Dag supplied. "Barr's, um . . . with me."

Barr smiled sunnily. Most young men did, when first exposed to Sumac. Most all men did, actually. The tears came later.

Sumac nodded all around and introduced her partner, or follower. "And this is Rase from New Elm Camp. I took a returning exchange patroller down to New Elm last fall, then stayed on a bit to help train their youngsters. Rase here is coming back with me to Hickory for his first exchange."

"I'm looking forward to meeting the famous Fairbolt Crow," Rase confided to Dag.

Dag quelled the impulse to say something unnerving, and chose instead, "You'll be made welcome. We send out far more patrollers than we ever get back." *We?* How easily that old habit of speech slipped in. "Fairbolt will also work your tail off, but it'll be good for you."

"So I'm hoping, sir." Rase nodded earnestly.

Blight, but trainee patrollers were getting younger every year . . . Dag's half-opened groundsense noted a primed knife in the boy's saddlebags. At least he'd come prepared.

About to turn and lead them out onto the road again, Dag followed Fawn's arrested look to Sumac's knee, and noticed for the first time a bouquet of a couple of dozen fresh rattlesnake skins hanging from her saddlebags—to dry, presumably. A similar lashing hung on the other side, tails down, free to swing and rattle interestingly as she rode. Barr choked. Arkady twitched his brows. Dag resolved not to be the first to break down and ask.

Indigo came cantering back to them. "Dag? Are you coming, or should we wait for you, or what?"

Dag waved at him. "We're coming."

Sumac's eyes lifted to the receding green-painted wagon. "You're with them?" she said. "But they're farmers!"

"It's another long story. We'll be making camp soon—care to join us?"

She glanced at her partner, and up the long road ahead. "We'd planned to reach—never mind. Of course. I wouldn't miss this tale for anything."

Dag let Fawn introduce her—absent gods!—new niece and Rase to Indigo, who rode off to let the others know what was happening. Barr fell behind to talk with Rase, not much younger than himself; Dag, Sumac, Fawn, and Arkady rode abreast at an easy walk.

"It's actually your fault I spent the winter at New Elm, Uncle Dag," Sumac confided to him.

"Oh? And me so . . . not there."

She grinned. "When has that ever stopped anyone from blaming you? No, it was your marriage adventure did it. Of course, Grand-mama's been pressing me forever to bring home a husband to help prop up the tent, and you know how much she *loves* me being in the patrol."

Dag nodded full understanding at this last sarcasm. Of all his sins, inspiring his niece to stay in the patrol was the one that most irked his family. And he hadn't even done it on purpose.

"Lately even Papa's been wading in on her side, or at least not on mine, not that he ever was on mine, but you'll never guess who put in the next oar."

"Omba?" With her elder son safely string-bound, and her two younger children apprenticed to makers and happily courting, Dag hadn't thought his tent-sister would be quite so concerned.

"Of course not Mama! You know when Redwings start to argue she just ducks out and goes to pet her horses. It's likely how she survived all these years. It was Fairbolt. Fairbolt!" Sumac shook her head at this defection. "I was joking around with him about when the next company captain place would open up—well, half joking, half angling, you know the way it is when you're trying to get information out of Fairbolt—and he flat out told me I'd be a shoo-in for it—as soon as I returned to the patrol from my child-years. Then he went on about Massape and Great-aunt Mari."

"Ah," said Dag.

"Without you to hide behind, it seems I'm the new prime target for the Redwing matchmakers."

"Well, you are destined to be the next head of Tent Redwing."

She jerked her chin, making her heavy braid swing. "Shouldn't that be Mama?"

"I'm afraid Cumbia's always thought of your mama as a sort of place-holder."

"I've long plotted that when Grandmama passes, I'll change my name back to Waterstrider. Just to show her, although I suppose it couldn't show her anything by then."

From the far right of the row, the intently listening Arkady made an inquiring noise.

Fawn turned her head to him and put in helpfully, "Dag's mama Cumbia only had the two boys, Dar and Dag. She persuaded Omba Wa-terstrider to change her name to Redwing when she married Dar, so's she'd have a girl to carry on her tent. It was sort of like an adoption, I reckon."

Sumac shook her head. "Mama being the youngest of six girls, there's no shortage of Waterstriders at Hickory Lake Camp. I have about a thousand Waterstrider cousins. And Grandmama's good for another forty years just for stubbornness, I guess, by which time I likely won't care. But she does make me so mad, sometimes. Uncle Dag never could do anything right for her."

Not that he wanted to discourage one of his few partisans, but Dag groped for his supposed maturity and managed, "Cumbia never had an easy life. Nor very rewarding. Or not the rewards she wanted."

Sumac shrugged, and sighed. "*I* know. Oh, feh, of all the ways Grandmama makes me crazy, the worst is when I end up going on about her like this. Don't listen, Dag."

You and me both, youngin'. "How're Cattagus and Mari?" he asked, to put her at her ease again.

She brightened. "Still wheezing and bickering. I love Great-uncle Cattagus. I'll give Fairbolt this, if I could make a marriage like Mari and Cattagus, or like Massape and him, it wouldn't seem half bad."

"So, um," said Fawn—it would be Fawn—"where'd you get all those snake skins, Sumac?"

Sumac's eyes sprang wide. "And if that wasn't the strangest thing I'd ever seen! We'd taken a short cut across the Barrens to reach the Trace, and went to ford a river, and found all these drowned snakes!"

"Half-drowned snakes," came a bitter voice from behind. Dag glanced over his shoulder at Rase, who seemed to be reminded of some grudge.

"I told you to use your groundsense," said Sumac, entirely without sympathy. "Anyway, we stopped to collect as many as we could. The skins will fetch us some useful coin at the ferry, I figure."

Rase put in, "It had us in a puzzle, how all those rattlers came to be washed up there. I wondered if there'd been a flash flood, but Sumac said there was no other sign of it. The Barrens are a queerer place than I'd thought." He shook his head in wonder.

Dag smiled benignly.

∽

Camp that night was lively with the exchange of tales. Dag eventually confessed to the snakes. To Dag's relief, Fawn and Barr took up much of the burden of explaining Raintree and their river journey. Sumac had less to offer, but her words seemed just as exotic to the entranced farmer boys, describing a quiet winter patrolling out of New Elm, a camp some forty miles west of the Trace that covered most of the territory between the Barrens and the Hardboil. Rase had been a trainee in her patrol, and showed every sign of the usual hopeless infatuation Sumac tended to engender in young men. Dag did not waste pity on his plight. If he was any good—and she wouldn't be taking him back to Fairbolt if he weren't—one of the younger Crow girls would doubtless make short work of him. One way or another, the boy might never see his home camp again. Dag stifled a grin.

Watching his niece across the flickering firelight, Dag found himself curiously unsettled. She was like a breath of bracing northern air to him, a song of his lost home. He did not regret his exile. One glance at Fawn was still enough to lift his heart near into his throat in wonder. He'd cut off the weight of his past like shearing through a towrope, and he had no desire to drag that barge again. But. Yet. Still. . .

Sumac threw curiously unsettled glances back. Ever since Dag had returned from Luthlia maimed and strange when she was rising fifteen, she'd made a bit of a hero of her only Redwing uncle. Unlike Neeta, she had few illusions about him—she'd surely seen him at his worst, many times—but everyone in the family knew she'd chosen the patrol over the knife-making apprenticeship her father had offered because of him. All her adult life he'd been the same dry patroller fellow, the one kinsman who never criticized her choices, as solidly planted as her favorite tree. She could not have been more startled if a hickory tree had risen up, shaken the dirt from its roots, and run off with a farmer girl. Leaving whatever hammock end she'd had tied to him lying forlorn upon the ground.

Despite any confusion in her heart, she was polite and even friendly to Fawn. As the tales of malices and river bandits, medicine making and

walnut magery wound on, Dag trusted she realized Fawn was his partner, not his pet. She managed choked but sincere congratulations at the
news of their impending child, and a wholly sincere gleam of evil delight
that was pure Sumac when she said, "I can't wait to tell them at home!"

∾

When Dag made his habitual bedtime patrol of their camp's perimeter
that night, Arkady fell in beside him.

In a voice remarkably neutral even for him, Arkady said, "Interesting
woman, your niece."

"She is that."

" . . . How old is she?"

Dag's brows rose. He'd thought Arkady shrewder at estimating folks'
ages than anyone he'd ever met. "Let me think. I was about twenty-two
when she was born, because it was the year I was patrolling up on the
Great North Road. So she must be, um, almost thirty-five, now. She's
Dar's second-born, see. Her arrival was greeted with much relief and
rejoicing in Tent Redwing, I can tell you. Omba's credit with our mama
rose immensely."

"She does not appear to be string-bound."

"No."

"Betrothed?"

"Not as far as I know."

"One wonders why not. No tragedies?"

"I'm not sure she would have said. She's certainly had serious suitors.
Omba calls them the String of Bodies."

Dag could feel Arkady's slow blink in the darkness.

Dag set aside a truly overwhelming temptation to tease Arkady, and
said seriously, "You're a subtle man, when it comes to folks' insides. If

you can figure it out and tell us, Tent Redwing would be grateful. I've patrolled with her a time or two. She doesn't hate men, she doesn't prefer girls. Granted, her first few dewy suitors were crushed by Dar, but they weren't up to her weight anyway. After that she kept 'em out of sight, naturally."

"Naturally."

"The family stopped worrying that she'd make a mistake some time back. Now I suspect the family has started wondering if even a mistake might be better than nothing." To think *Omba would know* was unjust. Sumac's parents were loyal to each other, even if Dar was a difficult man.

"She's more of a puzzle than she looks at first glance."

"Yep."

"Rather like her uncle, that way. Hm." Arkady wandered off into the darkness.

Dag watched him go. *Hm, indeed!*

15

A cracking thunderstorm, blowing in hard just before dawn, ended their nice dry spell. By the time everyone turned out to settle the spooked animals and recapture wind-scattered gear, gray daylight arrived, but it wasn't till midmorning that they set off through the trailing drizzle, bleary-eyed. Fawn let Dag talk her into riding inside the wagon; he and Barr were protected in the boatmen's rain cloaks Fawn had fashioned back on the *Fetch*. At least the boiling brown creeks in this more settled country were mostly bridged again.

Fawn wasn't sure whether to be surprised or not that Sumac and her partner elected to trail along with them at the wagon's pace "just till the ferry." Sumac rode between Dag and Arkady, chatting animatedly whenever the rain eased. Fawn supposed she and Dag had a lot of catching up to do. Arkady didn't seem to be saying much, but he didn't come up on the wagon box at all that day to continue Calla's lessons. Edged out of the prime spots at Sumac's stirrups by their seniors, Barr and Rase trailed a trifle disconsolately. But camp that night was not nearly the sodden misery Fawn expected, because

Finch and Indigo scouted out a run-down barn that its owner let to benighted Trace travelers. The roof leaked and the old boards thrummed in the gale, but it beat huddling together under the wagon all hollow.

The clouds broke up into a humid pale heat by the next noon as they came to the edge of the Hardboil Valley, quite as wide as that of the Grace. The shining ribbon of river wound through spring-green woods and fields that steamed with the recent rains. As they slithered carefully down the muddy road, Fawn caught her first glimpses of the ferry town, which bore the arresting name of Mutton Hash, and of the ferry itself, which seemed to be the familiar flat barge hauled from shore to shore by a rope-wound capstan. But here, two big boats worked in parallel, one coming while the other was going.

The water was wider than Fawn had imagined, over half a mile, and Mutton Hash the biggest settlement she'd seen for weeks, not a mere village but a lively river town. As they neared she could make out boat-builders and goods sheds, hotels and liveries, brewers, bakers, smiths, a ropewalk, tanneries, and horse dealers, and she marveled at how comfortably familiar it all seemed to her now. There was also, she discovered as they arrived near the riverbank, a line for the ferry backed up for two blocks. Besides local wagons, riders, and a lot of foot traffic, the entire forty-mule tea caravan had somehow got ahead of them again.

Such a clot seemed to be an expected thing, because the way down to the landing was lined with booths and hawkers selling food, drink, and goods to the bored and waiting travelers. Fawn stood in her stirrups and sniffed inviting smells: meat pies, funnel cakes, beer, honeyed tea. Sounds, too—someone was playing a fiddle quite as well as Berry did, quick and sweet. The fiddler started an old river song, the music dancing high and low, and Fawn's heart caught. She kicked Magpie closer.

The fiddler was a lean, tall woman standing on a stump to the side of the road, elbow sawing, her blond hair drawn back in a lank horsetail shining in the sun . . .

"Berry!" shrieked Fawn in astonishment.

Berry looked up and grinned across the heads of the crowd clustered around her, seized a breath before a repeat to whip her bow through the air in greeting, and continued with her tune. She looked much less surprised than Fawn felt. Hawthorn stood at her feet holding out Bo's shapeless felt hat. When he craned his neck and spotted Fawn, he plunked the hat down between his sister's tapping toes and elbowed his way toward her. By the time he arrived, she'd slid from her saddle and was able to give him a heartfelt hug, which he didn't even shrug off in boy embarrassment. *Oh, my! He's taller than me!*

"What are you doing here?" Fawn demanded.

"Waiting for you, partly. Mostly waiting for Whit to finish fussing with his little pack train."

What pack train? "Is everyone all right?"

"Oh, sure. 'Cept my raccoon eloped, halfway up the Gray." Hawthorn frowned in memory of this defection.

Fawn didn't think there was any *oh sure* about it, but she gave up the urge to shake him as Berry finished her tune and cried, "Lunch break! Try Mama Flintridge's dried peach pies over there, best in the valley!" She jumped off the stump, stuffed her fiddle in its leather bag, grabbed the hat, and passed through the throng to Fawn, collecting a few more coins on the way. The hugs this time were mutual.

"Berry!"

"Sis! You made it! We figured if we were going to cross paths at all, this would be the place."

"Where's Whit and the others?"

Berry swung an arm toward the river. "He has a day job working the capstan on one ferryboat, and Hod's on the other. Bo's keeping an eye on our horses and gear at a place across the river. Farther from the taverns."

Dag and Barr dismounted and made their way to Berry, rather more easily than Fawn had, in time to hear this. Folks glanced at the tall Lakewakers and edged back, mostly—then stared openmouthed when they exchanged happy hugs with the grinning fiddler.

"How did you all end up here?" asked Fawn. "I thought you'd taken berths on a keelboat bound for Tripoint."

"We did, and I do believe upstream keelboat hauling was a shock to Whit—he'd thought he worked hard on a *farm*. Anyways, our fool boat boss managed to get his hull stove in by a floater just above the mouth of the Hardboil. We made it to shore and worked back to the village there, but it was plain that boat wasn't going anywhere for some time, not to mention we'd lost half its lading to the wet. Well, we heard there that the ice hadn't even broke up yet on the upper Grace, but the Hardboil was clear. So we found berths on another keel headed up to Mutton Hash, that being as high as we could get by boat."

Mutton Hash marked the head of navigation for the Hardboil River. The Trace crossed the Hardboil, not by chance, Fawn guessed, just below some thirty miles of impassable shoals and rapids, the hazard that gave the whole river its name. Legend had it there had once been a bridge and a city upstream at a narrow high point, but both were fallen into the mists of time, buried by the encroaching woods. Fawn nodded.

"Whit always was divided in his mind between the river and the road," Berry continued. "This way he gets some of both. I was agreeable, because I figure it'll cut three or four weeks off the trip home. If we're to build another flatboat before the fall rise, we'll need that time."

Might we get there in time to plant a kitchen garden, too? "Did you get the letter I sent you in Graymouth?"

"Yep, thanks."

"You didn't come all this way just on the chance of meeting us, did you? Because we weren't sure till the last we'd even be coming home this year."

"No, but we've been keeping a lookout all the same. We knew from asking at the ferry that you two hadn't passed ahead of us—Dag is memorable all by himself, and when the pair of you are together, folks notice. I won't say we haven't been lingerin' a bit in hope, but I want to start north soon. Before your brother buys any more horses." She made a face.

The ferry pulled into the landing with shouts and a rumble as the gangplank was laid out. Walkers and wagons heaved up the slope, and the crowd shifted as the new passengers hurried to take their place. While some of the tea caravan's younger and less jaded mules were taking exception to their offered boat ride, Hawthorn dashed down to tell Whit about the arrivals.

Whit came thumping up grinning like mad, hugged Fawn, and wrung Dag's hand. "You made it! Hoped you might! Hey, I bet I could squeeze you on right now."

"Thanks, but we're not alone," said Dag. "We're traveling with some other folks. Young homesteaders. Theirs is that green wagon up there."

"Sage is a blacksmith, going to look for work in Tripoint," Fawn added.

"Even better. Bring them along! I have so much to show you." Whit glanced back at the filling ferry; a big fellow guarding the gangplank, clearly the ferry boss, was glowering after him. "But I have to go back to work now. Can't quit in the middle of a day, it wouldn't be right. I'll talk to you more when you get aboard, unless you end up on Hod's boat, and then he'll tell you all about it. Berry or Hawthorn will take you to our digs, I guess. Where's Remo?"

Barr stiffened a little. "He stayed at New Moon."

Whit blinked. "Oh. Why?"

"There was this girl," said Fawn, as the simplest answer. Which had to suffice, as the ferry boss followed up his glower with a bellow. Whit waved and ran back to the boat.

Whit seemed both changed and unchanged. He was definitely broader in the shoulders. He plainly retained his sometimes-alarming enthusiasm for the new; if his ability to stick with a tough job to the end was improved by his marriage, so much the better. As Dag led them all over to introduce Berry and Hawthorn to the company, Fawn decided to save her most important family news for some less crowded moment.

Whit's ferry slogged all the way across the river and back again before their turn came to clamber aboard. Fawn thought the boat rode alarmingly low in the water when the ferry boss finally slid the gate pole across. Whit and the southern boys seemed to become instant comrades, Whit because he was a friendly cuss, and the others because they'd heard so much about him that it likely felt they already knew one another. Despite their growing up not thirty miles from the Gray, the Hardboil was the largest river some of them had yet seen, and they were agog with it. Under the ferry boss's amused eye they were permitted a few turns on the four-man capstan.

Dag's attention was mainly taken keeping Copperhead from picking a fight with all the strange horses jammed up around them. Some of the other travelers eyed the Lakewalkers suspiciously, but the ferrymen evidently saw enough of their sort as to excite no comment, at least not out loud. Well, Sumac drew covert stares, but if any of the men were thinking rude thoughts, the Lakewalkers doubtless kept their groundsenses furled in this crowd, and so could take no offense.

As she led Magpie across the echoing gangplank onto the northern shore, Fawn thought with a thrill, *We're halfway home!*

∾

Dag was unsurprised when Berry led them two miles off the Trace to another farm with a dilapidated barn, cheaper to let because it was not so near the road. It offered good pasturage, though, important as their mob of hungry animals joined the six horses that Whit had acquired. Since Whit had started this whole venture with a mere pair and the clothes on his back, it seemed good progress, except for his new beasts being near breakdowns. Yet on closer look, his selections were shrewd. Most of the animated racks of bones needed no more than worm medication, rest, and grain, which Whit had already supplied. A couple showed signs of prior abuse, now stitched, patched, and plastered.

"All mares," Whit, when he arrived from the ferry at sunset, pointed out to Dag. "By the time we get to Clearcreek, I'll know which ones I want to cull and which I want to keep for breeding. D'you think Mama's colt Darkling might be ready to cover them by next fall?" A light of equine enterprise shone in Whit's eye.

Whit was ecstatic to find that Sage was an experienced farrier, and the two promptly put their heads together on a problem of corrective shoeing for one of the mares. The company's animals being overdue for a rest, they also obtained an extra day of pasturage and shelter from the farm's owner in exchange for a promise to shoe one of his horses. It seemed to Dag that an uneven burden had fallen on Sage, but the young smith was willing, and the other boys all turned out to help him as best they could.

He's not afraid to get his hands dirty was praise for a man whether northern or southern; Arkady was let off from any ragging about his cleanliness when he supplied value by doing ground checks of all the new acquisitions to sort the serious from the remediable problems. As a result, Whit took one of his mares back to the Mutton Hash market the following morning and returned with a different one. So it was late in the afternoon before Whit whipped out his newest prize to show off.

It was a crossbow with a spring steel bow and a cranking mechanism for cocking, the work of some Tripoint artisan. "I got it in trade from a broke-down keeler back on the Gray," Whit explained eagerly, turning it in his hands to point out its notable features, which seemed to be all of them. The farmer boys were drawn to it as swiftly as if it were fresh apple pie. Everyone wanted to try it at once except Sage, who wanted to take it apart and see if he could copy the mechanisms, an operation Whit was unwilling to allow just yet.

"I only have seven bolts for it," Whit explained. "I used to have eight, but I lost one already, not having a Lakewalker around to help me find the misses." He made a sad face.

Fawn frowned, turning one of the short steel-tipped bolts in her hand. "I guess I couldn't make arrows for this bow. I suppose Sage might."

"Oh, hey, actually, I was hoping you would. Make me some wooden ones for practice bolts, that is. I don't want to lose any more of the fancy steel-head ones just on target practice."

Fawn brightened a trifle. "Sure. I could try, anyhow."

The mob of them went off to set up a target at the end of the pasture, then retreated to shooting distance to flip a coin for turns. The Lakewalkers leaned on the pasture fence watching, at least till the first frenzy wore off. As the rattle of the ratchet rose in the air, Dag could tell that Barr, Rase, and Sumac were all itching to try out the new toy.

Arkady was less impressed. "It's rather crude. The range is short, and the firing rate is slow. A Lakewalker bow maker could craft a much finer one."

Dag pursed his lips. "A lovely unbreakable longbow, yes—in about two weeks, plus a week to recover. But I've seen those Tripoint artisans' shops. Once they were set up for it, they could likely turn out one of those crossbows in a day. More than one, if they organized their hands."

Arkady sniffed. "Quick and cheap."

"Yeah, but if they can turn out twenty to our one, it wouldn't matter if a few broke or didn't work quite square. They could just swap out, and still be miles ahead. And that's no poor instrument as it stands—it's as good a working as my cuff bow, which has held up for years with just minor repairs." Dag considered his specially adapted bow, crafted to bolt into his wrist cuff in place of his hook, which had turned him into a tolerable archer again after his maiming. And his Tripoint-made arm harness generally, which had gifted him back his life as a patroller.

He dug in his pocket, found a copper cray, and handed the coin to Arkady. "Look closely at this."

Arkady, mystified, accepted it.

"If you found this somewhere, not knowing what it was, how would you judge the metalwork?"

"Well . . . the raised image of the crayfish is actually quite fine. And the lettering, of course, so tiny, but clear to read"—Arkady squinted—"*Silver Shoals City Mint, One Cray.* And making things perfectly round is harder than it looks, I suppose."

"Aye. Yet when we all visited the mint at Silver Shoals, back when we were coming downriver on the *Fetch,* we saw the machine that stamps these out a hundred at a time. One of these disks is a little work of art. Tens of thousands of 'em . . . become farmer magic."

Arkady raised his brows; Dag plowed on. "They're counters, memories of trade and labor that a man can put in his pocket and carry across a continent. They make things move. With my groundsense, I can summon my horse from a mile away. With enough of these, the folks at Silver Shoals can summon a forty-mule tea caravan from eight hundred miles away. And the ground density and complexity of a big river city like Silver Shoals is a making in its own right."

"You see a farmer town as a making?" said Barr, his forehead wrinkling at this new thought.

"I do."

"What about a Lakewalker camp, then?"

"That, too, of course."

Arkady made to hand the coin back; Dag grinned and said, "Keep it. There's plenty more where that came from." He paused a moment to contemplate the ratcheting, *thwack,* and laughter of the crossbow practice, and his smile faded. "Now imagine a city like Silver Shoals or Tripoint turning out those crossbows the way they turn out coins, and putting them into the hands of thousands of farmer boys like ours over there. And now imagine a city like that, and all those boys and all their bows falling into the grip of a malice. Blight, you don't even have to imagine. I saw the Raintree Lakewalkers last summer put on the run by a bunch of farmers even less well organized and equipped than that. The Raintree malice was wasting its farmer troops right and left from not knowing how to handle 'em yet, but it would have learned better, if we'd given it more time."

Sumac leaned forward on the fence to tilt her face at him, eyes cool and shrewd. "Huh. So there was more of a bee up your butt when you left Hickory Lake than just the way the Tent Redwing treated your farmer bride, wasn't there, Uncle Dag?"

Arkady winced at the crude but vivid turn of phrase, but by the tightening of his mouth, it was plain that he followed the argument.

"I wouldn't have learned that from Papa," Sumac went on. "He made out you were just besotted. I think Fairbolt gave me a hint there was more to it. And so did Mari."

"Fairbolt and I talked about the wider problems, just before I left," said Dag. "He understood. The shape of the world is shifting under us, and we can't go on standing still and not fall. Finding our new footing won't be a task for one man to finish, but it's surely a task one man can start." He took a breath. "I don't know if I'm doing the right thing, but I do know I'm walking in the right direction."

Rase hadn't said a word, but he was listening. At least that.

～

Spring peepers, the noisiest frog per half inch that Dag knew of, had taken up their earsplitting chorus in the farm's woodlot and pond when he rounded the corner of the barn to make his bedtime patrol. He stopped short when Whit called unexpectedly over the racket, "Wait up, Dag!"

His tent-brother, a lantern swinging from his hand, fell in beside him. Whit cocked his head, listening to the peepers. "Maybe I could stuff cotton in my ears tonight. I'm sure glad I didn't have to court Berry by squatting with my naked tail in a puddle and screaming for hours till she took pity on me."

Dag choked on a laugh. "You just had to put that picture in my head, didn't you? Maybe that's why the lady peepers pick their mates. To shut them up."

"That makes a persuasive sort of sense, you know?"

Dag started forward once more, only to stop again when Whit said, "Dag—does Fawn seem a little peaked to you? Not quite her usual cheerful self?"

Concerned, Dag turned to face him. "Does she seem so to you? Seeing her every day, I might not notice subtler changes. And of course her ground is so bright and busy right now with its making, it tends to overwhelm everything else. I'd thought she was holding up real well, all things considered, but if you think not, maybe I should . . ."

"Huh?" said Whit. "Making?"

"Didn't she tell you yet?"

"Tell me what?"

Well . . . Dag supposed he had an equal right to this announcement. "We're expecting a child"—would it be coaxing lumps from fate to say *our first child*?—"in the early winter. Fawn says she's hoping it'll be around my birthday, though I think that might be a bit early."

Whit stepped back a pace, eyes and mouth both wide, before he laughed in astonishment. "Hey! I'll be an uncle! And Berry will be an aunt! How about that? Oh, I can't wait to tell them at home." His black brows drew in. "Wait a minute. What of all those tricks you were telling me about, before Berry and I got married, for delaying things?"

Dag hoped Whit couldn't see the heat in his cheeks in this dimness. "Well. Nobody said they were perfect tricks. Accidents happen even to Lakewalkers, you know."

"I guess!"

"I was, um . . . distracted."

Whit, blight him, sniggered. Dag ignored him with what dignity he could muster and trod off once more, Whit tagging after.

"Well, if she's increasing, that accounts for it," said Whit, sounding satisfied to have his mystery solved. "Short-tempered, too, I bet, heh."

"Not noticeably," Dag growled.

They walked on in silence for a few moments after that.

An accident? Or accidentally on purpose? Dag hoped his own mind wasn't playing tricks on him to that extent. What threat had New Moon Cutoff offered him, after all, to make him want to claim his wife so irrevocably at just that moment? A threat of ease? He had to admit, the offer of a life like Arkady's gentle, protected usefulness was a real temptation, as much for the usefulness as for the protection. But not there, not in the south.

Dag counted time in his head. All those weeks and miles gone by already, and the tiny fire within Fawn's womb had not faded or faltered, but had clung with dogged, Spark-like determination. *Maybe it'll be a girl,* he allowed himself to think. *Strong like her mama.* Maybe it was finally safe to let himself start thinking of that new spark as a real person, original and astonishing. Maybe. *Oh, my heart.* It almost hurt to have it stretched so far beyond its former—safe, secret, shriveled—boundaries.

Yet by whatever chance they had arrived, he was not sorry to be on this road.

～

Five days later, Dag was rethinking that belief.

It hadn't been *wrong*, merely much too simpleminded. This was nothing like the northward leg he'd pictured back when he and Fawn had left Hickory Lake—a vision that actually took him some effort to recall—just the two of them, a lingering spring, and plenty of bedroll time together. Yet the whole point of this journey had been to put fresh pictures in their heads, because the old ones hadn't seemed up to the new tasks they faced. He could hardly complain because his scheme was working to excess.

He turned in his saddle to look back over the cavalcade. Sixteen people and twenty-five animals made nearly a full-size patrol, without a patrol's training. He wasn't quite sure how he'd been elected patrol leader. Still, his old system of giving as few orders as possible, because every time you did people would come to expect them, and then badger for them, and then grow too stiff to move without them, seemed to apply here as well.

This disparate clump of folks was blending better than he'd hoped. The river crew was used to frequent dealings with strangers, which helped ease the less traveled Alligator Hat boys. Sumac accepted the Bluefields as her esteemed uncle's tent-kin with barely a bump, and Rase wouldn't dare say boo to her, so that settled him. Arkady kept his own counsel as usual, but Dag knew he was taking it all in.

Berry, Calla, and Fawn had swiftly formed a sisterhood, and it was only now, after watching them pass tasks smoothly from hand to hand, helping one another and laughing together over various female jokes, that Dag realized how painfully isolated Fawn had been at New Moon Cutoff. The medicine tent had tolerated her for Dag's sake, but not one Lakewalker woman there had truly taken her up to teach her the ways of their inner world. Which led him to a very unexpected contemplation of Sumac as odd woman out in this company, neither farmer woman nor patroller man. Maybe that was why she rode so often beside odd-man Arkady.

But Fawn's eyes, wide with wonder as the company climbed day by day up into the true mountains, made his every effort worth it. The hillsides tilted up higher and steeper until, she noted with a flatlander's alarm, the sky had shrunk by half, as if stolen away. Tiny rivulets trickled over cliffs to fall like spun thread into secret crevices lined with pink splashes of mountain laurel. Fern fiddleheads unfurled into delicate fronds around dark and abundant springs. Green, ankle-high umbrella apples sheltered spring beauties and bloodroot, and the white and pink trillium after which Fawn's mother had been named cascaded in waves down the slopes, all familiar northern wildflowers that made her smile in recognition.

"I finally see why you wouldn't let us call those hills around Glassforge mountains," she told Dag.

"There are mountains up in northeast Seagate even bigger than these," Dag said. "So tall it's winter on top all year round, and the snow and ice never melt off."

"You're pulling my leg!" said Finch.

"Nope. Seen it with my own eyes," said Dag. "Floating up all white against the blue summer sky, the peaks and ridges like something out of a dream."

"I wonder if you could make a trade in that ice," said Whit thoughtfully. "Pack it down in the summer and sell it to folks."

"It would be a lot of work, climbing a mountain that high," said Fawn in doubt. "And ice is heavy. Maybe it could be slid down somehow . . ."

"Actually," said Dag, "folks in those parts cut ice from their ponds in the winter and store it in cellars packed in straw. It lasts longer than you'd think."

"That sounds a bit more practical," said Fawn.

"Huh," said Whit. "The things you learn travelin'. I might try that at home."

Once he'd carefully described what they would be up against, Dag let the farmer boys sort themselves out to tackle the first big mountain pass. That dawn, the four pack animals were unloaded and added to the wagon traces, and the wagon's cargo reduced. Bo was left at the foot of the pass to guard their gear, because he really wasn't quite as recovered from the belly stab of last fall as he made out, and Hod set to guard Bo. The plan was to make it to the top by midday and down as far as the first good stopping point, then send some of the boys and the unloaded pack animals back to Bo's camp for the night. The other half of the party would rest up till they arrived next day, then continue the almost equally painstaking descent, using rocks and logs to help brake the wagon's wheels and prevent a disastrous runaway. After that would be another four days of relatively easy travel up another long, running valley before they had to do the drill again.

Everything went according to plan till they were halfway up the hill at midmorning, and came upon another wagon blocking the road.

Dag, flanked by Indigo, rode around it to encounter a bizarre sight. The team hitched to it consisted of three mules and a skinny horse, blowing and marbled with wet and dried white sweat; one of the mules, a wheeler, was down on its knees, tangled in the traces. A woman knelt next to it, weeping, a burning brand in her hand.

A rough, weak voice issued from the depths of the wagon's raised canvas cover: "Light its fool tail on fire! That'll get it up!"

"Missus, what are you doing to that poor mule?" cried Indigo in outrage.

She turned up a red, tear-streaked face, crisscrossed by brown hair falling from its topknot in messy strands. She might have been any age between an exhausted twenty and an equally exhausted thirty, her shirt sweat-stained and skirt dirty. "It's fallen, and it won't rise and pull."

"I can see that," said Indigo. "If you got that rig up this far with just those spavined beasts, it's likely spent. You're crazy to try to drag a wagon that size up this road with only two pairs! Our wagon has five pairs and it's barely making the grade."

"It's all we have. One mule died two days back, so we put the horse in. They have to get us up. They're all we have . . ."

"Who you talkin' to out there, Vio?" came the hoarse male voice again. "Don't you go talking to strangers . . . !" From under the stuffy canvas, a child's voice began crying.

Dag reluctantly opened his groundsense as the man lurched out to the driver's box on his knees. His face was fish-belly white, his arms shaking as they propped him up. He peered around suspiciously. In addition to the man, the wagon seemed to hold two children. A half-grown girl, also sick, lay on a pallet. A toddler boy was tied inside by some sort of harness, likely to keep him from falling over the side and under the wheels, and he fretted crossly at the restraint. He'd likely howled before and would howl again, but just at the moment was still working up to the next spate.

The woman's gaze drifted to Dag. She recoiled. "Grouse, help, there's a Lakewalker fellow on this road!"

"Where? What—" The man staggered back inside, then crawled out onto the box waving a boar spear. "Keep away, you! You won't have our bones!"

"Is he crazy?" muttered Indigo.

"Fevered, I think," said Dag. Not that he couldn't be crazy as well. Dag wheeled Copperhead out of range of the wavering spear point, and bellowed back down the road, where Sage's wagon had halted and the other riders were starting to jam up, "Fawn! Berry! I need you here!"

The two women rode up and dismounted, taking in the scene, and Dag backed off slightly to avoid unnerving the distraught travelers further. Vio burst into ragged sobs at the sight of such friendly female faces. The man slumped to his knees behind the box, bent over the seat, still clutching the spear he could barely lift. Under Fawn's soothing murmurs and Berry's crisp questions, it wasn't long before their tale tumbled out.

The Basswoods were a poor couple with no due-shares from a village south of the Hardboil who had fled their life of drudgery in hopes of the rumored free land in Oleana. Sage and Finch left their animals and walked forward in time to hear most of the sad story. Fawn looked over their rickety rig with a shrewd eye.

"You two are a mite underequipped for homesteading. It's good land, mind, but it takes a lot of hard labor for better than a year, usually, before you could expect to live off it. Though I suppose if you could make it to the Grace Valley, you could get day work there and build up your supplies."

"That's the life we just left!" said Vio.

Grouse growled from his slump, "Not going back. Not going back to be scorned and made mock of!"

"Well," said Berry the ex–boat boss, who for all her youthful blond looks didn't suffer fools gladly, "if you can't go up and you won't go back, it looks like you'll just have to set and starve on this here hillside. Which'll save you steps, I reckon. But don't set that silly mule on fire. It can't tow you up this mountain nohow."

"It's best if you turn around now," said Dag, reluctant to draw attention to his scary Lakewalker self, but feeling the need to voice support of Berry. "Even if you somehow made it to the top here, there are two more passes farther along the Trace that are as bad or worse. You'll founder."

"Anyways, you still have to shift your rig to the side so's others can get by," said Berry firmly.

Vio's weeping increased. Inside the wagon the children, Plum and Owlet, heard their mother's distress and began to cry along.

Dag saw the sympathy in Fawn's eye, and guessed what was coming. "Sage," she said, "we're bringing half our animals back down for another go anyhow. What if you brought your team back later and hitched it on with theirs? Their animals could have a rest while they waited. Then, with seven pairs to pull, this wagon would go up the hill in jig time."

Indigo scratched his head. "Actually, if we hung together to the next pass, we could hitch on all our mules to each wagon in turn, and wouldn't have to do all that shuffling around with the packhorses."

Vio stopped sniveling and looked up in hope. "Would you? Could we? Oh, please, say yes, Grouse!"

The fevered man mumbled something about *Kill us in our beds*, which his wife ignored in her fresh concentration on Indigo. "Grouse'll make better sense when this bog ague spell passes off. One more day, I promise, and he'll be back on his pins. Oh, please . . . oh my, so cruel, oh, you shouldn't ought to have said it if you didn't mean it . . . !"

Which was how, that night, they all ended up camped at the top of

the pass in a chill fog, instead of lower down in some more pleasant lo-
cation, and Dag and Arkady were pressed into trying to force bog-ague
remedy into a half-delirious man who fought them every step. Grouse's
terror took the form of swearing and abuse, mainly. His wife was helpless in the face of it, but Berry lent a hand, and a voice, that settled him
as swiftly as a drunken keeler. Arkady was less taken aback than Dag
expected; his prior experience with difficult sick farmers seemed to be
wider than he'd quite let on.

Dag walked his perimeter patrol wondering if anybody was going
to stumble over a precipice while trying to take a piss tonight, and if
Arkady had any headache remedies in his pack. Strong ones . . .

He paused, arrested by the feel of horses and riders coming up the
trail behind them. Honest folks had little reason to dare the Trace after
dark, and sensible ones none, here in this mist only made more blurry
by the meager light of a half-moon. Bandits preyed on travelers in these
unpeopled stretches. He extended his groundsense anxiously.

A very familiar ground bumped his.

Dag strode down the road in time to see three riders loom up out of
the milky haze. Remo. And Neeta. And Tavia.

"Absent gods, Dag!" Remo's aggravated voice echoed weirdly in the
damp air. "It's blighted time we caught up with you!"

16

Dag was able to avoid the confrontation that night only because Arkady was already asleep in his bedroll, but in consequence he and Arkady were cornered by Neeta and her little company at first light the next morning. It would be optimistic to call it sunup; it was more of a brightening fog. Water droplets beaded on blankets, gear, and in everyone's hair, dank and chill. The crackling flames of the patroller breakfast fire, not quite out of earshot of the farmers' wagons, seemed wan and pale, much like the people clustered around it. In this orange-and-gray light even Arkady looked unshaved, road-worn, and bleary.

"I thought we'd catch up with you before you'd reached the Barrens," Neeta explained earnestly. "We might have, too, if only we'd been allowed an earlier start."

Remo said to Dag, "We wasted the first five days on Antan Bullrush's attempt to wait you out. I told him Arkady might be bluffing, but you wouldn't be. When he finally let me ride out to the Bridger farm to check, you were already four days down the road."

"Yes," said Neeta, "and then we wasted another two days arguing about it all. It took the camp council to finally overrule the captain. We should have gone after you courier-style, and swapped out the horses along the way, but Antan wouldn't even authorize that."

"We had good luck in the road and weather," said Dag. *I pushed us along.* He wished he'd had a few more days to push; the farther, the better.

"Anyway," said Neeta, "you've no need now to travel another foot north. We've won!"

Arkady squinted curiously. Barr, lurking at his shoulder, frowned.

"I'm pledged to the north, and to my Bluefield tent-kin," said Dag. "And these farmer youngsters are relying on me to be their guide on this road, which is all new to them. I've more or less promised to see them safe to the Grace Valley, leastways." He gave Arkady a hooded glance. "Naturally, I hope Arkady will ride on with us. I haven't even begun to show him all the north has to offer. There's a lot to see and learn, yet."

Neeta said, "No, sir, you don't understand! I mean we've won you *everything.* Dag to be let back in camp, and tent-rights despite the farmer girl, *and* the medicine booth at the farmer's market! Maker Challa's actually become very interested in that, since you've shown her all about your unbeguilement trick."

Arkady blinked. So did Dag.

Barr looked around. "I have a better idea. Why don't you all come north with us? At least for a while. We're better'n halfway there, and I was told last fall not to come home without you, Remo. I've a suspicion nothing about Pearl Riffle Camp will look the same to me, but I'd like to finish up proper, before making a clean start doing . . . whatever else. You might, too."

Remo shook his head. "You don't see. I've found a new place for myself—a place that doesn't think I'm dirt under its boot heels. I don't have to go back and crawl on my belly to get a place in a good patrol. New Moon really wants me!"

Shedding his imagined sins as a snake sheds its skin, along with his past and his faultfinding family—Dag could understand the appeal of the southern camp to the boy.

"Wants isn't the same as needs," said Barr. "New Moon Cutoff has enough patrollers. There isn't a camp north of the Grace that would make that claim." He glanced meaningfully at Tavia, who touched her lips in doubt.

Neeta tossed her head. "Barr can suit himself. We were sent to escort Arkady and Dag home." She did not, Dag noted, add Fawn to that tally. "Anyway"—she turned to Arkady—"surely you've had enough of living rough, sir, at your age. We can whisk you right back to your own comfortable house. It's all being kept for you."

Arkady rubbed his sleeve across his eyes. "Gods. I can't think when I'm covered with trail filth."

Dag didn't see that Arkady was any grubbier than anyone else, but he bit his tongue on saying so. Fawn and Sumac had been collaborating on rustling up the breakfast tea. Sumac rose and wordlessly handed the first sweetened cup to Arkady. He took it with a grateful grimace, and sipped.

Sumac looked Neeta over rather coolly. "No one's going forward *or* back for another day. If our animals are due for a rest, your mounts must be in worse case, from covering the same distance in two-thirds the time. Dag can't leave his party scattered over ten miles of trail—it would be very poor patrol procedure. At the very least, we need to get everyone safely to the bottom of this pass and reorganized. There's plenty of time to think about all this later. *After* breakfast."

Dag said, "I agree."

Arkady looked around the circle of faces and shrugged. "Dag's the trail boss."

Neeta doubtless sensed she was being outmaneuvered by the older woman, but couldn't muster a reasonable objection, since it was quite true about the horses. With the reminder of breakfast, the debate broke up amongst growling stomachs, and was prevented from re-forming by the bustle of breaking camp.

"After lunch," Dag overheard Sumac murmur to Arkady, "when we're lower down, I'll show you a patroller trick for finding warmer water to wash in."

"That would help," sighed Arkady.

It had taken a full day to get the party to the top of the pass, but only cost half that to descend the other side. It likely aided things that the cantankerous Grouse remained bedridden in his wagon, as his wife seemed the more sensible half of the couple. Ash and Indigo helped her out. They all made it to the bottom without losing any wagons over the edge of the twisty road, despite having to shift two fallen trees and a small rock slide along the way. Between the mist lifting and the lower elevation, it was a soft, warm spring afternoon by the time they'd found a new campsite in the valley. More bustle followed, to get the four southern boys and Whit fed and off back over the pass to fetch Bo, Hod, and the rest of their gear; they likely wouldn't traipse in again till the following afternoon.

When Dag finally went to look for Arkady, he was nowhere in sight. Nor in groundsense range.

"Did you see where Arkady went?" he asked Fawn.

"Um . . ." said Fawn.

"What?"

"Sumac took him off into the woods to find him a warm bath. She said."

Dag raised his brows at her.

"Well, Arkady did take his scented soap and his towels and razor."
She added after a moment, "Sumac had a blanket, which I guess you
could want for a bath." And after another, shyer moment, "Do you suppose they've gone to scout for squirrels?"

Dag drew breath. "Not sure."

Fawn eyed him uneasily. "You don't think it's your duty to go after
them, do you? On account as Sumac is your niece?"

"And get my other hand bitten off? No. Sumac is a woman grown.
And Arkady's . . . not an ineligible suitor." Arkady's maker bloodlines
were plainly as superior as they could be, and the age gap between the
pair was something Dag wouldn't have dared remark on.

Fawn sighed relief.

A slow smile lifted Dag's lips at a vision of Arkady and Tent Redwing tangling with each other, if he were to be dragged home as a prize
by Sumac. Dag had no doubt Arkady could hold his own—blight, Dar
wouldn't last five minutes. And Cumbia—well, Arkady would doubtless be exquisitely polite to Cumbia. But she wouldn't budge him half an
inch from any course he'd chosen.

Don't get ahead of yourself, old patroller. Arkady and Sumac were both
complicated people, which might or might not help them suit. They'd
not drawn each other out very deeply in front of Dag, Arkady seeming
content to listen to Dag and Sumac reminisce. Concealing his vulner-
able heart? A man would be wise to do so with Sumac, and Arkady was
a wise man.

Still . . . Sumac and Rase had meant to leave the company days ago,
back at the Hardboil, and be a hundred miles closer to Hickory Lake by
now. Maybe the reunion with good old Uncle Dag wasn't the sole reason for her delay?

And then had come Neeta, and the hot breath of competition, if of a rather indirect kind. Dag suspected Sumac wasn't used to rivalry over men, seldom a thing she had to deal with when they all followed her like ducklings. Though as a patrol leader, she was trained to quick thinking and action in an emergency. And if Arkady went south tomorrow, it was unlikely they would ever cross paths again . . .

"Poor squirrels," Dag murmured. "They haven't a chance."

Fawn grinned up at him. "Maybe we should go find some of our own. If Sumac can spot a warm creek in these woods, seems to me you could, too."

"A fine plan, Spark."

"I'll fetch our soap."

"And blanket. Which direction shall we scout?"

"Any but northwest. I think the squirrel menace is likely covered in that direction."

"Right."

When Dag, smiling, went off to find Barr and warn him of their afternoon's planned absence, he found Neeta and Tavia at the boy's elbow.

"Have you seen Arkady?" Neeta demanded. "I have to talk some sense into him."

"He went off to get his bath, I believe."

"Which way?"

"I didn't see him," said Dag, with perfect truth. And with less perfect truth, added, "Downstream, wouldn't you think?" Southeast, as the creeks ran here.

"Come on, Tavia," said Neeta. "Arkady shouldn't be wandering around in these woods on his own. It's not safe."

"I don't think he went far, and I doubt he'd care for your company," Dag observed. "He's a man who likes his privacy."

Tavia set her heels at the alarming thought of interrupting Maker

Arkady at his bath; the pair were sitting on a log still arguing when Dag and Fawn snuck away in their own right. Westerly.

᠊ᢆᢆ

The languid afternoon was everything Dag had dreamed of, back when he'd still been envisioning this as a wedding trip. Deep in the woods, he and Fawn found a creek trickling over clean rocks into a sunlit pool, as warm as the season could give, with their bedroll even warmer laid beside it on a sun-dappled bank of soft green horsetails. Mountain wildflowers abounded. But despite their decided lack of hurry, when they strolled back to the quiet camp Arkady and Sumac were still not there.

The mountain ridge they'd just crossed blocked the sun early, casting the woods into cool shadow under a still-luminous sky. Those shadows were thickening when Dag at last spotted Arkady and Sumac emerging from the fringe of the trees. He rather thought the pair supplied their own glow, leaking through their half-closed grounds. They stopped and unlinked hands, then Arkady turned to arrange Sumac's loose, drying hair, falling like night's shadow to her hips, combing it through his fingers. Fortunate fingers . . . It took Dag another moment to realize what was different about Arkady—besides the obvious. His silver-gilt hair was no longer in its mourning knot, but braided down the back of his head and then set in a loose queue to his shoulders. A northern style—Sumac's handiwork?

Nevertheless, and quite maddeningly, neither made any interesting announcements, but slipped back into the reduced camp's dinner routine almost separately. The Basswoods kept to themselves, but Fawn, Calla, and Berry teamed up to grill the trout Remo and Barr had collected from the nearby rushing river. Neeta watched Arkady in concern, but either had the sense not to badger him, or was too caught up in the evening camp chores and horse care to get the chance.

Dag, wondering if he ought to ask Arkady his intentions, decided that was the wrong end of the stick. As the stars came out, he cornered Sumac.

"Pleasant afternoon?" he inquired genially.

"Very. You?"

"Likewise. I suspect. Not to pry."

He could feel her smirk in the shadows of the tall blooming tulip tree they'd ducked behind. "You're dying to pry."

"Well. I do feel a certain responsibility for my partner."

Sumac tilted her head back and remarked as if to no one in particular, "I do like a man with clean hands. Who knows what to do with them."

"Should I ask you if your intentions are honorable?"

"Intentions are like wishes. You don't always get them."

"Arkady . . . is a right sensitive man. If strong in his own way. You could—if you—" Dag strove for neutral wording. "He could be hurt."

"I am aware." Her eyes, glinting in the shadows, grew serious at last. "We talked."

"Talked." Dag tried to imagine Arkady talking. It was an effort. "What about?"

"A lot of things. What we had in common, for one."

"Like what?" said Dag. They were not an obviously matched pair, for all that he suspected subtler compatibilities.

That dark smile, again. "I don't think I'll tell you. But you were right—the man's insight is unholy."

Dag cleared his throat. "Did he, um . . . tell you anything about his first marriage?"

"With Bryna? Oh, days ago."

"Oh." Dag stumbled on: "A week's not very long to make up your mind, after fifteen years of avoiding . . . whatever you've been avoiding."

"Yes, I'm off to a late start. And he's worried it could be his and Bryna's sorrows all over again. He does feel it might be better not to get string-bound till we're sure things will work out. So's I wouldn't quit the patrol and turn my life upside down for nothing. We'd both be glad of your blessing, though."

Not seeing why his blessing was worth a pig's whistle, it took Dag a moment to decode this. He imagined it: *Why, yes, Arkady, by all means, impregnate my niece! The family will be ecstatic!* Except that they likely would be, by now.

"It's time, you see," said Sumac simply. "After fifteen years, I've had so much practice at sorting out what I don't want, it doesn't take that long to see what I do. Even if I've never seen the like before. How long did it take you and Fawn to decide on each other?"

"Er . . . several weeks." Honesty compelled: "Well, two days. Several weeks to get up the courage."

A flickering fox-grin. "Well, then." She drew breath. "When I was twenty, I knew everything about my future. Now, I know nothing. But I do know your partner will go north when I do. So you can say, *Thank you, Sumac.*"

"Thank you, Sumac," Dag echoed dutifully. And added more gently, "All the joy in the wide green world to you two."

Her lips eased in quite the softest smile he'd ever seen on her tough-girl face. She nodded gravely.

∾

Sumac proved right about Arkady's sense of direction.

Neeta, however, did not give up and turn around, in part because

Remo had been argued into a tizzy of indecision by Barr. Tavia said little. But the upshot was that when the reunited company at last took the Trace north again, it was swollen to twenty-three people and an entire drove of horses and mules. Leastways, Dag reflected, it made them a more daunting target for bandits.

The Trace here ran for three days travel up a slot flanked by running ridges, vast green sky-blocking humps. It was a thinly peopled country. A few hamlets, carved out of what little flat land the valley offered, supplemented their meager livings by supplying the needs of travelers. Grouse, recovering from his ague attack enough to take the reins on his wagon box, eyed the land hungrily, but any vale with a creek bottom worth having was clearly already taken.

Inevitably, Whit saw and recognized the birthday walnut around his sister's neck. Rather than having to talk his tent-brother into being his next target, Dag found him to be an eager volunteer. Dag was at first inclined to seek some private spot for the trial, then recalled the show he'd put on with Crane and his first sharing-knife bonding. The memory was disturbing, and he disliked doing complex and chancy groundwork with an audience, but this crowd was captive and mostly friendly. His own words came uncomfortably back to him: *Never miss a chance to befriend and teach.*

Around the campfire that night, Dag took on his next major making. The first few minutes were spent sorting out whose hair Whit was to borrow to supplement his own too-short curls, his sister's or his wife's. They settled on Berry's. She made a face as Fawn did the snipping, filching a generous blond hank. Whit's thicker fingers proved considerably less deft at cord braiding than Fawn's, especially when his added blood made the mixed hair slippery. Everyone gathered around, the Lakewalkers watching more wide-eyed than the farmers when Dag straddled a log behind Whit and helped him draw his ground out into the growing length of braid.

"So that's how they did those wedding cords!" murmured Tavia. Indigo scowled in fascination, his fingers rubbing one another as if in troubled memory.

The little sack of black walnuts had ridden with Dag all the way from Hickory Lake, sifted to the bottom of his saddlebags and forgotten on the river journey. Taking up one now, he rolled it between his fingers, feeling an unexpected shiver at this reminder of home. He glanced up at Sumac, watching over Arkady's shoulder, and managed a smile. Any hard-shelled nut would likely do to anchor this involution, but Dag was glad of these.

Arkady knelt at their side, watching closely as Dag, hook harness removed, held his long arms around Whit, his chin resting on the boy's shoulder. His fleshly fingers worked with Whit's to slip the nut into the net of hair, while his ghost fingers shaped the involution out of their own substance, catching up and winding in Whit's ground.

"Suggest you ease down, Dag," muttered Arkady in his ear. "You'll turn yourself inside out going that deep."

Indeed, Maker Vayve, too, had accused Dag of overbuilding his groundwork; Dag eased down. He and Whit together lifted the hair necklace over Whit's head, and the walnut pendant fell to touch his skin, framed by the open collar of his shirt. Dag opened his ghost hand and let his involution go, setting his jaw against the tearing pain. His belly shuddered, and his feet went cold. Arkady breathed sharply through his teeth; Sumac's lips parted in a wince. Remo whispered, *Ow.* And smoothly, like a spreading stain, the shimmering ground shield spread out through Whit's skin all over his body. *Top to toe. Yes.*

"Well, now what?" asked Whit, fingering the walnut.

"Didn't you feel that?" asked Sumac.

"Not especially." Whit looked up and blinked. "What? Are we done already?"

"Yep." Dag eased upright and stretched and clenched his fingers, grimacing as the tension unwound in his back. Whit leaped up and capered around the fire, demanding that Barr and Remo describe what they saw with their groundsenses.

Grouse Basswood, apparently still waiting for the human-sacrifice-and-cannibalism part to start, blinked and said in a disappointed voice, "Is that it? He didn't do nothing!"

"Now do Berry!" said Whit in a burst of enthusiasm. "And Hawthorn."

Hawthorn crowed assent; Bo thumped him on the side of the head. Hod hovered, grinning hesitantly. "And me?"

Berry clutched her hair and laughed uneasily. "I'll be snatched bald!"

Arkady eyed Dag's slump on the log, and said, "May I try the next one?"

Dag's head jerked up, and he squinted in surprise; Arkady cast him a nod. Sumac's encouraging grip on Arkady's shoulder pushed him forward. Barr gave Dag a hand up; Dag staggered and stood a moment with his hands on his knees till his light-headedness passed.

Arkady swallowed, taking Dag's place on the log. Fawn repeated the operation on Berry's hair with her sewing scissors and a lot of female consultation about just where to cut to best conceal the growing back. "You Lakewalkers have to give me some of your ground reinforcements later on these here finger cuts," Berry said sternly as she seated herself with the hair strands laid out in front of her, "so's I can play my fiddle." At the chorus of volunteers, she nodded in satisfaction, and began. Berry's bloodstained hair braiding was considerably neater than Whit's, and swifter.

Arkady caught up her ground on his second try—Dag was impressed—and wound it into his involution with seeming ease. Arkady did complex and delicate involutions in his work from time to time; any sharing-knife maker or senior medicine maker, Dag thought, ought to be nearly as practiced and adept. His hopes rose. If more makers than Dag and the admittedly extraordinary Arkady could be taught this technique, it became far more than a stunt. *It might even be a solution.* Although even Arkady gasped when he let his shaped involution go, his face draining; Sumac caught his arm and held him upright till his breathing steadied.

"Best stop for tonight," said Dag. "That gives us three different samples to study." The groundwork on each was slightly different, and Dag wasn't sure which would be best. When he had perfected the skill, he decided, he would go back and redo Fawn's. Although he didn't think her shield overbuilt; if anything, he wanted to make it twice as strong, for her and for the child—he rather thought by now it was going to be their daughter, though the shield made it hard to be sure—growing so swiftly within her.

"That didn't look so bad," said Vio, watching Berry.

"This is just what they let us see," Grouse grumbled.

Berry and Barr then flummoxed each other when he attempted a ground reinforcement on her pricked fingers and had it slide off. Arkady was called over to consult.

"Well, the shield repels groundwork, all right," said Arkady, stroking Berry's hand and frowning. "It doesn't seem to care if the intent of the groundwork is good or not. You can break the shield by removing the necklace, but I'd rather you didn't, just yet."

Berry studied his slightly haggard face and nodded understanding. "My word, yes, it would be like sinking the boat you'd just launched. I'll just wash my fingers good and tie strips on them for the night. They're only little cuts. They'll be fine in the morning."

Dag caught Arkady's glance. "See why it won't be finished till I figure out how to make the shield something the farmer can take on and off?"

"Something to think about, to be sure." Arkady's shoulders were as bowed with fatigue as after emergency medicine work, but his coppery eyes gleamed with excitement.

"What I don't understand," said Grouse, "is why you Lakewalkers would want to do something that stops you from doing things."

"Really, this seems pointless," murmured Neeta.

"It's not Lakewalkers I want to protect farmers from," said Dag—*not entirely, leastways*—"though I expect that might have some interestin' consequences. It's malices. Blight bogles."

Grouse's face screwed up. Another farmer who didn't quite believe in a menace he'd never seen and barely heard of—or he wouldn't be so anxious to move north, Dag reckoned. Vio looked more wary.

The show over, the company broke up to seek their respective bedrolls. As the night breeze sighed in the trees, Dag hugged Fawn close. She cuddled in tight under their blankets and said, "That was well done, Dag."

"Well started, maybe. It all seems a long way from done to me."

"Mm," she said. "But stop and think about how far you've come since last year this time."

He hardly needed to sense her clouded ground to feel her little spurt of memory, a ripple of tension across her back under his only hand. "Hm?"

"How far we've both come," she went on more quietly. "Last year this time . . . I'd already made my big stupid mistake, and was just working up to running away from home in a panic. Well, not panic, exactly. Desperation, maybe."

He let his fingers seek those back muscles, rubbing the remembered strain out of them. *No more desperation for you, Spark. Not if I can help it.* "Me . . . let me think. Out walking my thousandth routine patrol, I suppose, before Chato's courier called us down to Glassforge. I'd spent too many years just about one bad night's sleep away from tossing it in and sharing, and was getting mighty tired of that state of mind. I do remember that."

Her slim little fingers chased bad memories out of his muscles in turn. "Could you have imagined us, here, now? Could you have pictured doing such a making as you did tonight?"

"Gods. No. Nor any other making. Not in my wildest dreams. My dreams mostly not being good dreams, see."

"There you go, then." Her lips pressed a warm circle on his collarbone, then curved up. "I s'pose the advantage of being a gloomy cuss is that all your surprises are good ones."

He snickered. "Point, Spark."

The following afternoon brought them to the foot of the next pass, where they made an early stop to sort out the most efficient plans for getting the wagons up it. With a dawn start, Dag hoped the whole company could make it to the bottom of the far side by tomorrow night. That vale, rugged and almost as unpeopled as the Barrens, was the last where this land humped up like a giant's blanket folds; the trail at its head would lead over and down into the settled country approaching the Grace Valley. Dag felt a funny little flutter in his belly at that thought. *Spark and I and our youngin' are coming home.* It would be a home to make, carved new out of unknown territory, even though their sort of homesteading was unlikely to involve chopping trees and pulling stumps.

On his bedtime perimeter patrol that night, Dag became aware he was being shadowed by Neeta. Maybe he needed to vary his habits; he was getting too easy to ambush. He reluctantly slowed his steps and let her come up to him, not anxious to reopen the argument about his direction of travel.

"Nice night," she remarked.

"Ayup." It was star-spangled, the cool darkness drenched with the green scents of spring, alive with bug and frog songs.

"You know . . ."—she touched his sleeve, her smile turning warm—"you'd be welcome in my bedroll."

What, had she been inspired by Sumac's ploy? Did she mean to seduce him into turning south? What *was* this, with all these lovely young women flinging themselves at his head this season? *And where were they all when I was twenty-two, and could have done something about it?* The depressing answer, *Not born yet*, presented itself rather inescapably. First Calla, then Neeta, although Calla hadn't hardly meant it. Neeta's was a dodgier proposition on that score.

"Well, that's a right flattering thing to say to a fellow my age, Neeta, but you know, I'm string-bound." He reached to touch the cord coiled on his left arm above his harness, incidentally shifting his right arm out from under her grasp.

Neeta's smile of invitation didn't waver. "She's a farmer. She'd never know."

Wouldn't be able to read the changes in his ground, Neeta meant. "That's not the point." He needed to nip this in the bud hard and fast, but not, perhaps, cruelly. *Forgive me, Kauneo, for using your memory so.* But Kauneo had been a patrol leader herself, and would understand. "I think you do not see, so I'll explain. Once only. I loved a patroller woman very much—"

"You might again."

"No. Never again. Never while I breathe will I trade hearts with a woman who I could have the duty to order into harm's way."

"You're talking about Wolf Ridge, aren't you? It was a great tragedy, but a great battle." Sympathy shone in her eyes like starlight.

"Actually, it was a pretty stupid battle. Since for two weeks afterwards I was too dizzy from blood loss to stand up, I had plenty of time to lie there and think about ways to have done it better. And one of the things I figured out was that if I had it to do all over, I would have sacrificed the whole company, and her brothers, and all, to save her, without remorse or regret. This is not a fit state of mind for a patrol leader or captain, which is why I never willingly took up those duties again."

She started to speak; he overrode her. "One of the things I love best about Fawn is that she's not a patroller woman, and never will be or could be. She's an opposite to Kauneo in every way possible. Short instead of tall, dark hair instead of winter-red, brown eyes not silver, not my equal in age or groundsense. Farmer instead of Lakewalker, how much farther can you get? I can look at her all day long and not stir up one painful memory." Except for the brightness of her ground; in that, his two wives were blazingly alike. He gulped at the thought, and wondered why he'd never allowed himself to think it before. "Give this notion over, Neeta. You'll just embarrass yourself and me to no good purpose. There are better young men for you."

"Young idiots," she snorted.

"They grow older in due course." Growing into old idiots? There was evidence.

She stood rigid. Dag wondered in despair how else he might say, *You're a cute young thing but your tactics are transparent and I wouldn't touch you with a stick* without offending or crushing her. He surely wasn't the most ornamental addition to any woman's bedroll, and he rather thought

Neeta hadn't thought of him in those terms till now—indeed, the first time they'd met, before she'd learned his ancient history, she'd looked at him like a spring beetle found crunched underfoot. But the tinge of hero worship was a dilemma.

Fortunately, before he could tangle himself up worse with his tongue, she raised her chin bravely, turned, and strode away. She was too much a proud patroller woman to flounce, which relieved him only slightly. Dag hoped he'd discouraged this approach to the argument about their direction of travel for good and all, although the possibility of Neeta sending in her partner as a second wave did cross his mind, and then he didn't know whether to laugh or wince. He trusted Tavia had more sense.

Neeta had a problem more pressing than what man she might or might not attach to her bedroll. Dag wasn't sure how much of a show she'd made of herself back at New Moon Cutoff to win both permission for the Arkady retrieval and command of it, but he had no doubt that for her to drag back to her camp without the groundsetter would be a considerable comedown. Still worse to return all alone, if Remo and maybe Tavia both bolted north, although Dag suspected Antan, at least, would be quite pleased if she came back without Dag and Fawn. Had her camp captain set her up to fail? Not a nice thought, though Dag could understand Antan yielding to the temptation to undercut his badgering young patroller and teach her a sharp lesson, the sharper for having brought it on herself.

So all in all, Dag was not surprised, come the dawn mist, to find Neeta and her little patrol saddling up to climb the next pass along with them. It was a long and busy day, fortunately, and by the time they'd been forced to cooperate on a dozen tasks, they'd established an unspoken pretense that the prior night's conversation had never occurred. At least she didn't seem heartbroken, and Dag could hardly fault her for her determination, even if it wasn't going to do her any good.

∽

After the labors of the pass, the following day's start was made later by a pouring rain. But the ragged gray clouds blew out by noon, the sun emerged, and a hot, bright, steaming stillness overtook the rugged country. Their cavalcade strung out along the miry road, just outpacing the first crop of mosquitoes whining in the woody shade. In the damp air, even quiet voices echoed off the rocks. Dag found himself riding together with Fawn, Whit, and Berry at the head of the line, everyone's feet dangling beside their stirrups. Despite the lazy heat he was pleased to note Fawn upright and staring eagerly around, not as fatigued as she'd been of late.

"How many folks live in Clearcreek, would you guess?" she asked Berry.

"Maybe seven hundred in the village, but a couple thousand up the whole valley."

"I was wondering what was the right size of place for Dag—Dag and Arkady, now—to set up their trial medicine tent. Too little, and there wouldn't be enough customers to keep them busy. Too many and they'd be overwhelmed. Likely Silver Shoals would be too much to start with. I don't know about Tripoint."

"It's bigger than Silver Shoals," said Dag. "I don't know if we'll have time this summer to take you up there and show you the city."

"It would be something, to have ridden the whole Trace from Gray-mouth to Tripoint," agreed Whit. "Still . . . I want to take Berry up to West Blue, too, and I don't think there'd be time to do both."

Whit was plainly eager to show his new bride off to his family. As well he should be, Dag thought.

"I've about got calluses on my backside from the Trace already," said Fawn. "Maybe you could bring back my mare and her foal, though. And my sack of plunkin ears, which Aunt Nattie was keeping for me."

"Oh, I thought we'd all go together," said Whit, sounding a little disappointed.

"Well, we'll see. How close is your place to the river, Berry?"

"Not much more'n a mile up the Clear Creek. We launched our yearly flatboat right into the crick from our land."

"So . . . you're really almost in the Grace Valley. Do boats—and rivermen—come in off the river? Is it like a river town?"

"Nearly. Clearcreek Landing, which sits at the crick mouth, is turning into a village in its own right, 'cept for washing away now and then in the floods. Are you thinkin' of more trade for Dag? It's a fact them river boys do themselves a world of hurt, time to time, even without the fevers."

"That," said Dag, "and something Fawn said once. That the river was like a village one street wide and two thousand miles long. I've been thinking for some time that if I want word to get around about what I'm doing, the river folks would ride courier for us."

Berry nodded in approval; if Dag was not a riverman, a riverbank man would clearly be the next best thing, in her estimation. "It would be a help to me and Hawthorn if you and Fawn and Arkady was to keep our house while we was gone down with the yearly flatboat—that is, if we get a boat built for this fall's rise. Whit still has a mite to learn 'fore I'm ready to make him boat boss and take up managin' the goods-shed. I'd like at least one more trip on the river 'fore I get landed on shore like Fawn." She jerked her chin toward her tent-sister's middle.

Whit smiled innocently.

"I don't suppose," said Fawn, "you have a pond on your place, Berry?"

"Why, we do, in fact."

Fawn brightened. "Really!" Planting plunkin in her mind already, Dag could see. Clearcreek, Oleana, was looming larger in his future every day. He began to think he might deal with it right well.

"My word, this is a strange country," said Fawn, looking around. "Where did all the trees go? There wasn't blight here, was there, Dag?"

The woods had opened out, with only a few tall red oaks, their bark laced with black scars, growing out of a riot of green scrub. "No, forest fire," said Dag. "There was a big summer drought in this valley a few years ago. It's all coming back real good, looks like."

Fawn peered under the flat of her hand at the new growth climbing the valley walls. "That must have been quite some fire."

Whit squinted ahead into the hazy distance. "Huh. Funny-lookin' fellow, there, wanderin' our way. Hey—is he *naked*?"

Dag followed his glance, opening his half-closed groundsense. A big, shaggy-haired man with oddly mottled skin was limping southward down the middle of the road. Dag's breath drew in, his back straightened, and his feet sought his stirrups as his mind burst in twenty directions at once, like a covey of startled quail.

"Blight, it's a mud-man!"

Dag stood in his saddle and bellowed over his shoulder, "Barr! Remo! We got us a mud-man! Fetch out the boar spears! Sumac—" Blight, where was Sumac? And Arkady? They weren't in his groundsense range. If a live mud-man was here on this road, its malice master could not be far off. *Not nearly far enough.* But Dag, straining, couldn't sense it yet. It came to him—gods, where had his wits gone?—that they hadn't been passed by any southward-bound traffic all morning. All the night before? *How long?*

"Fawn"—panic was making Dag's world turn red—"drop back to the wagons, make 'em stop, get all the farmers together, and *stay there*." One flying wit at least dropped a feather—"Explain to the ignorant ones what's going on."

Fawn had her reins tightened up while Whit was still closing his gaping mouth. "Right," she said simply, and yanked Magpie around.

Dag wheeled in the opposite direction, wrapped his reins around his hook, drew his steel knife, and clapped his heels to his gelding's sides. Copperhead bolted forward into the breathless light.

17

By the time Fawn reached the Basswoods' wagon, which was first in line, every patroller in the company was streaming past her in aid of Dag, weapons brandished. Barr and Remo had reacted the quickest, but Neeta, Tavia, and Rase weren't much behind.

Vio Basswood stood up on her wagon box, gripping the curved canvas roof and staring in horror as Grouse sawed the reins and brought them to a creaking halt. Her face draining, she screamed, "He's *killed* him! Ye gods, he just rode that poor man down and *killed* him!"

Fawn turned in her saddle and craned her neck. In the heat-hazed distance, Dag was pivoting Copperhead around the fallen mud-man. She abruptly realized what Vio thought she was seeing: Fawn's grim, hook-handed Lakewalker husband suddenly running mad and brutally attacking, without reason, an innocent, unarmed—not to mention unclothed—traveler.

"No!" cried Fawn. "That wasn't a man! It wasn't human, it was a mud-man!"

"A mud what?" said Grouse, glaring and scrambling for his spear.

"Malices make them up out of animals and mud by groundwork—magic. I've seen the holes they come out of. They make them up into human form to be their slaves and soldiers, and they're horribly danger-ous. You can't reason with them or anything, even though the malice gives them speech. They lose all their wits when their malice is slain—oh, never mind!" Grouse had his spear out, but was aiming it in the wrong direction, at Fawn, and at Berry who had ridden up panting. Fawn had thought Whit was behind her, but instead he'd turned again and followed the patrollers, if at a cautious trot. Inside the wagon, the toddler burst into wails at all the shouting.

"Mud-men *eat* children," Fawn put in desperately. "The shambles are dreadful, after." Did Vio need to know this? Maybe. She didn't need to be made more afraid—she seemed close to fainting—but she needed to be afraid of the right things.

Rase and Neeta came galloping back.

"Is it dead? Are there any more?" Fawn called.

Rase checked just long enough to gasp out, "That one's dealt with. No more within groundsense range, so far. Dag sent us to find Sumac and Arkady." He spurred on.

That pair had fallen behind more than once, lately, and Fawn hadn't given them a thought—at least, not about their safety. Between them, Sumac and Arkady were clearly proof against any predator these hills harbored—wolf, bear, catamount, or rattlesnake. A gang of mud-men was a different proposition.

All the other farmers in the company came up to cluster in the road, goggle, and demand repeated explanations. Pressed, Fawn finally said, "Look, I don't think I can explain mud-men to you." *Not and be believed.* "Just come look at the evil thing, why don't you?"

She turned and led them, wagons and all, up the road to the site of the gory slaughter. Dag and Whit had dismounted. Dag released

Copperhead's reins and prodded the body with his foot; Whit looked as if he was working up the nerve to do the same. "Blight it," Dag was saying, "this area is supposed to be well patrolled!" He glanced up. "Fawn, I told you to keep back!"

"No, Dag," she said firmly. "These folks have to see, just like your young patrollers."

"Oh." He scrubbed his hand—was it *shaking?*—over his face. "Yeah."

Fawn slid from her mare, took the reluctant Vio by the hand, and dragged her forward; the mob trailed. "Look at it, see? Look at its jaw, practically a muzzle, and those furry ears, and all that coarse hair—it likely started out as a bear, wouldn't you say, Dag?" She tried not to look at its bloodied throat, torn out in one slash of Dag's reaching war knife, with all the power of his arm and Copperhead's stride behind it.

"Black bear, oh yes," Dag agreed absently.

"He's . . . it's naked," said Calla hesitantly.

"Naked is good," said Dag. "Means it hasn't killed folks and stolen their clothes yet."

Fawn realized from their openmouthed staring that this was the first mud-man, alive or dead, that most of the young patrollers had ever seen, too. Dag pointed out a few more distinguishing features, still with the toe of his boot, then glanced up at his whole mixed audience. "This one is so crude and bearlike because it's the work of a malice in its first molt. The malice might even still be sessile, which would be good news for us. As a malice goes through molts and gets stronger and smarter, its making gets better, till you can't hardly tell a mud-man from a real human by eye. Lakewalker groundsense can tell at once, though. Their grounds are . . . their grounds are just not right."

All the young men jostled forward for a closer look, with the enthusiastic Hawthorn pushing through to the front; Fawn let Vio shrink back. Vio was trembling and teary from seeing, and smelling, the welter of blood, and her little girl, who came out from the wagon and grabbed her skirts, burst into tears in sheer contagion. The toddler tied in the wagon just howled on general principles. Grouse, clutching his spear and looking frantically fearful, his world suddenly full of new dangers but with no clear target to attack, turned on his wife and snarled, "Shut them up!"

It seemed mean, but Fawn had to admit Vio did get a better hold on herself, controlling her snivels and shuffling off to manage her children. A respite of sorts. Vio was beginning to learn *something,* Fawn thought, if only that the world was not what she'd imagined. Bo hadn't pushed forward, and he didn't look much surprised, but his seamed face screwed up in a dubious scowl. His glance of dismay was not at his Lakewalker companions, though, but at the surrounding ridges.

Dag, too, backed out of the crowd and stared up and down the road, gold eyes slitted. Reaching with his groundsense? A little relief lightened his features, and he muttered, "Ah, good, there's Arkady." Truly, in a couple of minutes the strays rode up.

Sumac jumped down and strode to him. "Sorry we fell behind, there. We were just talking."

From their un-disheveled looks, Fawn thought this was likely true. Though they both had the weights of character to appear unruffled even when half undone.

Arkady, eyes wide, dismounted and approached the corpse. His hand sought his belly, and his face worked as he swallowed. "That's . . . the most grotesque making I've ever seen."

"Yep," said Dag. "Try to imagine the power of the groundwork that can turn a bear into . . . well, this, inside of two weeks."

Intrigue fought the nausea in Arkady's face. "Can I dissect it?"

"Now? Are you mad?"

"No, of course not now! Later."

"We'll see," said Dag.

"With any luck, you can have your pick of the litter," said Sumac. "I'll bring you all the mud-men your heart desires."

"I'm not sure my heart desires any," Arkady admitted. "But it's . . . absent gods, but that thing's so wrong."

"Do you eat them?" asked Ash, hunkering down in fascination.

This won gagging noises from all the patrollers present, except Dag, who said only, "No. The flesh is tainted."

"Lakewalkers do skin them sometimes," said Fawn, remembering a certain bride gift.

"Not to use the leather," said Dag. "Just . . . in special cases."

When the pain was too great, and mere victory wasn't revenge enough, Fawn suspected.

Dag looked at Sumac, who looked back. Sizing each other up? Sumac cut across the moment, saying simply, "Well, what next, patrol leader?"

Fawn thought she could see the weight of responsibility descend like a hundred-pound sack of grain on Dag's shoulders. He sighed. "Scout, I reckon. North, wouldn't you say?"

Sumac's lips pursed. "That thing could have been running for home. But we haven't felt any blight sign, south of here. We don't have enough patrollers to split up and run a proper pattern."

"We haven't seen any traffic from the north all day," said Dag.

"Nor from the south," Sumac pointed out, "but I agree, north seems the best bet. Should we send a courier for help? Closest camp to here would be Laurel Gap, I reckon." She turned her head, and called, "Anyone else here ever been to Laurel Gap Camp?"

The other patrollers returned negative mumbles. Sumac muttered, "Blight. I don't want it to be me. But it might have to."

"Not yet, leastways," said Dag. "Right now we're in the middle of nowhere, knowing nothing, which doesn't make much to report."

Sumac's eyes glinted. "Indeed."

"Open your ground to me."

Her brows went up; a faint flush tinged her high-boned copper cheeks. But she evidently complied.

Dag looked her up and down, nodded without expression. "Pick a partner and ride up the road a piece. No more than five miles. See if you find any blight sign. I'll try to organize"—Dag's eye swept the company—"these," he sighed.

"Right." Sumac swung aboard her horse, looked over not the patrollers but their mounts, evidently judged Barr's the swiftest, and said, "Barr, follow me!"

Arkady's hand lifted as she wheeled away, but fell back unseen. The two scouts loped off up the road, mud spinning from their horses' hooves.

Fawn puzzled over that last exchange between uncle and niece. *Oh. Of course.* Dag had been checking to be sure Sumac hadn't conceived, before sending her out. It wasn't just his general protectiveness; pregnant women, as Fawn had painful reason to know, were preferred prey to a malice on the verge of a molt. The women's natural making made them beacons, walking bait. Their new ground shields might presently be protecting Fawn and Berry—she touched the walnut at her throat—but what of Vio or Calla? *The Lakewalkers would know even if the women didn't, yet,* she reassured herself. *They'd take precautions.* Children were a malice's next most favored morsels—she glanced uneasily at the Basswoods' wagon, where the crying had died down.

"All right," said Dag, raising his voice to carry, "everyone move up to that next little ford." He pointed toward a shallow creek crossing the road a hundred paces farther along. "We better grab the chance to water the animals. We have to make ready to run sudden."

That it shifted everyone farther from the disturbing sight and smell of the dead mud-man was just a bonus, Fawn figured. Setting an example, she retrieved Magpie's reins and marched along briskly.

❧

A quarter hour later, Dag found himself saying to Sage, "No, you can't take your anvil!" He ran his hand through his hair in exasperation. "If a malice is close, our best chance of escape is to abandon the wagons and run mounted. If you farmers get caught within range of its ground powers, it could seize your minds, and then you wouldn't believe how ugly things can get. You rescue each other first, then weapons and animals, then food if there's time. But no more. Absent gods, every Lakewalker child is taught this by age five!"

"The wagons are all we have!" cried Grouse.

"You can't stop to defend *things*."

"But my anvil!" said Sage. "It's everything to me."

Dag fixed him with a stern eye. "More than Calla?"

"Er . . ." Sage fell silent.

"If it doesn't fit in your saddlebags, *leave it*."

"Chances are," said Fawn, "we can circle back later and collect our gear again. If we live. And if we don't live, we won't need it anyway, right?"

Sage still looked torn.

Whit put in helpfully, "Sage, your anvil would be the last thing thieves would run off with. It takes two fellows just to lift it!"

"Not if it's still in the wagon. They can just take the whole rig."

"We'll have the mules," said Fawn. Cleverly not suggesting that a malice could just chain up its mud-men slaves to haul it all off, good girl. Dag gave her a grateful nod.

Sage wavered, then resigned himself to unhitching his team, Indigo helping. Dag hurried to greet Remo and Neeta, returning on foot from scouting up toward either ridge.

"Nothing up on my side within groundsense range," reported Remo.

"Mine either," said Neeta. "No physical signs, either. Just animal tracks and old travelers' camps."

Dag eyed the high ground overlooking them with disfavor; that there was no hostile eye up there spying on them now didn't mean there hadn't been an hour ago, or any time this morning.

"Should we feed folks while we can?" asked Fawn.

She was thinking, as always. Dag said, "Hand snacks only. Don't light a fire."

Everything waited on Sumac and Barr. The company was actually closer to the next big settlement riding forward than back, and the passes were about the same climb in either direction. At least the road behind was known to the farmers now. But until they actually located the malice, it was a guess which direction was truly safer. If the malice proved sessile he'd go after it with a quarter patrol without hesitation, Dag decided, but if it was more advanced, sense demanded they go neither south nor north, but cut across country west to Laurel Gap Camp and the nearest reinforcements. Or did it? Dag imagined dragging this whole gaggle of farmers over fifty miles of broken terrain, mud-men in pursuit, and bit his lip. He would certainly have to send a pair of patroller couriers swiftly on ahead. Reducing the farmer youngsters' Lakewalker guardians by two . . . He turned to more immediate calculations.

"Rase, let me see your sharing knife."

The boy already had it out of his saddlebags and slung around his neck, good. He pulled it out on its thong and displayed it; Dag ran his hand lightly over the sheath. *A good making.* "Seems sound," he said aloud. "If we take on a sessile, you'll be the centerpiece of the attack. This is the experience you came north to get; it just came on a little sooner than you expected, is all."

Rase's nostril's flared, in pride and fear. "Yes, sir."

"Whose heart's death is in there?"

"My great-grandfather's. About two years back."

"I see." Dag touched his forehead in respectful salute. "How's your ground veiling? Have you been keeping up your drills?" With Sumac as his patrol leader, Rase surely ought to have been.

"Yes, sir!"

"Good. I carry a primed knife, too, but I'll hold mine in reserve."

"It's lucky we have two knives in this patrol," said Rase.

"That wasn't luck, that was preparation. Know the difference. Preparation, you can control." He gave the young patroller an encouraging grip on the shoulder, which made Rase flash an earnest smile.

Reminded, Dag turned away to rummage through his own saddlebags. His new bonded knife came to hand first, and he slipped its strong braided cord over his neck and tucked the dark sheath into his shirt. Next, sifted farther down, he found his primed knife—dodgy, first, and unsupervised making that it was. The sheathed bone itself lay lightly on his chest, but the weight of ugly memories it held dragged like Sage's anvil. Well, if the renegade Crane's cruel deeds had any redemption, this was it.

He turned to find Fawn watching him, her dark eyes grave. Her lips moved as if to speak, then pressed closed; she gestured down the stream instead. "So, uh . . . what's the matter with Arkady?"

The maker sat on the creek bank in the midst of a patch of green horsetails, his head bowed to his knees.

"The mud-man, likely. The trained sensitivity that makes good makers also unfits them for patrol. Malice spoor hits them too hard."

Fawn frowned at him. "You've been doing sensitivity drills with Arkady for the past two, three months. What's that going to do to you?"

Dag sighed. "I'm not real anxious to test it. We'll just have to see."

She came nearer; her little hand rose to trace the walnut-stained knife sheath hidden under his shirt. "I suppose you have to wear this. Just don't . . . don't do anything stupid with it, all right? Remember what you promised."

Not while I'm aboveground and breathing, her words echoed in the hollows of his mind. "I won't forget."

She nodded sternly. Abruptly, he lifted her up, hugged her, twirled her around, and kissed her on the forehead.

"What was that in aid of?" she puffed in pleased surprise, righting herself as he set her back down.

"Nothing. Just because."

She ducked her head in a firm nod. "That's a good reason."

The farmers were bickering with one another and with the patrollers, but all were making steady progress at sorting out mounts for a retreat, so Dag didn't attempt to interfere. Packsaddles were rapidly refitted for riders, emptied of their loads and padded with blankets. Inevitably, Dag supposed, the Basswoods' so-called riding horse had no saddle. He wondered whether it would be better to distribute the two children with their parents, or with the best riders, which would be a couple of the patrollers. Assuming everyone headed in the same direction. He foresaw another argument, there. *Ah, gah.* His brain was doing that mad thing again, running unstoppably and repeatedly down every possible and impossible scenario, even though he knew blighted well that the world never delivered him his expectations.

Fawn brought him a chunk of cheese wrapped in cold pan bread left from the morning. He munched it along with a few swallows of flat, tepid water from his water bottle while he walked a tense perimeter along the turbid creek and around the too-noisy camp, his groundsense straining outward. It was still Arkady, and not Dag, who first lifted his head from his knees and turned his face north. Dag jogged to join him as Arkady stumbled out onto the road and looked up it.

Arkady's lips parted in horror, and he went greener than when he'd first seen the mud-man. Sumac's horse was galloping wildly toward them. The stirrups flapped and swung from its empty saddle.

Every patroller in range turned to stop the runaway with a summoning, so hard that the poor beast tumbled to its knees. It grunted up and stood trembling, lathered white between its legs and down its shoulders. Dag ran up, looking it over for blood or wounds, trying frantically to remember if Sumac had been wearing her leather coat when she rode off in the heat. It wasn't tied behind the cantle . . .

Arkady touched the empty saddle and groaned, "No . . ."

"She's a Redwing," Dag said through his teeth. "She lands on her feet. We are survivors . . ." He whirled and bellowed, "Whit! Fawn, Berry! Get those blighted farmers mounted up! Patrollers, to me!"

People scurried, yelled, stomped. Argued. The patrollers led their horses up and stood in a ragged line, awaiting orders. In an agonized voice, Arkady said, "Go!"

Dag looked up. A mile off, a horse bearing two riders popped over a rise into sight and his groundsense range simultaneously. "Wait," Dag said.

Arkady's face lifted, following his gaze. It felt almost uncouth to be watching an expression so painfully exposed, a man's last hope returned to him.

Gods, Sumac, Dag thought. *If the pair of us don't have heart failure before this is all over, it won't be your fault.* And then she could *inherit* her captaincy, clever girl. Agonizing minutes passed as the laboring horse cantered nearer.

As soon as they hove within shouting range, Barr called excitedly, "We found the malice! It's just up the road!" A ripple ran through the patrollers like the strain through a mob of horses milling at the start of a race.

Barr pulled up among them. Sumac more or less fell from where she clung behind Barr's cantle down into Arkady's arms. A drowning man couldn't hug his log any harder than he did her. Her braid was coming undone, tendrils of black hair plastered around her flushed, sweating face. Strained lines of pain framed her mouth and eyes, and she was breathing hard, but her gold eyes blazed like fires. She pushed Arkady away enough to find her feet, but didn't shuck off his anxious hand supporting her elbow, nor his tender one that prodded her scalp, though she did wince. She was wearing, absent gods be thanked, the coat; her ribs bore only bruises, though the knot on the back of her skull was swelling like an egg.

"This malice looks like it's just barely out of its burrow," she wheezed. "It's advancing down the road with a guard of twenty-two mud-men, but they're moving slow."

"Seventeen mud-men now," said Barr.

"They none of 'em have clothes or arms at all, except for rocks and sticks."

"And numbers," Dag muttered. "And the malice. Likely it means to supply itself with *our* weapons and gear."

"It'll have to think again about that plan. Dag, we can take it!" said Sumac.

"Looks like it almost took you."

"Oh, well." She tossed her hair back in a mockery of a feminine gesture, and grinned. "I didn't collect worse than a knock on the head, and you should see the other fellas. Grant you that malice is nasty."

"And strange, absent gods it's strange," said Barr.

"It's the first you ever saw," said Dag. "How do you figure?"

"Well, Sumac said, but even if—it's huge, Dag, seven foot tall at least, ugly as mud, but it can barely move for its great big belly sticking out. The whole time after we'd run headlong into its guards and were fighting our way back out again, it never stopped waddling along. It can't be covering more than two miles in an hour. So I make it two, three hours till it reaches here."

"The mud-men can move faster." Dag jerked his thumb over his shoulder. "As we saw by their scout, I reckon."

Sumac said, "The malice looks like a sessile about to molt, except for its being out on the road. I've never seen one that close to splitting, if so."

"Good for us if it's awkward, but its menace is in its ground powers, not its pseudo-body." Dag chewed his lip. Very few decisions left, here, till he committed them all irrevocably to action. "Rase, are you up for facing your first malice?"

"Yes, sir!"

Dag nodded, grinning darkly, the old excitement running molten through his veins. *I thought you were tired of this game, old patroller?* A live malice was never just a training exercise, but absent gods, this sounded close to it. *So, let's teach these youngsters a few tricks.* The better to keep them alive on the day when Dag would not be there, and the malice would not be so soft.

Whit, flanked by Fawn, had come up to the edge of the crowd when Sumac had arrived. Now he shouldered forward to say, "Dag, can I ride with you?" He touched the walnut at his throat.

Dag said automatically, "No. I need you to lead the farmers."

"Berry and Fawn can do that! What's the point of making this ground shield if we can't try it out?"

Indeed, that was going to be a problem, if he kept making shields for people he loved . . . "Blight, Whit. If I ever make shields for Reed and Rush, I'll happily stake them out as bait. Not you."

Fawn said, "If your shields are ever to make us farmers be partners to Lakewalkers, and not just backward children in your eyes, it has to start somewhere. Seems to me you've said a word or two about a man starting where he is. Well, here we are."

She *would* quote Dag back to himself . . . He weakened. "I suppose," he said, "someone has to hold the horses."

"Thanks, sir!"

"You be careful, Whit," said Fawn sternly. "Don't go turning that into the stupidest thing I ever said. I shouldn't like to explain it to Berry. Or Mama."

"Right, Sis!" Whit gave Fawn a hug and dashed off to collect his horse.

"Arkady goes with the farmer party, of course." Dag narrowed his eyes at the maker, who, praise be, didn't protest. "So do you, Sumac."

Sumac opened her mouth, hesitated.

"You're still dizzy from that knock on your head, your horse is spent, and if it all goes sour, someone needs to know how to get these farmers to Laurel Gap. Which reminds me, Barr, go swap out your mount for a fresher one."

Barr scurried. Miraculously, Sumac didn't argue, but allowed the concerned Arkady to lead her off. She was blinking rather hard, as if her vision wasn't quite meshing.

In minutes more, Dag was leading five patrollers and one West Blue boy at a canter up the road, while Berry and Fawn rousted the rest to ride south. Dag wanted to put as much distance between the attack and Fawn as he could, to give the farmers their best chance if they needed it; and if they didn't, well, one of the young patrollers could play courier and close the gap quickly enough. A mud-man troop, horsed, could do the same, but these all seemed to be afoot, so far. *And let's keep it that way.*

Dag's safe scheme to leave his tent-brother with the horses foundered at once on Whit's crossbow. His little patrol was too short on archers to forgo the weapon or its most experienced wielder. He reordered his plan of attack in his head yet again, in time with Copperhead's swift stride.

"Barr!" he called over the hoofbeats. "Where's our last good cover before we come up on 'em?" Which would be soon; already, and despite his closed ground, Dag could feel the dry shock in his midsection that told him a live malice was nearby.

"Depends on how much they've moved since we hit them," Barr called back. "Right up there, I think." He pointed to a rocky outcrop almost overhanging the road, the tail of a spur from the western ridge, sheltering a seeping rivulet. "Not many trees beyond, all fire scrub and brambles. We'll be able to see trouble coming."

So will the malice, Dag thought, but waved his hook in acknowledgment. They swung into the sheltered space, to find signs of its having been used as a campsite by many prior travelers. The patrollers dismounted and began arming themselves.

Dag flung himself off Copperhead and scrambled up the steep slope to the ridgelet, flanked by Barr. On his knees, he parted the blackberry canes and poison ivy with his hook arm and peered out into the hot green afternoon.

The road drew a groove through the recovering scrub, winding down to the next stream crossing and up again, an open space of a good mile. A quarter of the way across it, the malice's band trudged toward them. Dag could see the creature clearly, head and shoulders above its mud-men. Its body was indeed massive, its gut enormous, its gait clumsy and bizarre.

"Still on the Trace," murmured Dag. "I'd have thought you and Sumac would have driven them to cover. By the way, five down or no, I don't thank you two for teaching them to fear Lakewalkers, or how to fight us. Sumac should have known *scout* doesn't mean *alarm*."

"We were flying around a bend and ran into them quicker than we expected. Just beyond that next rise. They were more spread out, then," Barr whispered back. "They've only moved on about a mile since."

Dag squinted into the shimmer trying to number mud-man heads, gave up, and said to Barr, "Count 'em. Has it changed?"

Barr's younger eyes narrowed intently; his lips moved. "Twenty-six now. Hey! That can't be right."

Dag didn't think Sumac had miscounted. "It must have drawn in its scouts, for defense, and to replace the fallen. Which is no bad result." This close to the malice, Dag didn't dare open his groundsense to check, but he saw no sign of flanking mud-men moving through the nearby scrub. Any more distant mud-men were not a tactical consideration.

The enemy was closing the gap, if at a shambling pace. *Let them do most of the walking, good.* Dag slid back down to the clearing. The horses had been tied patroller style, that is, reins wrapped up so as not to trail, and heavily persuaded to stay together. Because you wouldn't want to physically tether a horse you might need to summon, nor risk leaving the poor beasts helpless if no one returned to release them. He rechecked Copperhead, then turned to order his patrol, keeping his voice low.

"All right. We have the advantage of this rise here, which I mean to keep. As soon as the malice and its mud-men are in bow shot, if they haven't spotted us and turned tail first, I, Whit, Tavia, and Barr will try to take down as many as we can till we run out of arrows. After that it's a wild pig hunt with spears and knives, except pigs aren't smart enough to gang up on you and mud-men are. Try not to get separated and become a target, and keep an eye out for anyone who does. Don't stop to finish off your mud-man if it's too disabled to move, but be aware they'll keep coming at you even when hurt as long as their malice is alive. And remember the mud-men are just a noisy diversion; the only target that counts is the malice, and getting Rase and his knife up to it. Try to circle behind it, Rase."

The patroller swallowed, set his shoulders, nodded. Forced his hand, clutching the knife slung around his neck, back to his side.

Dag drew breath and went on swiftly, "I'm shifting your usual partnerships around. Neeta and Remo both will partner with Rase, flanking him like linkers, because they have the best ground veiling to be that close to the malice, and Neeta has some experience."

Neeta flashed a nervous but pleased smile, and ducked her chin.

"That leaves Barr with Tavia, and Whit with me."

That pleased Barr, certainly. Whit blinked in shy pride.

Without Whit along, Dag would have partnered Rase, guiding him in to his first kill. Whit had slain bandits; mud-men wouldn't shake him unduly. But if the ground shield failed, the boy risked ground-ripping or—almost worse—mind slaving. If the latter happened, Dag hoped he wouldn't have to do more than clout his tent-brother on the head to put him out of the way till the malice went down, but that wasn't a task he dared leave to anyone else. He did not voice the risk, not wanting to put Whit off his stride.

"We don't have to worry about surrounding the malice once it's close to our position. It's moving so slow that when the mud-men are out of the way we'll almost be able to overtake it walking. But—listen close, Whit, because this is where it gets different than a pig hunt—taking on the malice is more like attacking a big bear, and not one of the cute black bears you find around here, but a big northern grizzly. It's strong, it swings around fast, and it can knock a man thirty feet if it connects with you. Only the sharing knife will kill it. So you concentrate on the mud-men, and leave the malice to Rase and his partners. Got it?"

"Yessir," said Whit, eyes wide.

"All right. Get a drink or a piss now if you need to, keep your grounds shut tight, no talking from here on. Tavia and Barr, find your best shooting positions. Whit, stay by me."

Dag went to Copperhead and collected his adapted bow and arrows. He hitched his quiver over his shoulder, unbolted his hook from its wooden wrist cuff and dropped it in the leather pouch at his waist, seated the bow in its place, and locked it down. He tested the draw: strings dry and sound. Whit came bounding up swinging his crossbow, and Dag thought to whisper, "Don't cock that thing till I fire my first shot. Noisy ratchet."

Whit nodded understanding. Except for an occasional faint clink of gear or snort from a horse, Dag's makeshift patrol was moving in proper uncanny silence. Now he had nothing to do but find a good line of sight from the cover of the rocky rise, hunker down, and wait for things to go wrong.

18

The malice stopped barely two hundred paces off, a little to their right where the road started to bend around the outcrop. It seemed to sniff the air, swinging its great hairless head back and forth. Seven feet tall at least, and Dag guessed from its livid, mottled skin that its initial lair must have lain among gray rocks, which didn't narrow it much; thousands of dells, cracks, caves, and overhangs lined this valley. The malice looked quite odd, standing out naked in the sunlit green space. It belonged hidden in cold shadow, where spring didn't reach and ice lingered and its monstrousness might be concealed.

Dag didn't know how much those glittering too-human eyes, lurking under brows like their own little limestone overhangs, could see in this light. He prayed the other patrollers had their grounds furled as tightly as his own. Shielded Whit would be an ambiguous glow in its ground-sense, a smudgy *something*, alive yet elusive. It could likely sense the horses by now, growing uneasy behind the rocks.

It certainly sensed something, because it snorted, and a dozen of its mud-men left the road and began to wade through the waist-high scrub toward the outcrop. Even the mud-men flinched from last year's thorns on the dry blackberry canes, which crackled as they fought through them. The angle between Dag's position and Barr and Tavia's was not as wide for crossfire as he would have liked, but their elevation was excellent. *Yes, that's perfect. Come closer, you suffering brutes, yes.*

Dag held his steel-headed arrow loosely nocked and waited some more. Whit was watching him, crossbow clenched and bolt at the ready, with his eyes going wider and wider, as if to cry, *Now, now . . . now?*

Dag knelt up leisurely, taking his first and last chance for a perfect shot. He would try for an eye on that approaching . . . possum-man? Or it might once have been a rabbit. The peculiar relaxation overcame him that occurred when all decision making was over, as when an arrow had been released but not yet found its target. Speaking of which . . .

He drew. Settled. Released. *"Yes,"* he hissed. Brain-shot; the possum-man squalled once, fell, thrashed, and went still. Dag nocked and drew again while the wild cranking of Whit's crossbow mechanism stuttered beside him. His second arrow flew just before Whit's first.

Dag's brows twitched up at the *thwack-crack* of Whit's heavy bolt striking a mud-man's arm. A belly or brain shot would have been better, but he could swear that bone just broke. Within its short range, the weapon's projectiles packed an impressive punch. From the corner of his eye he saw more arrows dart out. Two hits, followed by roaring and howling. The mud-men boiled forward, crunching madly up the slope, which was just fine as long as the arrows lasted.

Whit's next ratchet-and-thrum resulted in a clear miss, but after that was a hard hit that knocked a looming tuft-eared fox-man backward down the slope. Dag was not yet out of arrows when the few mud-men remaining on their feet began to turn tail, or at least withdraw toward their master. Dag didn't bother counting the ones down, just the ones still up. Some had arrows sticking out of them at odd angles, and shrieked in pain, but they weren't stumbling nearly enough to suit Dag.

The malice had actually knelt down, its vast gut resting on the road between its spread knees, but it wallowed upright again as its dozen remaining guards drew back around it. Dag let his bow arm swing down out of the way and drew his war knife. "All right. It won't get any better."

Out of bolts, Whit started to let his crossbow fall, but Dag said, "Hang it on your back. You might get the chance to collect a few of your misses. Or hits." Whit shrugged the carrying strap across his chest and took up the ash spear he had borrowed from Sage. The boy yelled once in excitement as they began to run, noticed that everyone else was advancing in dead silence, and clamped his mouth shut. Dag let him plunge ahead and spend his eagerness threshing a path through the thorny scrub, for which the waving spear proved unexpectedly useful. Barr and Tavia wove down the slope to his right, with the sharing-knife threesome close behind them.

They spread out around the malice; its mud-men responded by throwing rocks, with which this country was only too well supplied. Their whistling power was nasty, but fortunately the aim was mostly bad, though Remo yelped as one bounced off his shoulder. The malice turned around and around, roaring horribly, but did not retreat. Closing and careful, Dag expended two of his last four steel-tipped arrows putting mud-men down to stay. Another pair lurched toward them; one ran up on Whit's spear, ripping it from his hands but then falling over its impalement in a tangle. Dag's war knife opened his mud-man from groin to breastbone. Whit paused to yank back one of his bolts from the fallen creature's leg, shaking it free of gore.

A cudgel-waving mud-man charged toward Rase, bowling Barr over; swiftly, Dag sent an arrow after it as his threesome kept trying to circle behind the malice, who kept rotating to face them. Inspired, Whit raised his bow and shot his retrieved bolt at the malice. It thwacked hard into the creature's left shoulder. And vanished.

The malice screamed and heaved its awkward body around. On its left breast, its gray skin parted; from that mouth, the bolt spat into the malice's up-reaching hand. The skin rippled closed again while the malice was winding its arm back to throw the bolt like a dart. *It* would not miss; Dag stepped in front of Whit, who was gibbering, "Did you see that? Come flyin' out just like a watermelon seed! Should've gone through its *heart* . . . !"

Even through his tight veiling Dag could feel the malice reaching out to ground-rip his tent-brother. The power of it would pry open Whit's shield like a mussel shell, given enough time. Which of course was also true of ground veiling. The huge arm bunched . . .

Whit's shot had been futile as a blow but perfect as a distraction. In the malice's momentary and terrible shift of focus, Rase, face gone white, darted up behind it, shut his eyes, and thrust out the pale blade of his sharing knife.

The faint *crack* as the bone split and released its hoarded death into the malice was the sweetest sound Dag could imagine.

The malice's scream shot upward in pitch till it felt like hot needles thrust into Dag's eardrums. Whit clamped his hands over his own ears and bent, mouth opening and closing on words Dag could not make out. Rase, Neeta, and Remo all stumbled backward; Rase, grazed by the malice's deathly aura, was curling in on himself and starting to vomit already. Slowly, starting at the top of its ridged skull, the malice began to fall apart, pieces flaking off and spinning away in a stinking cloud. Destruction spiraled downward, faster and faster, yet slowed when it reached the out-thrust torso. The remains of the creature—god, man, monster, or some clot of all three—slumped in a pile in the middle of the road, several hundred pounds of slimy rubble. The sudden silence was a blessing beyond imagining.

Dag eyed the great formless lump, drew Crane's primed knife from the leather sheath hung at his throat, and advanced cautiously. He was going to have to open his ground just a hair to check this, and then he was going to regret it. The smell was bad enough. The lingering *wrongness* blasted through Dag with the force of a bitter wind in a Luthlian winter; his belly knotted and his mouth watered uncontrollably. But the new malice body forming inside the old one was dead, too, or never alive. Dag clamped his ground and his jaw shut again, put the knife away, and swallowed hard against his late lunch demanding instant escape.

Whit was shaken but standing. Barr was sitting on the ground holding his bleeding head; Tavia, with a bright red mark on her face that was going to be a dark blue bruise soon, knelt beside him trying to pull his hands away to check the damage. Rase was now on all fours, emptying his guts, with Remo bent beside him in concern and Neeta watching warily.

"Whit, Neeta," Dag called. "We're not done yet. Got to clean up all the mud-men within reach."

Easy reach, at least. Only a couple of the creatures had escaped across the road, trying to find concealment in the riverbanks or in the scrub up toward the far ridge. They were mindless now—or rather, and more dreadfully, returned to their animal minds trapped in their humanlike bodies. They would die on their own, but only after lingering agonies. The ones still alive in the broken brambles were making the most vile noises, animal screams mixed with almost human-sounding weeping. Dag paused to swap out his bow for his hook again, and drew his knife once more. The downed mud-men were still dangerous in their thrashings, so the three of them worked together, two to hold them down and one to slice through those pitiable throats, ending what should never have begun. It was rightful mercy and Dag hated every wretched minute of it. But the youngsters didn't need to see that, so he set a methodical and thorough example, for the thousandth time. They collected as many of everyone's spent arrows as they could find.

Dag made sure Rase wasn't vomiting blood, then set Remo to haul him back to the horses, away from the remains of the malice. Tavia supported Barr, who looked impressively gory—scalp wounds bled like wellsprings—but had suffered no skull cracks. Dag assigned Neeta to ride after the farmers and get them turned around once more. "Tell them we'll meet by the wagons!"

As the swift hoofbeats of her mount receded, Whit circled the smelly mound piled up in the middle of the road, shaking his head in new amazement. "That thing must have weighed six, eight hundred pounds. Did Fawn's malice look like that one?" he asked Dag.

"Pretty much. Except the Glassforge malice was more dangerous, not being on the verge of a molt." The Glassforge malice had also acquired language; this one seemed not to have, which suggested hopefully that it had not yet taken any human victims.

"How do those molts work? You keep talking about them like they was a bad thing."

Dag shrugged. "You understand how mud-men are made, right? The malice places a live animal in the soil, and alters the creature's ground to impel its body to grow into a human form."

"I heard Fawn describe the ones she saw in Raintree. I wouldn't rightly claim to *understand* it, but I guess I get the picture."

"Ground is the underlying truth of the world. The malice turns it into a lie, or at least, into something else, and the matter labors to match it."

Whit looked much blanker; Dag swiftly gave up on maker theory. "It's like the malice uses its own body as a mud-pot to grow its new one in. A newer, better, more advanced, usually more human-looking one. Depending on what people or animals the malice has found to consume. Ground-rip, that is. A malice uses those grounds to teach its new body how to grow."

Whit's nose wrinkled. "You're saying the malice gives birth to *it-self*?"

"There's a reason we call it molting and not birth. When it reaches full size, the malice abandons its old body, which dies around the new one, and the new one, er . . . fights its way out of the old skin. The new body is usually near as big as the old, so a malice on the verge of a molt is sessile—immobile. It holes up for days or weeks and doesn't move till the process is complete. They're pretty helpless at that stage, and easy—well, easier—to slay."

"What about when it gets more human, like the one you saw in Raintree? That you said was so beautiful?"

"Same process. Messier, I guess. They tend to molt less often as they advance."

Whit stared at the pile of rubble and scratched his head. "Huh. You wouldn't want Fawn to see that just now, I reckon."

Trust Whit to blurt out what was better left unsaid. Dag didn't know whether to laugh or sigh. "No," he agreed. "I sure wouldn't."

But Whit was already in pursuit of another thought. "So—back when you two met near Glassforge, Fawn did what Rase just did, more or less?"

"Yes. She slew a malice, with a primed sharing knife. Just like that."

Whit was silent for a very long time. "My little sister," he finally said. His tone was not especially readable, but Dag thought it might be wonder. Or awe. "Huh."

∿

Fawn was relieved to camp that night back at the shallow ford where they'd left the wagons, despite the exhausting trek to regain it. Grouse wasn't the only farmer to grumble about having ridden twelve miles down the road only to ride twelve miles back, just the loudest.

"It was a long day's work to end up right back where we started. What did we gain?"

"Practice," said Sumac, without sympathy. "Practice is never wasted."

Once Fawn had convinced herself of Dag's uninjured state, she viewed the victorious but battered patrol with what concern she had left over. Whit assured her that Barr yelped far more for Arkady stitching up his head than he had for the mud-man hitting him with the original rock. Remo moved stiffly, and couldn't raise his right arm higher than his shoulder, but made no complaint. Everyone including Tavia seemed to think the bruise on Tavia's face was more showy than serious.

Rase, untouched by any blow, was by far the sickest. Fawn gladly shared her dwindling stock of anti-nausea medicine with him, but it was after sunset before he could keep so much as a sip of water down. Dag seemed unalarmed, but made sure the boy stayed in his bedroll. The Lakewalkers all agreed Rase deserved a proper bow-down, a party patroller-style to celebrate his first malice kill, but that it would have to be put off till he was in shape to enjoy it, which Dag said could be as much as a week.

The patrollers collected around the fire after supper to piece to-gether Rase's spent knife and carefully wrap the shards in a makeshift cloth shroud until it could be returned to New Elm Camp for burial. They didn't seem grave enough for Fawn to call it a ritual, nor cheery enough to call it a celebration, but Sumac led them in a song Fawn recognized from the bow-down she'd seen back in Glassforge—not with a bone flute this time, just with naked voices. The words turned out to be not about malices or death or sacrifice, but about a garden by a lakeside where two lovers met. It ought to have sounded lyrical, but somehow came out more like a hymn. Fawn could not have said why, but she felt the tune must be very old.

Berry, listening as the verses found their culmination, drew her hickory-wood fiddle from its bag and, despite her healing fingers, took up the melody in winding variations each sweeter than the last. The flickering firelight gleamed off tracks of tears on Rase's face as he listened from his bedroll, and when she finished, he murmured, "Thank you," very sincerely. Fawn wondered how close to his great-grandfather the young patroller had been.

Berry lightened the mood with a brisker reel, inspiring Plum to drag her little brother Owlet to the fireside in a valiant attempt to dance. The two held hands and swung arms with more enthusiasm than grace, and Owlet squealed his delight as Plum twirled her skirts. In this warm weather Owlet ran about dressed in a cast-off shirt, as good as a gown on him, and nothing else; below the hem his dimpled knees pumped and his little bare feet tromped the dirt, and even Bo and Dag smiled.

After Berry shook out her hands and put the fiddle away, Bo offered a tale or two, both outrageously unlikely, which led to some reminiscing from the patrollers, the likelihood of which was harder to judge. A few hoarded bottles passed from hand to hand. Arkady's contribution won the most respect; the one sip that Fawn dared went down like liquid fire. Even Grouse took a swallow of that one.

When the moon rose, Fawn lay in their bedroll and listened to the munching and muffled snorting of the grazing animals, scattered up the creek side. From the way he'd picked at his dinner, she thought Dag shared some of Rase's queasiness, but she wasn't sure how it compared with how he'd felt after the Glassforge malice, as she'd been in no condition then to notice. So had Rase's ground veiling just been unpracticed, or would he grow into a maker someday, too? Dag walked his perimeter patrol very wide; it was a long time before he joined her. They found their familiar positions, legs interlaced beneath the blankets, face-to-face in the silvered dark.

"Was it a hard fight today?" she asked, stroking his furrowed forehead, winding her fingers in the unruly curls of his hair in which no gray strands yet gleamed.

"No. As straightforward as any other sessile, truth to tell."

"Did Whit's shield work right?"

"As far as I could tell. Well, I don't know how long it would have stood up to a serious attempt at ground-ripping, but it resisted mind slaving. If only because it made Whit's ground so blurry the malice couldn't figure out what he was. We didn't give it time to puzzle out the problem."

"Your patrollers were all right?"

"Oh, yes."

Fawn said carefully, "I'm not sure they know you think that. You've been sort of grim and glum tonight."

His brows lifted. "The youngsters did very well. Whit, too. He pulled his weight, and they all saw that he did. Won't any of 'em look at farmers quite the same way again, I daresay." He was silent a moment. "It's the malice bothers me."

"Why?"

He drew breath, let it out slowly. "I don't know. It just . . . niggles. Every malice is akin, yet every one is a little different. Why was it out on the road like that?"

"Maybe it was just changing its lair. Looking for a better place to molt."

"Possibly." Dag didn't sound convinced. "But this one seemed awfully aggressive for a pre-molt. Usually by the time they reach that stage they just lay up and let their mud-men bring them their prey."

"Maybe . . . I don't know. Maybe it ground-ripped some rabid animals?"

"I don't think it would work like that." He shook his head, hugging her in close as she turned to fit the curve of his body. "But I'll say a few good words to the youngsters tomorrow. They earned it."

∾

The next day dawned clear; the company made a creaky but willing enough start shortly thereafter. Rase had recovered enough to sit his horse, although he had to let Indigo saddle it and two of his comrades help boost him aboard. Four miles up the road came a delay when everyone who hadn't been on the battlefield got dragged over it by everyone who had for a blow-by-blow description of the fight. Fawn watched from atop Magpie, a trifle worried about the effect any lingering blight might have on her child. She was waiting eagerly for the first flutter of quickening, down there deep in her belly. She had not confessed even to Dag her unfounded conviction that if only she could bring this pregnancy past the point where her first had failed, it would be a sign of hope, like breaking a curse. To encounter a malice just *now*, bringing back such evil memories, had shaken her more than she'd let on.

But Whit and the patrollers finished babbling about their every bow shot *at last*, and they moved on.

Late in the morning, they came upon the spot where Dag said the malice must have first turned onto the road, and Dag led a mixed party of patrollers and farmer boys up toward the eastern ridge to search for the lair. Sumac stayed with the wagons to watch over Rase, with Neeta, who had seen lairs in Luthlia, assigned as support. Bo also declined the treat, and Hod as usual stuck by him.

Berry, grinning, leaned across her saddlebow to whisper to Fawn, "I expected Bo to have a worse head than this, come this morning. At midnight last night he was swearin' to me he'd seen bats the size of turkey vultures flyin' over the moon."

"Were they anything like the hoop snakes he told me southern folks used as wagon wheels?" said Fawn. "Or the alligators hitched up in teams to draw racing boats in the swamps? Or the time it rained so hard that he saw catfish swimming up the road overhead, and fellows caught them in their hats?"

"I expect so. This fish wasn't biting, though."

Fawn snickered, and kicked Magpie along. She wouldn't be surprised if Bo had seen vultures; those unburied mud-men corpses stank, and would draw scavengers soon. Did vultures search for carrion by moonlight?

The fire scrub ran on for miles, and Fawn tried to imagine the size of the blaze that had leveled these woods. How fast had the wind whipped the orange wall of death? She was reminded that malices were far from the only great uncaring hazard in the world. Between being burned to death or blighted, she could see little to choose. Yet the fire scars were recovering in years, not decades or centuries, and from the point of view of blackberry brambles and fireweed, might almost be considered a blessing.

Her ruminations grew darker when they stopped for lunch at a stream crossing by what was plainly a burned-out village, destroyed by that same three-years-back fire. The lack of settlers in this valley seemed suddenly explained. She walked among the traces of houses and sheds, blackened char sticking out from the green weeds like bones through skin.

"We could stop right here," said Grouse, eyeing the bit of flat land along the feeder creek that had doubtless been what first attracted the burned-out folks.

"I'm not stopping in *this* accursed country," said Vio sharply. "Monsters and fires and bear-men and who knows what all . . ." She had to break off to run and rescue her toddler Owlet from a determined attempt to fall headfirst into an old well. As she was snatching him away from death, and he was thrashing mightily in protest, she glanced down and shrieked.

Fawn hurried to her side, as did Sage and everyone else in earshot. The sun overhead lit the well shaft, revealing a mess of bones at the bottom all tangled together. The flesh was gone, but a few scraps of hair and clothing still showed.

"They must have gone down into the water there to try to get away from the flames," said Sumac, coming over to look, "and suffocated when the fire passed over."

"Or drowned," opined Bo, "if they climbed on each other."

Fawn swallowed and walked quickly away. Several sizes of bones, down there. A family? A couple of families, maybe.

"Wasn't there anyone left even to bury these?" asked Calla.

"Maybe the survivors decided to let this be their grave," offered Sage. "Not wanting it for a well anymore."

After some debate, it was decided to leave the well-grave as it had been found. Fawn had lost her appetite for lunch, and was glad to be gone from the haunted place.

The malice lair expedition dropped down to rejoin them a few miles farther on. Dag had told Arkady he would be sorry if he came along, and the maker looked it, his face clammy with a Rase-like paleness. Sumac hurried to help him, but he just shook his head. The two parties traded fire-village and malice-lair descriptions, equally gruesome, and for once Bo offered no silly tales to top them.

Late in the afternoon, Fawn found herself riding between Dag and Finch at the head of the company. Everyone was starting to keep an eye out for a likely spot to camp for the night. Dag said that they might reach the pass at the head of this long valley late tomorrow. A debate was afoot whether it would be better to rest the animals for a day before or a day after the climb, but Fawn thought most folks were in favor of after. No one much liked this country anymore.

Finch was still full of his first sight of a malice lair. "Never would have believed! Everything dead gray for two hundred paces around. And those pocky holes where the mud-men came out, just like you said, Fawn!"

"Was it very bad?" Fawn asked.

Dag shook his head. "Nothing you haven't seen, Spark. And less. It still puzzles me." He turned in his saddle, frowning. "I sure wish we'd seen some other traffic today. Either direction."

Sumac was riding behind them, along with a recovered but rather quiet Arkady. "That reminds me, Dag," she remarked. "We should log a report at Laurel Gap Camp. They should have cleaned out that malice before we found it."

"Writing a patrol report, ah, yes," said Dag. "That'll be a good thing for you to teach the youngsters how to do."

She stuck out her tongue at him.

He grinned unrepentantly, but added, "We can leave it at the courier drop point in Blackwater Mills, when we get there. No need to go out of our way."

"Though I'd sure like to know where their patrol has got to," said Sumac.

Dag grimaced. "Aye." His puzzled gloom returned.

Inspired, Fawn sat up in her saddle. "What if that malice wasn't attacking us, Dag? What if it was running *away* from something?"

"What does a malice have to run away from?" asked Finch.

Fawn brightened further. "Patrollers! Maybe we'll run into those Laurel Gap patrollers up the road a piece."

"Will they be mad that we poached their malice?" asked Finch. Who hadn't been there when the malice had been slain any more than Fawn had, but somehow Whit as representative farmer cast a reflected glory on all the boys. Fawn didn't think it a bad thing.

"After a time," said Dag, "you learn there're plenty to go around. We don't hoard them."

Sumac said, "Though I trust the Laurel Gap patrol will be embarrassed. In fact, Uncle Dag, I believe I will write that report. Just to make sure of it."

Dag's smile flickered, but faded again. "I shouldn't think that malice would've run from a patrol. In the first place, it was so new-hatched it wouldn't have known to, and in the second, malices regard us as meals on legs. It'd be like running away from your dinner. We try to make the sharing knives a surprise to them."

Which gave Fawn a peculiar picture of her next meal leaping up off her plate, grabbing her knife, and attacking her. She shook it from her head. She didn't want to try to imagine what malices thought; she was afraid she might succeed. Maybe she needed a nap. She glanced up at Dag, and her belly went cold. His face had gone absolutely expressionless, as if he'd just had an idea he really, really didn't care for. "Not likely . . ." he breathed.

What isn't likely, beloved?

The fire blight was at last giving way to patches of never-burned trees. A quarter mile up the road, Fawn could see a clear line where the woods closed back in. Had sudden rain saved it? Or a change of wind direction? The sun's rim touched the western ridgetop, whose eastern slopes were already in shadow. She squinted at movement near the road at the tree line, doubly dusky.

"I'd vote for the first good stream past the trees for camp tonight," said Finch, peering too. "Huh. What is that? Turkey vultures have got themselves a party, looks like."

Half a dozen dark, flapping shapes surrounded a carcass. "A goat?" said Fawn. "A dog?"

"Maybe a fawn?" said Finch, then snickered at her peeved expression.

Dag stood abruptly in his stirrups, staring hard. "That's not a goat. It's a mule."

"Can't be," scoffed Finch. "That'd make those bird wings ten, twelve feet across."

"Those aren't birds. Sumac? Lend me your eyes. And your ground-sense."

Sumac kneed her horse forward, peering along with Dag. Her breath hissed in. "*What* the . . . Dag, what *are* those ugly things?"

"Mud . . . men?" His voice sounded remarkably unsure. "Mud-bat . . . things. No feathers. Joints are wrong for birds. Bat wings."

"Malices can make bat-men?" said Finch blankly. "Why didn't you say?"

"I've never seen the like," said Dag. "Wolf-men and dire wolves, yes. So why not bats?"

Fawn could think of a dozen good reasons why not bats, right up there with why not alligators? *No, ick, eew!*

"Absent gods, they're *huge*," said Arkady, who'd ridden up to look. His voice held a very un-Arkady-like quaver.

At the mule carcass, one shape was driven back by its feasting friends. It spread long, leathery wings, and vented a sharp snarl like a mill saw jamming.

"More leftovers?" said Fawn. "Like the ones you said got away over the river?" She hoped fervently that these were leftovers. Because the alternative. . .

What in the wide green world would a malice have to run from?

Nothing.

Except—a worse malice.

"Are those *hands* at the tops of those wing joints?" said Sumac. "With . . . claws?"

"*Blight*," said Dag. "Fawn, Finch, ride back and stop the wagons. Sumac, round up the patrollers. I'm going for a closer look."

"Not alone, you're not!" said Sumac sharply. "Arkady, you alert the patrollers."

Arkady gulped, nodded, and wheeled his horse. Reluctantly, Fawn followed, turning awkwardly in her saddle to watch over her shoulder.

As Dag and Sumac cantered up to the carcass, the bat-creatures scattered from it, making more jamming-saw noises. They were awkward, crawling on the ground with their wings trailing like half-folded tent awnings. Two clawed their way up nearby trees. Others made for a pile of rocks, scuttling up one after, or over, another to gain height. Another turned and screamed, rearing up and flapping its wide leathery wings like a crowing rooster; both Dag's and Sumac's horses spooked, pivoting and trying to bolt. Dag couldn't force Copperhead close enough to slash with his knife, but did persuade his mount to spin and lash out with both hind legs. The shod hooves connected; Fawn could hear the bone-crack.

The bat-creature screamed again and flapped over the ground trailing its broken wing. Copperhead bounced wildly.

The bat-creatures who'd made it to the rock pile took off one after the other in great noisy wing flaps, barely clearing the ground before they started their climb into the air. They *could* fly, oh no! Roughly bat-shaped, with flat, oddly rectangular bodies like a flying squirrel's, heads large, with backswept, pointed ears. Fawn couldn't see the shapes of their mouths from here. Worse, they could fly *well*. Gaining height, the nightmare trio sped off over the woods.

Sumac gestured, mouth moving; Dag nodded. Both came galloping back to the wagons.

"Get everybody turned around!" Dag gasped.

"Not again!" wailed Grouse.

Fawn hesitated. "Dag—it's open country for miles behind us. If those things can drop down out of the air on us"—and it sure looked like they could—"wouldn't we be better off amongst the trees, where they'd tangle their wings?"

He stared at her openmouthed, eyes dilated. "Ah," he wheezed. "Point."

"At least," called Sumac, whose horrified horse still fought her, "close up under the trees till we can scout and take stock. Knives are going to be no good on those things. We want spears and bows."

"Axes, too," suggested Fawn. *The ones with the good long hafts.*

Everyone who was mounted rode up and clustered around to listen; Sage left their team's reins to Calla and came running up to hear as well. Shrewdly, he bore his long-handled sledgehammer, though his hands shook as he clutched it.

The wagons lurched forward once more. Fawn stuck close to Calla's. All the patrollers except Rase, and half the farmer boys, rode forward to make another attempt at slaying the mud-bats. They closed rapidly on the fallen one; when they parted, the shape lay still, like a collapsed tent. The remaining two seemed to have snared themselves in their tree branches. A rider might reach one with a spear, but the horses wouldn't go near; Whit had already dismounted. Fawn could hear the ratcheting of his crossbow, and see him exchanging gestures with Sumac about the angle of his shot.

So Fawn had a clear view when a black cloud of about fifty of the bat-things burst over the eastern ridge and stooped upon them.

She'd never been much for shrieking, or making squeaky girly noises, but she screamed in earnest now. Magpie reacted to the vast flapping wings much like the other mounts, plunging under Fawn and almost unseating her, carrying her away from the wagons in an all-out attempt to bolt. If only the mare had run *toward* the trees, Fawn would have let her carry on. Fawn sawed the reins, trying to get Magpie's head turned around in the hopes that her body would follow.

Water streamed from Fawn's eyes and whipped away in the wind as she bounced in her saddle. She gasped in terror of falling hard and maybe losing the baby, till she realized that at this speed she was more like to break her neck; the thought was oddly liberating. She gripped with her legs, felt herself slipping with every hard stride, then abandoned her reins to grab her pommel.

Every animal in the party was bolting or trying to. The Basswood's wagon was slowed because the two leader mules were tangled in their traces, and Sage and Calla's wagon was jammed behind it. Grouse had evidently fallen off, but he leaped after his rig jabbing upwards at mud-bats with his spear. Vio was braced on the box with one hand around the roof hoop and the other swinging an iron skillet. The wagon was covered with swarming bat-creatures, much as they'd mobbed the dead mule. They used their wing hands to hold on, mostly, but tore strips out of the canvas roof with their clawed feet, reaching down as if feeling around inside. Vio banged her skillet down on the clutching claws like a hammer, which made them jerk back, and whanged other mud-bats in the face or body as she could reach. She drove off some, but more came.

Vio's screams shattered when a bat-creature beat its wings and began to rise, clutching her toddler in its two feet. Owlet's mouth went square with terror and pain as he was lifted into the air, his shirttail flapping wildly around his churning knees. From the corner of Fawn's eye she saw a patroller boy, she wasn't sure which one, unseated and pulled struggling from his horse. Three mighty wing beats, and he fought free, only to fall with a cry cut off too sharp and a sickening bone-crack noise. Arm, leg, neck? Yanked around by Magpie, Fawn couldn't see where he fell.

A stench and a hot wind buffeted Fawn in the back, and suddenly a clawed foot anchored itself in her shoulder. Her cry of pain came out a stretched wail, *"Go away! Go away! Go away!"* as she beat at the creature with her hands, only to have it grab her around her other arm and flap its vast wings again and again. Its claws were like iron, its thin muscles like cable. Without the grip on her pommel, she began to rise from her saddle, and frantically wrapped one foot into a stirrup strap. Galloping Magpie jerked them along as if the mud-bat was a kite and Fawn the kite string. If the creature let go and she fell she could be dragged by her ankle, but if she let go she could be carried off like Owlet . . .

Copperhead, half bolting, half bucking, appeared in the right of Fawn's vision. Dag was somehow still aboard, gasping for air, gold eyes demented. There was no sign of his steel knife, but he swiped frantically with his hook and connected at least once, tearing a strip from a leathery wing beating against his face. The mud-bat yelped and drew its foot claws from Fawn's right shoulder, which welled with blood.

At Dag's next swipe the mud-bat caught his hook in its foot and held hard, releasing Fawn's left arm, too. She grabbed at her saddle as she fell, ripping several fingernails half off, but yanked her ankle from her stirrup strap and came tumbling to the ground on her feet and not her head, rolling in the damp earth and weeds. She scrambled to her knees, rearing around dizzily and trying to spot Dag again.

Magpie shied away. Copperhead, made frantic by the flapping monster fixed overhead, got his head down and gave a mighty twisting buck that would have launched his rider into the air even without the aid of a mud-bat. A second mud-bat swooped near.

"Take leg!" screeched the first as Dag wrenched, kicked, punched, and struggled. The second mud-bat got a claw into one of his boots, then brought its other foot down for an iron grip on Dag's ankle. Somehow, the two sorted themselves out so their beating wings didn't knock into one another, and rose higher.

They talk! They have wits! They work with each other! Oh no, no . . . Fawn staggered along beneath the swooping shadow. She thought she was crying, but no sound seemed to be coming out of her bone-dry throat.

Higher overhead, Dag twisted, heaved, swore. Fawn remembered the falling patroller, and screamed upward, "Dag! Don't fight them till you're closer to the ground!"

He stared down wildly at her, seemed to realize how high he'd been dragged, and abruptly froze. *He heard, he understood, oh thanks be!* With his hand, still free, he clawed at his throat. Snapped the leather thong that held Crane's knife.

"Spark, take the knife!"

She stared up openmouthed, bewildered. The sheathed knife fell, turning in air, into the weeds, where it bounced unbroken in soft soil. She looked up to see Dag rising higher, higher . . .

In the distance, the howling toddler was being carried eastward; behind him, a madly flapping mud-bat seemed also to have Tavia, although it was struggling for altitude with her greater weight. Fawn didn't think the evil things could weigh more than forty pounds, wings and all, but the biggest ones seemed to be able to lift upwards of a hundred. Fawn weighed less. She squirmed in the dirt and sought a well-anchored sapling to grip as more mud-bats swooped overhead, but they didn't appear to be able to take prey right off the ground without fouling their wings. Once fallen and awkward, they could be outrun even by her, she thought.

She raised her head again. The wagons and the riders had reached the shelter of the trees, a litter of dead or injured mud-bats left in their wake. The slaughter was no consolation. Tavia's horse was down, making dreadful noises, gut-gouged and bleeding. Some mud-bats were attracted to its helplessness like the swarm around the dead mule, but most of the survivors took to the air and followed their comrades bearing the captives, screeching garbled abuse and clear calls to *Come!* at the hungry lingerers. Along the woods' edge to the east, Fawn thought she glimpsed Sumac spurring her horse in and out of the trees in a futile effort to follow.

Fawn crawled forward and gathered up the sharing knife, gripping it with trembling, bloodied fingers.

Whit galloped back out from under the trees toward Fawn, slid from his saddle, threw her up, and climbed after. She drew breath in stuttering gasps, unable to speak, but stuffed the knife in her shirt as they dashed for the woods once more. Beneath the screen of the branches at last, she slid down, then down to her knees, shaking too hard to stand. She wanted to faint, to escape this horrific moment, but she'd never mastered that trick. She was going to have to get up and deal with whatever came next.

"He giv' you his knife! Why'd he drop you that knife?" Whit wheezed. "Last thing!"

Neeta, scratched, bleeding, and wild, strode up. "I saw. Madness! Dag's got as good a chance of using it as we do—better! Absent gods, it's the only sharing knife we have left!"

Fawn stared fearfully up through the leaves at the luminous, empty sky, and thought, *No. He's got one other.*

19

People had dreams about flying, Dag had heard. He might have nightmares about it in the future, if he lived. Just now that wasn't looking . . .

. . . *down*. He shuddered for breath that would not come. The world wheeled wildly beneath him, like a map grown green and alive. The mud-bats' flapping wings were as thunderous as a tent coming loose in a windstorm. Horses looked strange from this angle, legless ovoids with questing heads. Copperhead and Magpie were running off riderless and bucking. Had Fawn fallen? Where? *There*. Too still? No—she lunged up, scuttled, dove under a little tree that seemed much too scant a cover. *Alive*. So far, so far.

On the next whirl he glimpsed Sumac, face raised, whipping her horse in and out of the fringe of the woods. She fell behind. The mud-bats lurched and swooped at a terrific pace, unimpeded by any barrier. *No, wrong*. The mud-bats were laboring hard to clear the eastern ridge.

Dag abandoned thought of the knife in his boot in favor of getting his hand around the other ankle of the mud-bat that gripped his hook.

It would not be able to drop him *wholly* at its convenience . . . the mud-bat shook its back foot and made an angry screeching noise, but in this position was almost as helpless to fight as Dag. The feeling that his skull was exploding in his panic eased slightly with this doubtless-false sense of control.

Fawn had seen the problem at once, while his head had still been swinging around. If he fought free at this height—*the blurring fall, the hot crunch of impact*—even Arkady wouldn't be able to put the pieces together again. *Blight, I only look like I know what I'm doing because so much of it is the same doings of the past forty years.* The truly new uncovered his weaknesses. Such as now, when he wanted *down* with a desperate desire, but *not that fast* . . .

He stiffened his neck and tried to look in some other direction. Most of the surviving mud-bats had winged ahead, but the burdened ones lagged. The screaming toddler—*oh, I hear you and agree, little brother*—was not far in front of him, if higher up. At least Owlet's mud-bat seemed to have its back claws locked around the child's thin arms, not cruelly piercing them the way the other had caught Fawn's shoulder.

Tavia was ahead and lower, struggling. She, too, had hit on the notion of wrapping her hands around her captor's back ankles; she twisted and kicked air, dragging her mud-bat closer to the ridge, which seemed to rise below them. The gray rocks looked bony and lethal, the trees like pit-trap stakes. Could Dag force a similar descent without being dropped or falling? Once they wobbled across the high line, the ground would fall away again. *Best chance.*

If he could somehow get rid of the mud-bat holding up his right boot, the other would not be able to support his weight. He kicked, without effect but to elicit some nasty hissing and a tighter grip that hoisted his right leg higher at a more awkward angle.

How close was the malice? The mud-bats strung out ahead seemed to be aiming to clear the next ridge as well, a good four miles off. *At least that far.* Dag dared to ease open his groundsense, reaching upward into the mud-bat bodies as he would examine a distressed patient. Their thin-walled chests heaved, their big hearts pounded with their exertion. Their grounds were a horror, but he ignored that. He focused on the second mud-bat, closer up and deeper in, deeper in . . . The ridge was coming up fast. There was no time for—there was no time.

He organized a projection, reached in, and ground-ripped a pinhole in the great artery exiting the mud-bat's heart. Three straining flaps, three thumping heartbeats, and the vessel split asunder. The mud-bat's mouth opened on a pained roar, its eyes rolled back, and it fell away, its clutching claws tearing loose from Dag's boot. It tumbled into the trees. Dag's remaining mud-bat lurched in surprise, redoubling its efforts.

Owlet's mud-bat turned and swooped nearer, calling in confusion, "Come, come!"

It's this or the poor tad is malice food. Dag had once been partly ground-ripped by a malice; as painful deaths went, there wasn't much to choose between that and plummeting onto rocks. Dag reached again, at his fullest stretch. This time he went for the big vein entering the heart. A touch slower to take effect, maybe . . . ? He felt the *pop*, withdrew at once. Owlet's mud-bat shrieked, choked, flapped more slowly . . . began spiraling down . . . crashed into whipping branches. Owlet's screams stopped too suddenly.

Dag's mud-bat was falling, too. It released its grip on his hook, tried to shake him off. But the release gave Dag back a weapon. He clawed upwards, catching and ripping skin from the creature's short rear legs, tearing tatters in the lower edges of the leathery wings. Blood spun out like a shower of raindrops, bright red.

The branches of a beech tree came up around them with a whoosh and crackle. The mud-bat's twisting wings caught, jerked loose, caught, jerked; together, mud-bat and prey descended in a neck-wrenching stutter and a shower of leaf bits and twigs. Just when Dag was figuring that his next greatest danger would be the mud-bat falling atop him, his sweaty grip was yanked loose from the bloody ankle, and *he* plummeted. He tried to take the impact on bending knees, rolling, but lost everything on the steep slope; a looping root, strong as a hawser, caught his right ankle and wrenched it violently. But it stopped him tumbling tail over teakettle down the mountainside.

Then the mud-bat landed on him. Snarling.

In a world beyond pain, Dag fought his way out from under the choking black envelope of those wings. His hand closed on the first stout weapon he could find, a broken branch. He swung it high and began beating in the creature's thin skull with frantic strokes.

On the third swing, he caught his first close look at its big brown eyes, blinking up at him. *"Ow,"* it said, in a miserable voice. *"Hurts."* A human voice, an animal's eyes, a child's bewilderment as to why these terrible things should be happening to it.

The mud-bat shuddered, choked, and died.

Dag, chest heaving for air, bent over and heaved in truth. There wasn't much in his belly. *Small favors.*

Oh, absent, absent gods. He folded in a boneless heap. He supposed, from the wet and slime on his face, that he was crying, although some of it might be blood. He didn't care. He put his arms over his head and bawled.

∾

His regained control of his breath and wits in a few minutes. *Overwrought* didn't *begin* to describe his state of mind. And body, which shuddered like Grouse in the throes of his ague. He lifted his right hand and found the wedding cord wrapping his left arm, and gripped it through the torn fabric of his shirt. *Alive, Spark's alive. She needs you. Start with that.* Upon that foundation, he could stand.

Or at least . . . sit up. His wrenched ankle was throbbing under his boot. He eyed it with disfavor, turning his groundsense upon himself, although it sent another wave of nausea through him. He was fairly sure no ankle was ever supposed to fold as far sideways as that one just had. He unlaced his boot and, with difficulty, extracted the bent steel knife, staring at it in wonder. *There's why my anklebone's not busted clean through.* Not exactly the way he'd pictured that knife saving him, but it would do. He re-laced the boot for support before the joint could swell further.

Ripping the mud-bats had left a greasy stain in his ground—Arkady would doubtless disapprove—but hadn't larded him with poisonous black blight like the time he'd ground-ripped a malice. The contamination would render him unfit for gifting ground reinforcements for weeks, which was likely all right, as he was more wishful just now to receive some. At least he hadn't traded a swift death for a slow one. Yet.

In the distance, somewhere down the hill, a child began crying. Weak, muffled. Dag went still. Opened his groundsense, reached out.

Alive. The tad had survived his fall!

Dag felt around himself, found a long, stout stick, and stripped side branches from it with his bent knife. With it, he levered himself onto his feet and began to make his way down the hillside. As swiftly as he might with due care, because he didn't think another tumble would help much. The shadowless light was graying, concealing detail, although the sky above the leaf canopy was still luminous, shot with pink streaks of high cloud. The crying grew louder as he skidded from tree to tree. *There.*

The black shape of a fallen mud-bat lay like a discarded cloak, half wrapped around a hickory trunk. The weeping was coming from underneath the folds. Dag leaned his stick on the bole, reached down, and heaved the carcass aside to reveal Owlet, curled up and shaking. The little boy looked up at Dag and burst into howls.

Dag's groundsense flicked out anxiously. No broken arm, leg, head, neck, or spine. Both eyes still blinking. Lungs clearly in working order. Scratches and gouges in plenty, though, a torn ear, and tumbled bruising. Dag lowered himself with a pained grunt. The child flinched away. A memory flashed in Dag's mind of the second time he'd met Spark, in a rough rescue from a violent assault; too dizzied to tell friend from foe when she'd been flung at him, she'd tried her level best to scratch his eyes out. "I guess I'm not a very reassuring sight," he said ruefully to Owlet. "But I do mean well."

The howls stopped, perhaps in surprise. Then started up again, though not as loudly.

"Absent gods," hissed Tavia's voice. "Can't you shut that child up? It'll have every mud-man for a mile down on us. Up on us. Whatever."

Tavia descended the slope, lurching from sapling to sapling, and fell to her knees beside Dag, winded. No broken bones there, either, clearly; but bruises, cuts, branch-whipped wheals, red-brown braid undone, a hank of hair torn out and her scalp oozing blood. Copper-brown eyes wide and wild and pulsing. Dag suspected his were, too.

"Welcome back down," he murmured. "Glad you made it in one piece."

"Absent *gods*," she said. "Nobody *ever* said the *north* was *full* of *giant bats*." She glared at Dag as if this were somehow his fault.

Dag stifled the impulse to apologize. "Surprise to me, too. What happened to your mud-bat?"

"When it couldn't clear the ridge, it scraped me off in a mess of dogwood scrub and got away." Her jaw set in frustration. But she seemed to have made a softer landing than his, fortunately.

"And, um . . . how are you with tads?"

"I was the youngest in my family," she returned at once, eyeing the crying toddler with alarm. "I don't know anything about little children. Farmer or otherwise."

"Ah." Dag sighed and extended his hand. "Here, Owlet." The child recoiled farther. "Eh." Tavia was right about the noise. Reluctantly, Dag opened himself and shaped a persuasion for the shocked boy. *It's all right now. I won't hurt you. You want to come to Dag and let him make it better.* He left the beguilement in, too, for good measure.

"Mamamama," Owlet blubbered.

"Sorry, the only mama-shaped person here doesn't want to play. She's just a youngin', too, you know. I'm afraid you're stuck with me." *Come here.*

"Mamama . . ." But Owlet stopped inching away.

Dag reached over and pulled the child into his lap. Owlet abruptly reversed his opinions, hiccupped, and buried his slimy face in Dag's shirt, gripping like a baby ba—possum. Dag didn't think it would do what was left of the garment a mite of harm.

"How did you do that?" asked Tavia. Whispered, actually, perhaps influenced by the sudden end of the clamor.

"Cheated," said Dag.

"Ah." Tavia glanced fearfully upward, seeking black motion over-head.

"Don't open your ground," Dag warned.

"No, no. But can they see us in the dark?"

"Not through trees. Rocks would be better. You and I can veil, but the tad here can't. He'll be a beacon."

"Do those bat things have groundsense, do you think?"

"Might." A grim thought. Their maker malice must have taken a human or humans, or it wouldn't have been able to gift its creations with speech. Had it yet taken a Lakewalker, stealing deeper powers? "We'll have moonrise in a while. While we can still see, better find us a ledge or cranny to hole up in. With water near." The grown-ups could go without their dinners, but Dag was parched with his late panic, and Owlet likely was, too.

She looked at his ankle. "How is that?"

"Not good."

"I'll scout, then."

"Aye."

Tavia slipped off in best patroller fashion; Dag waited, contemplating his new burden. Owlet now lay on his side, head pillowed on Dag's knee, in a false calm. Hysteria still lurked beneath, like fish circling under a frozen lake.

Tavia returned fairly soon, thankfully, and they set off through the dusk along the steep hillside. Ledges and crevices there were in plenty. Water was harder to come by at this height, but Tavia had found a mossy trickle that would doubtless become a stream farther down. It more seeped than flowed, but it did collect in a natural stone bowl before slipping away. They took turns putting their heads down and sucking it up. Owlet was harder to persuade into this novel form of drinking, but he got the idea at last, then was inclined to play in the puddle, and then objected to being dragged away and tucked in the far back of the crevice. Dag would have taken the outside position, but Tavia clearly wanted a spacer between her and the unhappy farmer child.

With an overhang at the back, the cleft was blocked from both vision and groundsense from five out of six directions. Dag was less certain that it would be blocked from invading mud-bats—they folded rather well when they weren't tangled in trees. But the creatures' clawed hands and feet, though dangerous in themselves, didn't seem built to carry weapons—not that all of this malice's scouts were necessarily of the same design.

Blocked perception unfortunately worked both ways. Dag wished they'd landed on the other side of this ridge, overlooking the Trace. If he were alone, he'd be up and over that ridgeline already, bad ankle or no.

"Where did those horrible bat-things come from?" asked Tavia, peering nervously out past the narrow rock walls of their temporary refuge. In the slice of purple sky, Dag could see one lonely star.

"They were mud-men. A malice made them. Not the one we slew yesterday."

"I could tell *that*."

Dag squeezed his eyes shut and open a few times, trying for coherence. "It's been over thirty years since I exchanged in these parts, and that only for a season. But this whole region all the way north to the Grace River is limestone country in its bones, shot through with sinkholes and caves and caverns. And some of those caverns harbor bats."

"Thousands of bats?"

"Oh, no, not thousands."

Her shoulders slumped in relief.

"Millions."

Tavia's mouth fell open. In a tone between hope and dismay, she said, "That's a Bo story . . . isn't it?"

"No. The biggest bat caverns are amazingly dangerous. Besides the risk of rabies, which some bats seem to carry, when they gather in such numbers their droppings poison the air. People who've stumbled into one of the big caves have choked and died on the fumes. Though skunks and raccoons do go in to catch baby bats, in the dead dark—nobody quite knows how they do it."

Tavia's face screwed up in mounting horror.

"Now, the local patrols do search the caves, but only near the surface. It's dangerous to go deeper, though they say there's galleries and passage-ways running for miles underground. But no malices have ever emerged from the deep caves, either because they were never seeded down there, or because there's no life for them to get started growing on. Except—I have a notion—that if a malice finally chanced to come up near or right in one of those big bat caves, it would have found a feast laid out for it from the get-go. Off to a very fast start, which could explain how it was missed between one patrol and the next. That's my best guess, leastways."

Tavia poked tentatively at her hurts. She could do with a stitch here or there—they all could, likely—but no one was doing more than ooz-ing by now. Treatment would have to wait. She glanced up. "What has that child got in its mouth?"

Dag looked around. Owlet was sitting up looking very scruffy and battered, with an appalled expression on his face, his jaw working and drool dribbling from his lips. *"Peh,"* he remarked. Dag went fishing with his little finger.

"Inchworm," he remarked, holding up his green catch. "Actually, more of a two-inch worm."

"Ugh!"

Dag smiled. It felt strange on his set face, like dry leather cracking. But welcome for all of that. He dug down in his pocket and drew out a dark strip. "Here, tad. Chew on this."

"What is that?" asked Tavia, peering in the dimness.

"Dried plunkin. I always keep a few strips in my pockets. When they start to look good despite the lint and sand stuck to 'em, you know it's time to eat 'em."

Owlet regarded the plunkin with considerably more suspicion than he had the worm, but shortly broke down and began gnawing. His false calm was beginning to be replaced with real calm, Dag thought, for all that Dag had pulled the initial persuasion out of his own ear. When the child crawled back into Dag's lap, it was as soothing as holding a purring cat. Moods were contagious in more than one direction, it seemed; which was why a leader should never break down in front of his patrollers. He was grateful Tavia hadn't found him any sooner.

His back to the warm stone, Dag felt strung tight between nerves and exhaustion. He decided to cultivate the nerves, because if the exhaustion overtook him he might not get up again for a week. And they had to move again soon. He felt his marriage cord for reassurance, *still alive*. But surely the malice would mount its forces for another attack—the Trace must seem a moving picnic to it. Unless the Laurel Gap patrollers were alerted and gathering, putting on pressure north of here. *There's a hope*. And not a fool's hope, either, but—he contemplated the unsubtle difference between *arrive eventually* and *arrive in time*.

"We'll have to work out some way to carry the tad," he said to Tavia. "He can't climb these rocks, dark or moonlit. I'm thinking we could rig a sort of sling with my shirt and your vest, to tie over my shoulder."

"What about your bad ankle?"

"Well, I'm thinking . . . one of us needs both hands free in case of trouble, and that's already not me." He hesitated. "We're not going to be hunting this malice, but there's no doubt it'll be hunting us. If it catches us"—he drew breath—"just so you know, I have my bonded knife around my neck."

She stared at his throat, at her hands.

"If the job has to be done, it'll be at the last moment, because, well, because. But that means you won't be able to hesitate. Can you do the needful?"

"I . . . don't know," she answered honestly.

He nodded. "You'll find your way if you have to." He made his voice confident, unwavering, bland. Such situations had come up before, of course, though more common in legend than fact. For the first time he wondered if any of those prior ill-fated heroes had been as desperately unwilling to share as he was right now. *Likely.* A year ago, this would have been easy, his barren future scant grief to give up. Things seemed to be coming at him out of their time.

Fatherhood, for one. He wanted to watch over his late-come little girl as a live papa, not as a dead legend. Not even as a living absence, as his own father had been. *I want to see how her tale comes out . . .* The sudden thought of her at the mercy of strangers, as Owlet now was at his, made his heart go hollow.

No need to burden Tavia with these reflections, no, nor any fraught last words, either. "The malice," he said, "will give you all the gumption you need. Trust me on this."

She nodded unhappily.

~

It was upwards of an hour before Sumac dragged back. Whit almost shot her.

Fawn looked up from the far side of the little fire where she was attempting to help Calla attempt to help Arkady with Barr. As the ominous shape loomed out of the dark and the dual gleam could be made out as Sumac's eyes, Whit lowered his quivering crossbow. "Give some warning, why don't you?" he gasped.

"I bumped grounds with Neeta," Sumac said, voice flat. Neeta was off in the woods somewhere, trying to guard their whole perimeter by herself. Sumac's hair was in disarray, her face branch-whipped and strained. She added tightly, "You can see that blighted fire for a hundred paces through the trees. And smell it. Put it out."

"Not yet," said Arkady in a blurry voice, from deep in his trance.

"Need the boiled water . . ." Sumac looked around, taking in the scene in some dismay, Fawn thought.

Barr lay on a blanket, right boot off and trouser leg cut away, his lower leg held across a towel on Arkady's lap. Arkady's hands hovered over the bloody mess. The hideous pink bone ends that had been sticking out through his burst skin earlier had been pushed beneath it once more, mating up under Arkady's most powerful groundsetting. The maker had seemed unshaken by the bone break—the worst Fawn had ever seen or imagined—but had complained bitterly, back when he'd still been able to speak, about all the dirt he had to work in. Barr's face was the color of suet, and he looked as if he wished he could pass out again, as he had a couple of times so far. Remo gripped his white-knuckled hand and wiped his sweating forehead with a wet cloth.

The rest of the group was scattered back under the trees, taking care of the animals and one another. When the last of the mud-bats had vanished over the eastern ridge, the shaken company had pushed forward a quarter mile into deeper woods, then turned off the road at a shallow stream and struggled up it as far as they could drag the wagons. The boys had pushed the two wagons as deeply under the cover of some spreading oak trees as they could be squeezed; Fawn doubted it was enough.

Sumac ran an aggravated hand through her escaping hair. "If you . . . oh, blight. Keep the fire. With all these unveiled farmer grounds and this *herd* of animals, nothing with groundsense could miss you, dark, trees, or no. Blight, have a party and dance."

"I'll pass," said Barr weakly from his blanket.

It might almost have been a joke; the wheezy bark it won from Sumac might almost have been a laugh. The laugh leached away as she met Fawn's anxious eyes.

"I couldn't catch them—couldn't get near them," she said. "Other side of the river, up the ridge, those rocks rise up in ten- and twenty-foot blocks. No way for miles either side to get a horse up. Fawn, I'm sorry."

Barr squeezed his eyes shut.

Mutely, Fawn held out her left wrist, wrapped in its wedding cord. Sumac's lips parted; she strode around the fire and gripped it. "Ye gods, he's still alive!"

"Yes. Remo and Arkady said. We keep checking."

"His patrol always claimed Dag was a blighted cat, but this . . . ! How can he—*where* can they have—"

A jerky wail interrupted her as Vio ran out of the dark. "My baby! Did you find Owlet?"

Judging from the spasm of her hand, Sumac barely kept herself from flinching away. She dropped Fawn's wrist and turned to the desperate woman. "No. I lost them over the ridge. Couldn't follow."

"How can you have lost them! You're a Lakewalker, you're supposed to be magic!"

Sumac stiffened. "I can't blighted fly!"

Fawn pushed herself up to stand between the pair, hitching up the torn fabric of her shirt. Left-handed, because her right side wasn't working too good. With Arkady drawn deep into the urgency of the bone break, Fawn had to wait for her turn, so Berry had done her best to clean out the deep gouges fore and aft in her shoulder, wrapping them in a strip of torn cloth. It would hold for the moment. Fawn wasn't about to complain of the throbbing pain with Barr down there gritting his teeth on much worse.

"We think Dag's still alive," Fawn said. "If he is, he'll go after the child if he can." If he hadn't been dropped on those rocks like Barr, and left lying up there in some broken agony.

"How do you know?" Vio demanded.

"Because . . . because he's Dag."

Vio's mouth thinned. "Can't we send out searchers?"

"Are you mad?" said Remo.

"I'll go by myself, if none of you big men and Lakewalkers will!"

Grouse, coming up behind her, said, "Don't be a fool, Vio."

The girl Plum hovered—skinny, hollow-eyed, dark hair straggly. Her distraught mama, earlier, had screamed at her for not helping hang on to her baby brother; her frantic papa had hit her for crying. She was pretty quiet now, creeping to cling once more to her mama's skirts, because no matter how bad it got, where else did a five-year-old have to go?

Vio gave her husband a hard look. "I don't see anybody else volunteering, now, do I?"

Fawn put in more quietly, "We all lost folks. Neeta her partner, Sumac her uncle, me, well. And if Barr gets to keep his leg it'll be a miracle."

A disagreeing grunt from Arkady. All in a day's work for him, was this?

"If this is a contest, I don't think much of the prizes," Fawn finished, ignoring that last. "What we *need* is to work together."

Vio stared venomously at her. "You can't know what it's like to lose a child."

On the list of pointless things to say to the woman, *Yes, I do* seemed pretty high up. So Fawn said nothing, and was shortly glad of it when Vio's hard voice broke. "Owlet's so *little*."

Sumac started to rub, then winced and dabbed, at her scratched face. "There's not a lot of question in my mind Dag would have wanted me to turn back and look after you all." Her glance at Fawn added, *Especially you.*

In an effort to be practical, because someone needed to, Fawn put in, "We found another dead mule along the road. I don't know if you had time to notice, but didn't neither of those mules have their harness taken off. If they'd died natural, those tea caravan boys wouldn't have left their loads on 'em, nor the hides either, likely. That says to me they must have been attacked and forced away or run off. But we haven't spotted any human bodies yet."

Sumac's brow furrowed. "Sounds like trouble to the north, all right. Besides no traffic coming down, I 'specially don't like that we haven't even met anyone running away our way."

"Except for that first malice," Fawn pointed out.

"There was that." Sumac grimaced. "Going forward seems a bad idea. Going back is no better. We'd be open targets in that burned-over country. Staying here's no good, either. We hit that mud-bat pack hard. No question they'll be back looking for more. But I know the *worst* would be to scatter into the woods with no blighted plan!"

The others had trickled up around the firelit debate, looking more mulish than their mules.

"We should round up our weapons," said Ash.

"We should," agreed Sumac, "but we're too many to hide and too few to make a stand."

"I'm thinking," said Fawn, "that those muleteers could have been mind-slaved." She looked around at the array of faces, some blank, and explained, "That scares me way more than mud-men. I talked to folks at Glassforge and in Raintree who went through it. It's like you still have your wits, you keep all your know-how, but suddenly you want to do whatever the malice wants of you. If it wants you to attack your friends, or eat your own children, it seems like a fine idea at the time. And you *remember,* after. The most important thing, whatever else we do, is to keep everyone out of range of that malice."

Sumac bit her knuckles, seemed to gather herself, and spoke in the most no-nonsense voice Fawn had yet heard from her. A patrol leader's voice, for sure. "All right. This is what we're doing. The wounded can't run or be carried. They'll have to be hid in the rocks on the valley side no matter what. Lie up till rescue can get to them. That'll be Barr, Arkady, and Rase."

"I can fight," Rase quavered. To Fawn, he looked as if he could barely stand.

"Good," said Sumac heartlessly, "because if you get found, you'll have to. My best guess is that the malice lair lies to our east. So that leaves west. Happens there's a Lakewalker camp almost due west of here at Laurel Gap. So we set the animals loose, pull together what food and weapons we can carry—and ropes, we'll want ropes—and skedaddle west over the ridges on foot. Tonight." Her voice slowed. "It might be best to leave Plum with Arkady."

"No!" Vio wailed.

"Your decision," said Sumac. "You have one hour to think about what this retreat'll put her through. And who's going to carry her fifty, sixty miles over mountains at a run." She turned on her heel, taking in the rest of the stunned company. "We want to make sure we have all the bows and arrows into the hands of folks who can use them."

"Tavia's bow was broken when her horse fell on it," Fawn said. "Neeta got back her quiver."

Sumac nodded. "Remo can take Barr's bow, Neeta can have mine. Whit, you have yours."

Putting the distance weapons, Fawn noticed, solely into the hands of people who could ground-veil or were shielded, and did not risk mind slaving.

"We can fight those things!" said Finch. "We drove them off once!"

"Speak for yourself, boy," growled Bo. "Looked to me like they just left 'cause they got bored."

"But we can't fight their master," said Sumac. "This wants the Laurel Gap patrol. Blight, this wants every Lakewalker camp in the hinterland!"

"I have Dag's primed knife," said Fawn quietly. "He dropped it to me. Last thing."

Sumac's eyebrows rose. "Well," she said. "That gives you two good reasons to stick tight to me."

Fawn swallowed. "Dag might come back. Looking for us. Or maybe Tavia."

"Then they'll be able to join up with Arkady's group," suggested Sumac. "Hide out till we can send help." Fawn thought Sumac drew more consolation from this notion than she did.

Arkady looked up, squinting, and said in an underwater groan, "Needle. Dressings. Splints."

Calla and Fawn hurried back to his side, Fawn rooting in the medicine pack.

"You all right?" said Sumac, in what was for Sumac an amazingly diffident voice.

"I'll do. Just don't bring me another like this for the next three days, eh?" He grimaced at her.

"In case you didn't hear, we're going to tuck up your medicine tent back in the rocks. Your job will be to all stay alive till we send a patrol to dig you out of your burrow again."

He nodded. Not sorry, Fawn guessed, that it would be Sumac's duty to run away from this place as fast as she could drive her farmer flock.

Sumac packed off the splinted Barr on a sapling-and-blanket stretcher carried by Remo and Whit, with Arkady leading his packhorse bearing the medicine-tent supplies and Rase staggering along after. Vio didn't send Plum with them. Again, Fawn noticed, no one without either ground veiling or a shield would know just where they'd gone to earth, and so could not betray them even under a malice's persuasion. The company scattered to gather its gear.

20

Two hours after sunset, the lopsided moon rose to bathe the eastern-facing ridge in milk and ink. Under normal conditions, Dag would have found it as good as daylight. *Not tonight.* Staggering along with his only hand full of walking stick, trying to peer over the squirming burden of Owlet tied to his chest, ankle screaming at every step, it took Dag twice as long to reach the crest as he'd planned. He could sense Tavia's growing impatience.

"Maybe I should take the tad," she said as they made the top and Dag stood gasping and bent.

He waved an acknowledging hand. "A minute." He stared out over the valley, seeking, beyond the silver ribbon of river, the fainter line of the Trace. Nothing moved along the road. No curls of luminous smoke rose from the woods to the north, either. He dared to open his ground-sense, reaching, but it was well over two miles to the valley floor, beyond his range even at his best. *Fawn's still alive,* his marriage cord told him, but *where?*

The cool damp of this black-white-gray world, falsely serene, felt clammy on his sweating face. Something unexpected pricked his senses, not below, but north along the ridge. Faint, thready . . .

"Tavia, open and check along the ridge to our right. Maybe half a mile."

"That's right at the edge of my—wait. A patroller? Not one of ours . . . ?"

"No ground I recognize. Hurt, I think."

She nodded; they began to pick their way between scrubby bushes, around jutting rocks, through weeds. Plants bruised by their passage gave up a sharp green smell in the dark. The trees rose around them as they descended, making the shadows more treacherous, though they did give Tavia handholds. Dag found that anchoring his hook on a passing sapling proved more pain than it was worth. His left arm was wrenched and sore, his stump swollen and uncomfortable in the wooden cuff, but he hardly dared remove his arm harness for fear he wouldn't be able to get it back on.

Tavia forged ahead; he caught up to find her crouched and peering over a twenty-foot drop. A huddled man-shape lay at its foot.

A dry, hoarse voice rose from below. "Someone . . . up there? Help!"

"We see you," Tavia called. "We're coming down."

"I think my back is broken," the voice returned.

"Don't try to move!"

"I *can't* . . . blighted move!"

They crept along the outcrop till Tavia found a steep scramble down. Dag was forced to go a little farther and then work his way back.

A patroller, yes, Dag saw as he limped near. Spare of build, middle height; a few threads of silver gleamed in his dark hair, mostly undone from its braid and scrambled around his head. He lay faceup, legs limp, hands clenched. A marriage cord, frayed and faded, circled his left wrist. His lips were dry, cracked, and bleeding. His ripped shirt was stained with dark, dried blood; already Dag recognized the pattern of mud-bat clawings. And he was right about his back. At least two vertebrae fractured, about halfway down.

"Water," he whispered to Tavia as she bent over him. "Oh, please . . ." The man's patting hand found a leather water bottle at his side, empty and flaccid, and thrust it toward Tavia.

"Dag?" she said uncertainly.

"Yes. He's dangerously parched. Careful getting it off."

She unwound the strap from his neck, untangled it from his hair, and sped away. Dag lowered himself with a grunt. Sleepy Owlet whimpered protest; Dag off-loaded the child and rolled him to the side, where he curled up in the dry dirt, stubby hands relaxing again in sleep. How did youngins *do* that, go from squirming whirligigs to limp little rag dolls in a blink?

"Who're you?" whispered the injured man. "Patrollers? Not ours. Help from outland . . . ?" He squinted up at Dag in brief hope, took in his battered appearance, his arm harness, his stick, and answered his own question with a deflated, "Not . . ."

"Name's Dag Bluefield N—" Dag swallowed the *No-Camp*. "Traveling north with a mixed party of farmers and Lakewalkers. We were attacked just before sunset by a flock of those flying . . . things. Mud-bats. They tried to carry me, Tavia, and the tad over there across the ridge, but we fought free of 'em. We're trying to get back to our people, but I don't see where they've gone."

"Lucky. I . . . was dropped . . ." The man's eyes rolled anxiously as Tavia reappeared out of the moon shadows. "Ah-please . . ."

"You can help him raise his head," said Dag, "but don't lift his shoulders or jostle his back."

Tavia nodded, and spent the next few minutes getting the entire skin of water down the desperately thirsty man without choking him, much.

"Ah," he said as she let his head down again. "So good. Gods. *Hurts . . .*"

"How long have you been up here?" asked Dag. The man's bladder had given way in his paralysis long enough ago for his trousers to have pretty much all dried out again. That actually wasn't a good sign, but the water should fix it.

"Not sure. I keep fading in and out, and waking up not dead. Surprises me. One day, two? It's been dark and light and dark . . ."

"Where you from? Laurel Gap?"

"Aye. My patrol—we'd heard strange reports, just arrived at the head of the valley and started to sweep, when those mad things fell out of the sky on us."

"North of us, then. How far?"

"Maybe ten, fifteen miles? There was a strong west wind . . . whenever. That nightmare that carried me off rode the updraft along this side. It kept trying to cross the ridge like the rest, but couldn't stay up over there, so it was forced along farther and farther south. Lower and lower. It finally got so exhausted, it just . . . let me go." A shaken breath. "For an instant, I thought I was going to get lucky, but I slammed off that rock face and landed wrong, way too hard."

"Can you feel anything below your waist?"

"Weird spurts of pain sometimes, but mostly not."

"Did any of your patrol get away to warn your camp?"

"Gods, I hope so."

Then Laurel Gap should be alerted by now, if anyone had escaped and *followed the blighted patrol procedure,* as Dag so often hadn't. He felt a sudden new warmth toward the rules. "It sounds like your mud-bat was trying to carry you back to the malice's lair, same as us." Which suggested the malice was still *in* its lair, hopeful thought. "It's a ways east of here, I reckon. Did it capture anyone else?"

If this malice had succeeded in ground-ripping a Lakewalker, it was primed to grow immeasurably more dangerous, but the mud-bats plainly had trouble transporting prey as large as a full-size patroller.

"Not sure. That thing took me off early in the fight. I didn't see much except . . . gods. I used to *like* high views."

Dag grimaced in sympathy.

"You haven't . . . run across any of the rest of my patrol yet?"

"No, sorry. You're the first."

"If I'd had a primed knife"—the man's voice dropped low—"that thing could have carried me to the malice with my goodwill. If I hadn't left my own bonded knife in my fool saddlebags, wherever they are, I'd have shared by now. It'd have to hurt less than this. With this back, I'm a dead man sooner or later. You'll never get me down off this ridge alive."

"Maybe your luck just got better," said Tavia. "Dag here's a medicine maker."

The man's eyes widened. "With one hand?"

"I'm just an apprentice. My wife partners me when I need two hands, but she's"—Dag lifted his head to peer out through the trees, but couldn't see much—"back with the others." He added, "What's your name, patroller?

"Pakko. Pakko Sunfish Laurel Gap."

"Right." Dag opened himself, dropped down and in.

The break was every bit as ugly as his first impression had suggested, two vertebrae cracked and pushed out of alignment. The spinal cord was twisted, with bleeding and swelling pressing upon the nerves and creating excruciating pain. One wrong move with enough force, and the nerves could be sheared through or torn outright. Pakko's foresight was shrewd.

Likely the very best they could do was to get the man home to die there. Dag wasn't sure that was a kindness. His own father had shared while taken sick on patrol, and been buried where he'd died, sending nothing home to his family but a clean bone blade. Would his return have merely plunged his tent into strain and grief and helpless anger, to the same end? No mercy there. *No mercy anywhere, at the last.* But Pakko didn't have his knife, and Dag was almost glad of it. Though not for Pakko's sake.

Dag came up and out again from his exploration to find the patroller staring at him with wider eyes. *Groundsense. What you see, sees you.*

"There's a better medicine maker with our party, a groundsetter. If we can get him up here, I expect we can get you down." Dag did not promise, *Save your life.* But what Arkady might do with this mess he scarcely dared guess.

Dag was not above plunging in and trying single-handed, if things were dire enough—he'd once done crude groundsetting on a man with a spurting cut throat, knowing much less than he knew now—but with water and someone to care for his immediate needs, Pakko didn't look to be dying just yet. Dag was sure he could preserve the man long enough to give him the chance to share. Arkady might be able to get him back to his camp and walking well enough to live and work, if not patrol, for many more years. Forty or fifty years of a man's life were too much to hazard on Dag's own impatience.

Dag glanced aside at the sleeping heap of Owlet. *These are not the responsibilities I want right now.* But they were the ones he'd been handed. He sighed.

"Tavia. I need you to refill the water bottle, then help me slide Pakko here further under this overhang, without putting strain or pressure on his back. I'll stay here with him and the tad. You try to find Arkady and the others, and bring us help."

About time, Dag thought he saw her breathe. Tavia had been wild to do just that, earlier, but had been stuck with Dag's limping pace. That he might now be sending her alone into a death trap . . . *there are no good choices here.* But there were less stupid ones.

She nodded and scrambled up. Glumly, Dag resigned himself to getting no further tonight.

∾

Sumac was right about the rocks. There was no way to haul a horse over this terrain, and Fawn wasn't too sure about a gaggle of frightened farmers, either. Or frightened Lakewalkers. Their air of patroller grimness might conceal their anxiety from the others, but she'd been around Dag too long to be fooled by it.

Getting them all in motion in the same direction—*disorganized for retreat* as Sumac tartly put it—took an agonizing amount of time, by Lakewalker standards that Fawn found herself sharing. Sumac was rendered speechless when she found Sage at work fastening a chain around a tree and fixing it to his wagon axle, to daunt possible theft. But since half the others weren't ready yet either, she let it pass. Indigo wept to let loose the mule team and his riding horse.

"If we make it back alive," Remo said, "I'll help you find them again."

"What if those mud-bats eat them?"

"Better them than us."

Indigo didn't looked convinced.

They tramped five miles north through the woods to come up even with a saddle on the ridgeline that Sumac figured they might get over. Plum stumbled along for the first mile till she started to cry, was carried by her papa, still weak from bog ague, for the next two, then was passed off to Vio, and finally, as the family fell behind, was handed on to big Ash. Fawn figured the relay: between Ash, Sage, Finch, and Whit, they could likely pack the poor slip of a child over this barrier. The young men could spare the gift of energy, now. But later? *Let's hope there's a later.*

The moon rode high, lighting their way. Such as it was. Their line of seventeen people began to snake up the steepening slope. Neeta and Remo, ahead, scouted paths by eye and groundsense, breaking the trail and dodging dead ends and drop-offs. Sumac, tense and wary, brought up the rear. Fawn trudged just ahead of her.

As Fawn bent and climbed, the sharing knife swung and bounced on the end of its cord, and she tucked it inside her shirt, below the walnut pendant. That didn't stop the distraction. The sweat between her breasts made the cord slippery, and the sheath rubbed against her belly, bringing to mind her other burden. So welcome—till now, when all her fears seemed doubled. Her pregnancy had drained away a freedom to take risks that she'd scarcely been conscious of before. Lakewalker customs of knife sacrifice were so careful about binding and assent. Her own state seemed a strange inversion, binding her not to death but to life. When she'd lain with her husband she'd made an irrevocable choice, and she could not now go back on it.

She rubbed her marriage cord. *Where is Dag?* Prisoner, injured, escaped? Was he struggling to get back to her, just as she was going away from him? The thought hurt her heart, thumping hard and fast in her chest.

Fawn spared a glance upward to find the company strung in a zigzag across an exposed patch—whether burned over in the recent fire or always barren, she could not tell in this milky light. Across the weedy slope, a shadow rippled, like a wavelet on water. Then another. Fawn blinked rapidly, wondering if she was passing out from the breathless climb. Then she realized what she was seeing, and spun around, looking up toward the high blue face of the moon. Across it, another shadow fluttered, and stars winked in and out.

"They're back!" she gasped. Mud-bats, a dozen of them. Of *course* they could fly at night.

Sumac followed her gaze. Rasped, *"Blight."* Raised her face and bellowed up the incline, "Archers, alert! Everyone, close up under that outcrop! Grouse, give that blighted boar spear to someone who can swing it"—Grouse had mainly been using it for a walking stick, poling his shaking legs up the hill—"trade with Ash, take back your youngster!" At the shouting and scrambling, Plum began to cry again.

People abandoned the path and started to climb for the twenty-five-foot-high face of stone, silver gray in the pale light, that promised some protection. Hod and Hawthorn shouldered under Bo and boosted him upward. Sage grabbed Calla, who grabbed Indigo, and they chained over the rugged rises. Remo, Neeta, and Whit slid down toward Sumac, bows brandished.

Out of the sky, disturbingly quiet, a vast shape descended and settled upon the outcrop overlooking them. It had twice the wingspan of the other mud-bats. It stretched out its arms to the sides like black sails, and folded them in again. A whiff of its unmistakable scent, a dry cellar smell, rocked Fawn back in realization.

That's not a mud-bat. Oh gods, oh gods . . .

The malice turned its dark, chiseled, elegant face upon them. Great eyes glimmered in the moonlight, and pointed ears twitched against its faintly ridged skull. Soft, batlike fur covered its body; its legs, anchored by clawed feet, were longer and more manlike than those of the mud-bats. The weight of its gaze fell like a war hammer.

Fawn had seen the Glassforge malice face-to-face, an early molt, ugly as mud. The Wolf War malice was said to have acquired a strange man-wolf form before its end. The Raintree malice had been breathtakingly beautiful, Dag had told her, a tall warrior shape of surpassing glamour. This malice, too, had its own appalling beauty. Fawn stared upward, entranced with terror.

Sumac, frozen beside her, made a weird little noise that might have wanted to be swearing, but was squeezed thin by awe. She found her voice only to whimper, "It *flies* . . ."

But her words broke both of them out of their shock. Fawn was already scrambling in her shirt as Sumac hissed, "The knife, give me the knife!" As Fawn fumbled it into her hands, Sumac's legs bunched to launch her up the slope, angling around the rock face.

Three bows lifted, aimed uselessly at the commanding figure staring down over them in cool curiosity. Remo was so shaken that he almost tried to shoot it anyway, but at the last moment turned and found a circling mud-bat instead. His arrow tore through a wing; the creature shrieked and fluttered sideways. A few more mud-bats darted near and banked away, not so much seeking to grab prey off the hillside, Fawn thought, as to drive it before them toward their master. The spread-out company's dash in all directions changed to a drawing-in.

Fawn saw it coming before Neeta and Remo did. Ash, upslope, turned and raised the boar spear. Took aim, but not at the malice or the mud-bats.

"Remo, duck!" Fawn screamed.

The heavy, steel-tipped pole hissed downslope. Remo dodged barely in time; the point grazed his shoulder instead of lodging in his throat. The spear clattered to a stop against some rocks below. At least Ash had thrown away his weapon, temporarily. He looked confused, blinking and shaking his head. Finch, Sage, and Indigo drew up beside him. Only Calla tried to back off, jerking like a balking horse, but ended up falling to her knees.

Above, Sumac burst onto the outcrop. The malice merely spread its wings and fell forward, sliding away as she swung wildly. Two buffeting flaps and it rose, wheeling upward once more. Sumac pitched over the edge, breaking her own plummet with skin-tearing grabs at bushes clinging to cracks in the rock face. The bone knife spun from her hand, rising futilely after the malice and arcing outward. Fawn gasped and tried to move beneath it—*if that bone breaks on the stones*—with a crackle of twigs, the knife came down in a buckthorn bush. Fawn raced to retrieve it. Whit, after a moment's hesitation, followed after her, crossbow swinging in his grip as he ran.

Sumac landed in a shower of leaves, rolled downward past the farmer boys, found her feet, and kept on going, braking from handhold to scrubby handhold. Sage, looking puzzled, knelt and picked up a rock, and threw it after her. Finch and Indigo, after a moment, followed in clumsy imitation. Hod and Hawthorn turned back to join them.

"Hawthorn, no!" screamed Berry in dismay as he, too, scooped up a missile, launching it with rather better aim. It clipped Remo's ear.

Neeta's bow wavered around to point at the farmers.

"No!" yelled Sumac, breathless, still scrambling wildly downward. "We can't fight them! Cut and run!" Remo had half fallen; Sumac pulled him up, stared around, spotted Fawn scrabbling through the buckthorn after the knife. Tried to make for her.

A line of mud-bats went for Sumac, one after another, and she broke the other way, ducking through the scant shelter of the scrub. All the mud-bats circled to concentrate upon the three Lakewalkers, who retreated southward.

"Berry, over here!" yelled Whit. Berry's white face turned, saw him; she gave up yanking at Hawthorn's arm just barely in time to evade Ash and Sage closing in on her, and bounded down the hillside toward them. Whit caught her as she almost plunged past, the walnut pendant bouncing on her collarbone.

"The malice." Fawn, scratched bloody, clutched the knife to her heaving chest. "The malice has taken everybody's minds." She stared at her brother and sister-in-law, gaping back in horror. "Except ours . . ." In the moon-washed dark the mud-bats whirled; their master soared above them, so close, so out of reach. "Sumac's right. It's time to run."

"But—Hawthorn," choked Berry, looking back as Fawn turned north toward the nearest trees. "Bo . . ."

"We can't help them now," Fawn gasped over her shoulder as Whit grabbed Berry and dragged her along. "They'd turn on us, too. Best hope is to all stay alive till the local Lakewalkers arrive and bring down the malice." Would the local patrol be expecting *this*? Did they even know about the night-sky terror that had burst upon the Trace? What if the rest of the company was made to be soldiers against them? Unlike Sumac and their own Lakewalkers, the Laurel Gap patrollers wouldn't see the farmers as captured friends, only as dangerous enemies. Tears tracked down Fawn's face at the vision, but she bit her lip and dodged onward. The ground came up like blows under her fleeing feet, and whipping strands of her hair caught in her open mouth. Running beside her, Berry looked just as wind-wild.

They stumbled into the shelter of the trees and looked back. The Lakewakers had vanished on the south side of the clear space, a couple of hundred paces away, but Fawn thought she could mark them by the mud-bats dipping and swooping above the trees over there. The malice appeared to be following them. The rest of their company stood in a bewildered huddle, temporarily undirected by their new master.

"Keep running," said Whit, shouldering his crossbow to free both hands for their next burst—or rather, one hand to fight through the undergrowth, the other to clutch Berry's in a death grip that she returned. Fawn longed for a hand to grip as well—*just one's all I need*—but Dag seemed as beyond her reach right now as the moon overhead. She swallowed, nodded. The three of them toiled north along the mountainside.

∾

Dag peered into the night. This rock ledge above their overhang offered a broad vantage, down over the tops of the trees. The angle gave him a dizzy shudder, and he ventured no closer to the edge. The moon was full enough to infuse the whole valley with a blue glow, but it wasn't bright enough for him to see clearly at a distance, even without the rising mist. The widest cast of Dag's groundsense wouldn't make out what was happening eight or ten miles off, nor did sound carry that far. But beneath that saddle in the far ridge, he thought evil specks whirled. Unless his eyes were full of floaters, like that time Copperhead had thrown him . . . but by the ugly quaver in his belly, he thought not. The mud-bats were abroad, and had found new prey. Fawn and the company? Some other hapless Trace travelers?

The faint hum of Spark's live ground in his marriage cord was no reassurance. Because if it stopped, it would already be *too late* . . .

He clenched his teeth and hand and snarled helplessly. Even if he were to ruthlessly abandon Pakko and Owlet to each other— and he was feeling pretty ruthless right now—it would take him four, five, *six* hours to limp from here to there. Whatever was happening would be long over, or moved elsewhere, and he'd be wrecked, wholly crippled instead of just half. Was Tavia seeing any of this? She might have crossed the river by now, but if she was under the trees—and she should be— her view would be worse blocked than his.

His every heartstring twanged *go*. What was left of his wits said, *stay*.

I'm going to go mad before this night is done.

~

Fawn sat panting on the dirt floor of their crevice. A tiny patch of moonlight lay at her knees like a rivulet of spilled milk; she and Whit and Berry edged back from it, as if the moon were a malicious eye that might stare in and see them cowering.

"You think this is enough?" Whit wheezed, staring around; Fawn could just see the gleam of his eyes in the shadows.

They'd run maybe two miles north, angling downward mainly for speed's sake, before Fawn realized they would run out of rocks if they descended farther, and started looking instead for a bolt hole. "Ground-sense doesn't go through thick stone," she said. But malice groundsense was in every way stronger than Lakewalkers' . . . Fawn tried for optimism, because the alternative was a panic they could ill afford. "I expect Sumac tucked Arkady and Barr and all up somewhere a lot like this. And I don't think she'd take chances with Arkady."

Whit breathed reluctant agreement with that, relaxing slightly. Berry nodded, her blond hair a glimmer in the gloom.

Fawn traced the two cords around her throat; her hand clenched on her birthday walnut in its hair net. "They worked! Do you realize, Dag's ground shields worked!" At least long enough for them to run away from a malice distracted by other events. Long enough to live to tell the tale? "We got away!"

"The others didn't." Berry's voice was flat—not with censure, Fawn thought, but just to keep steady.

Whit scrubbed his face. "Why didn't that malice just ground-rip everyone right then?"

"It was chasing after the patrollers," said Berry. "I reckon it's circled back by now." Her voice quavered at this last.

"Maybe not," said Fawn slowly. "That malice you fellows brought down the other day was a lot like my malice at Glassforge, a lumpy first-molt. This one seems more like the one Dag saw in Raintree, advanced, except mainly eating bats instead of people, so it's advanced . . . oddly. It was so crisp and fine and fresh-looking. If it just lately *had* a molt, maybe it's only now able to fly and get around. It might not be looking to start another molt right off, especially as that would weigh it down so's it couldn't fly anymore. Maybe it might want to, like, save its prey till it's ready for more."

"Like a spider?" said Berry. Fawn could *hear* her grimace.

Fawn frowned, trying to think it through. "If it's mostly been eating bats, it might not be too bright yet." Bats didn't keep larders, as far as she knew. Would the malice think like a bat, or like a person? *A mad person.* She brightened. "But it can't get too far away from its mind slaves. Remember what Ford Chicory said back in Raintree, how he and his fellows would ride in and raid the malice's army, catch folks and bring them back out of range, and then they'd get their wits back? I think this malice will want to gather all its captives in one place, except then it'll be stuck—if it flies too far away from 'em, they'll all come to their senses and escape."

"Think it'll try to march everyone to its lair?" asked Whit, puzzling it out, too.

"Maybe. Though this one doesn't seem tied to its lair anymore."

"Now what do we do?" asked Berry. "If I had six good feet of water under my hull, I'd take on anything, but I barely know this dry-foot country. Should we try to get back to Arkady?"

Whit shook his head. "We'd not be that much safer, and we'd be all exposed trying to get there."

Fawn thought of the pale flash of bone knife, spinning through the air in Sumac's last, futile effort, and let her hand curl around its sheath. "Whit, you got any of those crossbow bolts left?"

"Just three."

"Give me one."

Whit rustled around, extracted a bolt from the short quiver, and handed it across. It glinted in the strip of moonlight. Fawn held it, traced it, tested its balance, fingered the feather vanes. Drew the bone knife, compared length, diameter, heft.

Whit saw her drift at once. "Um . . . if that worked, wouldn't Lake-walkers already have invented sharing arrows? Sharing spears, for that matter?"

Fawn shook her head. "Actually, Dag says patrollers do fix their sharing knives to spear hafts sometimes, in the field, but not often. In the close quarters of a woods or a cave, a spear's not much more use than a knife, and they all are right terrified of anything that risks breakage."

"Like poor Remo," Berry agreed. "So cut up when he broke one by accident that he ran away from home."

"Yep," said Fawn. "It's not just a handy sharp point on the end of a stick. It's someone's life. Death. Hopes. And it has to be the right shape to carry around with you for years, and something you could drive into your own heart even if you were caught out dying by yourself. A primed knife can be made into a spear easy enough, but I think a patroller would faint dead away if you suggested a sharing arrow. Think of a miss hitting a tree or a cave wall hard."

"Mm," said Whit. "Your grandfather's ghost would haunt you for-ever, I expect."

"Now this"—Fawn held up the knife—"would just tumble and be

useless if you tried to shoot it from your crossbow. But if I put vanes on it and balance it, I think it might fly straight. Enough. For a short ways." She touched Whit's bolt, showing where she meant to scavenge the vanes.

"How would you make it balance?"

"I'd need to carve away some of the bone."

Whit made a choking noise.

"Won't that destroy it?" asked Berry doubtfully.

Fawn stared down at the length of carved bone, turning it in the moon patch. "I watched Dag bond and prime this knife. The groundwork he did seemed mainly concentrated on what used to be the bone's inner surface. The end is just carved this shape to be handy for a grip. If I pare it down . . . See, if it doesn't break, it's not broken."

"Huh?" said Berry.

"It's made to bust open from inside by the groundwork when it comes in contact with a malice. If it doesn't crack apart while I'm fooling with it, that means the priming is still sound." But Fawn ruined her confident-sounding claim by adding, "I think."

"And just who," said Whit warily, "do you picture doing this shooting?"

"It would have to be you."

A fraught silence. From two directions.

"You've had way more practice 'n me," Fawn forged on, "and besides, my shoulder's hurt." Hot and aching from the mud-bat's clawing. She would deal with that *later*. "Best to be as close as we can get, in case you only get one shot. But all the bone bolt has to do is fly more or less straight and hit anywhere, and go a little ways into the malice's fake skin. I didn't shove Dag's old primed knife point more'n an inch into the Glassforge malice"—she suppressed a shudder of memory—"and it worked just fine."

"That's taking an awful risk with our only primed knife," said Whit.

"Yes, but if we sit hiding out here with it, it's just as useless as if it's busted. Better to try something fast. Before the malice flies somewhere out of reach. Before it starts snacking on our folks. Everything I've learned about malices says it's better to get them sooner than later. Like putting out a fire."

Into the continuing silence Fawn added desperately, "And if it fails, well, it was only *Crane*."

"That," said Berry, after a cool pause, "is a real good point."

Whit sighed, partly agreement, and partly . . . well.

They would shortly lose what little light they had as the moon advanced over the ridge. Fawn held the bolt in the patch of moonlight and picked apart the threads winding the vanes, laying the feathers out carefully, one, two, three. She then drew her steel knife from her belt. One of Dag's earliest gifts to her; he'd insisted she wear it at all times, and kept it razor-sharp for her.

She balanced and rebalanced the sharing knife in her hands, turning it over and around. Set the steel to a knobby bit on the hilt. Pressed. The bit flew off with a faint snap.

Everyone held their breaths. But the bone blade stayed intact.

Fawn swallowed, set her steel to lift a longer sliver, and leaned into her next cut.

21

The scent of a campfire, drifting in the chill dawn air, warned Fawn, Whit, and Berry to get off the Trace and take to the woods once more. *Sumac was right about smoke smell carrying,* Fawn thought, then wondered if Dag's niece was still alive. Earlier they'd discovered where the remains of the company, herded by the malice's mud-creatures, had tromped back onto the road, right enough, but if the patrollers were still around they'd left no mark. Following the slight acrid whiff upwind, they came to what was plainly a long-established stopping place along a creek— and found their quarry. *No, not our quarry; our bait.*

Prior travelers had stripped the woods of burnable deadfall near the big clearing, but Berry, scouting ahead, found a pile of old rotting logs, too damp and punky and moss-grown to burn, shaded by huge old mountain-laurel bushes and a spreading white pine; by the time they crept beneath to take stock, color was seeping back into Fawn's vision as the last stars were swallowed by the steely sky. The day would turn hot and fine once the sun rose above the eastern ridge, but right now all was a shadowless damp. And an eerie quiet. A whimper from Plum, quickly muffled by her mama, came faintly to their ears, and Fawn was reminded that sounds carried both ways.

More than their captured company huddled around the fire; maybe a dozen tea caravan muleteers and a few other unlucky Trace travelers were also collected, sitting or lying down in sodden exhaustion, or snoring. In the meadow opening out beyond, mules munched and crunched, big gray shapes moving through the wet grass. They seemed to have their harnesses off, so evidently the muleteers had retained enough of their wits to care for their animals. Fawn wasn't sure if that was good or bad.

"See that malice anywheres?" whispered Whit.

Fawn peered over the mossy log. Balanced on a dead tree branch on the other side of the clearing, what seemed a tall cloaked figure moved, and she caught her breath, but then she spotted another, draped from a lower branch like dirty washing, and realized they were only a pair of mud-bats. The one above shuffled in an irritated way, then swung to hang head down; the one beneath whined uncomfortably, and clawed its way back upright. Neither seemed to like its new position any better.

A couple of big, naked shapes sat cross-legged at the far edge of the circle of captives, and Fawn realized they were ordinary mud-men—new made, or seized from the other malice? Their lumpish forms made her think maybe they were spoils of the earlier clash, the one that—it was hard not to think of it as *our malice*—had been fleeing.

Berry followed her gaze, gripped her arm. Breathed, "Can they sense us?"

"I guess not," Fawn breathed back, when none of the dozing creatures roused in suspicion.

Dag had said their shields didn't make their grounds as invisible as that of a fully veiled patroller. Were these early creations lacking groundsense, or did the smudged grounds simply not catch their interest? *Maybe we look like rocks.* Fawn tried to crouch as still and rock-like as possible, to keep up the illusion.

"When d'you think the malice will come back?" whispered Whit into Fawn's ear; she had to strain to make out the words. At least she didn't have to warn him to keep his voice down.

She also made her reply as voiceless as she could. "Not sure. If it's past the stage of ground-ripping everybody on sight, and it seems this one is, next thing a malice does is try to gather forces to make attacks. 'Cept there's nothing around here *to* attack. It'll have to march everyone forty miles up the road to even reach the next village." She hesitated. "The Glassforge malice started to dig a mine, pretty early on, but that might have been 'cause it ate—ground-ripped—a miner. If this one's been eating muleteers and traveling folks, it may just want to traipse away up the Trace."

"Huh." Whit settled in tighter to the earth.

They might have a long wait till their ambush. That would be bad. Fawn could feel her nervous energy leaching away in exhaustion. This was a well-watered country, so they hadn't gone thirsty in the night, but no one had eaten since noon yesterday. Or slept. A wave of nausea swept her, but it wasn't as bad as the sick chill from being reminded of what she risked. Oh gods, if the baby made her throw up, could she do so in utter silence? *Don't think about it, it just makes it worse.* She swallowed and breathed through her mouth.

To distract herself, she counted heads. All their company seemed still to be here, and together, except, disturbingly, Calla and Indigo. An ice lump formed under her breastbone as she realized that the four bodies in a huddled heap near the road weren't sleeping. But all were strangers. Had the muleteers redeemed their comrades for burial, or were the mud-men just saving the corpses for breakfast? She swallowed again, harder. If the mud-men were properly frugal, they ought to consume the oldest meat first, before starting on a more tender morsel like, say, Plum. *Only if the malice has ground-ripped a good farmwife, I suppose.* And, *It might still get that chance.*

Whit shifted uncomfortably, readjusted the lie of his crossbow. Touched the cord of the sharing-knife sheath, now hung around his neck. "If it flies around, how do we lure it close enough to get a good shot?"

"I figure our shields will puzzle it, if it sees us. It'll fly closer to look. Then we get it. You get it," Fawn corrected herself.

"Maybe you two better draw back."

Berry shook her head. "Somebody might have to keep attackers off you till you get your shot." Her hand tightened around a long, stout stick, which Fawn had no doubt the riverwoman knew how to use.

Fawn felt less useful. If Whit's first shot missed, but fell without breaking, she might be able to scurry and retrieve it. Depending on whether anyone, malice or mud-men or mind slaves, realized what was going on. Giving Whit not one chance, but two. *But probably not three.* She did not mention the dodgy scheme aloud.

The light grew; from the woods, a redcrest trilled incessantly, *cheer-cheer-cheer,* and was answered by another. A few figures around the smoldering fire stirred, lay back down. Fawn spotted some, but not all, of the company's packs and bedrolls lying scattered about. Would the muleteers share their food? Would the malice realize it needed to feed its new troops? If so, would it bring people food, or bags of bugs . . . ? Fawn blinked rapidly, fighting a soft slide into the hallucinations of dream. This was nightmare enough with her eyes wide open. Maybe the bat-malice only came out at night. They would have to withdraw and hide till then; there was no way they could stay awake and undetected till nightfall in this . . .

Whit's breath went out in a guarded huff. Fawn looked up through the laurel leaves.

A bat-shape circled in an un-bat-like graceful glide. She could not guess its size against the blank blue sky, but its bone-shaking aura rolled before it like sea waves. She wanted to run *now,* but of course it was too late. It wasn't courage, nor any fancied usefulness, that kept her crouching. *Papa always said Mama should have named me Cat, because my curiosity would kill me someday.* Maybe today? Yet beneath her fear, curiosity refused to surrender. *Will my stupid-farmer-girl idea work?* She wet her lips and waited.

"All right," Whit muttered. He fumbled the modified knife out of its sheath—Fawn took it back from him so he wouldn't drop it while he was cranking his bow—stood up, and stepped forward. Breaking cover too soon, maybe, but oh gods that he could stand up at all . . . Fawn scrambled after and pressed the bone bolt into his sweat-damp hand.

The malice circled overhead, looking down curiously. Too high? Moving too fast? It flapped it vast wings and went higher. "Whit, wait," Fawn gasped as he raised the crossbow, wavering after its target.

Instead of the malice descending, the company rose to its feet. Turned faces their way. Started to move in a stumbling bunch. Finch called anxiously, "No, you don't have to kill them! Just pull those walnut necklaces off them, and they'll be fine!"

Oh gods . . . !

Berry took a grip on her stick and stepped forward grimly. Fawn, desperate, jumped out and waved her arms frantically skyward. "Down here, you stupid bat-thing, you malice bat . . . stupid thing! This is what you want! Come and get it!" She danced back and forth. *Oh, come and get it.* "Stupid malice!"

Whit gulped as the malice, with another lazy wing flap, dropped suddenly closer, eyeing them. Still beyond reach of any knife or spear. More wing beats sent gusts of cellar smell tumbling toward them as it hovered, legs drawn up. Fawn wondered how long their shields would stand up to the malice's full concentration, then realized she was about to find out, because they had surely won all its attention now. Its legs extended—it was coming in for a landing. The morning grew darker, like a cloud drawing across the sun, but the sky was cloudless and the sun wasn't up over the ridge yet . . .

The shaking crossbow steadied, Fawn knew well at what cost. *Yes, Whit!* A snap of release, a deep thrum from the string, a white flash as the bone bolt flew upward. A *thwack-crack* as it entered the malice's abdomen, spread broad as a target as its wings stretched to scoop the air.

The malice's surprised shriek pierced Fawn's ears, dimming abruptly as darkness descended on her eyes. *Am I being ground-ripped? But Dag said it would hurt . . .* Through the boiling black clouds, Fawn saw the malice's wings blow off in both directions and tumble earthward as its body disintegrated. Rank matter showered down. The blackness shrank inward, hard and tight. Was this death? *Oh baby, oh Dag, I'm sorry——*

∽

Dag came awake on a sudden, indrawn breath, and stared around, heart thudding for no reason that he could discern. All was quiet, the woods fog-shrouded, but the world had lightened since he'd dozed off under this ledge in a black chill. The sky shaded upward from gray to pale blue. An hour after dawn, perhaps? It would be at least another two hours before the sun cleared the ridge and began to warm them, but already the mist was shredding away as the air began to stir. His two charges still slept; or at least, Owlet slept, and Pakko lay in a pain-hazed doze that Dag could find no reason to disrupt.

Fearfully, Dag tested his marriage cord coiled on his upper arm. *She's still alive.* At least that. The tiny hum seemed disturbingly muted, as it had ever since Dag had anchored Fawn's walnut shield into her ground.

Was it more muted now? Why? Was Fawn traveling farther from him? Ordinary distances had never affected their cords before. Dag tried to encourage himself: *Sumac will know to look after her,* but the dire part of his mind that wouldn't shut up had to add, *If Sumac is still alive.* Would his scout Tavia find any survivors at all in the valley, let alone Arkady?

He rolled his shoulders, propped uncomfortably against the rock wall, and scowled at his right leg, stretched out before him. He'd finally loosened his boot for fear that cutting off circulation would lead to cutting off his purpling foot, and as he'd expected, the ankle was now too swollen to tie it again. Soon he would need to get up and go refill their water bottle. He tried to muster a proper medicine maker's concern for his charges, instead of frustrated rage for being fixed here. He and Tavia had made Pakko as clean and comfortable as possible before she'd left last night. Dag's last reserve was one strip of dried plunkin in his pocket. Pakko's body was the most depleted, but his pain muffled his hunger, and keeping Owlet silent might prove the more urgent task . . .

With his thoughts chasing their tails like crazed cats, all hope of dozing off again faded. As silently as possible, Dag levered himself to his feet with his stick, gathered up the water bottle, and began hobbling down the hillside. This was going to take a while.

When Dag at length returned, Owlet was awake, cranky, and fearful. Pakko was eyeing the farmer child with a glazed sort of alarm. Even in his dreadful pain, the patroller was holding a tolerable ground veiling, which won both Dag's gratitude and respect; Owlet, of course, blazed like a beacon.

"Oh, good, you're back," said Pakko. A tension in his tone reminded Dag of just how long Pakko had lain up here alone, lost and hopeless.

Dag settled himself by the man's side, leg out. "Ayup. Water?"

"It'll just make me piss myself again." Pakko grimaced, looked away, hiding helpless shame.

"I'm a medicine maker. I'll deal with it." Dag revised this slightly. "You help guide the bag, I'll hold your head up." He slipped his hand behind Pakko's head; Pakko raised an arm, though it made him gasp. Together, they managed to get another good drink down the injured man. *Absent gods, what a pair. We're not half a patroller between us.*

Owlet circled around Pakko and crept into Dag's lap; Dag gave him a drink, too, with rather more spillage, but the threat of howls passed off with only a few sniffles.

In the daylight, Pakko squinted at Dag in new curiosity, Dag hoped not too tinged with dismay. "Except for the hand, I'd have taken you for a patroller."

"I was, once."

"Is that why you went for maker, instead? How was it you were traveling with farmers?" He looked over at the scabbed and grubby Owlet as if the child were the most unlikely part of all this.

"It's a long story. A couple of long stories."

"I'm not going anywhere." Pakko's air of indifference was a bit too carefully held. Some tale-telling would keep his rescuer safely planted under his eye, right.

Dag sighed. "Yeah, me neither." But before he could choose a beginning, a ragged motion through the trees snagged his eye. He sat up, squinting, then grabbed his stick and clambered abruptly to his feet; Owlet, dumped, whimpered in protest. "'Scuse me."

He ducked out from under the overhang, and dared to flick open his groundsense. *Mud-bat!* He snapped closed again. Limped a few dozen paces along the hillside to where a rock slide had plowed open a wider view of the sky, and of the treetops falling away.

Several hundred paces below, a laboring mud-bat crashed into the branches, fought loose, and struggled for altitude again. It was flying very badly. Injured? Burdened with a load or a captive? It was too far off, Dag thought, for him to pull yesterday's risky trick with a precisely placed ground-rip, yet if it was taking a prisoner back to its malice, he'd have to try *something*. But as the creature pumped frantically upward, Dag saw that its back claws were empty.

It lurched nearer. Had it seen him, was it attacking? One bent boot knife and a cut sapling weren't going to be enough to bring it down. Dag took a breath, opened himself again, reached.

Stood stunned. There was nothing in the mud-bat's ground but bat, natural bat. Voiceless, wordless, stripped of reason. Terrified and confused to find itself in this all-wrong, too-heavy, dying body. Frantic to reach the cool refuge of its dimly remembered cave, far to the east, out of the horrible hurtful light. In the hot speed of its flight, with no support from its malice master, its disintegration was proceeding rapidly.

There was no mistaking the ground of a mud-man that had lost its wits; Dag had seen the little tragedy played out countless times, most recently two days ago.

Someone has dealt with the malice!

A good half of the thousand pounds of worry weighing Dag's heart lifted. His mouth opened, and his lips drew back in an uncontrollable grin.

The mud-bat crashed again, rose again, and finally tumbled out of range over the ridgeline. Dag tottered back to their shelter. If he could have, he would have danced the distance.

"Hey, hey, hey, Pakko!"

"What is it?" Pakko clutched the only weapon he had, the water bottle.

"No, good news! Your patrol must have found the malice's lair! Its mud-men are skinned of their wits and scattering. If we just hold out, help has to come. My people might get up here by the end of the day.

Yours could even be out looking for you already! They were what, you said, only about fifteen miles north of here when you parted ways?"

Pakko made a sound of profound relief. His head fell back limply. Despite everything, his lips, too, stretched in a grin.

With a sense of joy, Dag flung his own ground open wide, releasing that cramped, deaf, blind, *No one here* and changing it for a flag of welcome, *Here we are! Come get us!* Pakko's grin went wider. Even Owlet looked up and cooed, bemused by the sudden cheer of the mysterious, scary grown-ups.

Dag escorted Owlet back to the streamlet for an overdue morning cleaning, then settled himself again and offered the child a celebratory half plunkin strip, which was grabbed with alacrity. Pakko accepted the other half. The child climbed back into his lap refuge, to gnaw and drool happily. "So, let me see." Dag thought he might be babbling, but he didn't care. Pakko was surely the most captive of audiences, and Owlet seemed to find the rumble of Dag's voice soothing. "You asked for my life story."

"I sure do wonder how you stumbled onto me, I'll say that," Pakko allowed.

"Well, I'm from Oleana, originally, but I took a walk around the lake . . ."

∾

Later, Dag passed some time tricking a few luckless squirrels and a mourning dove into becoming lunch, a process that both fascinated and fed the fretful Owlet. Peeled, cut up, and cooked on a toasting stick, the game produced hardly a mouthful, but Owlet's was a little mouth. Dag was more worried for Pakko, who seemed barely able to swallow.

It was midafternoon when Tavia arrived with Arkady, wonderfully sooner than Dag had dared hope. Unexpectedly, they also brought Calla, Indigo, and pack loads of supplies. Dag ducked out from under the ledge, where Owlet was napping, and hobbled forth to greet them.

Arkady, still catching his breath from the climb, grabbed Dag by the shoulders as though he didn't know whether to hug him or shake him. "I never thought I'd see you alive again! Ye gods, what horrible things have you been doing to your ground this time?"

"Did a little surgical ground-ripping on some mud-bats. That's how we all ended up here and not as meat in the malice's lair. Arkady, we're saved! Someone's done for the malice!"

"Yes, we saw." Tavia nodded vigorously. "There are dying mud-bats scattered all over the valley. We passed two on the way here."

"Where's Fawn? And the others," Dag added conscientiously.

Arkady and Tavia looked at each other in a way Dag didn't much like. Arkady said, "After you three were carried away, we made it to the trees, and the attack broke off. A mud-bat tried to take Barr, too, but it dropped him and shattered his leg. I put it back together as best I could, but there was no moving him far, so Sumac had me, Barr, and Rase hide up in a cave. Of sorts. Sumac decided she'd take everyone else west over the ridge, try to reach Laurel Gap."

Best patrol procedure, get the children and women out of range of the malice, spread the warning. Or, efficiently, both at once. "Good for her." Was Fawn safe on her way to the Lakewalker camp, then?

Evidently not, for Arkady added, "After that, Calla had better tell the tale."

The half-blood girl took a deep breath. "We were partway up the hill last night, trying to cross that saddle, when the mud-bats came back. The malice came with them. It was *flying*."

Dag's belly chilled, but he reminded himself that however appalling this malice's form, it was dead now.

"It looked sort of like a mud-bat, only bigger and, and . . . more beautiful, I suppose. Once you'd seen it, you wouldn't ever mistake it for anything else, not for a second."

Dag nodded understanding.

"It took our minds. It was the strangest sensation. Like I was calm on top, but screaming underneath." Her tremors were long gone, in this bright afternoon, but Dag sensed a bone-deep exhaustion left in their wake; a familiar state, after dealing with the terror of a malice.

"It didn't keep hold of her mind the way it did ours, though," said Indigo. He, too, was pale with more than the night's exertions.

Calla scowled in memory. "It was like all these wild ideas kept fading in and out of my thoughts. Arkady thinks I was trying to veil myself."

"Anyway," Indigo went on, "the mud-bats chased Sumac and Remo and Neeta off, and Fawn and Whit and Berry got away, too." He seemed about to say more, but swallowed instead.

"Together?" Dag asked in hope. Was Fawn safe with Sumac?

Indigo shook his head. "They ran opposite ways. We think those walnut shields of yours must have worked."

"The malice marched the rest of us north up the Trace in the night," Calla continued, "but I kept falling back. Dragging as much as I dared."

"I kept trying to make her keep up," said Indigo. "It seemed like my own idea at the time. It was just . . . something we had to do. But we got farther and farther behind the others, and then . . . it was like my mind cleared. *Then* we turned tail and ran."

"I hoped we could find Arkady, and that the Lakewalkers would protect us," said Calla. "I've never been so scared. We were searching along the ridge about where I thought Sumac had put him, when Neeta found us instead. She was all by herself. She said the patrollers had veiled themselves and shook off the mud-bats, and hid up in a cranny. Sumac was frantic by then, but finally decided someone still had to warn Laurel

Gap Camp. So she took Remo and lit out westward, and left Neeta to hunt for Fawn and try to get her back to Arkady."

"But Neeta said she couldn't," said Indigo. "Find Fawn and Whit and Berry, that is. She said it was a good sign, because if her groundsense couldn't find them, neither could the malice's. She hoped they'd have the sense to stay hid."

Dag ran his hand through his hair, and tried not to scream. "Then what?"

"I came out of the cave to fetch water, and found Neeta and these two blundering around," said Tavia. "I'd reached Arkady a couple of hours before."

"Tavia was our first word of your fate," Arkady told Dag. "It was a relief to know the local patrol was on the hunt, but absent gods, what a mess."

Tavia went on, "We were trying to decide what was best to do for you, since we didn't have near enough hands to carry an injured man down this ridge, or any better place to hide him if we did. And then we saw the first dying mud-bat, and then, well, the whole situation was changed."

"It was plain it was going to be easier to get the medicine maker to the injured than the other way around," said Arkady. "Or so I thought, before I climbed this benighted mountain. I left Barr with Rase, which I don't quite like, but they've no need to hide themselves now. They should be all right."

Tavia said eagerly, "Neeta recovered her horse, so she decided she'd ride north and try to find the others, wherever they'd gone after Calla and Indigo got away, and maybe make contact with the local patrollers, get us more help."

All as good and sensible as it could be, under the difficult circumstances, but *where was Fawn?* Plainly, no one here knew.

Dag led the party around to their near-cave under the ledge. Arkady knelt down by Pakko, opening his ground to the man's injury in that keen daunting way of his. "Interesting," he murmured.

Dag, familiar by now with that particular tone of voice, sincerely hoped his sprained ankle would qualify as *boring*. He made introductions, which he hoped the glazed-eyed Pakko understood, and went on, "I didn't think it was good for the break to sit untreated this long, with his muscles in spasms around it like that, but while I'd have been willing to go in after the bone alignment, I wasn't too sure of those disrupted nerve cords."

"Right on all counts," said Arkady. He sat back on his heels and frowned at Dag. "You should be a patient right now, not an assistant, but need drives all. His skin is unbroken, bar some abrasion, and I'd like to keep it that way. That means we do it all by groundsetting techniques. I want you to do the heavy work, go in and carefully realign the two vertebrae, and place ground reinforcements across the fracture lines. Are you ready?"

Now? Dag's relief having arrived, *now* he wanted to go search for his wife, blight it! *And child.* Yet Fawn wasn't out there alone, he reminded himself. She'd had her kin with her . . . his thought snaked on, *when last seen.* Dag eyed the helpless, hurting Pakko, and controlled his frenzy of impatience. Fawn's phrase, *Soonest begun, soonest done,* drifted through his head. "Just a moment." Carefully, he sat on Pakko's other side, laid his bad leg out, undid his arm harness, and set it aside.

While Dag was pulling body, mind, and ground together, Arkady called, "Tavia, Calla, Indigo, set up camp here. We won't be moving this patient tonight. It wants six fit fellows, and we're going to need to fashion a rigid board carrier to tie him to, first."

Pakko swallowed, and said, "If I'm not going to walk again, sir"—he did not say aloud, but Dag understood, *If I'm just going to be lying in a bedroll pissing myself*—"I'd rather you found my knife."

Arkady gave him an enigmatic look. "You'll have time to make that choice later. Ready, Dag?"

Arkady could scout the lay of his land and choose his tactics as swiftly as Dag, and for the same reason: forty years of experience. Despite his weariness, Dag found himself relaxing into that trusted leadership. He stretched his fingers, real and ghostly; sight and sound dropped away as he sank into the shared hinterland of flowing ground.

It was not healing so much as making ready to heal. Pain moved with hot red violence. Muscles cried. The sculpted bones themselves were cool, solid, reassuring, yet like strange lace down and in, alive with blood both flowing and blocked, bruised and clotted. Arkady handled the much more delicate nerves, like ropes and whips and threads of fire, down and in, down and in . . .

"Hold up," Dag murmured, following with a ground-touch; Arkady gasped and broke out of his beginning ground lock. Dag couldn't have fallen into a lock right now if all their lives had depended on it; his heart was too outwardly drawn, wild to regain the world and all it held. It made him a good anchor, he supposed. What Arkady was doing was *complicated*, a fiendishly difficult task accomplished with as much grace as any dance, and a strange sort of pleasure to observe just in its own right, apart from any consequences.

"Thanks," muttered Arkady. "Good job. You can pull out now . . ."

Dag inhaled, blinked, sat up as their mountainside refuge rushed back into his senses. How much time had gone by? The sun seemed notably lower.

"He passed out a while back," reported Calla, wiping Pakko's clammy face with a damp cloth.

"I'm not surprised," said Dag, and rolled away, pale and shaking. *That was good!* he thought with elation. *Gods,* he liked this work. Magery at full stretch. *Allowable* magery. He crawled to prop his shoulders up against the cool rock wall of the overhang, and let other people do everything else for a few minutes. Tavia brought him water, and a dried strip of ruddy New Moon plunkin.

Surely this discharged his last obligation to fate; as he was Pakko's good luck, perhaps someone else would be Fawn's, passing the debt around. Now it was Dag's turn to pursue his own ends. And no one had better get in his way.

Just as soon as I can stand up.

"Will Pakko walk again?" asked Tavia diffidently.

Dag shook his head. "Too early to say. It'll be a week before the swelling goes down enough to tell the permanent damage. But he'll live to see his wife again."

When Arkady, at length, rolled back and propped his own shoulders, looking much like a wet rag, Dag said, "I need to go look for Fawn."

"Tomorrow," said Arkady. "I promise we'll get you down off this mountain first turn."

"I can get myself down."

Arkady made a rude noise. "How, fall? I grant you it would be quick."

Dag touched his left arm. "Something's not right."

Arkady's gaze flicked, quick and keen; he frowned, but did not argue that particular point. It disturbed Dag that he did not. "I suppose I can't stop you, short of tying you up."

"That wouldn't stop me, either."

"Absent gods, Dag, if you've half the sense of a plunkin, you'll wait for help."

I am the help. Dag frowned.

"And falling downhill or not, it would be dark by the time you could get to the wagons," Arkady added. "I suppose that's the one known meeting place, at this point. Otherwise you'll have this whole valley to search."

"Mm," said Dag trying to think it through. Everyone here was just as exhausted and short of sleep as he was. Calla was also missing a spouse. Dag would have quashed any half-crippled patroller of his who suggested a jaunt so plunkin-brained. Still . . . he touched his marriage cord again, rubbing it through the rips in his shirt, but it gave him no further enlightenment. Changed, yes, but what did that *mean?* Perhaps his and Fawn's questionable cord weaving was simply running down naturally.

No. This is wrong.

Dag found an unexpected ally in Owlet, who had awakened during the groundsetting session. Flustered by the influx of strangers, the child began crying again for his mama. Dag ruthlessly let him. Tavia quickly handed him off to Calla, who had no better luck calming him. Arkady, returning from washing up in the streamlet, winced at the noise.

"Best to get this child back to his family," Dag observed over the ruckus. "Before he cries himself sick or takes a tumble down the hill. There's no need to keep him up here in the cold another night."

"Who are you volunteering?" said Tavia. "You couldn't carry him!"

"I could," said Indigo unexpectedly. "Go with Dag and help look for the Basswoods." A glance exchanged with Calla added, *And Sage and Finch and Ash.*

"Huh." Tavia rubbed a hand over her weary face. "I guess Calla and me between us would be enough help out up here tonight. I mean, with Arkady and all."

Calla added, bouncing the child to no other effect than to give the wails a waver, "His parents have to be crazy with worry and grief right now. Cruel to leave them that way any longer than needed."

"Where would you look?" said Arkady, weakening under the on-slaught.

"There's been a tail of smoke coming up from the woods near the Trace all day, 'bout eight, ten miles north, looks like," said Dag. "I've been checking it. Seems like a campfire, and on the route Calla and Indigo said our folks took. If not our people, it's *some* people, who might have seen them."

"And you plan to walk two miles down this hill, cross a river, walk another mile to the road and more miles down it, with a sprained ankle, before dark?" inquired Arkady. "Lugging this little screamer? You're not heroic, Dag, you're mad."

Getting there. For the tenth time today, Dag hobbled to the drop-off and cast his groundsense out to its farthest, thinnest reach.

For the first time today, he received a response: far below, a long, plaintive whinny echoed up the ravine-slashed slopes.

Dag grinned. "Who said anything about walking? Seems my ride's turned up. If Indigo can get me down this hill as far as I can summon Copperhead up, I'm back in the saddle."

∽

To Dag's surprise, his saddle *was* still on Copperhead's back, though his saddlebags were gone, scraped off somewhere in the woods. He'd have to spend a day hunting for them, not for the first time in his career. Not to mention his war knife, lost in the clash. *Later.* Copperhead hadn't managed to pull off his bridle, and his bit was slimy and crusted with browsing. His mane and tail were full of burs. But in all, the horse was in vastly better shape than his owner.

Bemused, Dag handed back the blanket he'd begged from Indigo, with which he'd planned to pad the gelding's murderously serrated backbone. "You didn't unsaddle the horses before turning them loose?"

"The others, sure!" Indigo, indignant, stepped prudently out of range of cow kicks as Dag led his mount to the nearest fallen log. "This one ran off after he dumped you in the fight. We never caught him."

"Embarrassed, I hope. Eh, old fellow?" Dag scrubbed the chestnut ears; Copperhead snorted green slobber and rubbed to be relieved of his bridle, in vain. He laid his ears back in protest as Dag tightened his girth. But Dag made sure the horse sensed this was no time for tricks. It was an awkward heave to get himself up, but Dag blew out his breath in relief as his haunches settled into their accustomed place once more, and he allowed his throbbing right foot to dangle. He hurt all over, and his vision seemed to pulse in time with the pain in his ankle. Arkady, though also exhausted and still disapproving, had spared him a small ground reinforcement to his sprain before he'd left, muttering, *I suppose Sumac's halfway to Laurel Gap by now*, to which Dag had replied, *I'll keep an eye out*.

Dag lowered his hook, toward which Owlet reached out grimy hands; swinging from it had been a game they'd invented earlier in the day, which had worked for a while to turn wails to giggles. "Upsy-daisy, little brother." Indigo boosted him upward, and Dag tucked him in the blanket and disposed him as securely as possible before him in the saddle, left arm wrapping his little chest. Owlet made a noise halfway between fascination and dismay at this elevated view of the world.

Dag glanced out across the river valley, and said to Indigo, "Copperhead will outpace you."

"I didn't figure you'd be waiting." Indigo helped Dag slip his stick under his saddle flap.

"Do you want to follow, or go back up to Arkady's camp with Calla?"

Indigo shook his head. "I'll check the wagons, first. They really are the sensible meeting point. If no one's there yet, I may follow you up the Trace. Or I may just flop down and wait. But north's your best bet, right enough."

Dag nodded, and turned Copperhead westward with the pressure of his knees. It was slow work picking through the woods, spitting out spiderwebs, but they found a river crossing that didn't come up higher than the horse's belly just as the rim of the sun touched the western ridge. Dag reckoned the luminous mountain twilight would last till he reached the source of that smoke curl up the road; after that . . . well, it would depend on what he found. There was a very real possibility that he might be attempting to deliver Owlet to parents ground-ripped and dead in a ditch.

He tried for optimism; it was equally likely that the bat-malice had been mustering farmer troops to meet an attack from the patrollers operating to the north, in which case it would have been conserving its captives, not feeding on them. His optimism faltered with the thought, *I hope our folks didn't run into the patrollers before the malice went down.* Although that might well have been how the malice had met its end, because clearly the creature had not been tied to its initial lair. Dag had been on the other side of that scenario, a couple of times, fighting mind-slaved farmers. He didn't have to imagine the horrors; he could just call up the memories. He jerked up his mazed brain as if it were a balky horse. *No. We're not having that here.*

When they reached the road, Dag turned Copperhead north and touched him into his long, rocking lope; of the horse's many defects, that gait was not one. Owlet squealed with astonishment and glee as his curls ruffled in the wind. *At least one of us three is happy.* Actually, Copperhead didn't altogether seem to mind stretching his legs, and Dag let him stretch them a little farther. As a result, Dag came within ground-sense range of the smoke camp while the sky was still bright.

Yes! he thought as he touched the first familiar farmer ground. Still half a mile out, he let blowing Copperhead drop to a walk, and began hurriedly counting heads. Bo, Hawthorn, Hod, good. Sage—*oh, Calla, everything's going to be all right for you now.* Finch and Ash. The Basswoods, very distressed, but absent-gods-be-thanked Plum was still with them. He'd been especially worried for Plum, a high-ground-density morsel of little use as a soldier. A great many strangers, or near strangers—he was almost sure he recognized some of the tea-caravan muleteers they'd been playing leapfrog with for weeks. He sorted through again. Were those dim smudges Whit and Berry, behind their shields? Surely there was a third? Yes, dimmer still.

Dag pressed Copperhead into a grudging trot as orange firelight flickered through the graying shadow of the woods. He turned into a broad clearing, with a broader meadow opening out along a creek, to find a couple of dozen folks in a makeshift camp—muleteers, yes, and the larger part of his own company. Finch, lugging in an armload of deadfall, saw him first, dropped the branches around his feet, and yelled in astonishment, "It's Dag! He's alive! And he's got *Owlet* with him!"

A female shriek of *"What?"* came from the clearing's far side. Dag had just time to spare a powerful thought of *Behave or you're wolf meat* to Copperhead before a dozen pale, excited people swarmed up around him. Copperhead lowered his head and snorted, but stood dutifully still.

Without being asked, everyone parted to let Vio run up to Dag's saddle; Grouse and Plum hurried behind her. The ragged woman stared up openmouthed with all the joy lighting her face that Dag could have wished, her arms reaching as if for stars. He persuaded Owlet to hang on to his hook arm, lifted him from his saddlebow, and lowered him into his mother's grasp.

"Dag, Dag, Dag," chortled Owlet. "Plunkin, plunkin. *Blighdit.*"

Vio was laughing, shining tears tracking down her face. "My word, but he's *filthy*!"

"No worse'n Dag!" Grouse exclaimed, hugging wife and child both. As he took in the return of his son, all unexpected, from what had surely seemed certain death, his face bore a naked wonder unlike any expression Dag had ever surprised there. Dag grinned. *And what do you think of Lakewalkers now, Grouse?*

Dag's gaze swept the upturned faces, but didn't find Berry, Whit, or Fawn.

"Where's Fawn?" he asked.

Silence spread out from the crowd clustered around his knees, as though his words had been a stone thrown into water.

Vio looked up; her face drained of joy, leaving just tears. She clutched Owlet harder. "Oh, Dag. I'm so sorry."

"What?"

"The poor little thing was so brave and bright, and then so stiff and cold. If we'd guessed you were still alive, we'd have waited for you."

"What are you talking about?"

Bo, shouldering forward, swallowed and swung his arm to point across the clearing. "That bat-malice-thing kilt her, just as Whit got it with his bow. Them muleteers was buryin' their own dead, so we laid her in alongside 'em. Not an hour ago, I reckon."

"Buried?" Dag's heart began to hammer. He gripped his marriage cord and stared in foolish bewilderment at the mound of fresh-turned earth beneath a cluster of slender ash trees. "But she's not dead!"

22

Dag found himself atop the low mound, clawing at the dirt with his hook, with no memory of how he'd got there. He didn't have his stick. "We've got to get her out of there! She can't breathe!"

"Dag, man!" Finch pulled at his shoulder. Ash clamped a big hand on the other, lifting him more effectively; he wavered unwillingly to his knees, still clawing dirt, then clawing air.

"It's no good, Dag!" said Sage. "Give it up, please!"

A woman's voice, Vio's, in the background, calling in distress, "Oh, help! Grief's gone and turned his wits!"

"I did not," Dag gasped furiously, shrugging off the hands, "survive a fight with mud-men and a night on a blighted mountaintop, climb two miles back *down* the mountain, and ride ten with a busted ankle, all to find my wife, to stop *six feet short!*"

"Does he want her bones?" said an unfamiliar voice—one of the muleteers?

"They say them Lakewalkers eat their dead—it's like a funeral feast to them—but I'm not having with that here!"

"She was his wife, though. Maybe we should let him . . ."

"Well, he ain't eating *my* brother, nor stealing his bones neither!"

Dag fought free; more hands clutched him. Bo called out, "There's no use to this carryin' on, Dag—let her rest in peace. We done her all the respects, I promise you."

"She's not dead! I don't know what's going on, but she's not dead! She *can't* be dead! Not Spark!" He whirled, shedding men. *Farmers.*

"Dag, stop, this is madness!"

"Blight it, help me!" he cried, anguished. One-handed shoveling was not one of his better skills. But somebody must have had tools to dig the grave, so there must still be tools around to dig it up. He didn't expect the strangers to understand, but surely the southern boys . . . ? A muleteer shoved too close; Dag almost swiped at him with his lethal hook, just managed to slug the man instead. Six more helpful muleteers jumped Dag and wrestled him to the grass. Gods! He couldn't ground-rip them like mud-bats . . . *Yes, I could.* The unwelcome thought slowed him a little.

He wept in his frustration, water blurring his dizzied view of shadows, firelight, men's frightened faces. "Look, fetch another Lakewalker! Anyone with a speck of groundsense! They'll testify I'm right!" A knee pressed on his chest, making him think of the dirt that must be pressing down on Spark's. Had they stamped down the grave mound? "Absent gods, did you cover her face? There'll be dirt in her mouth—in her eyes—" They hadn't sewn her eyelids shut, had they? He'd heard that was a farmer funeral practice, some places . . .

Bo's voice, would-be-soothing but for the quaver: "Dag, there weren't no mistaking. She was cold and stiff. We couldn't feel a pulse. There weren't no breath mistin' on a knife blade."

"It was a hot day, of course there wouldn't be breath on a warm blade! Where's Whit? Where's Berry? Get me Whit, he'll understand!"

"He's too sick to stand up, Dag, and Berry ain't no better," Hawthorn's voice called anxiously from beyond the circle of looming faces.

Wrong, wrong, what was wrong? With a mighty lunge, Dag wallowed to his feet, knocking aside muleteers.

Oh gods, thank gods, a man was running up with a shovel. Dag's heart lifted in joyous relief. "Yes, yes, help me——!" He reached out his hand for the wildly swinging tool. Saw, too late, its intended purpose as the broad blade swept around his head and clouted him hard. Faces, firelight, spinning branches above, all dissolved in hot bright sparks.

ᕯ

He came to himself wincing, sick to his stomach. Pain pulsed like forge-hammer blows in his head, ankle. Lungs. Heart. He breathed shallowly, then more deeply. Made to touch his head, only to find his hand caught. He wrenched around, or tried to, to discover he was sitting with his back to a slender tree, his hand and hook tied behind it. He hadn't been stunned for long—his tears were not quite dried. It felt as if snails had been crawling across his face, and he jerked his arm again, desperate to wipe away the sensation.

Turning his wrist, Dag felt rope. He could ground-rip through rope, if he had to—it wouldn't kill him to rip anything he could eat, Spark had figured that out, *Spark, no!* Not that gnawing down a mouthful of hemp would be *good* for him. He panted, trying to collect his scattered wits, because they seemed to be his last resource. Struggling for calm, he extended his groundsense. The dim sensation in his marriage cord was unchanged. That, at least. The shadowy blur under the mound at the meadow's edge had not disappeared. Whatever had happened wasn't growing worse. Yet.

He looked up to find Finch, Ash, Sage, and Bo all crouched around him in a half circle, staring apprehensively. Hod hovered behind Bo. He'd been crying, too, judging from the snail tracks down his spotty face.

Dag swallowed, moistened dry lips. Croaked, "I'm better now. You can untie me."

Bo's eyes narrowed. "I'll be the judge of that, Dag."

Subterfuge. He should have gone to subterfuge right off, instead of alarming the whole camp with a display of deranged Lakewalker. Screaming—more screaming, gods, his throat was raw—would not be helpful. *Stands to reason, stands to reason,* and he choked down a shattered laugh at Spark's favorite turn of phrase, because inexplicable cackling would not be helpful, either.

The sight of Sage's strained face reminded him. "Sage. I saw Calla and Indigo. They escaped last night all right, and made it back to Arkady. Indigo's gone back to the wagons, to catch anyone who shows up there, and Calla's up on the east ridge with Arkady and a hurt patroller that Tavia and I found. Tavia, she got away from her mud-bat, too. Whole, we're all whole. Well, I got a little bent."

Sage almost melted before Dag's eyes, as a man had a right to who'd just learned he would not be burying his new bride. Not to mention his tent-brother. And all, and all. *Save for Spark.* But this level-voiced report seemed to reassure his audience in more ways than one.

"Please. All I want . . . all I want is to see her face again. One last time. Is that too much to ask?" Dag would have crawled on his knees to beg, without hesitation, but until he convinced them to untie him he couldn't move. It wasn't enough just to break free and run off. Now that he'd recovered his senses, he could think of three ways to escape, quick as a cat. But he had to have help—willing, careful help. *Right now.* He gulped again, to hide his mad-looking desperation. "Fawn and me, we've done a lot for you folks. I know it's late, and you're all tired, but . . . but please. I just want to look at her. One last time."

And if it really was the last time, well, he still had his bonded knife slung around his neck, didn't he? Formerly when he was in desperate straits that thought had calmed and heartened him, in a bleak sort of way. Not tonight. *I want Fawn, I want our baby, I want, I want . . . I want life.* Years and decades and heaping plattersful more of life. It was *not* too much to ask. "For pity's sake," he whispered.

He tried to compose himself enough to muster a persuasion, or more than one, unfit for groundwork of any kind though he was in this distraction. But then he saw the hesitation in Sage's face, and waited, one heartbeat, two, three.

"Maybe it'll settle him down," Sage said.

Dag quelled a howl of agreement, *Yes, yes!* Made his voice humble, mollified. "It's all I want. Please."

Bo's brow wrinkled. Finch's mouth twisted in doubt.

Ash, whose size had made him the victim of every cry of *Need some help liftin', here!* since they'd left Alligator Hat, sighed, and said sadly, "All right. I'll dig."

ஃ

There was only the one shovel, belonging to the muleteer who'd belted Dag with it, and who gave it up dubiously. But even with the three southern boys to take it in turns, it would be agonizing minutes before they uncovered the hopes they had so prematurely buried. More frantic urging to *Be careful!* would do nothing but re-convince them that Dag was mad. Since he was terrified that they might yet stop short, and he couldn't watch without screaming, he took himself across the clearing to see Whit and Berry, limping so stiffly that even Bo hurried to put a helping hand under his elbow. Dag did not protest.

His Bluefield tent-kin were laid out together on a thin blanket, just at the edge of the circle of firelight. Hawthorn crouched by his big sister and brother-in-law, looking forlorn; he shuffled back as Dag approached. Berry, muzzy and weak, levered herself up onto one elbow. Dag knelt awkwardly by her side. From this distance, now that he'd settled a bit, he could at last see what was going on. The pair had not, as he had first thought, been partially ripped by the malice, a crippling unpleasantness of which Dag had firsthand experience. Or . . . not exactly. But their shields had closed down so tightly under the impact of the malice's attempt to do so that their grounds were actually partially withdrawn from their bodies, drained from their extremities into quivering, defensive balls.

Dag huffed in astonishment and fascination, and reached to grasp Berry's walnut pendant and pull it over her head. She whimpered in protest.

"No, it's all right. It's done its work." Not only done, but nearly drained. The thinning groundwork was close to failure. In a few more hours, it would likely have fallen apart, freeing her ground from its shell, leaving her exhausted but alive. As he coaxed its cord from her hair, the deep connection pulled reluctantly apart in sheets like maple syrup just turning to sugar, and her ground flooded back out into its normal form, congruent with her skin.

Berry took a ragged breath, raising her hands to clutch her head. *"Oh."* She struggled to sit up. "What was that? Oh, Dag, what a night we've had! Whit—" She turned urgently to her unconscious young husband.

"Just a moment." Dag half crawled around them. He stole a moment to study the effect of the other walnut shield. It, too, had held against the malice's attempt at ground-ripping, but was clamped even more tightly. And was very close to failure. Whit wasn't going to be his friskiest after it released, but his abused ground would recover in a few days.

I trust. Dag drew Whit's braided cord over his head in turn, and felt the link shear apart.

Whit groaned, and mumbled, "I feel *awful*. Bo, what did I drink?" His gluey eyes peeled open to stare without comprehension up at Dag. Blinked. Came abruptly to awareness. "Dag! You're here! The malice— Fawn—she carved up your knife, put feathers on it—"

"We got the malice, Whit!" Berry told him.

"Did we . . . ? Yes, I remember. Its wings blew off, wildest thing— Dag, your shields! They must have worked!" Whit felt all down his body as if surprised to find it still attached to his head.

"Yes, though it seems they still need some refinin'. You just rest, patroller boy. You've done your job."

Whit settled back, pleased. "Hey, I did, didn't I? Heh. Wait'll Barr and Remo hear about this!"

And a great many others besides. Two dozen people had witnessed Fawn's farmer patrol shoot down the terrifying malice. Dag suspected that this was one tale he wouldn't have to labor to get across to folks. It would fly on wings.

Whit's and Berry's voices tumbled over each other to tell him the story of the past rough night, of all they'd done from the time they'd been driven away from the mind-captured company till their dawn ambush of the bat-malice. Dag barely listened, his groundsense straining toward the grave. If Fawn's shield failed before she was unearthed, releasing her ground back into a body buried alive . . . That certainly would have happened, Dag thought, sometime before tomorrow morning. Absent gods, and he'd almost let Arkady talk him into spending the night on the mountain. *Don't scream, don't scream.*

At the mound, the boys had stopped digging with the shovel and were leaning in, reaching down with their arms. Working something stiff and small up out of the soil. Dag found his stick and pushed to his feet again, turning hastily away from Whit's urging that he go look for the fallen wings, and Berry's woozy, belated query of, *Hey, where's Fawn?*

Dag fell to his knees beside the opened pit in time to receive his wife in his arms, Ash's face looming in sympathetic sorrow. She was every bit as stiff and cool as a real corpse, he had to allow the farmer boys that much. Her powerful shield had drawn her ground in deeply, centered on head, spine, chest, and especially belly. There'd been no shroud to wrap her in—she'd been buried in her shirt and shoes and riding trousers—but absent gods be thanked, someone had donated an old handkerchief to spread across her face. It lay dimpled and moist across her mouth and nostrils, which at least were not packed and blocked with dirt. He pulled the cloth away. Her face was set, her lips much too pale, but *not* the drained lavender yellow of a corpse's. Her closed eyes were undamaged, the lids traced with the pale violet lines of her veins beneath the delicate skin, her black lashes lying in a curving fan above her cheekbones.

His hand shaking so much he could hardly get a grip, Dag found the walnut and drew it over her head. Its cord caught in her dark curling hair, thick with dirt clumps, and he had to stop a moment lest he tear away strands of her hair, too, in his terror. Gently, gently . . . the bond sheeted apart the way Whit's and Berry's had, and he flung the walnut from him with enough force to make it bounce halfway across the clearing.

Her rigidity changed under his hand to a shuddering stretch. He bent his head and kissed her forehead, cheekbones, all over her face, but not her mouth, for she needed that to take a sudden breath, then another, and another, long gulps of air. Color flooded back into her face, and his world. The lashes fluttered faintly . . .

❧

There had been voices in the darkness, distant, as though heard from the other side of time.

The poor little thing!

Oh, the pity of it. . .

It's almost a blessing, that he's gone first.

Yeah, he wouldn't of took this well. . .

She'd wondered, in muzzy indignation before the voices faded out of hearing, where were her *congratulations*?

Pressure then, stealing her breath, and pain from the pressure, and panic from the loss. Air seemed absorbed through her skin, not her slow gaping mouth, seeping into her lungs and hot busy belly. Where had Dag gone off to now? She *needed* him, she was sure of it. Something was very wrong . . .

Time leaked away in the black. Hours? Years?

At last, mumbling sounds returned to her clogged ears, breaking up the worrying too-much-silence that had made her fear she'd been struck deaf. She felt suddenly heavy and dizzy, and only then realized how *nothing* she'd felt before. Almost, almost . . . there! Air!

Her eyelids fought apart onto the most welcome of sights: Dag. His eyes were turned their tea color in the graying shadows and flickering firelight, but a few gold flecks still glinted. From their crow-foot corners shimmering lines traced around his cheekbones, like inlaid silver wire beaten into a copper vessel. His cheeks were stubbly, face bruised and haggard, and his dirty iron-black hair stuck up every which way. For once, he actually looked his age. *Still looks good to me . . .*

Her hand struggled upward to touch the silvery wetness as she at last caught her breath. Despite his wild eyes, his grin nearly split his face. Her fingers traced the rough beard, his stretched lips, bumped over his slightly crooked teeth with the dear familiar chip out of a front one. His kisses found her knuckles, imprinting each one. Her hand slid across his jaw, around his neck, found a grip on his collar, and oh *my* what had he done to his good cotton shirt she'd made for him? More rips than cloth, she swore.

Kisses renewed, on her forehead, cheekbones, chin, mouth at last. *This is better.* She was still stiff and hurting under her collarbone and in the track of the gouges across her shoulder blade from the mud-bat's claws, but beneath her shirt, Calla's plasters seemed to be holding, tugging on her tender skin when she moved. She had still been able to carve . . . they had . . . wait, what . . . ?

"Dag! There was this huge bat-malice—it *flew*—but we got it!" She paused, worked her throat to clear the croak. "*Whit* got it, would you ever believe? And your shields, they must've worked! All those poor mice didn't die in vain . . ." Her free hand searched her neck for her hair-and-walnut necklace. *Best birthday present ever.*

"Yes, yes, and yes, *Spark.*" A fierce hug with this last, which she didn't quite like as much as usual, because the weight of it brought back her stifling nightmare—had she been asleep? Knocked unconscious?

"I knew you couldn't be dead—you looked too *mad* to die, when those awful flying mud-bats were carryin' you off upside down and backwards." At her wriggle, his grip finally loosened enough for her to sit up. "Hey, is this evening? It was morning—did I sleep all day? I don't feel so good. Was I out cold? Why am I all over dirt? My hair . . ." Her fingers, feeling among the dirt clumps, encountered a long, sticky, cool object that she withdrew from her curls with difficulty. An earthworm, big ol' nightcrawler. She flung it from her with a heartfelt *Eew!* "Did Whit put worms in my hair while I was asleep? I'll get him . . ." Her fingers searched her scalp in renewed alarm.

Bo's voice, broken and maundering as if he'd been drinking again— "Sorry, I'm so sorry . . ." Amazed murmurs joined with Bo's mumble, and Fawn looked up from the circle of Dag's arms to find their tender reunion had an audience, crowding up around them: Bo and Hawthorn and Hod, Ash and Finch and Sage, unfamiliar Trace travelers—no, wait, she thought she recognized some of the tea caravan muleteers, nice fellows, if a bit rough around the edges.

Whit shouldered through the mob, crying, "Buried her? *Buried* her! What'd you want to go and do a stupid thing like that for?" He knelt and pulled her away from Dag long enough to give her a hard and quite unprecedented brotherly hug. Dag tolerated this briefly, with a weird benign smile, then drew her back.

"Whit," said Fawn in suspicion, "did you stick that fishin' worm in my hair? You'd reckon a fellow your age would've outgrown such things!"

A muleteer's voice rose in a quaver. "He raised her! That Lakewalker sorcerer raised her up from the grave!"

"Don't think about it," muttered Dag into her now worm-free hair. "Don't think about it." As if to protect her from nightmare visions— hers, or his?

Another muleteer, one of the young ones—what was his name? Spruce, that was it—went to one knee on their other side, and held out a hand quivering in entreaty. "Mister, Mister Lakewalker Bluefield, sir . . . would you raise my brother too? He's younger'n me, it was his first trip, and I surely do dread taking the word of this back to our mama . . . oh, please!"

Dag stared back in bewilderment, his face as blank as if someone had hit him over the head with a shovel. Only Fawn felt his flinch as some realization slotted in. "Oh. No, you don't understand. Absent gods. No one is *that* good a medicine maker. Fawn was never dead in the first place. You blighted fools buried her *alive*." His arms trembled, tightened. "I can't help your brother. I'm sorry."

Fawn began to piece it together. She supposed she ought to be horrified, but really, her outrage echoed Whit's. "You buried me and didn't even wait for *Dag*? Bo!"

"We thought for sure he was a goner, too," Bo said in shaky apology.

"You could tell by my marriage cord he wasn't! We told you that before!"

"Mebbe one o' those other Lakewalkers could've, but we didn't have none of them. Nobody thought to ask that girl who rode by, Neeta, she was in such a hurry 'bout that hurt patroller stuck up on the hill."

Dag gave Bo a sharp glance, but he was distracted by the muleteer pulling on the remains of his sleeve.

"Please, sir, he weren't but twenty years old, and dead without a mark on him. Just like her . . ." The muleteer nodded eagerly at Fawn.

Dismay, pity, and horror chased one another across Dag's face.

"And my friend Bootjack . . . ?" said another muleteer, joining the first down on one knee. Fawn and Dag were suddenly surrounded by a mob of supplicating men. One tried to reach out to touch her, but his hand fell back, daunted by Dag's renewed clutch and glare.

"You don't understand," Dag repeated, and under his breath: "Oh gods, I'll have to *talk*."

Beleaguered, Dag began a halting explanation of ground, malices, the walnut shields, and his hopes for supplying the defense to more farmers than just his Bluefield tent-kin. Someone gathered up the discarded necklaces and placed them in a pile at his knee; at Fawn's urging, they were passed around the crowd so that the men might grasp with their hands what they did not quite take in through their ears. Some looked very interested, though the close friends and kin of the dead muleteers plainly wanted a different answer, and kept trying to get it through amending their questions. Bo and Whit and the Alligator Hat boys all testified to the parts they'd seen, which seemed to help; between that and Dag's obvious exhaustion, the press around them eased from dangerous desperation to mere disappointment. One or two stared at Fawn in a lingering alarm that seemed disproportionate to her small, rumpled self.

Her small, rumpled, filthy, *triumphant* self. She and Whit and Berry deserved the bow-down of all bow-downs, Fawn thought. So when the argument about walnut shields and raising the dead ran down at last, she clambered up, eager to show Dag the remains of their malice.

The cool spring night spun crookedly around her head as she straightened; she groped for Dag's arm, which he wrapped around her again, dropping his stick to do so. Only then did she discover what Dag had done to his ankle. His bare right foot was twice its normal size, colored a streaked deep purple that would have looked fine on a petunia but was very wrong for human skin. She led him in a mutual stagger over to show off the decaying traces of the wings—Dag made sure to warn everyone not to touch the poisonous blight of the malice's remains, and no souvenir taking, either. He plainly didn't even want to camp so close to it, but the deepening dark and everyone's utter exhaustion looked to keep them all planted in this clearing till morning.

Everyone in Sumac's party had carried light bedrolls and food with them, for the failed flight to Laurel Gap, and most folks had hung on to them despite their forced malice march. While Dag looked after his horse with the help of Sage, being careful not to let Fawn out of his sight, she nibbled a piece of hardtack till her stomach settled, then was able to get down a couple of strips of dried plunkin. The meal made her cold shakiness pass off. She was reminded of the very first time she had met Dag, with his firm belief in grub as a cure for shock, and smiled a little.

Her bedroll had contained a wedge of soap, and despite the hour she wanted a bath above all things. They borrowed a lantern from one of the muleteers and made their way across the road and around a crook in the creek to a pool of sorts. It was too chilly for lingering; they stripped down and splashed quick, although Fawn soaped up and rinsed her hair twice, holding her breath and shaking her head underwater, to be sure. She fussed over Dag's ankle, not to mention his impressive new collection of gouges and bruises, and he fussed over her shoulder. They could do no more with their filthy clothes than whack them against a tree trunk and shake them out before skinning damply back into them. It would be better when they got back to the wagons and their gear. Meanwhile, this . . . helped.

It wasn't till they were lying down together between two thin blankets on the grass that her mind began to turn over the events of the past day, imagining other, grimmer outcomes. *Then* she cried, muffled in Dag's shoulder. Mostly, he just held her, but then, he'd hardly let her out of his arms since . . . since she'd . . . *been dug up out of her grave.* Which seemed horror enough, till she dwelled on *not* being dug up. To have come all this way, and survived so much, only to be killed on the last leg, not by bandits or mud-men or malices, but just by an ignorant *misunderstanding* . . .

"Shh," he murmured into her hair, when her shudders renewed.

She swallowed to control her sniffling—was she crying too much?—and managed, "Is the baby all right after all that, can you tell?"

Under her hands she could feel the familiar stillness of his concentration as he went deep with his groundsense. "Yes, seems to be," he said, coming back up and blinking at her, eyes a mere gleam in the firelight and shadows. "Far as I can tell, leastways. She's no bigger than your little finger yet, you know. But I'll have Arkady check when we meet up again, for luck."

Fawn melted with relief. But—"She? You sure, now?"

"Yep," he said, and if his voice was tinged with a faint, smug glee, well, that was all right by her. As she shivered again, he said blandly, "We'll name her Mari."

His gentle teasing was a deliberate distraction from her grave thoughts, and she was grateful for it. "Hey, shouldn't you ask me about that?" She cogitated. "What about Nattie?"

"Dirla's a nice name for a smart strong girl. Or Sumac."

"Too confusing, if Sumac's going to be around with Arkady. Maybe for later."

"Later," he murmured. "Ah. I like later."

"No baby animals, that's for sure. I do sometimes wonder what my parents were thinking." They'd certainly never pictured her as a grown-up woman—then or later. "Can you imagine a grandmother still named *Fawn?*"

"With great delight."

She snickered, and poked him fondly. "Just don't you ever start saying, *Yes, Deer.*"

She could feel his smile in her curls, and finally grew warm enough to stop shivering. She wondered when a thin bedroll on plain grass had started to seem such unutterable luxury. *As long as Dag is in it with me, and we're safe.* The safety, not the coverlet, was the true source of her comfort, she realized. And the comfort of all the folks with them, too, so nearly lost to one another, sleeping close in blanketed lumps around the fire tonight for more than warmth. She cuddled in harder and, for all her hurts and wobbling thoughts, slept.

23

Dag woke in gray light to the sort of drowned lethargy that generally followed great struggles. *Yeah, I've been here before.* He wasn't so weary that he didn't reach out to reassure himself that Fawn was still in their bedroll, warm and asleep under his hand as she should be. His hazy mind shuddered over all the might-have-beens that he'd forbidden her to dwell on last night, and it struck him anew how very little interest he had in saving a world that didn't have her in it.

Well, and Berry and Whit and the rest of Tent Bluefield. And their friends, and they needed their neighbors, he supposed, and the tangle widened ever outward and he was back to where he'd started. Maybe a fellow didn't have to love the whole world—Grouse's voice, raised in complaint about something across the clearing, grated on his ear—maybe just one short heartening person would do. Dag stared up through new beech leaves at the pale blue sky. It would be a clear, warm day once the valley mist burned off.

Fawn stirred and sat up, looking dauntingly perky, all things considered. After supporting his hobble to the woods to take care of the morning necessities, she parked him back on the blanket with his purple foot prominently displayed, which served admirably to fend off any other demands upon him. Was it malingering, when you really couldn't hardly stand up? He was in any case content to lie low behind this excuse and watch the others deal with the day.

A couple of stray muleteers had arrived in the night, and a few more came with the dawn, with yet more recovered mules in tow. One beast, unfortunately, had another body draped over it. In addition to the muleteers, the camp included a trio of trappers who had been captured by the malice while taking their furs south to Mutton Hash, and another family of five grown siblings and their mama who'd been snatched while heading north for homesteading. They all assembled to pay what brief respects could be devised. The gaping maw in the earth that Fawn had escaped was filled after all, which made her sober all over again.

Dag was glad for the delay when Neeta rode into the clearing, guiding a half patrol from Laurel Gap detailed to bring Pakko down off the ridge. Her shock at finding Fawn afoot was swiftly cloaked by her closing ground. She looked almost more taken aback to find Dag.

"I thought you'd still be up on the mountain with Arkady! I brought extra fellows to help carry you!"

"I came down on my own. Copperhead did the rest." *I'll deal with you later.* He couldn't do it now, so soon after yesterday; he was too exhausted, and didn't trust himself. At the very least, he wanted Sumac with him, for all sorts of good reasons including a check on his wits. But the uproar that ensued when the dozen Lakewalkers trailing Neeta discovered just *who* had taken down the fearsome flying malice that had scattered three of their patrols across the upper valley, and *how,* was sufficient diversion.

Dag hardly had to open his mouth. Twenty-five farmer eyewitnesses plus Fawn, Berry, and Whit were couriers enough to carry the tale.

Everyone was led around to marvel at the tattered wings, handle the walnut necklaces, see and touch the pieces of the spent sharing bolt—collected by Berry and preserved in a cloth—and be marched through all the steps of the dawn ambush, Whit brandishing his crossbow and acting it out. Dag, limping after with his stick, had to allow that farmers and Lakewalkers were sure talking to one another now. And, better still, *listening*.

A field medicine maker traveling with the patrol cornered Dag back on his blanket, intent on the walnut necklaces. While Dag wasn't quite up to a live demonstration, the young maker did seem to follow his descriptions, and promised to carry them back to her camp medicine and knife makers. She was excited about unbeguilement, too. Dag attempted to show her, and at the same time relieve one of his worries, by having her put a general reinforcement against infection into Fawn's shoulder, but the maker was so open to the farmer heroine of the hour that she didn't leave a beguilement for Dag to clear. He considered, grimly, having Neeta work an example, but . . . no.

"You can pass the word amongst your makers," he told the young woman. "Anyone who wants to learn how to unbeguile or make these shields can find me and Maker Waterbirch at Berry Bluefield's place just outside Clearcreek, up on the Grace River. We'll take all comers. We haven't quite worked all the kinks out of the groundwork yet, mind . . . could be a few more folks chewing on the problem is just what it needs."

In all, it was noon before the Laurel Gap patrollers cantered off again, with many backward glances, and an hour after that till Dag's own party assembled itself for the long walk back to their wagons. Dag rode Copperhead with Owlet chirping on his lap, Fawn clinging behind, though after a time she climbed down and put Plum up instead, relieving Ash from playing pack pony. It was still light out when their straggling company arrived to find Indigo in calm possession of their abandoned goods, firewood collected and tea water on the boil, with a couple of the mules and his riding horse rounded up already.

Whit led two of the boys and one of the mules off to collect Rase and Barr out of their hidey-hole. Arriving back, they laid out Barr on the blanket next to Dag, where, Dag had to admit, Barr's busted leg far outshone his bent ankle. The groundwork Arkady had done on the break made Dag whistle.

They'd not finished dinner when the Laurel Gap patrol came in leading their mounts, six men hand-carrying Pakko on a rigid litter, Arkady supervising. Calla ran crying and laughing for Sage and her brother, and they exchanged heartfelt hugs. Tavia strolled after, looking tired. With darkness descending, the patrollers made camp for the night beside the farmers, and there followed much swapping and repeating of tales all round. Arkady made an admirably authoritative lecturer. Dag, thinking about the fad for wash-pan hats and cook-pot helmets along the upper Grace, not to mention his unwanted new reputation for raising the dead, had no illusions about how their story would twist as it spread, but at least it would *start* straight.

∾

Arkady wanted to keep Pakko under his eye a little longer, so the next day was welcomed as one of rest by the Laurel Gap patrollers, who were exhausted from their own strains. Their breathless tales of the fight at the north end of the valley, with their rising realization that a routine patrol had become an emergency, then a looming disaster, felt all too recognizable to Dag. Calla and Fawn helped Arkady with caring for Pakko, whose fellow patrollers in turn helped the farmers find their scattered animals, so that all the surviving beasts were retrieved by nightfall in fine fettle from their bout of freedom.

The wait proved a benefit, for the next morning, while Arkady, the patrol leader, and the patrol medicine maker were still debating rival merits of a hand versus a horse litter for transporting a spinal fracture, Sumac and Remo arrived. They rode strange horses, and two new patrollers accompanied them.

Sumac and Arkady more or less flung themselves at each other, which raised a few eyebrows from those who'd only seen Arkady in his austere mood. Dag grinned. One of the young patrollers turned out to be Pakko's son.

"The day after the malice scattered us, me 'n Remo hadn't made but fifteen miles cross-country," Sumac explained, "all frantic and footsore. We'd just found the patrol trail over the next ridge west when we ran into reinforcements on their way from Laurel Gap. So getting the word out was already a done deal, which if I'd have known . . . well. Anyway, we joined up with them and circled back into this valley. When we caught up with the patrols north of here, news was spreading that the malice was brought down, which we could tell from the dying mud-bats we found. Pakko's son had been in the first relief patrol, and was pretty distraught at the tales of his papa being carried off like you were, Dag. Then the word came, which I guess Neeta brought, that his papa had been found hurt. So we volunteered to guide him here in exchange for a ride, which speeded things up considerably." She and Arkady exchanged rather loopy smirks. Well earned, in Dag's opinion.

The horse Remo rode was Pakko's, recovered along with all his gear. His bonded sharing knife was indeed still in his saddlebags, but, the son confided later to Dag, he wasn't going to let his papa have it till his mama said so. Dag and the medicine maker—and Pakko— had enjoyed, or endured, a number of practical lectures yesterday from Arkady on the subject of nerve damage, which even Dag took as guarded hope for the man's walking again; he rather thought Pakko might well be a great-grandpapa before that meeting with his bone blade took place.

All the tales had to be told again to the new people, so it was after lunch before the Laurel Gap patrol headed back to the Trace once more, at a walking pace with men taking it in turns to carry Pakko's litter smoothly. The wagon camp fell much quieter, and folks bent their thoughts to their own road. Dag counted up the days of delay, and was surprised how few there were—he felt as if they'd been trapped in this burned-over valley for months.

Tavia was left horseless. Since Barr would be traveling the next stretch in the back of a wagon, he offered her the use of his mount—which, actually, belonged to Arkady—if she'd come north with him. After a sidewise glance at Dag, Neeta renewed her urging to Remo to come south with her; the boy seemed confused by her sudden warmth. Which brought Dag to a task he'd been dreading. His shiver of rage was still anchored by doubt. *Let's have the truth out, then.* And if it was as ugly as cleaning up mud-men, maybe it was as needful, too.

∾

Dag selected a spot just out of sight and earshot of the camp, near the chattering streambed. He sat on a rock and dug in the ground with his stick, while Sumac leaned on a gray beech bole, arms crossed. Her mere presence, he trusted, would be enough to block any embarrassments like his last private talk with Neeta. His other invitees settled cross-legged around him: Remo, Tavia, Neeta. Finch and Ash, also summoned, shuffled and stared uncertainly.

"What's this all about, Dag?" asked Remo. "Patrol business, you said."

Dag held up his hand to spare the last pair from settling. He'd have picked Sage for this testimony, as the most levelheaded of the Alligator Hat boys, but in the aftermath of the malice kill the young smith had been distracted by worry for his wife and tent-brother. "I won't keep you long. The day Whit shot the malice, that afternoon, what all was going on in camp when Neeta rode by? As exactly as you can remember."

"Oh . . ." Finch ran a hand through his hair. "It was such an uproar at first. Berry'd got out just about enough words to explain what had happened, or at least, enough for us to explain it to the rest. We were all worried for her and Whit. Bo'd looked over poor Fawn, and said she was a goner. Hod and Hawthorn were crying. It was plain we wouldn't be staying there long, and most of us figured you for a goner, too. So when we told the muleteers your tale, they dug space for her as well."

"As a sort of gift," Ash confirmed.

"Neeta came cantering up the road in a hurry, but she saw us and reined in."

"Before or after the burial?"

"Oh, before. We had those four poor muleteers and Fawn laid out on blankets, and were sort of looking at one another wondering what to say. Neeta said she'd been sent to find the local Lakewalkers and get help for some hurt patroller. That she'd seen Tavia, who'd hauled Arkady up the ridge to rescue you both—you were hurt, too, but she didn't know just how bad."

"It didn't sound real good," said Ash. "We got that somebody had a broke back, but we weren't sure which."

"We told her Whit had shot the malice, but I don't know as she really believed us. She rode around and looked at the wings, anyway. Never got down off her horse. Then she was gone at a gallop before Vio even got to ask about Owlet."

Neeta started to speak, but, at Dag's upflung hand, fell silent. Her eyes pinched. Did she see what was coming? Dag was afraid so.

Dag said, "Did she know you were about to bury Fawn?"

"Oh, sure," said Finch. "That is . . . we didn't talk about it, but it was all laid out there, the corpses and the grave half dug and all. I wouldn't think you could miss it."

Ash gave a slow blink, and started to open his mouth. Dag cut in: "Thanks, boys. That'll be all."

The two wandered upstream toward the wagons, looking curiously over their shoulders.

Dag scowled across at Neeta.

She raised her chin. "She looked dead! Ground-ripped, I figured. How was I to know those shields of yours would do such a crazy thing? And anyway, I had my ground veiled on account of the malice blight."

Dag said slowly, "It's your word alone as to whether you were open or closed. I can't prove you're lying. You can't prove you're telling the truth." *Can you, Neeta?*

Red spots flared in Neeta's fair cheeks: indignant, or scared? "Well, I like that!"

"She could open now," said Remo doubtfully.

Dag and Neeta traded a long, long stare. His heartbeats felt hot, and too far apart. Odd. He'd thought his world would be tinged with red by this point, but it was just blue and distant. "No," said Dag at last. "I think not. Unveiled, I could kill her with a thought, you know. Just like I did Crane. It'd be almost as easy as murder by silence."

A ripple of dismay ran through Remo and Tavia, a flinch from Sumac, but no one spoke. Or dared speak?

Neeta's gaze fell, slid away. It was all the answer Dag needed. Or wanted, really. *And you thought this was your duty, old patroller, why?*

Wearily, he ran his hand over his face, rubbing at the numbness. "Go home, Neeta. Patrol there. You owe New Moon for your raising, and Luthlia for your training. You'll be a long time paying that debt back. At the end of your lifetime, share if you will. Just don't come north. The north does not need you."

Remo stared at her in bleak doubt.

"It's not fair!" she began, then clamped her jaw shut. *Right.* Best advice for someone at the bottom of a deep, deep hole: stop digging. *Apt turn of phrase, that.* Well, he'd never thought the girl was *stupid.*

"What about me?" said Tavia. She had gone very pale, staring at her partner.

Sumac stirred on her tree bole. "I'd recommend you to Fairbolt Crow at Hickory Lake, if you want to take a turn exchanging north. My word with Fairbolt is pretty good coin. I'll be speaking for Rase as well, you can bet—I expect he'll be all recovered by the time I get him up there. His recent malice experiences are going to make him very much in demand, I can tell you. Yours, too."

Tavia looked at the ground, looked narrowly at Neeta, who stirred uncomfortably but said nothing. Tavia finally replied, "I think I'll report in at home, first. Be sure the story is told straight. Make my good-byes properly. But I'll take you up on your good word after that, if the offer holds."

"It holds."

"Tell Rase I'll be along come fall, then."

Sumac nodded.

Rase? thought Dag. So much for poor Barr's hopes. Well, Barr was resilient. Remo looked downcast, again. *Blight, that boy can't win for losing.* Both were so very young . . .

"And you, Remo? Which way you ridin', tomorrow?" asked Sumac.

Remo let out a long breath. He did not look at Neeta anymore. "North," he said.

No one spoke on the short walk back to camp.

~

In the morning, when they'd finally wrestled the wagons back down the creek bed and onto the Trace, two silent riders turned south. Arkady had lent Tavia a horse, also lading her with a long list of his possessions to bring back with her when she returned. Dag didn't know what all Sumac had confided to Arkady last night, but he was formidably chilly to Neeta in parting. Tavia turned once in her saddle to wave farewell, a gesture earnestly returned by Rase. Neeta, her back rigid, did not look around.

~

To Fawn's joy, Blackwater Mills harbored a hotel almost as fine as the one in Glassforge, if smaller. Better still, it had a spanking new bathhouse. She gladly pried open their purse for a room—as, after one look at the bathhouse, did Arkady. Doubling up with Sumac for frugality, no doubt. As for Fawn, she looked forward to a few days of eating food someone else had fixed, and no squinting in the cook smoke. The swelling in Dag's foot had gone down in the four days of travel since they'd left the burned-over valley, but its color—colors—were even uglier. They both could use some time in a real bed, she reckoned. All to themselves.

The town held sadness, too, for this was a place of parting. It lay on a barely navigable tributary of the Grace River, but more importantly it was where the Tripoint Trace crossed the old straight road that cut up toward Pearl Riffle, with its Lakewalker ferry and camp. Sage, Calla, and Indigo would point their wagon east up the Trace; the rest of them would take the northern way, from which in turn sprouted the back road that led to Clearcreek.

The Basswoods stopped abruptly short, when Vio dug in her heels and declared she'd had enough and wouldn't go one more step. Well, in this busy place Grouse would have no trouble finding day labor, likely more successful for him now he was cured of his recurrent bog ague, and, really, Fawn expected the couple would do better with town life than with the demands of homesteading. Selling their rickety wagon and a pair of their mules would give them enough to start out on. She grinned, though, to overhear the phrase *Our Lakewalkers* fall from Grouse's lips when he was explaining their adventures to the hotel horseboys.

She would miss Plum, who had somehow ended up under her wing, and she rather thought Dag would miss Owlet. He seemed vastly amused by his grubby *Little Brother* of the mud-bat adventure, and Owlet seemed to return the compliment. Though she suspected Dag used his groundsense to cheat—unless it was his arm rig that so enthralled the child, who had developed a passion for buckles. *Well, I'll just give Dag a toddler or two of his own, and he'll do fine.* Could she really object when the cheating would be on *her side*?

But the most important thing that happened in their stopover in Blackwater Mills, almost as good as a bow-down in Fawn's view, was when a patrol that had come from a neighboring camp to reinforce the Laurel Gap folks—though they'd arrived after the fight was over—rode *miles* out of their way home to catch up with Dag and Arkady to have the tale firsthand. They seemed a little taken aback to get it mostly from Fawn and Whit and Berry, complete with a display of the sharing-bolt shards and crossbow. But their captain, as shorthanded as every other patrol leader, was highly interested in the notion of farmer help that couldn't be mind-slaved by a malice, even if the farmers did no more than hold the horses. Dag tried to make it very clear that his walnut shields weren't quite perfected yet, but the captain left with a gleam in his eye nonetheless, after making sure of the directions to where Dag and Arkady planned to roost.

〜

Later that night, Fawn rolled over on clean sheets atop a yielding feather mattress and snuggled up to Dag. The bedside lamp cast a gentle glow over their quiet room. Slow spring rain sounded through the real glass windows, open just enough for a cool breeze to stir the cloth curtains. Just being *inside* when the rain was *outside* seemed pleasure enough for any sensible woman, but she had plenty more blessings to count. Her fingers reached up to flick over his quizzical eyebrows, *one, two,* comb through his unruly hair, *three.* This tally might take a while . . .

"Will it be enough?" she murmured. "Those patrollers tonight? Seems to me they listened to us better than any Lakewalkers yet. Or is this just another stone in the sea?"

Dag's lips softened in a smile. "The world's a pretty big sea. For all our travels, we've only seen a slice of it. Enough . . . no, not yet. But it's a start. And *this* time, our rocks will make ripples." He leaned into her hand to kiss it in passing. "Best part is, I don't have to go around like a stump speaker trying to *talk* folks into being nicer to each other, one by one. Which really would be like throwing pebbles into the sea."

He stretched over and picked up her spent walnut necklace from where it lay by the lamp, turning it thoughtfully in his hand. "These will bring folks to us, for their own reasons, and I don't even have to know what all the reasons are. Send enough farmers out with enough Lakewalker patrols, and they *will* learn all about Lakewalkers, and bring their true tales home."

"Well," said Fawn, "only if the Lakewalkers can resist trying out patroller humor on them."

His lips twitched. "I'd think any fellow raised on a diet of Bo stories would be able to sort it out . . . Maybe not on the first day."

Fawn giggled. "Those river boys should do well on patrol, then. That learning won't be all one way, I expect."

"Indeed, I'm counting on that." He held up the necklace, squinting at it. "I do wonder about what Whit and Bo said, back on your birthday when I first showed this off . . . that it wouldn't be a day, after I set something like this loose in the world, before someone figured out how to misuse it."

"I'm afraid that's true." Fawn sighed. "But if there's enough folks . . . Those river bandits we ran into were awful, sure, but most of the rivermen were good enough fellows. The river has a reputation, but that doesn't stop folks from going on it anyhow, and getting plenty of good from it, too. If there's enough grease, some grit won't stop the whole wheel from turning."

"I hope that's so, Spark." He set the necklace back and found a better use for his hand, stroking over her shoulder, which made the skin of her arm stand up in happy goose bumps. "I guess we'll find out."

She eased back onto her pillow, and his warm palm traced over her belly in a flatteringly interested fashion. She raised her head and squinted over her torso, frowning impatiently. Her waist was still disappointingly slim down there. Six months from now she'd likely be wondering why she'd been in such a hurry to expand, but still. "Is Nattie-Mari all right in there?"

"Seems to be happy so far. Despite all her adventures with her mama." He tried to keep his voice light, but just a tinge of remembered desperation leaked through.

She drew a breath, then stopped to consider just how to phrase this so's he wouldn't take it wrong. "It's been a pretty amazing wedding trip. Most fellows only claim they want to give their sweethearts the world. You really did."

This won a trail of light kisses from her temple to her chin, which was very agreeable, but she couldn't let herself be distracted yet. She caught his head between her hands before he could work down farther and rob her of words. "So don't take this as any sort of complaint, but can we try staying *home* for a while?"

He laughed. "I'd say you took your turn traveling with a patroller. It's my turn to stay put with a farmer." He sobered a little, though not too much, good. "It'll be a fine, fresh new thing for me, staying home. I've never done that before."

"I'll try to see you don't faint from the excitement of it all."

Being kissed through a grin was good, too. His lips drifted down her throat and struck south, and they gave up talking for a warmer exchange.

∾

After a few more days of rest in Blackwater Mills, Arkady pronounced Barr able to ride again, suitably splinted and at a careful plod, on a mild-eyed mare borrowed from Whit. Dag, remembering his own much less severe broken arm last year, figured Barr was still in a quelling amount of pain, confirmed by the boy's wan smile and lack of complaint about the restrictions. Well, a quelled Barr was not altogether a bad thing.

Even at their gentle amble, the straight road north brought them all too soon to their next parting. Barr, Remo, and Rase were to ride on to Pearl Riffle. There Rase would play guest, observe a northern ferry camp in operation, and not least add his testimony to the tale of their malice kills back on the Trace, until Sumac caught up with him again.

Finch and Ash, too, planned to cross the Grace at the Pearl Riffle ferry; they carried a stack of fat letters to West Blue that would guarantee them room and board for quite a while, with lots of sound advice for homesteaders thrown in, most likely.

Sumac's own plan was to ride with Arkady to Clearcreek, ostensibly to see him safely settled—but given the glitter in her ground, Dag would have bet cash money the couple had more intimate reasons for sticking to each other like burs for the next few days. Sumac herself was vague on whether she meant to leave Arkady at Berry's and come back to fetch him in a few weeks after presenting Rase, and her resignation, at Hickory Lake Camp, or take him with her straightaway to exhibit to her parents, rather like a hunter returning home with a spectacular bag of game—Dag kept trying not to grin—or have a string-binding on the spot with her uncle Dag doing the blessing and tying, just to make sure, before exposing her husband to his new tent-kin. Dag was happy to stay entirely out of that decision.

Remo turned in his saddle and stared up the shade-dappled road toward his home, his brow clouded with doubt.

"Your kin and camp will be glad to see you," Dag told him, not entirely recklessly. "Word of how you two helped put down the bandits at Crooked Elbow had to have reached the Riffle months ago, and if a patrol circular about the Trace malices hasn't got ahead of you already, it'll be along soon. Grab your forgiveness while the excitement is still high, and you'll do fine."

Fawn, atop Magpie, raised an eyebrow at him. "Speaking from experience, Dag?"

He touched one finger to his temple in wry acknowledgment. "Just don't try to pull the returning-son trick too often, is all. It does wear out with repetition."

Barr eased his horse forward and observed, "With this leg of mine, we can each take credit for getting the other home. I guarantee to hobble and yelp a lot. You'll look good."

"Home camp's not going to look the same, I promise you," said Dag. *Both of you.*

"Neither does the view in my shaving mirror," Barr muttered, and maybe it wasn't just the leg making him sober. He turned his head and said seriously to Dag, "I've learned a lot, since that night in the rain when I first caught up with the *Fetch,* so mad and cold I could hardly stutter. Thank you."

Dag's head cocked back in surprise. And, he had to admit, sneaking gratification.

"Yeah, Dag has a way, that way," said Whit. "I daresay he's been teaching me new things ever since that first night my sister dragged him into the kitchen at West Blue. Did I ever say, *Good work,* Sis?"

"It was luck, mostly," said Fawn. "That, and grabbing onto my luck with both hands and not letting go again."

Or even one hand. Dag nudged Copperhead around next to Magpie.

Sumac, by now well acquainted with Remo's darker moods and listening with some amusement, put in, "It'll be fine, Remo. And if it's not—Fairbolt's always looking for healthy young patrollers. He'll need at least two to replace me, I figure. I'll put in a word there if you should need it."

Remo brightened slightly at this prospect of an honorable bolt hole if his return went ill, which Dag thought profoundly unlikely. In any case, when Barr shook his reins and started off, Remo followed. Finch and Ash called their good-byes and fell in behind, pack animals trailing.

Dag watched them out of earshot before he said to Sumac, "You really intend to inflict that pair on Fairbolt?"

"Fairbolt has nothing to do with it. I promised the Crow girls when I exchanged last fall that I would bring them back some cute men. As it seems Rase is bespoke already, I have to make my word good somehow."

Dag considered Fairbolt and Massape's array of black-haired grand-daughters, lovely one by one, formidable in a mob.

"There's enough of them, one's bound to like a gloomy boy and another a flitter-wit," Sumac went on cheerfully. "Feed them to the Crows, I say."

"What a fate," murmured Dag, brows rising at this riveting vision.

"Just so's the girls don't get them switched the wrong way around," said Fawn. "Again."

"I trust Massape," said Sumac.

∾

Berry was by this time wildly anxious for Clearcreek, so they picked up the pace.

"I hope the place is still standing," she said, kicking her horse along between Copperhead and Magpie. "Papa leaves—left—two of his cous-ins to look after it—aunts, I call them, 'cause they're older than me, one's a widow and one's never married. The widow has a son who comes around a couple of times in the week to help with the heavy work."

Fawn pictured a Clearcreek version of Ash Tanner, and nodded en-couragement.

"I wrote two letters—Whit helped me—one after Crooked Elbow and one after we was married in Graymouth, and sent them upriver with keeler friends. Bad news and good. I hope they got there." She added after a reflective moment, "In the right order."

"If Clearcreek's as much of a river town as you say, the word about Crooked Elbow will have got there one way or another ages ago," Fawn pointed out. "They'll have had months to get over the bad news. If the good news only arrives when you do, well, that'll likely be all right."

Berry nodded, and slowed good-naturedly when Fawn complained that if they did any more trotting, either she or Nattie-Mari was going to start hiccupping.

Nevertheless, Clearcreek came into view over the lip of a steep wooded climb the next afternoon, with two hours to spare till sunset. The valley spread out in gold-green splendor before Fawn's eager eyes, with long blue shadows growing from the western hills. Off to the left, the broad Grace River gleamed beyond the feeder-creek's mouth. A tidy village . . . homesteads scattered up the vale with evening cook fires sending up gilded threads of smoke . . . and a stream, Fawn saw as they descended the long slope and clopped across it on a timber span, that earned its name. Fawn stood in her stirrups and gazed out under the flat of her hand as Berry eagerly pointed out landmarks of her childhood. Even Sumac and Arkady, riding behind engrossed mainly in each other, closed up to listen.

They rode along a split-rail fence enclosing a narrow pasture, with a craggy, tree-clad hill rising behind. "Look, there's the pond!" Fawn said in delight. And a placid-looking cow, a few goats, and some chickens. They rounded a stand of chestnut trees into a short lane also lined with split rails, and the house spilled into view.

It was an unpainted warren, looking as if a hive of flatboat carpenters had worked on it for years. Instead of having its stories neatly stacked, like the house in West Blue, it was as if a load of crates had been tossed down the hill, connected by chance one to another. Half a dozen chimneys stuck up here and there. It must have held a much larger family a few generations ago, and looked as if it hoped to again. *What a splendid place to grow up in.* For all its rambling oddity, it had quite a proper front porch, long and railed and roofed, and if it looked a little like a boat deck, well, that was all right.

Hawthorn whooped and galloped ahead. Hod stuck close to Bo, looking shy and hopeful. Fawn could only think that Berry's letters must have got here in the right order, because two stout women ran out onto the porch, both looking excited but not surprised, and waved vigorously. Hawthorn jumped from his horse and bounded up the steps, and one of the women dried her hands on her apron, hugged him, and made universal signs to head and hip and heart, *My, how you've grown!*

The other shaded her eyes; Berry grinned fit to split her face and pointed emphatically at Whit, *This one's the husband!*

The aunt in the apron clasped her hands over her head and shook them in a gesture of shared, if not downright lewd, female triumph that actually made Whit blush. As they rode close enough at last for voices to carry, she cupped her hands to her mouth and called, "Welcome home!"

Fawn glanced at Dag, who was looking very bemused and a little bit wary—just like a Lakewalker dropped down among strange farmers. *Welcome home to a place we've never seen before.* But if a place was home because it held your past, wasn't it equally so if it held your future? She stretched out her hand to him; he shifted his reins to his hook and grasped it in a swift squeeze.

In the sunset light, his gold eyes glinted like fire.

Epilogue

Footsteps clumped on the stoop; at the knock on the kitchen door, Fawn grabbed a cloth, pulled her pot on its iron hook away from the hearth fire, and hurried to answer. She hoped it wasn't another emergency. But the door swung open onto a damp and chilly afternoon, and Barr. He wore patroller togs, smelled of horse and the outdoors, and walked without a stick. Mist beaded in his dun-blond hair, gleaming in the watery light.

"Hey, Fawn!"

"Well! Aren't you a sight for sore eyes! Come in, come in!"

He shouldered through into the pungent warmth, staring around. Fawn spared a look-see out at the sodden brown landscape. Warmer air had moved up the valley of the Grace last night, breathing wisps of low-lying fog across the sad streaks of dirty snow. The gray tailings wouldn't be lasting much longer. If not quite spring, this was definitely the tag end of winter. No other riders were waiting in the yard, nor approaching on the part of the road she could see from here. She shut the door and turned to her unexpected guest.

Barr rubbed chapped red hands and moved gratefully toward the fire, reminding her of the very first time she'd ever met him. He was much less wet and cold and distraught this time, happily. He sniffed the air. "*What* are you cooking?"

"Medicine."

"Oh, whew! I thought it was dinner, and was worried."

Fawn laughed, and pointed to the volume propped open on the kitchen table. "Remember that blank book Hawthorn 'n Hod gave me back on my nineteenth birthday in Graymouth? I used it to write down all the recipes for the remedies they were making up in the medicine tent at New Moon Cutoff, and drew pictures of the plants and made notes about the herb maker's groundwork, too. It came with me in my saddlebags when we went north, you bet. Arkady was so surprised when I pulled it out. He hadn't realized how much I had in there. "

Barr eased out of his deerskin jacket and hung it over the back of a chair to dry. "Yeah, I ran into Sumac when I went to put my horse away in your barn. She looked downright cheerful. And, um, bulky. Floating around like those boats we saw down on the sea." He made hand gestures to indicate a bellying sail.

"It's the feather quilt I padded her coat with, when Arkady got to fretting about how much time she spends out with the horses in the cold. She's less alarming out of it. It won't be long till their baby comes, though." She smiled. "It would make you laugh how much Arkady fusses for her, if you didn't know his history. Instead it's sort of sad and hopeful all at once. I must say, I suspect it's no bad thing for a man to wait till he's older to have his children. He seems to *appreciate* things more."

Barr smiled briefly. *Bleakly* . . . ? Fawn shook off the odd fancy and went on: "Fortunately, Sumac doesn't much put up with his coddling. A lot like her mother Omba, I'd say. She's pretty much taken over all our horses, and manages the barn the way Omba used to run Mare Island. Or still runs it, I guess. Did you see my Grace's filly Dancer when you were out there? Isn't she a sweetheart?"

"Yep, Sumac made sure to show her off first thing."

Fawn swung her pot back closer to the coals. "Are you out with a patrol?" The valley of the Clear Creek lay at the easternmost edge of Pearl Riffle Camp's patrol territory. She wondered if she should offer the barn loft for bedrolls, except that Sumac would surely have beaten her to it. "Or are you courierin'?"

"No, I'm on my own. A private visit. Came to see Dag. And you."

"Leg troubling you?"

"No, it's—oh!" Starting to drag a chair noisily toward the hearth, he spotted the big basket tucked in the room's corner and lifted instead, setting the legs down two by two with exaggerated care. In a whisper, he said, "Is that Nattie-Mari, then? Asleep—will my talking wake her up?"

"Likely not, as long as you don't yell or drop things. She just fed, so she's for dreamland for a bit yet. It won't matter if she does wake up—she sleeps better through the night if I don't let her nap all day." Fawn yawned. "And so do I. There's so much to do, though, it's tempting to let her sleep too much."

She stepped up as Barr peered down into the basket in vague masculine alarm. She did lower her voice. "She's still round-faced like a Bluefield, though I'm hoping for Dag's cheekbones in time. Her head's grown a lot this past month. And her hair, thankfully." She bent and touched a finger to the black fuzz. "You can hold her, later on."

"Um . . . thanks." Barr backed carefully away from the basket and found his chair.

Fawn took up her wooden spoon and stirred her gray-green goop, which was thickening nicely. "Papa brought Mama all the way from West Blue, slogging through the mud—they got in just two days before Nattie-Mari was born. Stayed for three weeks, then Mama had to go back for Clover's first. Mama says she doesn't approve of men in birthing rooms, but Arkady won her right over. I think she was relieved, really—despite all the children she's had, midwifery isn't her best thing. Dag was pretty excited, but he kept his head real good, I thought. Better than I did, some stretches. It was the most pain I'd ever done, but I got a real fine baby out of the deal, so I figure it for a fair trade." Barr stirred uncomfortably, and Fawn kindly decided to spare him all the terribly fascinating details. Other people's babies, as she recalled, were much less interesting than one's own. A little silence fell.

"Dag and Arkady should be back soon," she offered. "They were called out for some fellow who'd hurt himself down at the landing, and meant to stop on the way back and look in on a neighbor woman with lung fever. I don't ride out much just now on account of Nattie-Mari, but I am Dag's other hand when folks stop in here. I do try to go along when I can, or Dag will get all wound up in the *interesting* parts and forget to ask for money. I swear Arkady's rubbing off on him. And the other way around—Arkady's getting quite used to having *dirty ground* these days." Arkady hadn't actually said, *On me, it looks good*, but Fawn thought it was implied.

"So . . . your medicine-making-for-farmers scheme is going well?"

Fawn wasn't sure if Barr was trying to draw her out, or avoid talking himself; in either case, she rattled obligingly on. "It was slow to start. Having Berry as a wedge to get us in did the trick. I can't imagine how it would have gone if we'd just plunked down in a place like this as strangers. But Dag and Arkady did a few things for her kin and friends, and Bo and Hawthorn and even Hod talked us up all over town. The first night someone we barely knew knocked on the door for help was a big step, you'd best believe." Her brows drew down in consideration. "But the most important thing, I think—this is going to sound strange to you, I know—the most important thing that happened this winter was losing some patients. Because makers must, you know—over enough time, it has to happen. Not the fellow who'd been dead for two days when they brought him to the door on a plank, no one blamed Dag for that one, though he did have words. Never saw him look so harassed." Her lips twisted at the memory, which would be funny in a black way except for the distress of the dead fellow's friends. "But people we'd got to know a bit." The old man with the broken hip, the child with the strange raging fever, the woman who'd miscarried and bled dry almost before Dag had arrived, though he'd raced Copperhead to flying foam. "Dag tries his hardest, my word, he about turns himself inside out with the trying . . . but sometimes, it just isn't enough. The sensible folks have seen that clear, though, and straightened out the couple of less sensible ones. It's a tricky dance, but we all seem to be learning the steps, us and the folks around here both."

"Huh." Barr tilted his head. "I always knew you had to learn to be a medicine maker, but I never thought you had to learn how to be a patient."

"Lakewalkers in camps teach those tricks, and that trust, to each other as offhandedly as how to swim, and as young. We have the ways of farmer midwives and bonesetters to follow up, but no one knew exactly what to expect of us at first. Not even us, so we've all had to learn together."

Barr stretched, scratched his chin, looked around. "Did Berry and Whit get their fall flatboat built and launched after all? I didn't spot them anywhere when I rode in."

"Oh, they left months back—took Bo and Hod and Hawthorn for crew, though Bo claims this'll be his last trip. It's not quite time to be looking out for them, but soon. They weren't sure if they'd be coming home by the river or the Trace. I hope it's the river, and I hope Whit brings me an iron cookstove. Which I wouldn't expect him to carry in a packsaddle, although with Whit you never know."

"Whatever he brings, I imagine it'll turn a profit. I don't know how he does it."

"Nobody in our family would have guessed that talent of his back home. Neither one of us had much chance to shine there, I reckon." The town of Clearcreek was only about twice the size of the village of West Blue; Fawn wasn't sure how it managed to seem worlds larger.

Barr cleared his throat. "You, ah . . . ever hear anything more from Calla and Indigo? And Sage," he added in afterthought.

"Oh, yes! Calla sent letters twice. I'll let you read them, later. We get mail up and down the river fairly regular."

"How are they getting on?"

"Well, Sage got work in a foundry, and he's learning lots of new things, just as he'd hoped. Calla says he still wants his own place in due time. Indigo found a job driving a delivery wagon, and his boss thinks the world of his way with the horses, though Indigo doesn't much care for town life—too crowded. He says it makes him feel funny and tense. We wrote back that he'd be welcome in Clearcreek, but he hasn't taken us up yet. But here's the best thing—Calla got so interested in medicine making in her time with Arkady, she went and apprenticed herself to this midwife in Tripoint. Her bit o' groundsense gave her such an edge, she finally 'fessed up to her half blood. And instead of throwing her out on her ear, the woman took her to someone who knew one of the local Lakewalkers, and now Calla goes and trains one week in the month with the medicine makers at the Tripoint camp—same place Fairbolt was born, if you can believe it!"

"Oh!" said Barr, brightening. "That's . . . good." His brow wrinkled. "Unexpected."

"Was to me, too, till I got to thinking about it. Seems Calla was tested to be let in to her papa's camp back south, but she wouldn't join up because they wouldn't take Indigo, too."

"Huh. I didn't know that." Barr looked very pensive, which was not an expression Fawn was used to seeing on him. Before she could ask what was troubling him, another set of clumps sounded from the stoop.

Fawn looked up eagerly. "Ah, here's Dag!"

As the door swung open, Barr cast her a crooked smile. "You developing groundsense these days?"

"No, but I'd know those boot steps anywhere." *Like my child's cry, or my own hand in the dark.*

Dag ducked through, straightened up, and grinned broadly. "Hey, Barr! What brings you here?" Things must have gone well with his patients; he wasn't drooping with fatigue, or low with gloom, or spattered with blood.

Before Barr could answer, Nattie-Mari stirred in her basket and meeped. "Be right with you, Sparkle," Dag called to her, and hastily slipped off his jacket and went to wash his hand in the basin in the sink. The meeping grew more anxious, if not yet a full-throated cry. Dag tossed the towel over the sink rim and went to gaze down into the basket a moment, his expression curious and tender. Barr, brow furrowing, watched him pick up his child and position her on his left shoulder, hand spread securely over her little back, and take a comfortable seat in the rocker on the other side of the hearth.

"Is she wet?" asked Fawn. "Hungry?"

"No, she just wants to join the party."

"She likes the rumble of Dag's voice," Fawn informed Barr, and, reassured, went back to her stirring. "I do wonder that Lakewalker children ever learn to talk, with the grown-ups able to figure out everything they want by groundsense."

Dag shook his head. "Not everything, I assure you. The little ones have to train us up just like farmer babies train their parents. Don't you, Sparkle? You're teaching your old papa all kinds of tricks, aren't you?" Nattie-Mari settled in her new perch with an air of ownership, little fingers flexing, eyelids half shutting. Her eyes had been rather muddy at birth, but lately had cleared to a deep brown, with exciting red-gold flecks. Dag added to Barr, "How are things at Pearl Riffle? How's Maker Verel doing with my ground shields?"

"Better, since Whit came by last fall, puffed off his walnut pendant and his malice kill in every tavern in the Landing and the Bend, and had Verel quadruple the price. Which last also settled the camp council— and *increased* the number of farmers wanting to try one, which I don't understand but Whit said would work."

"Whit has that knack," said Fawn complacently. She tapped her wooden spoon on the pot edge, readjusted the pot's distance to the coals, and settled on the hearth edge by Dag's knees to listen.

"Verel's taken on two new apprentices to help out," Barr continued. "So the shield work doesn't put him too far behind."

"Good," said Dag. "And Captain Amma? Was she willing to try our experiment yet?"

"Yeah, finally. She sent four farmer boys out with my patrol, with me detailed to ride herd on 'em, since she said I knew farmers better than any other patroller she had. Two of 'em quit after their first stint, when they found out how boring and uncomfortable it is, especially in the winter, and no sign of a malice anywhere, of course. And all the dirty work piled on, though I kept explaining that *all* new patrollers get the dirty work. But the others stuck it out, and two more came on. We're to go again next week."

Dag said, "You know, Arkady trained Hoharie in shield making when he was up to visit Hickory Lake Camp with Sumac, same as I trained Verel."

Barr nodded.

"Well, half a dozen Raintree boys—survivors of their malice out-break—heard the rumors and turned up at the gate to volunteer. Fairbolt claimed it was a patrol matter, and made sure the camp council was too divided to overrule him. He had the boys partner with Rase and Remo to teach them how to go on, which answered fairly well. The boredom and grind didn't daunt them, with kinfolk to avenge. I had a letter from Remo just last week—they've survived their first test with a real malice. It was just a little sessile, but Hoharie's shields held, and none of the dire predictions of the naysayers came true. So far, so good."

"Will you ever go back there? To Hickory Lake?"

Dag shook his head. "Not soon. I don't have *time*. So far, Arkady and I have had eleven different makers from nine different camps turn up here to learn our tricks, shields and unbeguiling and more. New folks come every week, seems like."

"We got so we keep a bunk room ready for visitors," Fawn added. "We'll put you up in there tonight."

Barr nodded gratefully.

"That's in addition to all those long descriptions Arkady wrote up for Hoharie and Verel to send out all over the hinterland with their medicine-tent circulars, and for Fairbolt and Amma with their patrol circulars. Even if Copperhead achieves his lifelong ambition of bashing me into a tree tomorrow, the ideas are out there."

"Does Remo sound happy there, up at Hickory? As happy as Remo ever gets, that is," Barr added.

"Seems to be." Dag smiled slowly. "Tioca Crow got mentioned three times in the letter. She was a good-looking girl, in a strappy sort of way, as I recall."

Barr shook his head. "I hope he has better luck in love this time."

"If it's really Tioca, I expect she'll see to that."

"He didn't have to go, you know. Amma was all ready to put him back in the Pearl Riffle patrol. I suppose it was better that he did things in order and transferred properly, though. He's always happier when he thinks he's following the rules."

Dag's eyebrow twitch made provisional agreement. "Rules aren't actually made to be broken. They're generally invented because someone made a mistake or a mess, and folks didn't ever want to have to clean up after another one like it."

Barr cleared his throat. "Yeah. About that."

Now he's getting to it, thought Fawn. She didn't think Barr would've ridden a day and a half in this raw weather just to party with Nattie-Mari. Something was preying on his mind, for sure.

"You know, I could be a bit of a blight, when I was a younger patroller."

Fawn supposed it would not be polite to agree too wholeheartedly. She hunkered on the hearth, *don't let me interrupt.* Dag limited himself to an encouraging, "Hm?"

"I thought most of the rules were stupid. And, I suppose, I was still new to my powers, wanting to test them out. Like boys running races, or lifting logs, or something. Anyway, I did this thing . . ." His eyes shifted Fawn's way. "Fawn's not going to like this."

Fawn rubbed her lips. Not that she exactly wanted to make it easy for him, but . . . "If you're talking about the time you persuaded some farmer girl to go out to the woodpile with you, and then tried to talk Remo into seducing her sister, I already heard."

Barr's lips made a silent *Oh.* "Uh . . . when?"

"Remo told us, back before you first came on the *Fetch.* When we were all trying to work out unbeguilement."

"*Remo* said!" Barr sat up, looking betrayed.

"He was still plenty mad at you about the accident with his sharing knife, recall. You two only fell into that ambush in the first place because that flatboat girl led you there by the nose—or whatever she led you by—and he followed you."

"Oh. Um. Yeah." Barr shot another look at Fawn. "Was that why you wouldn't hardly give me the time of day, when I first came aboard?"

"Well, let's just say it didn't help your cause."

Barr gave up betrayal in favor of glum. "Well, it was true. That farmer girl wasn't *un*willing, mind, even before . . . er. And then Remo pitched such a fit, I never dared it again. And so much has happened since, I'd almost forgotten about it, till this last patrol. Took us back through that same little village. About thirty miles northwest of the Riffle."

Dag leaned back, looking very bland. Fawn was chilly but silent; she'd get no tale if she rushed to judgment.

"It was a joke, almost. At the time. I thought."

"I doubt it was such a big laugh for her," said Fawn.

"Yeah. I found that out."

Fawn sat up. "She didn't go and hang herself, did she?"

Barr's eyes flew wide. "Hang herself! Do farmer girls really *do* that?"

"Sometimes. Or drown themselves."

"No, it wasn't that, um . . . bad. Kind of the opposite. I asked the blacksmith, after I saw her . . . she'd got married. And had a child."

"One of those seven-months children with the nine-months hair?" said Dag. "We get them around these parts, time to time."

"I think they get them everywhere," conceded Fawn. *I might have had one myself, once, but for some strange mortal chances.*

"We ran into each other outside the village smithy. Cold day, but bright, the sort you sometimes get just before the first thaws. My patrol'd stopped to get a couple of cast shoes fixed. She was carting away some tools that had been repaired. She recognized me right off, but she pretended not to know me. Like I was invisible, or she wished I was. She had her little girl toddling after her, about Owlet's size, blond-headed, curls everywhere, in this knit cap with a long pink tassel. She kept tossing her head to make it fly around, and giggling. Dag, she was *mine*."

Fawn scowled. "How can you be sure? Just from her age and hair color?"

"No, from her ground!"

Fawn cast Dag up a doubtful look; he returned a nod. "Barr would know, yes."

"Then what did you do?" Fawn asked in worry.

"Rode after her, of course. I caught up with her cart the first bend out of sight of the village. First she said she didn't know me, and then she told me to leave off because she hated me, and go away or she'd scream, and I said the little girl was mine, and she said no she wasn't, and I said yes she was, and then the girl started to cry from the yelling and her mama finally stopped the cart to talk." He added after a moment, "She'd named her Lily."

Barr took a breath and went on, as if afraid that if he halted he wouldn't be able to get started again. "She said she had a good life now, and a good husband, and I didn't have no call to ride after her and wreck her world."

"Again," murmured Fawn.

"And I said, did this fellow think my girl was his? And she said yes. And she offered me all the money in her purse to go away quiet."

"Did you take it?" asked Fawn sweetly.

Barr glared, outraged.

"Now, Fawn," chided Dag.

Fawn sighed. It was much too late for a traditional farmer horsewhipping to do Barr the least good, after all. Or anyone else, she supposed. He was learning his lessons in other ways, possibly no less painful.

"So she said if I wanted the other favor from her she wasn't going to give it to me, because she was pregnant now, and this one was her husband's, and I said no, I didn't, and yes, I could see, it was a farmer boy, and healthy, too. She seemed glad to learn that, and calmed down a little. But she said that I should ride away and stay away, because I'd done her enough harm for one lifetime." Barr blinked. "She didn't actually look like she was suffering that much."

"How would you know?" said Fawn tartly. "You weren't there to see the bad parts. Just because you survive a hurt doesn't mean you didn't bleed plenty at the time."

"So what did you do?" Dag's deep voice cut in before Fawn could expand on this theme.

Barr's face scrunched up. "I didn't know what to do. So I turned around and rode off like she wanted. But Dag—that little girl—she could've, should've, might have been my, my tent-heiress. In some other world."

"Too late for that, I think," said Dag.

"I know. But all the way home, I kept thinking about her. And about Calla and Indigo. I don't know that I would have understood the problem, before I met Calla and her brother. What if Lily grows up with ground-sense? What's she going to do, come eleven, twelve years old, when all those strange things start happening in her head—you know how it feels when your groundsense first comes in, all in spurts—with no one to tell her how to go on? What if her mama's husband comes to suspect, and, and . . . doesn't treat her right?" He hesitated. "What if I come to some sudden end, out patrolling, and no one knows she exists?"

Dag said, "You did not, I take it, see fit to inform your parents they have a half-farmer granddaughter? They having the next closest interest by right."

Barr shuddered. "Absent gods, no!"

Barr was still, Fawn was reminded, very young by Lakewalker standards. He might change his views on that later.

Dag grimaced. "Well, we don't know them, you do; I won't argue with your judgment on that."

Barr ducked his head gratefully. "But I thought . . . someone had better know about Lily. In case. And if there was anybody who could tell me what to do next, it would be you two. So . . . I rode here."

Dag shifted in his chair, and Nattie-Mari on his shoulder; she whuffled faintly, smacked her lips, and fell back to dozing. "What do you want to do?"

"Well, first off . . . no harm."

"Then you'll do best to leave that poor woman alone to live her life," said Fawn. "It seems she's found a way to survive . . ." She wasn't sure whether to say *you* or *without you*, so said neither. "You daren't take that away from her unless you stand ready to replace it, and I don't think you can. And nor does it sounds like she much wants you to."

"No, I guess . . . not."

Dag sucked on his lower lip, tapping his hook gently on the rocking chair arm. "But you shouldn't, I think, leave little Lily alone without any watching over at all. Things change. Parents can die—hers *or* yours, come to think—fortunes reverse. Families up-stakes and move. At the very least, you owe the child a discreet—and if you don't know how to be discreet, it's time you learned—check every now and then. So you can spot if she ever needs any help."

Barr said slowly, "I could do that, I guess." His strain was easing, now that he had his confession out. And if it was replaced by a nearly Remo-like glumness, well, it would do him no permanent harm. Barr's gaze lifted to Nattie-Mari, flopped happily on her papa's shoulder, and Fawn finally recognized his odd look as a kind of envy. He added apologetically, "My father is a pretty good one, mostly, for all that we used to butt heads till Mama threatened to drown us both in the Riffle. He spent a lot of time with me and my sisters, teaching us things . . . it's strange to think that I won't ever . . . well."

The silence that followed was broken only when Nattie-Mari stirred and squawked. Dag looked down at Fawn and smiled. "Two-handed chore, coming up."

"Huh. Funny how your dexterity comes and goes, medicine maker." She scrambled up, stirred her pot once more, swung it to safety, then bent and retrieved her daughter. Yep, leaking. Dag was entirely unmoved by the damp spot left on his shirt, though he did stretch his arms and roll his shoulders. She might offer to teach Barr how to do this cleanup chore sometime, if he hadn't yet learned on one of his younger sisters. Not just now, though—later on, when his heartache had eased a bit. Earlier in their acquaintance, she'd often wished for someone to hit Barr over the head with a plank and adjust his self-centered view of the world. It seemed little Lily finally had, but the results weren't as much fun to watch as she'd imagined.

When Fawn came back, Dag gave up the old rocking chair by the fire for her to sit with Nattie-Mari, taking her place on the hearth to continue his earnest discussion with Barr. New ground-shield designs, and teaching unbeguilement, and how many camps had sent inquiries, and how many makers had promised to pass the word. Arkady blew in then with Sumac, stomping his feet and complaining as usual about the deadly northern cold, which was actually quite mild today, and the talk turned to medicine making Clearcreek-style, and the new apprentices begging for places, and horses in foal, and plans for the spring.

And if hope for their wide green world grew as slowly as a baby grew into a mama, well, no one had ever said raising either was a task for the faint of heart, or the impatient.

Fawn rocked, and fed the future.